Sydneysider Melissa James is a former nurse and has worked as a waitress, store assistant, and perfume and chocolate demonstrator. A highly successful Mills & Boon author, Melissa has over 20 romance titles published. Four of these were romantic suspense with Silhouette Intimate Moments (two of which won *Romantic Times* Top Picks). Under the name Lisa Chaplin, Melissa writes Napoleonic and ancient historical fiction.

MELISSA JAMES

BENEATH THE SKIN

mira

First Published 2017
First Australian Paperback Edition 2017
ISBN 9781489232373

Published by
Harlequin Mira
An imprint of Harlequin Enterprises (Australia) Pty Ltd.
Level 13, 201 Elizabeth St
SYDNEY NSW 2000
AUSTRALIA

Cataloguing-in-Publication details are available from the National Library of Australia
www.librariesaustralia.nla.gov.au

Printed and bound in Australia by McPherson's Printing Group

MIX
Paper from
responsible sources
FSC® C001695

To Kate de Brito, my first critique partner—you were the first to read this book.

To the people whose stories in my UNE course, and at Survival Day concerts, so inspired me that this is my third published book telling your stories: the Aboriginal people of Australia. Elly and Rick are fictional, but they're part of all of you. Survival brothers and sisters, beneath the skin.

PROLOGUE

Medical Clinic, Pitjantjatjara Lands,
Central Australia

'There you are.' The doctor covered the ragged line of stitches on the boy's leg with a dressing. 'Don't get them wet.'

The dark-skinned boy on the examination table grinned. 'Thanks, aunty.'

The young woman with honey skin and an almost-beautiful face acknowledged the courtesy title with a nod and smile. 'No worries, nephew.'

The boy's father stood at the opening of the modified humpy house just out of the blazing desert sun, head down and feet shuffling, waiting until the elder of the clan spoke. The old man standing just inside the clinic reminded her of the land that surrounded them: wiry and tough, with a straggling beard, minimal clothing and a sudden burst of unexpected colour in the red, yellow and black bandanna around his head. He smiled in her direction, showing the gaps in his teeth. 'You been good help durin' your stay. We're glad you come by, niece. The nurse here is good, but a doctor's always needed.'

The doctor smiled back. 'I'm glad I could help. Forgive my not knowing the Arrernte language. I'm one of the Eora people.'

'Almost nothin' left of that language,' the elder remarked sadly. 'All fadin' now.'

She nodded. 'We're city folk now, the Sydney people. We have our stories and memories, but …' She shrugged, not knowing how to finish.

'The Dreamin' keeps its power, niece, even now,' the old man said, voice gentle. 'Better times will come for us. We know how to wait. Five year ago, this town was a mess. Now we're doing better. It will happen for you, too. Just believe.'

She glanced up, remembering just in time not to look into his eyes. The Pitjantjatjara people of Central Australia considered looking into a person's eyes an unpardonable rudeness—the eyes were mirrors of the spirit, and belonged to each person alone. 'I hope so, uncle, but the way is hard to see.'

'There's a place here for you, niece, if you wanna stay.' His offer was made with a sense of delicacy.

She gulped, pressed her lips together hard, as if in pain.

The old man flicked a swift glance at her. 'You'd be safe here. Nobody could find you, if we didn't want 'em to.'

At his insight, she gasped and withdrew further into herself. She shook her head, but could not—or would not—speak.

'We would help you, if you ask.' There was compassion in his voice.

'I can't put you all in danger, uncle,' she whispered.

'You're not blockin' just us, are you? Keeping everything to yourself's a way of life now,' he said very quietly. 'You give and give, but won't take anything back but a place to sleep, some food. Won't even give us your name.

'Common enough thing,' he went on. 'I seen it with loads of the Stolen Kids. Even if they find their way home, most of 'em don't know who they are or where they fit in.'

She shook her head, keeping it bowed. 'I wasn't stolen, uncle. I was one of the lucky ones.'

When he didn't answer, she glanced at him.

'Not so lucky, I'm thinkin'. You say nothin', but the silent screams are louder than words.' His gnarled hand patted hers. 'Damage.'

She closed her eyes. 'I can't burden you with my problems, uncle.'

'Or put us in danger,' he repeated. 'Seen this before, too. Whoever he is, runnin's like breathin' to you now. You bolt from one place to another, changin' your looks and your name, but still only feelin' safe when you're alone.'

In less than twenty words, he'd stripped her life bare. She only knew she was reaching to twiddle her missing hair when he said softly, 'It's gone, niece. Thinkin' it'll take a few years to grow back, too.'

Her hand dropped to her lap, and didn't move again.

After half a minute of silence, the elder spoke again. 'It's all right, niece. I know you gotta go. Don't worry about us. I'll prepare the people for whatever comes this way when you're gone.' He stood, and put a hand on her hair: a moment's benediction. 'Go with a blessing, niece. You're not alone.'

With a strangled thanks, the young woman fled the hut.

CHAPTER

1

Macks Lake, Southwestern New South Wales

A commotion erupted outside his office.

Detective Sergeant Adam Jepson frowned, taking in the scene through the window between his office and Macks Lake Police Station reception. Their rookie constable, Simon Wynn, and Senior Constable Barry South—Baz for short—were leading in a woman in handcuffs.

What could she have done in sleepy Macks Lake to merit the cuffs? They hadn't used them on a woman since they'd found the girlfriend of an ice dealer holed up in a bush cabin with the guy and all his equipment. The girlfriend had gone berserk during the bust, beating the crap out of Adam and his drug squad mates, who'd come down from Sydney for the nick.

This woman wasn't fighting her cuffs; she seemed to be having too much fun to bother. Her laughter touched the office with the ripe colours of an outback sunset, and Simon and Baz had dopey, almost drooling grins on their faces.

After three years on an inner-city beat before transferring to the Federal Police, he knew the look: her skin, the hue of dark honey, and her big, coffee-coloured eyes were a dead giveaway to her background, though her dusting of freckles showed European heritage too. About five-nine or ten, late twenties, with a lush body that showed her indifference to the half-starved look dictated by fashion. The outfit was over the top: the faded denims clung to her curvaceous bottom, and the white crop top was too short, leaving far too little to the imagination, and a hooker on his old beat could have worn those chunky-heeled boots. The hair didn't suit her, either – the loose chestnut curls didn't match the rich tone of her skin, or her eyes.

The whole look sat wrong.

He was missing something. Something about her … She didn't seem the type to want to draw attention to herself with dyed hair or tight, sexy outfits. If she was, she'd have packed on makeup, too, but she was bare-faced.

As Adam watched, he thought he caught a moment of dread hiding beneath her impish sparkle. *She's terrified of something—or someone.*

He strode out to the open office, breaking the party atmosphere. 'What's going on here?'

'… so that's when I—oh!' The woman turned and smiled in the friendliest way. 'Hi, Adam! Long time no see!'

So that was her tactic, playing everyone's best mate. It might work on some men, but he wasn't one of them, letting his hormones do the thinking.

Hold on, how did she know his name? He hadn't worn a uniform in years, and had no name badge … He frowned. 'That's Detective Sergeant Jepson to you, Miss—?'

'Oh, come on, you can do better than that, Old Sobersides.' A roguish dimple appeared as her mouth quivered.

His brows snapped together at the annoying nickname his station-mates had given him. He sent a brief glare to Simon and Baz, who both took a prudent step back. 'What's her name, and what are the cuffs for?'

'Don't blame them, Adam. It was my idea.' The woman's voice was deep and husky, a rich, throaty alto that hit his nerve endings with a gut punch. She wasn't quite beautiful—more memorable than pretty—but she was making him react in ways he didn't want to remember. 'I wanted to see if being in cuffs was as much fun as you said it was.'

Me? He barely held in the incredulous question, but smothered chuckles filled the office. Another glance at her caused something inside him to shift, leaving him off-kilter. No—she'd had him on the back foot from the start. It was like a dream he'd had once of flirting with a stranger in a corner of a crowded, smoky party: he could hear the others, could see them in his peripheral vision, but he and this woman in cuffs before him—it was as if they were alone. What was it about her that left him so disturbed? Beneath the rare burst of masculine hunger her presence had generated in him, the sense of dread grew.

His best mate in Macks Lake stepped forward. 'Hello, Miss—um. I'm Senior Constable Rick Mendham. And you are …?'

The woman didn't even look at Rick, or notice that he, too, was of Aboriginal descent. 'Talking to Adam … sir,' she said curtly.

So she has a problem with men. Yet for some reason, she trusted Adam. Only God knew why, but the certainty grew. She'd come here for him.

'And did you have fun, ma'am?' he drawled, trying to shake off the desire he knew was bloody unprofessional as well as stupid. But he couldn't shake the sense of desperation every time he looked at her. The feeling wasn't his, but hers—and his instincts whispered that dismissing her would be more than stupid. It'd be downright dangerous.

Help me, Adam. Don't tell anyone.

'Mmm.' She sighed, her expression dreamy. 'We're more alike than I'd imagined.'

The smothered chuckles around the room made him tighten his jaw again. They weren't alone. 'What the—what are you talking about?' Him and thrills, compatible? Yeah, right.

Not for years, at least …

Even thinking about his past made him frown. If he'd once been a stupid kid, he'd buried that part of himself years ago. And it wasn't getting a resurrection any time soon.

The woman flashed him an odd look, a mixture of reproach and shared mischief. 'Has it been so long for you? What about the time you cuffed your mate to that flagpole, naked, at the academy … not to mention what you and your best man did with the cuffs and that, um, *exotic* dancer on your buck's night?' She grinned. 'But maybe I shouldn't mention that in front of all these cops. You can still get pinched fourteen years after the deed, can't you?'

He felt a hot flush cover his face as laughter erupted around them. How did she know about that? Those stories had been beneath the sod so long, even he'd forgotten them. 'I don't know where you got that from, but stick to the point. What's your name, and why are you in handcuffs?'

A comic look twisted her face. 'Uh … speeding?'

A crack of laughter broke from behind the open door of the senior sergeant's office.

Adam blinked. 'You were brought in by these constables—you were *cuffed*—for speeding? I don't think so. What's really going on?'

Help me. Please. Her silent cry screamed so loud in his brain now, he could almost hear it, and yet she was laughing, along with everyone else in the station. But he knew something was terrifying this woman, and she couldn't afford for anyone else to know. So she was hiding it with this ridiculous practical joke. But why had she chosen him, of all people, to be her confidante?

He *must* know her from somewhere. But he could swear on a stack of bibles he'd never met her.

The woman's eyes sparkled as if she'd heard his thought. 'It was *serious* speeding, Adam—thirty over the limit.' Beneath the laughter, her eyes begged. *Go along with me. Please.*

There was no DUI involved—she was stone cold sober. 'Nobody's cuffed for thirty over the limit,' he barked, and wanted to kick himself when he saw her eyes darken further. Terror. Pleading beneath the smile. *Help me.*

'Then they frisked me!'

'They did *what?*'

Simon fled to the doubtful security of his desk. Baz, at least twenty kilos heavier and a fair bit shorter, held his ground. Almost. One or two more steps away, until his back was against the counter.

'I asked them to,' the woman replied, managing to sound earnest and merry at once. 'I wanted to know what it felt like to be arrested and frisked. It was properly done, according to the book. And it *was* exciting, being a crim for an hour,' she added, grinning in cheerful apology as the laughter erupted again. 'There'll be no repercussions. I promise. I'll pay my fine like a good girl, and I won't mention my little adventure outside the station.'

Adam flicked a look at Baz and Simon. In this quiet country station that only had six cops because it covered a few hundred square kilometres, boredom was the norm. No wonder she had 'em wriggling like fish on a hook.

'You realise these constables would lose their jobs for going along with your so-called fun, if word of it ever gets out?'

She smiled again, but it held a touch of pity in it, like the popular kid in school wanting to share her fun with the class nerd. 'C'mon, Adam, this will never go outside the station walls.' She sighed, her coffee-dark eyes filled with something akin to compassion. 'Poor Adam. She really did a number on you. You don't trust people anymore, and you've forgotten how to laugh.'

The quiet words shocked him into silence. Whoever she was, this woman had known his wife. Who was she? Why did the fear behind her eyes lock him into her game, compelling him to play? He didn't know, but whatever danger lay hidden behind the jokes, she desperately needed him to play along—for now.

His mind raced, trying to find the right answer. 'You'll be laughing from a cell if you don't cut out the act and give me your name.'

She clicked her tongue, but her eyes softened with relief. 'Adam Stephen Harold Jepson, you've forgotten the good manners Aunt Irene and Uncle Adam taught you to display before a lady. Shame on you.'

He reeled back. 'How do you know my grandparents—and my middle names, for that matter? Who the hell are you, woman?'

Rick stepped forward again. 'Hi, Miss—um. As I said, I'm Senior Constable Rick Mendham, and you have the apologies of the Macks Lake Police Service for Detective Sergeant Jepson's lapse in manners. He usually isn't so rude to old friends.' He clicked his fingers, and a sheepish Simon handed him the keys to the cuffs. 'You know, the PR that might come out of this little adventure of yours would be awful. You wouldn't want to make trouble for us poor country coppers, would you, sister?'

Another flicker of dread shadowed her eyes. It hovered for a split second, then she grinned at Rick, so carefree, Adam wondered if this woman was an actress. 'No booze or drugs, and no resisting arrest. Better watch your back—and your job, eh, brother?'

Rick's smile warmed and softened. 'Where do you hail from?'

Now the smile was genuine, yet Adam was still haunted by all she was keeping unspoken. 'My grandmother's Eora, from the La Perouse mob. I'm a Sydneysider. You?'

A moment's hesitation before Rick answered. 'The Mendhams are Paakantyi people, from the Darling River near Broken Hill.'

Adam frowned. So she was from Sydney? She knew his family; that much was obvious. She had to be related, if she'd called his very conservative grandparents aunt and uncle; but if any of the hundred or more relatives he had in Sydney had Aboriginal background, he'd never heard of it.

Whoever she was, he'd had enough of her game. 'Well, now you've had your fun, Constables Wynn and South can give you your ticket. Then you can cause trouble for the cops of another town, and leave us to our boring lives.' He didn't like this woman—he was almost sure of that—and he sure as hell didn't like her effect on him.

She only winked at him. Coupled with that megawatt smile, her lush sensuality hit him like a perfume. The other scent—a fear so primal he couldn't ignore it—sat with even less comfort. *Please help me.*

'But I came all this way to enrich your boring life. It's been thirteen years since we last met, and you trussed up in a monkey suit. It was the most tedious affair I ever had to sit through. I thought my good mate Claudius's wedding would be a right old hoedown. You shouldn't have let Sharon and the Jepsons bully you into the boring conventions.'

Claudius? Only one person had ever called him that stupid nickname—and a sudden burst of memories he'd kept dammed up too long became a flood. Everything made sense, right down to the ridiculous outfit and cheeky smile. *'Elly?'*

'In the flesh.' Her shimmering eyes alight with affection, she ran around the counter, flung herself on him and snuggled right in.

He swore silently as his body tightened in swift, hot reaction. Well, after all these years, it was comforting to know he was still a man, but his libido picked a hell of an embarrassing time to let him know it was still a functioning part of his anatomy. He was so hot and hard against the softness of her belly there was no way she could mistake his reaction, even through his jeans and hers.

You bloody moron. This is Elly!

But almost any man would react to the lush breasts pressed against him, and the soft perfume of baby powder and warm sunshine in the feathery curls tickling his nose. Just the normal reaction to the touch of an attractive woman—and the most basic of needs submerged way too long, resurrecting to sudden life.

But this was *Elly*. He had no right to desire her—not now, not ever. And yet, it wasn't a conscious choice; it was as natural as breathing. Like the myriad times she'd climbed up to his window to taunt him into joining her in her next adventure, her cheeky little face a challenge he could never resist. *Coming, Claudius?*

Little Elly, the best friend he'd never had before her, or since he'd left her life.

How the hell had he ever left her behind? Half a lifetime …

He looked up, still holding her. Every man in the station watched him with half-wistful and knowing grins—except for Rick. The man who'd come to Macks Lake a few months after Adam, and who'd become his best mate soon after, seemed far from happy. His eyes were narrowed in acute assessment and a suspicion that was too damn accurate for Adam's comfort. And something else, almost like resentment.

When he glanced over again the look was gone, leaving only shadows of doubt behind.

He tried to put Elly at arm's length, but she pulled him right back to her. 'No, you don't get off that easy. I haven't seen you in thirteen years, *Detective Sergeant Jepson*.' Full lips, warm and moist, brushed the side of his mouth. 'Howdy, Claudius.' The mock-hillbilly accent was spiced and softened by her natural velvet huskiness. 'How're y'all?'

Adam's throat was dry, the rest of him in pain. He conjured a smile from the humiliated depths. 'Howdy, Elly-May. Still collectin' the critters?'

'Still a-s-stutterin' with the purty w-w-womenfolk?' she shot back.

'Ah-ah-ah ... yep.' He laughed with the memory of where he'd got his nickname. 'Right. Everyone, meet my—'

'He's no relation to me, anyway,' Elly interjected, laughing.

'You would deny it, even if we were family.' He grinned at her. 'Then what are we?'

'Foster aunt and nephew?' Elly suggested.

He rolled his eyes. 'Yeah, that works, seeing that you're almost five years younger. Okay. Everyone, meet my, um, I suppose my—'

'And after that pathetic non-explanation by my non-related and no longer furious childhood friend, you still have no idea who I am. I'm Elly Lavender.' She held out a hand to Baz, with that big, friendly smile of hers. 'How do you do, Constable South? I believe we've met, but I was ... um ... tied up at the time.'

The members of the station crowded around her, laughing. Under the cover she'd provided, Adam's mind raced. Yeah, she was good. Quick and smooth, that interruption, with a laughing reference to her 'arrest' to distract them. And the ruse worked—except on him. For he alone knew Elly wasn't her real name. Neither was Lavender.

And yet Simon and Baz, who must have demanded her licence, weren't arguing.

Rick was standing slightly apart. Adam saw the same frowning doubt on his face. Rick knew she was lying, too, but though his friend was an excellent cop, he couldn't know that Elly had always refused to answer anyone else who'd tried to use her nickname, as he'd done with Claudius. The names were theirs alone during their time at his grandparents' farm.

Now she was using it in public. Worse, she must have made the name legal. The boys would have looked her licence up on the database, so it couldn't be a fake.

Elly Lavender.

Although they'd been apart almost half a lifetime, and she'd gone from child to woman, he knew her too well to believe in this game of charades and shadows. They'd been inseparable during almost four years of holiday time, and spent hours on the phone and emailing every day when he'd had to go home. They'd been so close they could read each other's thoughts half the time. He'd always known when she was hurt or upset, as she'd done with him. An email had always come when he was going through a hard time: *Want to talk about it?*

He ought to have listened to the deep-honed instinct that had been screaming at him since she'd come in, but the personality she was projecting had no correlation with the girl he'd known, and she looked almost nothing like her, either.

You haven't seen her in years; what would you know?

But it nagged at him. Surely, she couldn't have changed this much?

Unless something happened to her to force the change. He watched her closely, but she wasn't looking at him, her back almost turned to him now. The same way she'd done when they were kids, and she wanted to hide something from him.

Homing into the instincts he never used except during arrests or interviews, he glanced around the room, feeling it. Yeah, something else was wrong. It didn't take long to find the source—Rick was watching Elly with far more intensity than a stranger should.

Damn it. He hadn't seen that kind of look—almost possession— in his mate's face since his cheating girlfriend had skipped town seven months ago.

The screen door opened with a shuddering squeak, reminiscent of the effect the voice that followed it always had on him, with its deliberate girlishness and helpless high pitch. 'Adam, I need to see you—alone. I've been molested in broad daylight!'

He turned to the woman leaning over the counter, showing a hint of cleavage. There was little sign of distress in her smile, or in her lithe, slender body—but then, there never was. Jennifer Collins was a woman on a mission: to get him into bed. Feeling the usual mix of distaste and unwilling half-arousal; it was another of those times he hated being a man. 'I'm too busy for this today, Mrs Collins. If you have a genuine complaint, make it to Senior Constable Mendham. He'll check it out.'

'But Adam ...' the woman purred—and then, seeing Elly, she frowned. 'Who's she?'

'None of your concern,' he snapped, and turned back to Elly. 'Come into my office.'

CHAPTER

2

'So are you going to tell me what's really going on? What are you doing here, Elly?' Adam asked as soon as he'd established their privacy.

She shrugged, reaching over the neat stack of paperwork that had to be on the regional inspector's desk tomorrow to take his hand in hers. 'It's been a long time, Claudius, with no see at all—almost half a lifetime. Can't I come to the back of beyond to visit my long-lost childhood mate without getting the Spanish Inquisition about it?'

His gaze roamed her face. Her transition from a short, scrawny Little Orphan Annie with wild, waist-length black hair to a tall, curvaceous woman with short, loose chestnut curls—and a face like that—still stunned him. His tree-kitten had always made him smile. From the day they'd met, she'd invited him to come and run in her own private jungle, but now, as a woman, just meeting her again had shifted something in him. Something fundamental he couldn't name.

He released her hands and sat back to try to gain some rational perspective. 'Maybe. If you'd introduced yourself as Jane Larkins out there.'

Silence answered him.

He lifted a brow. 'I can find out all about you in seconds on the COPS database.'

'You got me there, Claudius.' She grinned, then looked around, mouth turning down. 'Your office is very—plain. Sterile, even. All grey and white and files, and a dark desk. Aren't you allowed to have anything personal?'

He stared at her. 'It's my work space. It doesn't need to be aesthetically pleasing.'

'I've always thought a work space says a lot about how a person feels about their job.' A frown at him—assessing, weighing him on unseen scales. 'Yet all you ever wanted was to be a cop.'

And yeah, he'd been found wanting. In all their history, she'd *never* criticised him. It was so unexpected a hit he felt his whole body stiffen. 'Yes.' He unlocked his jaw after the word. 'And since I am a cop, I know when someone's avoiding my questions. So why did you introduce yourself as Elly Lavender?'

She must have known she'd pushed him too far, for she pulled a rueful face. 'Maybe I got a yen to change my name? It's all legal, I promise.' She handed him her driver's licence. The legend above her unsmiling face—the only time he'd seen her without a smile since she'd re-entered his life—read *Elliana Angelina Lavender*.

He handed the plastic card back. 'How many times have you felt that "yen" before?'

The flush creeping up her rich skin came out the dusky rose of the outback sky at sunset. 'So I don't like keeping to one name,' was all she said; but he sensed something—some dark ugliness—lying hidden beneath her words. Emotion not quite buried, but not in the open.

Perhaps he'd already hit close to the truth? Given their history, he knew he'd have to dig to get her to talk. 'Once upon a time you hated the name Elly, too.'

She laughed, but the sweetness of it rang false. 'No, I just hated anyone but you using it. And you have to admit, Elly-May suits me. You know, the hillbilly kid with the critters. I never did like Janie. Bad connotations, Claudius. You know, plain Jane and all that.'

She really means that. It was so ridiculous he couldn't believe she didn't know. Okay, so she'd never win any beauty contests; she wouldn't be every man's cup of tea. But in his eyes, Elly was—was—hell, he didn't know … But she had such vivid, fiery life inside her it felt like she'd burst into spontaneous combustion any moment.

Or maybe it was him who was ready to explode. Denial was useless, and he refused to lie to himself; nobody knew how useless that was more than he did. Wanting to run his fingers over her dark-honey skin, taste every inch of it … and find out how far down those tempting freckles went.

He wanted Elly like hell. He'd never have her. End of story.

So move on to why she's here.

'Plain Jane. Right. I don't think so,' he said, dry to the point of brittleness. 'You must know you're a bloody attractive woman, Elly. You must have had plenty of men in your life tell you that.'

The deep rose bloomed in her cheeks again, but it was a flush of discomfort. Her eyes showed a quick flash of dread, even fear, before her gaze fell to her lap. She folded her hands, weaving shadows of calm around herself like mist.

She'd shut him out for a simple compliment. How could his calling her attractive scare her?

'And your hair? Wasn't it black, and much curlier, the last time I saw it?'

She remained shrouded in a tranquil silence that hit him as wrong. Practised.

He pursued the subject with dogged determination. 'Black hair's very difficult to lighten, I hear. I've interviewed women who do it—the bleaching and colour, and the straightening treatment. A woman must have a very strong desire for … change … to put herself through all that. The other women I've interviewed were on the run from violent partners, or criminals.'

She lifted her chin and faced him down with a smile, her eyes cool, unreadable. 'Are you interviewing me, Claudius? Really?'

'Those women were all on the run,' he persisted, holding her gaze.

She only sighed, as if she was bored. 'Maybe they were. Maybe I just had a yen for change all round.'

Shadows of the past were locked deep inside her eyes, and worry hit the alarm bell on his slumbering life. 'Elly, talk to me. It's obvious you're in trouble—'

'I was so sorry to hear of your father's death, and Sharon and Zack's accident,' she said, her voice subdued. 'I know how much you loved your father and Sharon—and little Zack, only a month old. It must have devastated you.'

He took the hit without word or movement, until he realised it wasn't a ploy to open him up; it was an obvious change of subject. His father's death to cancer eighteen months ago hadn't been unexpected, but he'd kept the sudden deaths of his wife and newborn son buried beneath a blanket of silence since it happened. He didn't like his wounds being probed, and nobody knew that better than Elly. Yet she was putting her finger right in them.

Then it hit him—she'd been there when he'd first known loss. Eighteen years ago she'd given a faltering prayer at the grave of Abe, his beloved dog—and if she hadn't truly changed, he knew she'd never open up if he didn't first. He conceded her right to open the subject with a curt nod.

'Is that why you left Sydney, and the federal police?' Her voice was gentle, as it had been at old Abe's grave.

Sick with relief that she wasn't going deeper, he nodded again. 'I was only in the Specialist Response Group for three years—and you're partly right. I left because I got shot just above the lung in a drug raid two years ago.'

Her gaze lowered to her lap, her fingers twining around each other. 'I heard. I wish I could have come to you when you were in hospital. I wish I could have helped you through.'

'So why—' But seeing the shadows in her face, and her classic gesture when feeling uncomfortable or guilty, he closed his mouth. Who was he to ask? She could have been married, murdered or become famous the past thirteen—really, fourteen—years, since soon after he'd met his wife, and he wouldn't have known a thing about it.

Because you never asked. You got out of her life so fast you left skid marks on the road.

When his wife and father had made it too damn hard for him to ask his grandparents about Elly, the easy option had felt like the only option: walking away and never looking back. And he'd done it so bloody thoroughly he'd almost forgotten she'd existed.

'Anyway, I realised how unstable an environment I was putting Zoe in,' he said, hearing the abruptness in his tone. 'The element of constant risk in the SRG is better handled by guys without families. So I quit, joined the New South Wales police, and applied to come somewhere slow and quiet, for Zoe's sake. There had never even been a detective here, or a plain-clothes cop, but there was suspicion of drugs being made in this region. So I was sent here to investigate, using the truth as a cover—I was a single dad looking for a preschool and a house to buy. By the time the case was done I'd bought the house, and Zoe was happy here.'

Her brows lifted, but whatever she'd been about to ask, she changed her mind. 'So how is Zoe?'

Glad to leave the subject, he grinned, though his heart still felt rimmed by darkness and shadow. 'She's fine—better than fine. She's four and a half now, and a holy terror.'

Her eyes lit with that impish grin. 'Like father, like daughter? She couldn't have inherited that from Sharon!'

His mouth tightened. *Stop it. Don't say her name!*

His brother Jared, his mum, his cousins—everyone had been trying ever since the accident to bring up his dead wife's name, or Zack's, hoping he'd talk out what they assumed to be his grief. Now Elly was doing it—but somehow, it didn't feel the same. She hadn't been in his life for years; he hadn't even seen her since the day he'd taken his marriage vows with his dainty, golden-haired bride. Elly was probably assuming he was far enough from the trag-edy for his sorrow to have dulled—and she'd be right, if it were sorrow alone he felt.

'The image of her mother, the heart and spirit of her crazy dad,' he agreed, wondering if she'd press it.

Her answering smile was sweet, pensive. 'You still crazy after all these years?'

Relieved again that she was reading him so well, he grinned. 'Mum and Dad, Grandma and Grandpa—the whole family—wouldn't believe you said that. As you seem to know, they call me "Old Sobersides" around here. You're the only one who ever believed me crazy.'

'Maybe because they don't know you like I do.' Her brow lifted, that twinkle back in her eyes, daring him to deny it.

She was right. He *had* been crazy when he was with her. Those summers had been—still were—the best times of his life. Stealing food from Grandma's kitchen for unauthorised picnics, taking forbidden joyrides on Grandpa's tractor, fishing with lines and reels made from Coke bottles, sleeping in the bush. Coming back from their adventures covered in mud and slime, bringing injured wild creatures home in makeshift cages to care for them. Every day with Elly had been one adventure after another, each more addictive than the one before it. Helpless to resist, and against the will of his stiff-necked father, who'd disliked Elly from first sight, Adam had returned to his grandparents' farm every holiday he could, and emailed, texted and called her between. No one in his family understood that need to just *be*—the utter relief of being with someone who accepted him, just as he was.

Stop it. That ended long ago. You're not a kid anymore. You have a child to raise, a responsible job. Those days, those pranks are over.

Again, as if she'd read his mind, Elly changed the subject. 'You don't need to let loose after your experiences? You scared me at times, the way you were so single-minded about being a cop. And you're still a cop after everything you've been through. Surely you need to—'

'How do you know what I've been through?' he cut in, not wanting to hear the lecture from her, of all people. 'We haven't seen each other in thirteen years.'

Her grin was sheer impudence. 'Aunty Hat.'

He groaned. His great-aunt Harriet had immersed herself in Jepson politics and romance since her fiancé's death early in the Vietnam War. 'We can escape Interpol—'

'But Aunty Hat will find a Jepson descendent to pump information from, no matter where we run.' She finished the family joke.

He chuckled. Then, thinking it through, he frowned. 'Did she send you here? Are you checking up on me?'

Her left brow rose. 'Why for, Claudius?' Yeah, she knew why he'd asked, all right, and wouldn't make it easy for him. 'Have you been up to mischief again, despite your denials, and this shrink-worthy office? Do you need checking up on?'

'By you? What good would you be?'

She laughed. 'Times change, people change, old friend—as you must have noticed, since you didn't even recognise me.' He winced at the deliberate needling, but she only grinned, and wiggled her brows. 'These days, I think I could surprise you with how useful I can be, in the most unlikely of places.'

His eyes narrowed, hating that kind of obvious remark, before he realised it was no come-on. She was teasing, taunting him with affectionate memories—the methods he'd used once to draw out a grieving, withdrawn little girl, his grandparents' misunder-stood foster child, and bring her out of hiding up a tree. It struck him that while she knew so much about him—even down to the handcuffs incidents—he knew nothing about her in the years since she'd left his grandparents' farm to live with her paternal grandmother.

'So what do you do with yourself these days?'

She leaned back in her chair. 'Me? I wander the vast red outback in a BMW.'

'A Beemer?' he asked, diverted despite knowing she'd thrown him another red herring, one that her childhood mate would fall for immediately.

'A four-seater red convertible, custom made.' Her tone was soft, beguiling. 'Six-cylinder turbo. She goes from zero to a hundred in under eight seconds, in the sweetest purring quiet you ever heard in your life.'

'Oh, man,' he breathed, moving around the desk to her. 'What model? Where is she?'

She stood up, coming to his chin. At six-three, he'd had so few women do that. Last time he'd seen Elly, she'd barely reached his waist, and was as flat chested as a boy, and as adventurous. So many changes—no wonder he hadn't recognised her.

She looked up at him. 'Want to come see her? If you're a very good boy, I might let you take her out for a spin.' Her smile was all friendly guile, one childhood friend challenging another. There was nothing in her manner to match the provocative words, despite being close enough to breathe in the fragrance of her. Simple powder and shampoo—but when the combination radiated from Elly, who wore the scent of earth and sensuality like a second skin, he'd never inhaled a more seductive scent in his life.

He looked down into her upturned face. 'What does "very good boy" entail?' Hearing the odd huskiness in his voice, he coughed to cover it over, even grinned. 'Are we talking deals, Miz Elly, like we used to?'

'If you like.' Yet her smile faded. 'No more questions would be a good start.'

'You need me, Elly.' Now his tone was rough, almost angry. Absurd to be jealous of his younger self—but he was, jealous that she wouldn't trust him as she used to. 'I don't mind a few mysteries, but you're in trouble. Isn't that why you came here? Why you got my attention by getting cuffed in the first place, and wearing that ridiculous outfit?'

Her expression closed off. 'I thought I came to see a friend.' When he didn't answer, she sighed. 'Okay, I dressed this way for you, and got arrested. It was just harmless fun. I wanted to wake you up, and find Claudius, lost in Old Sobersides—and Simon loved driving my red baby ...'

This game was getting ridiculous. 'Maybe you did—but you also did it because you knew I wouldn't recognise you. You did it so when you jumped in with your new name, I'd be too confused to say "Janie Larkins", or correct you.'

Her gaze flew to his, then fell. She flushed, but didn't speak.

Exasperated, he lifted her chin with a hand. 'Come on, talk to me, Elly. I'm the guy who sat in the tree with you when you cried for your mum, the one you covered for when I pinched Grandpa's tractor. We've been in trouble together, roamed the mountains, and shared everything as we nursed your critters through the night. If you can't trust me, who can you trust?'

Great fawn-like eyes met his, wide and wary in a face pale beneath its warmth. Memories of the day they'd met hit him. The child Janie had been all hurting, raw emotion, less refusing to talk than unable to talk.

He found himself mumbling, 'I'm sorry, Elly.' *Sorry for so many things. Sorry I never kept in touch. Sorry that my family only saw you as an embarrassment, and thought you were bad for me. And more than anything, I'm sorry life never taught you to trust anyone.*

She shrugged. Whatever trouble she was in, he'd only know about it when she chose to tell him. 'I—thank you,' she said. When she looked up, his heart almost stopped at the pure fear crouching beneath the illusion of calm she was trying to project. 'Don't tell anyone my real name, or look me up on the database. Not yet. Please.'

'Elly—'

'Please.' A quiver ran through her. 'A day or two of fun. That's all I'm asking.' Her voice was a bare whisper. Then her fingers groped at her waist, before her hand dropped slowly to her lap.

A sudden vision blinded him: the little girl sitting in an enormous gum tree outside his grandparents' farm, still grieving for her mother, and twiddling her waist-length curls whenever she felt stressed or miserable—a habit no amount of nagging could break.

So she'd only recently cut her hair. She'd dyed it. A professional hand had tamed its wild tangles. She'd changed small, but characteristic gestures—and she'd changed her name before she came to him, someone who'd had no contact with her for thirteen years.

'C'mon, Elly, at least tell me if you need help.' He frowned again, all she'd left unspoken assuming sudden and massive proportions in his mind. 'Are you a protected witness?'

CHAPTER

3

How had he *done* that? After half a lifetime apart, he'd come so close to the bone, and far too soon. The jolt to Elly's system was like an electric shock, hitting all of her. Whatever she'd expected in coming here, it hadn't been *this*.

She shook her head, giving him a half-smile that offered nothing. But the look that created instant distance with most people only made him lift a brow. The way her cousin Kara always had, too—her only other real friend.

'Then why put yourself through all this change … Janie?'

Don't react. That's what he wants. She managed to speak, clear and cold. 'My name's Elly.'

Worry filled the eyes she'd never forgotten, the silver-green of eucalyptus leaves in the forest near his grandparents' farm, with flecks of earth brown. 'What made you hate your own name, Elly? What happened to you?'

A ball of pain took up lodging in her throat. She coughed, but it wouldn't clear. 'Nothing. I'm fine.'

He only shook his head. 'No, you're not. Come on, Elly. You can trust me.'

She felt herself rear back a little, a slight bitterness like gall rising from her belly, tight and hard. 'I haven't seen or spoken to you in years. How could you know if I'm fine or not? How could I know who or what you are any more?'

'Because it's me and you. Some things don't change. You wouldn't have come here if you felt that way. Something or someone's got you on the run, and you turned to an old friend with no connections to you for a long time. A friend who happens to be a cop.'

His insight unnerved her, but she said, 'Hey, don't overthink it, Claudius. I hadn't had a chance to feel like a charity kid in years … and there was a Jepson close to hand. So I thought, why not?'

'Liar. I never saw you that way, and you know it. So why don't you stop stonewalling me?'

Something in her darkened, a flame blown out. 'No, you didn't see me that way—then. But times change, people change. As we grow older, we often take on the attitudes of our families—and partners. After all, you did stop talking to me.'

At last she'd deflected him—yeah, he winced at her emotionless comment. Some of the more thoughtless remarks his family had thrown at her echoed through her mind. The words Adam's girlfriend-then-wife Sharon had said to him, the careless cruelty she'd never meant for her to overhear: *She's not one of us.*

But even Sharon hadn't known how right she'd been. Janie Larkins or Elly Lavender, the nowhere child had become a nowhere woman.

Janie's life of isolation had begun when she was three, when her father disappeared, taking her older brother with him. She didn't remember what they'd looked like now, or even their names—but she knew all about her father's desertion, thanks to her mother's bitter comments. Her mum's job as a fruit picker meant they had travelled from place to place, struggling to survive, her mother teaching Janie to read and do basic maths outside of working hours. Life was the two of them, morning and night, and Janie reading and playing on her own through the day.

Then they'd come to the Southern Highlands when she was ten. The nightmare still came to Elly as if in slow motion: one of those vivid, technicolour things you can't wake from or forget when you're awake. Playing in the backseat of the car with Amelia, the rag doll she'd had for years, Janie didn't see the Jepsons' prize bull when it wandered onto the road. She didn't see it charge at their car. She only heard Mum's high-pitched scream, and felt the hard jerk of her own head, and then her body slamming against the seat-belt when the car swerved into a power pole.

The stupid bull came after them, charging the car over and over, hitting the driver's seat. Janie wailed with the pain in her head and shoulder, with the stink of smoke in the car, crying for help. 'Janie, be *quiet*! Don't move,' her mother had whispered, a horrible, wheezy sound that terrified the child into obedience. 'No matter what happens, stay in the car, *and be quiet.*'

Boom. The bull hit the car again. Mum's door buckled further. Her gasp was a long, sucking sound. She made a weak, frantic attempt to undo her broken seatbelt, but her hands didn't seem to be working right. After a while, she'd stopped trying.

More smoke, not thick, but enough for the burning rush to come up Janie's throat. Vomit all over her, over Amelia. Where was her water? 'Mum, where's my water? I need water, *now*!'

'No! Don't scream, Janie.' It was a hiss pushed from the deepest part of her. The last part left. '*Don't make a sound.*'

The driver's door buckled. Mum flopped around like Amelia did when Janie made her doll dance: her head jerked sideways almost to her shoulder. Then she didn't move again.

And still the car jolted a few more times, pushing off the pole, rolling into a ditch. Janie's head smacked against the window. Pain and blackness and she couldn't breathe. Everything hurt.

When she woke, pain ripped through her arm and head and Amelia had lost her head, and she was scared, so scared. Holding tight to what was left of Amelia, she'd scrambled out of her belt and over to the front seat, throwing herself onto her mother for comfort.

The only response was a long, rattling gasp.

Don't scream, Janie.

'Mum, wake up,' Janie had whispered. Nothing. '*Wake up!*'

Even shaking her mother did nothing but make her head flop. 'Wake up, Mum,' she'd whispered one more time. 'Mum, where's my water?' But there was nothing but smoke and vomit, a broken doll and a hand that got colder, no matter how long Janie held it.

When emergency crews showed up at last, they had to use a machine to open the passenger door. A man's head popped in through the hole.

'Hey, sweetie, what's your name?'

Be quiet, Janie.

'Come on, sweetie, you're hurt. We need to get you to hospital. Is this your mum? What's your name?'

They were going to take her mum from her, and she couldn't even fight them off because her stupid arm wouldn't work. She kicked him, and he didn't even get angry. Kind and patient, the man sat beside her, strapping up her sore arm while she fought him. He kept asking her name. He even found Amelia's head, and promised his wife was great at sewing and would fix her.

Don't make a sound.

'The engine's gonna blow!'

She still remembered the prick of the needle going into her arm. The thin scream tearing from her throat, fighting sleep because—because she knew—

She'd woken up in hospital, a drip in one arm, and the other arm strapped to her body. Everyone was calling her Jane. A stranger in her own body, in a place she didn't recognise, among people she didn't know, and no Mum. Mum had gone to heaven, they said.

Liars, she screamed inside her head. *If she's gone away, she'd take me! She never goes anywhere without me!*

When Steven, the paramedic, laid a repaired Amelia on her chest, Janie couldn't move beyond caressing the doll with her cheek. *Mum, come back! Take me with you!*

Don't move, Janie. Don't make a sound.

Then some old people with beautiful clothes came to visit. They said to call them Uncle Adam and Aunt Irene, and she was coming to live with them on their farm.

No! Tell me where heaven is. I want to go with Mum!

Some more people came, with folders and pens, writing stuff down. They said they were from Child Services. 'You're so lucky to have a good home to go to, Jane.'

I'm not Jane! I want my mum! The screams in her head, the memories of Mum's last moments, were so loud she didn't even know she wasn't talking. Not for weeks.

'Elly?'

She'd forgotten the way Adam could make her feel—and remember; but it was second nature now to will away the memories. They were hers alone, not to be shared with anyone. Not even the boy who'd become her foster brother, her first real friend—and then … everything.

Not that he'd ever known, or wanted to know what he was to her.

She made herself grin. 'What?'

'Have you changed?' Adam asked patiently, as if he'd already asked a few times.

Still feeling the waking dream, she found her current reality a relief. She thought about his question, instead of pushing him away. 'I suppose I have. Living with my family taught me to believe in myself. I'm not ashamed of who and what I am.'

'There never was anything to be ashamed of,' he said, low. Shame crouched behind his chair, the Jepson elephant in the room. His burden to bear.

So he hadn't changed as much as she'd feared.

She felt the smile grow from deep inside as better memories flooded in: the first day he'd come to the farm, and though he was just getting over a serious illness, he'd climbed the tree to sit beside her. Then he'd let her share his dog, and the screams in her head had slowly become murmurs. Instead of seeing her mother dying day and night, Mum's twisted, bloodied face began to smile. *He's a good one, Janie. He's not one of them.*

Just like she wasn't.

'I'd better find a place to s-stay.' Her tongue tripped, she needed to get away from the bright-burning candle of emotion he lit in her. Friendship and love twining in painful beauty, always hurting like lost possibilities. Being with Adam was always too much, and never enough.

'The Rose and Thistle's a good pub. Zoe and I stayed there for a few weeks when we first came.' He spoke abruptly. Feeling her need to get away, but not understanding. So it still hurt him when she withdrew from him. 'I'll send Simon with you to make sure you don't get lost.'

A shadow passed the outer office window—and though the day was clear and warm, she felt the memory of all she ran from, cold and lost, a physical presence hurting her. The screaming silence took over inside her, the need crawling beneath her skin—the reason why she hated the name her mother had given her.

Janie ... I'm coming for you. This time, it's forever. You'll never leave me again.

'Elly?'

Safety in a nickname, and a voice of velvet over gravel that brought her back from the darkness. Sensing Adam's intent gaze, she turned away from the glass. 'Sorry, I went off into la-la land.' She laughed a moment too late, the sweetness a touch too false.

'You don't have to tell me. I can wait,' he said, too quiet. He was deliberately *not* probing, giving her space, but she felt his worry and fear.

She'd come here expecting to find a Jepson. Instead, she'd found Adam—*her* Adam, still alive within the confines of everything his family had wanted him to be. The caring and the respect in his words overwhelmed her.

She had to clear her head.

I should never have come here in the first place.

So she laughed, distance in denial. 'You know better than to worry, Claudius. I've always done things myself. I could always ride better than you, and round up Uncle Adam's cows—'

'Stop it.' It seemed he'd felt it, too, the broken pieces of all they'd once been, an imperfect fit over the people they'd become—and it hurt far more than she'd believed it could. 'I told you I get it. You don't want to tell me yet, fine—but please, leave out the fun-girl act you put on for the rest of the station.'

Walls of silence, years in the building, threatened to crumble with a few rough words. How did he always do this to her?

Then another shadow passed outside the window, blocking the sun. A moment, and it was gone. Was it real, or had she imagined it? Did she even know what was real any more? No matter where she ran, he kept coming, the broken man-child reaching for her each time he fell.

Was he here now?

'Elly.'

When she turned, Adam was still watching her. 'You're cringing away from the window.'

Her eyes ached from staring at him. How could she have forgotten the downside to his knowing her so well—that he *did* know her?

When he went on, he spoke like a cop sure of his ground. 'Your whole "arrest" act was to make me feel your cry for help in a way nobody else would be able to see or hear. So know I'm here, waiting. Whenever you're ready for me, Elly.'

Now her mouth couldn't even open. The child who'd died at his wedding thirteen years ago came to sit on that big, thick wall she'd built around herself, and the weight of little Janie's loyal heart dissolved the bricks—no demolition, no implosion. And behind the wall was all that the woman she'd become couldn't afford to show.

One by one, her muscles stiffened until she was straight backed, square shouldered, her chin up and her eyes cool. A soldier facing an unexpected battle—but for her, the fight was against the tenderness she'd never thought to know again, not from Sharon's husband.

As if he sensed her need to run, he changed tactics. 'So tell me what you do nowadays. That can't be a state secret.'

'Maybe it is.'

'Time for the big guns.' The grin was there in his voice, and lighting his eyes. 'Info works both ways with Aunty Hat. She'll give me the lot in five minutes flat.'

The child standing beside the ruins of her wall smiled. *Do it, Janie. You know you want to.* Elly laughed before she knew it. 'All right, Claudius, you win. I'm a GP. I've been treating outback people, mostly Indigenous—doing immunisations, eye treatments, wound treatment and basic surgery—for the past couple of years.'

He sat back in his chair, brows lifted. 'Somehow it doesn't surprise me. You always roped me in on your critter hunts on the farm, saving the rattiest animals—poor Grandma was—'

Something inside her iced over. 'My people aren't *animals*, nor do they need to be saved. They need basic health care and services, food and family and respect, like any other human being.'

His eyes and mouth pressed shut. Little splotches of red and white appeared on his skin, a patchwork she'd seen often in her years with the Jepson clan. 'You know I didn't mean it like that,' he said, too late.

'I *don't* know,' she retorted, keeping it low. The tension shimmered in waves, a tangible barrier she'd never known with him when they were kids. Before *she* came, Sharon the pretty, perfect fiend, and little Janie had lost her beloved Adam. He'd vanished into a world she could only ever view from the outside.

Janie had been the Jepsons' failed social experiment before she'd even left the hospital after the accident. But all her education and being exposed to the Jepson belief systems and morality hadn't made her one of them. How could it? The Jepsons' charity had always been loaded, because it was built on superiority and guilt. No matter what she did, they'd always close the window into their world with a smile, or lock the door when she was a step from opening it.

Which was why Adam's unwitting betrayal had cut her to the bone. He'd been the only one to *see* her, to *know* her, to *love* her as she was, and he'd walked away. He'd never know, never understand, the hole he'd left inside her, filled with a name. *Sharon.*

But when he spoke, his voice was rough with hurt. 'You *do* know me. I haven't changed. Give me a chance before you judge me.'

Damn him for still being Claudius—*her* Adam, deep inside. Why couldn't he have become like the rest of them, locking those doors and windows of their superior world in her face? Then she could walk away with a clear conscience.

'I'm here.'

Slowly, he smiled at her, and its uncertainty left her floundering, as jumbled as flotsam from a sinking ship. A few words, a smile, and he'd destroyed her resolve. 'Stay, Elly,' he said softly. 'Don't go.'

She gave a wordless nod, but the question remained. What was she doing here?

'I'd love to invite you to stay with us, but Zoe …' He paused. 'She's only four, and bringing strangers home upsets her.'

'Of course,' she said, remembering the few times her mother had made friends, and how threatened she'd felt. 'I'll be fine at the pub.'

His whole body relaxed, and he smiled at her, the man and the boy tangled inside him. 'I've got reports to finish. If you come back at four, you can show me your red baby, and I'll take you to meet Zoe. We'll have dinner at my place. You can tell me about your work. It sounds like a bloody hard job—the travel, the isolation involved.' He looked at her. 'You must get lonely.'

'It is hard, at times.' She walked to the door, refusing to answer his second observation. 'I'll see you later.'

As she passed, he said, 'Zoe's rather clingy. She may not like you.'

A hard pain sat in her belly. Poor little Zoe—they were sisters of loss beneath the skin. Elly opened her mouth, but her words weren't what she wanted to say. 'Who would understand that better than me, Claudius?'

He didn't answer. They both knew he didn't need to.

Jerking to his feet—his marionette movements soothed her with their familiarity—he walked to the door. He held it open for her, a whisper of balm over the unhealed wounds of emptiness inside the little girl who'd never doubted Adam would be there for her for life.

The men in the office looked up as she entered. The Paakantyi brother glanced at Adam and nodded, as if receiving a message. 'I'll get the lunches today.' He smiled as he crossed the room to stand with her. 'The Rose and Thistle, right? It's only a few hundred metres from here. Might as well leave the car here, if you're coming back. I'll help you with your bags.'

Something about his patter left her off-kilter. Was he always so effortless with strangers? She flicked a glance at Adam. He trusted this man. With an uncomfortable smile, she nodded.

★ ★ ★

'So are you here for a holiday, or looking to find a new home?' the brother asked as they walked down the unpaved footpath toward the hotel.

Though the question was friendly enough, Elly stiffened. Before she could put a civil tongue in her head she had to remind herself a few times that he was a cop, and questions were a way of life for him. 'Just visiting an old friend.'

'Rick,' he reminded her, gently. 'Or Ricky, if you prefer.' After a moment's silence—*what a weird thing to say*—he went on. Where have you come from? Who are your people?'

Friendly questions. Normal stuff for a brother. He doesn't mean anything by it. Yet it didn't *feel* right; she could sense the burning deep inside this man, the agenda he was trying to keep hidden. 'I told you already.'

A tiny pause, and though he kept walking, she felt the shadow of the office window again, hovering over her, eclipsing her, though he couldn't possibly be here yet.

'I don't think so,' Rick said. 'Who are you trying to protect, Elly? Them, or yourself?'

As surely as she felt the heat of the January day on her skin, she knew this man, a stranger to her until today, was interested in her beyond casual friendship. He wanted something from her … or he just wanted her.

Not again. Never again. 'Excuse me?' she said quietly, but with a distinct chill.

A long silence, in reality only a few seconds, but it felt like minutes. 'My name's Rick … Elly,' he repeated. She felt him watching her, the intensity of his need not hidden well enough. The wanting was on him like scent, like his woodsy aftershave.

'Rick.' It felt odd on her tongue. Something wrong about it. She wished she knew why.

'You're safe with me … Elly. You're a sister, and I'm Adam's best friend here. Whatever trouble you're in, you can trust me to help.'

He kept pausing before naming her. *He knew.* How could he know, so soon?

The sense of too much held in, the simmering anger and passion beneath—it was screaming from him. Fighting the urge to throw up, she turned and grabbed her bag from him without looking up. 'Thank you for showing me the way, senior constable. I'll be fine from here.'

'I mean it, Elly. You're safe with me. Whatever you need, I'm here.'

Against her will, her eyes lifted. Rick Mendham was the epitome of what women wanted: tall, dark and with a handsomeness that bordered on pretty with those big, dark-fringed eyes. But, blazing with sincerity, fierce and protective and *wanting*, he overwhelmed her. 'Thank you. I ... I—' She stumbled to silence, but he wouldn't take the hint, and the emotions he kept hidden so imperfectly grew bigger and bigger, another shadow putting her out of the sun. What was it about her that caused this reaction in men? 'Excuse me.'

She fled down the squeaking, uneven corridor of the pub to reception.

★ ★ ★

'I'm so glad you're here, Dr Lavender.' From the other side of the desk, the thin man with stooped shoulders and a shock of spiky white hair shook Elly's hand. 'It's a little difficult for me to reach the more remote outlying areas of the upper Murray these days.'

'I'm glad too, Dr Schumacher.' She smiled at the white-haired man. In his thin, pale face was the palpable relief of the overworked doctor. Setting up her clinics, her life's vocation, settled her nerves like nothing else. And they needed settling now—something about Rick Mendham wouldn't let go. The intensity, the sense of possession ...

Just like Danny.

She willed the thought away. If she let him dominate her thoughts, he'd won, and she might as well give in.

'How long do you think you can stay?' Dr Schumacher asked.

She wished she knew the answer to that. After months of this work, she understood the medical staff's desperate need for help wherever she went. The patter came without difficulty. 'If you'll let me know which of the Aboriginal communities are in greatest need, I'll make the arrangements. Which of them has a resident nurse, and which only has visiting nurses?'

Accepting her subject change, Dr Schumacher let the matter drop, taking what he could get. Even if she visited two outlying towns, it would give him a month's respite.

From there the discussion grew purely medical. Once a list had been made, and Schumacher had called the nurses for their current reports, Elly stood, shaking his hand again. 'Please remember to be discreet about my time here, Dr Schumacher. I have reasons for needing my presence to remain under the radar.'

'Of course, Dr Lavender. Anything you need.' In the outback, many professionals had their secrets, a past they were running from; it was almost expected. She'd relied on that reputation to help outweigh normal human curiosity. 'Do you need any of our stock before you head out? Of course, we give our outreach nurses whatever they need, and they escort patients here or to Dubbo by flying ambulance, but—'

She nodded. 'Of course.' Invaluable as the outreach nurses were, there were intricate procedures they couldn't do by law. 'I'd appreciate it.'

Dr Schumacher offered to take her to the medical storeroom then and there—but Elly shook her head. A female Indigenous doctor stood out like a sore thumb anywhere, but the last thing she needed right now was the bush telegraph working its magic. She handed him a list. 'I'd prefer for you to collect the stores, and I'll sign for them at your house in the morning, early.'

Schumacher's face lit with curiosity, but he only nodded at the unorthodox, almost illegal, request, such was his need for an extra pair of hands. 'Of course. Call back tomorrow morning, and I'll have everything ready for you.'

'Thank you.' She nodded, and shook his hand.

As she headed out of the hospital, she felt the weight of curious stares from other members of staff, patients and relatives. She didn't look at any of them, keeping her head down and her shoulders hunched, trying to look shorter. Hopefully they'd think she was a patient. *That* was a common enough sight. So when the private detectives came sniffing around asking questions, they'd only find out that a new Aboriginal woman was in town, no more. But that was more than enough—and the detectives would come.

Less than a day in Macks Lake, only an hour with Adam, and the walls were already closing in.

CHAPTER

4

Adam thought of Elly without ceasing, unable to sit still or work. The voices grew louder, more intense, until after a brief struggle with his conscience, he dialled his infamous great-aunt's number.

At the sound of his voice, Aunty Hat cried, 'Adam, is Janie with you?'

'She was here an hour ago,' he said slowly, hating that he wouldn't need to ask a thing. That this was the first non-duty call he'd made to Aunty Hat since coming to Macks Lake wouldn't make the slightest difference—his aunt *knew* she was a pain in the proverbial, and didn't apologise for it. Her family was her life. And family included Elly, it seemed.

The rushing sound of his great-aunt's expelled breath came down the line. He could almost smell the soft attar of roses she always wore. 'Oh, darling, I'm so glad!'

Ding ding ding ding ding … the alarm bells grew louder every second. He didn't have to be a cop to know Aunty Hat was dying to unload her truckload of worries. 'She's in trouble.'

'I think so. She left her people in Sydney after her residency finished in a city hospital. She joined the Flying Doctors—that was two years ago last December. It was what she'd planned to do since she met her family, you know, dear. She arrived at Moongallee Creek.' Adam noted down *Moongallee Creek*. 'She called a few times saying she loved the job, then she didn't contact me for a year. When she calls me now, the number always comes up "Unknown ID", and she won't leave a forwarding address or number. I called the Flying Doctors clinic at Moongallee. They said she'd only been running the clinic three months, then disappeared without trace. Something's happened to Janie, Adam, and it frightens me.'

If Elly's situation scared Aunty Hat, who looked as delicate as Dresden china, had the inquisitive, unshockable nature of Miss Marple and the heart and spirit of a Mallee bull, then it was far worse than he'd even imagined. 'Why send her to me?'

'You were so close once, dear. You were her entire world when you were children. I thought she might talk to you. And you're a policeman. I think … perhaps she might need help in that quarter?'

'Why didn't I ever know about her Indigenous background?' he asked, feeling his way through the tangled labyrinth rising in front of him with each step he took into Elly's life.

The hesitation was tiny, but noticeable. 'When we learned her only living family was Aboriginal, we contacted the authorities and offered to keep her—you know, give her a good upbringing. We told everyone she was Italian, and the local people accepted that.' She spoke simply, with the Jepsons' old-school, upper-middle-class mentality, the instinctive loathing of anyone who was not of Northern European background. 'But after you began dating Sharon, Janie barely spoke again, or ate. After your wedding, she sat in her tree day and night, only coming down to tend her animals. She grew thin and ill, pining for you so badly we feared for her. We contacted her father's family in Sydney. Her father had died years before, but we hoped she'd find a new friend among her own people.'

Shame ripped through his gut. He could see her: his poor, lost wild child sitting alone in her tree, mourning his loss while he made a life without her. Little, forgotten Elly. At fourteen, she'd lost her childhood, and the only friend who understood her. What kind of friend had he been, to push Elly from his life?

'You should have called me!'

'We offered to while she was up the tree, dear—just before you came back from your honeymoon. She disappeared for two days. We gathered that meant no.' The silence was more delicate this time. 'Janie was such a sensitive child, Adam. I think she wanted you to remember her without our prompting you … and she must have felt Sharon's dislike of her. It was fairly obvious to us all.'

He sighed, remembering Sharon's amused words when he'd first suggested Elly visit them in the city. *I wouldn't know what to do with her while you're at work. There aren't enough trees to climb into around here.* And every time he'd suggested it, Sharon had had a reason, another excuse, until her light-hearted contempt became accusations and near-hysteria, and he'd stopped mentioning Elly. No one in the family wanted him to keep the friendship going, least of all his delicate, upper-middle-class, prejudiced wife.

He blinked, realising that for the first time in over three years he'd thought of his wife's name without—

And there it came, the anchor dragging him down into the depths. The soft angel's voice, absolving him even as she lay dying: *It wasn't your fault, Adam … it's who you are.*

His voice curt, he thanked his aunt, promised he'd call her with updates, and hung up. Before him, the computer monitor went into screensaver mode. *COPS* rolled across the screen.

Yeah, it is who you are.

And that made temptation too strong to resist. His heart and gut told him Elly would be on the COPS database, that she was someone's case file. With two fingers, he typed in 'Moongallee Creek', with the date set to two years ago.

The first revelation was sickening enough to make him close his eyes. *Oh, Elly …*

And the updates on the case not only told him his every screaming nerve was right, but that he had to get Rick in on this case, the entire station, Public Operations and Police Affairs—not to mention bringing in detectives with emotional distance—before all hell broke loose.

He snatched up the phone and dialled a number in Western Australia.

'Mackleton Police Service, can you hold?' said a terrified-excited young female voice down the line—and Adam knew, even before he was taken off hold, that all hell was already coming for them.

Mackleton Minimum Security Prison, Western Australia

It was almost time.

Crouched behind sacks holding laundered sheets and blankets, he waited.

Where is she now? How many men are looking at her? Is she ... tempted? If any man dares touch her—

She doesn't want it, fool, he told that stupid voice in his head, the violent one he hated. *She's so innocent, so caring—*

And so alone, the voice said, softly. *The kind of woman men will take advantage of, leaving her sad and bleeding. She needs protection, even from herself. She gives too much. She needs a quiet life.*

He clamped down on the sound of the voice that his shrink had told him wasn't healthy to listen to. Anyway, in thirty-six minutes he'd begin his plans. Trusting no one on the inside to help get him out, he'd crafted his tiny masterpieces with painstaking care within twelve days of sentencing. This time, he'd make her understand ... he wouldn't frighten her.

That voice, the one he didn't like, had led him a bit too far. Janie didn't yet understand the beauty of what he'd done. Next time he wouldn't listen to that other one—and he wouldn't touch her until she was ready. He'd go slow and gentle, show her he'd take care of her for the rest of their lives.

Why had he never fully realised how innocent she was? Smart, to have a house with a panic button—she needed the protection— but she'd pushed it before she'd realised who he was, and when the sirens wailed and lights flashed half an hour later, he'd had nowhere to run. When he'd tried to make her understand that he'd come to save her from the world and all the people who were using her, she'd knocked him senseless and run out to the police.

He'd almost lost faith then. But he'd forgiven her when she'd refused to give evidence. If she had, he might have been given a much longer sentence than thirty days in minimum, no mat- ter what Granddad did to protect him. He'd frightened her—he really believed now he must have done that—but she still wouldn't hurt him.

Granddad was wrong. Janie wasn't a faithless slut like all the oth- ers. He'd be gentler with her next time, come to her in daylight. He'd show her how a real man protects his woman.

Thirty seconds—twenty—ten—

The explosion came right on schedule—a freak accident in the kitchen.

Tossing the bags into the back of the truck, the laundrymen ran out to discover the cause of the commotion.

He looked up and saw the blinking light of the CC-TV camera wink off. Fifteen seconds until they turned it back on. He flitted from the shadows to the truck, diving in. When he was hidden from view, snuggled behind four huge bags of clean linen, he worked on the second device.

A few minutes later the laundrymen returned, accompanied by the two guards his granddad had paid very well to smuggle in the ingredients for the explosive devices, make sure the camera was turned off for fifteen seconds, and overlook him when they checked the truck. With his impeccable sources, the old mongrel had found out which of the guards was neck deep in gambling debts, and which guard was being sued by his ex for defaulting on child payments after a nasty divorce.

'You're clear to go.' That was the one whose gambling debts ensured a deadened conscience. The other's eyes were troubled, but he kept silent, tossing in a marked laundry bag containing spare clothes, right on top of where he hid, following instructions to the letter—the guard would get the large bundle of unmarked notes Granddad would send via the usual channels on top of the two grand he'd sent as temptation.

There were advantages to Granddad being an unscrupulous bastard with unlimited funds. Though Janie's background guaranteed his misogyny had reached explosive levels, Granddad would do anything to get a legal heir who could stay out of prison. He was obsessed with getting another boy to own and screw over, all under the promise of inheriting Gundawin.

He grinned. He could just imagine how Granddad would feel when he realised his omnipotence had failed him for once.

The laundrymen threw the rest of the bags in the truck and closed the doors. Seconds later the engine fired, and they were through the gates.

He put two tiny devices in place before they could reach the linen service in town. Moments later the first shattered the glass window of the cab behind the men. The truck careened across the rutted road on the outskirts of town, hit a wood and barbed-wire boundary fence, and came to a screeching halt.

Seconds later the second device blew the back doors open.

Hopping through the fragmented exit and walking around to the truck's cab, he peered through the shattered glass of the windscreen. The driver's head lay at an awkward angle on the wheel, a jagged blade of glass in his neck. Unlikely he'd live. The other wouldn't stop screaming as he tried to pluck a shard of glass from his head—he'd pass out if he succeeded.

Neither would know anything about him, nor would they see him leave. He'd be long gone before the cops knew the truth of the 'accident'—and by the time they connected today's events to him, connected the truck to him, he'd be safe in a non-extradition country with Janie.

I wish this hadn't been necessary. Janie won't like it, won't understand.

Then she should be here to stop it, the other voice whispered, just loud enough to hear.

She'd have risked her life to save them if she were here, he argued, with some defiance.

Which only goes to show how much she needs protection. Charles Darwin was right. Life is the survival of the fittest. That means there's no such thing as murder, or embezzlement, or fraud; there's only the brightest outwitting the less intelligent. That's obvious, isn't it? Men like you are born to rule, while others obey or die.

It was a persuasive argument.

And if Janie doesn't like what I do, she should be here to stop it. She knows she's the only one who makes me go quiet. She shouldn't have pushed the panic button in the first place!

Shut up, he growled to the voice. *I'm not supposed to listen to you. I have work to do.*

He picked up two long, thin shards of glass from the broken windscreen, wrapped them in towels from the linen service and packed them in his new backpack. Zipping the pack up, he walked to town in the purplish-red haze of a gathering outback evening. His genius lay in the creation of simple explosives he'd made from basic chemical and household ingredients, checked by the prison officials on their arrival at the prison and sent on to the laundry. Three explosions that seemed so much like unrelated accidents; they wouldn't be connected until he was long gone. A homemade peroxide dye applied in the truck to his hair and green-tinted contacts—you really could buy anything in lockup, if you had the money—and he was a new man.

Five kilometres northeast of the accident, off the coastal highway and on the road to Tom Price, he thumbed a ride with the next empty miner's truck. He was on the way to diamond country: the remote Kimberley region, where the diamonds were as magnificent as the heat and dust and rock formations. Where women were as scarce as fresh water, the fights as plentiful as the beer, and doctors flew in from far away to sew the locals' crazy heads back together.

The air grew drier, the heat intense. The road became red and rutted; choking dust filled the cab of the truck. The town names changed from Anglo-Saxon to Indigenous. Moonyoonooka. Yalgoo. Meekatharra. Finally the sign flashed before his eyes. *Mullalabuk—58 kilometres.*

He was on his way to find Janie. And this time, they'd be together for life.

CHAPTER
5

Coming into the station from the sun blinded Rick for a moment. The old house, with its mullioned, stained-glass windows, cool and dark, could be refreshment from the heat, or a shock to the system.

Today was a day of shocks.

With a single look at her, a sense of belonging had overtaken him, so strong it was almost terrifying. He hadn't known love could be like this. One look, and he'd do anything for her. She wasn't exactly beautiful, but she was perfect to him. One look, and she was everything he'd never realised he'd been searching for all his life.

But he'd frightened her off. He had to slow it down, take it easy, show her how special it was going to be for them. Then, when she was comfortable with him, he'd tell her. She didn't know yet how much she was going to need him in her life.

'Your friend's in trouble,' he said to announce his presence in his mate's office. Unless Adam had someone in with him, Rick knew he never had to knock. The two of them had hung out after work and at lunchtimes since Rick's first week in Macks Lake. With his cloak of isolation shrouding him and the coldness scaring most people off, Adam had needed a friend more desperately than he'd known. Rick, alone in town and wanting a friend, had taken up the challenge—and he'd found a mate unlike any he'd ever known.

The words shook Adam from a reverie. He waved Rick into a seat. 'I know.' After a moment, he spoke again, with a thoughtful frown. 'What do you know? What did she say to you?'

'Nothing. She didn't have to.'

A searching look. 'You like her.'

More blunt perception. Usually he liked it, since it saved his needing to answer, or search his own emotions, but this time he felt the wrong kind of examination beneath, and it stopped him from telling the truth, or making the obvious retort, *So do you.* Was all he felt so obvious? He didn't mind Elly sensing it, since it was their private business, but it was none of Adam's, mate or not. He made himself shrug. 'She's a sister. I've been the Aboriginal liaison officer too long *not* to have seen the look before.'

Though Adam nodded, he didn't relax.

'If nothing else, the look on your face—and hers—told me,' he said. 'She was like a rabbit at the dingo fence from the moment we left here. She bolted into the pub as if she expected me to attack her.'

He waited for Adam to speak, to explain why; he knew his friend well enough to know he'd already looked Elly up on the database. Adam had knowledge of her that Rick could never have, though admitting it galled. But he could make use of it, if he didn't push too hard.

Adam didn't answer, just kept watching him with eyes that showed no emotion, though the challenge was there. So it was going to be like that?

He stood to leave the office. Then Adam said, 'Look at this.'

The relief felt like finding cold water in the desert; he wouldn't have to force the issue by using his position as Aboriginal liaison officer. Adam still trusted him. He walked around the desk, leaning over Adam's shoulder as he brought up her page. It was a long report, but two sentences were enough to get the gist.

One man is dead, another fighting for his life in hospital in a truck bombing. Prime suspect is Danny Spencer, who has escaped Mackleton Minimum Security Prison.

'So what are we doing about it?' he asked, grim with fury. 'What's the plan?'

'I was about to talk to Sarge about calling in backup. We can't do this alone.'

It was what he'd known Adam would say; it was procedure, it was right. And what else was there to do? Yet it was as if his life went into slow motion. The whole situation was unreal, like snow falling in the outback, and just as confusing. Only one thing stood out, in shining clarity. As Aboriginal liaison officer, he knew how few times women made formal complaints, and how often the trickle of complaints that were made were shelved in a computer file that went nowhere.

Like Elly's case. For almost two years her complaints had been shelved. Now a man had died, the case couldn't be overlooked any longer, and heads were going to roll. Like a confused mystic he saw the future: dead bodies scattered across Australia, from the Kimberleys to here. Every plan they made wouldn't be enough, because they'd all look at Spencer's history, his problems, his family. None of them would think to research why he'd fixated on Elly.

That's why she came to Adam — the only cop likely to actually listen to her.

Elly was the heart of this case, far more than any woman in a case he'd taken part in. And ignoring that fact would be a disaster not just for her, but for the entire town.

He had to keep her safe.

'Go,' he said to Adam, because there was no other choice. And because it was expected of him, he added, 'I'll check out the networks.'

After a relieved and somewhat embarrassed smile, Adam shoved back his chair. 'Thanks, mate—talk to her family, too, if you can. I didn't even know Elly was Indigenous until today.' A difficult sentence for Adam, he could tell, with the air of confession. *How could you not have known?* he wanted to ask. He again felt Adam's background rising like a horror-movie villain to strangle his mate. He had a feeling that particular monster had already done all the damage it could do to Elly, or she'd have gone to Adam when Danny Spencer first began stalking her.

He didn't have to ask how Adam felt about the discovery of Elly's heritage. The way his mate had helped him with local kids of all backgrounds, forming a football team and raising money for shirts, the way he let Zoe be the boys' mascot, the laughing references to Zoe's massive crush on him all screamed Adam's creed in flaring red letters: *I am not my family.*

Or was it: *I am not my wife?* There was no way he could ask. After a year, he didn't even know Adam's dead wife's name—and with no mention of her to guide him, he'd decided to let that particular ghost rest in turbulent peace.

But on one matter, he had to speak. 'Do you think you should have sent Elly to stay at the pub, mate? Isn't she going to think …?'

At the door, Adam shook his head. 'She understands about Zoe, probably more than I do. She lost her mum when she was ten. That's how she became part of my family.'

Another phantom pain he'd seen in his Adam's eyes from the start. Now he'd pinned the tail on that donkey. The knowledge of Elly's family loss filled him with a mixture of pain and sadness, and a resolve to call his mum that night. He'd been one of the lucky ones. 'But checking into a pub leaves a trail Spencer can follow.'

Adam swore. 'Why the hell didn't I think of that?'

He decided not to ask what had brought Elly to the Jepsons—or what had made Adam forget her so thoroughly he hadn't even recognised her today. He'd learned his friend offered information in tiny bites he could put together in time—but given the urgency of the case, he had to push in another direction. 'Go and talk to Sarge, mate. I've got a bad feeling about this one.'

'A very bad feeling,' Adam agreed quietly, and opened the door.

Left alone, Rick read the open case file on Adam's computer one more time.

After a minute, he took out his phone, and began taking shots of the screen – just in case. Given Elly's panicked response to his slightest push today, he had two choices: to back right off and wait for the right moment, or go deeper, harder, and find the information she wasn't telling, even if he had to push her buttons to do it. And if he did find the info he sought—which might just save her life—he had a feeling she'd make sure he was locked out of the case altogether.

And though she'd regret that decision one day soon, it wouldn't help if she was dead.

★   ★   ★

In the hazy heat of late afternoon, Elly wandered around the pretty little riverboat town. Most of it was preserved in Federation style. No mall dominated any street corner or block, and the new housing estate on the western edge of town had been kept right away from the town centre. The police station was a big old red-brick house with leadlight windows, carved door and lintels, and the school had the solid look of having been built well before the prefab box-shaped buildings of the sixties and seventies. Even the hospital had a semi-disused wing that dated back to Edwardian times, with leadlight windows over the doors, which gave a harlequin-like effect in the hallways when the sunlight hit them.

But five years of El Niño, just reversing with a recent cycle of heavy rain, had halved the oval-shaped body of water that gave Macks Lake its name. Twisted tree roots and dead branches poked like broken hands reaching for help from the muddy water; half-withered mangroves sagged around its banks, bowing down as if in defeat. The orange and olive trees that had been the town's livelihood for a century had green shoots and new leaves twisting up, reaching for the sun from sad-looking branches: a smiling defiance after a long dance with death-dealing drought. A shopkeeper had told her—with an air of warning, as if she was a developer looking at their land—that a dozen or so farmers who'd left their land fallow to find work and pay staggering mortgages were returning. But with so many of the next generation gone to Sydney, Melbourne or Adelaide for university or work, the town was fighting to stop a century-old way of life from disappearing.

She turned from the lake, heading back towards the police station. It was almost time to meet Adam. She dreaded the questions she couldn't postpone much longer. *I can't lie to him. He already knows I'm in trouble.*

So does Rick.

She shut the thought down. She'd met brothers before who'd claimed instant knowledge of her, or the right to attraction or even a relationship, based on culture or DNA, but she'd come to her heritage too late in life to believe in that kind of thing. She respected the culture, as she tried to for all people, but she didn't know if she *believed* in it.

So what do you believe in? Or, who do you believe in? a little voice taunted.

The song of her life. She wished it—*she*—was different, but she'd have to be hatched over again to achieve it. She cared for people—it was her vocation—but she loved very few. Liked even fewer. She hated that she couldn't open her heart to strangers, couldn't bring herself to trust them … and she hated still more that those who managed to break the chains around that stubborn organ snuggled right in for life. She couldn't let people into her heart, and she couldn't let those inside get out.

Like Adam. Though it was the last thing she wanted or needed, he was still in her heart—still the friend she'd never found anywhere else.

Liar.

She'd known long before his marriage that he was far more than her best friend; but since she'd been only fourteen when he met Sharon, of course he hadn't felt the same way. Never had, to judge by the way he'd forgotten her. And yet she'd never met a single man that even began to fill the vacuum he'd left in her life.

And now she'd met him again, she doubted any ever would. A taut bowstring of a man, with a stern face softened by a mouth that always seemed to be fighting a smile, and eyes like a eucalyptus forest touched by sunshine. She'd adored him as a girl, but as a woman, the child's yearning to have someone special to love had become something big and deep and wide—an endless abyss created with a single look.

What was wrong with her? All these years, she'd been unable to give up the dream, though he was long gone. Why couldn't she just let go, move on, find another man?

A feminine voice floated out from the open window of the rowdy pub. 'We'd better get back, or the boss'll sack us.'

Elly's head snapped up.

'Yeah, I s'pose,' a male voice muttered. 'What great jobs—stockman and ringer and you, a kitchenhand instead of head cook.

That's worth keepin', after what we had.' The door to the pub slammed open. 'We should just go home and go on the dole.'

'And let that bitch win? It's what she expects. Bloody brown-gubba with her degree and her scholarship, lordin' it over us,' the woman snapped. 'This gig's well paid, at least. And if she ever comes here …'

Elly drew into a shadow between buildings and watched the young couple walk past. Just as she'd been thinking of people who couldn't give up or move on, here were Wirrah and Lani Miraki. Could her luck be worse? How, why had they come to this tiny outback town where Adam lived? She didn't believe in coincidence to this degree.

She closed her eyes, remembering the last words Lani had spoken to her with such hate in her eyes before they'd left Moongallee Creek: 'Gubba! You're not one of us, and you never will be!'

The cruellest taunt Elly had ever known. How many times had she heard that, or felt it, in her life? 'Gubba' meant 'ghost'—the original term their people had for the whitefellas when they'd first entered the land and the Eora people thought the pale skin meant they were spirits. Now it had much harsher connotations, much like the German *auslander*. That was how so many people saw her: a foreigner, or outsider. A lot of her own family had seen her that way, less for her mother's half-English background than for her upbringing with the Jepsons, while the Jepsons had never seen her as anything but a blackfella.

A lifetime of standing on the outside, looking in. Caught in the crosshairs between lives and cultures, loved but never understood, cared for but never able to fit in. Even Adam had left her. He'd known and loved her as no one else had for the four years after her mother's death, but then he'd forgotten her as if she didn't exist. He hadn't even recognised her today. She'd turned him on, but so what? It meant nothing beyond the usual male reaction to a woman.

Being who she was, she'd always known the hope of fitting in to any culture had always been tenuous; she'd accepted it. But she hadn't realised until now how hard she'd held to the hope of rediscovering *something* with Adam. But now it too had walked into the mist of disappointment on quiet feet, and vanished without sound. Within an hour, it was over.

Picking up the broken pieces of her childhood love would be no hardship; she'd done it for years. A week or so, and she'd be gone—because this time, disappearing didn't mean just giving her peace of mind.

Adam's life could depend on it.

Gibson Desert, Western Australia

'Yeah, I've seen that girl a couple of weeks back. A boonger, right? Pretty one, with freckles, and great boobs.'

Don't call my Janie a boonger. Don't look at her body!

Danny watched Bert with eyes that didn't feel like his own. He couldn't explain it even to himself. The other entity inside him was growing stronger, and *that* Danny worked out every nuance, planned for any eventuality. *That* Danny—the shrink had said that if he named him something besides 'the other Danny' it would make him real, and he, the real person, would be lost—that other Danny knew one thing.

Kill something, someone, or I'll take over, it whispered.

'You gave her a lift?' Danny asked, keeping it casual. Hands in pockets to hide the shaking.

'Yeah.' Bert grinned at him. 'I give rides to lots of people. Makes life interesting when you're on the road. Someone to talk to besides yourself, you know?'

He nodded. He could hardly believe his luck. He'd been catching rides with truckers up and down the region, from Tom Price to Laverton, from Mount Magnet to Halls Creek. He'd expected it would take a few weeks to find the right trucker, but in eight days, he was with the man who'd taken his Janie away from him.

'Where did you take her?' Still cool, casual. Fingers twitching in his pockets, curling over.

A knife ... yes, cool and soothing, the feel of it in our hand as we rip through his skin ...

She'll hate me for it.

There are sheep in the back, use them, another voice sounded in the back of his mind, with something like regret for what he hadn't yet done. The one he called his voice of reason—his voice, the one who wanted Janie's good opinion.

But the other one was growing stronger, the nameless one who wanted to punish Janie for running away, the one who would take Janie and lock her away somewhere safe, where no other man would ever see her and she'd be his, all his.

Just like the man in Austria that raped his own daughter and kept her in the cellar for eighteen years?

His fingernails dug into his palms. Even the other Danny felt sick thinking of that.

Janie isn't your daughter, other Danny said, and real Danny felt his triumph. *You won't do that to your own kids. And when she's had a baby and you're sure it's yours, yeah, she can come out then. A baby bonds a woman to its father for life. You won't have to force her then. It's just for a little while.*

I had a vasectomy, moron, he told other Danny.

So? It can be reversed. You can do IVF. All easy. She'll have our child either way, and she'll be ours for life.

The relief of it, the pain fleeing his hands as his fingers relaxed. Janie would only be unhappy for a little while. Then he'd make her so happy ...

That's it, Danny, you have him now. Control, keep it calm and he can't take over. Granddad can't win, either.

Just watch me, the other Danny said. *And you know Granddad always wins. He knows where Janie is, and isn't telling us until he thinks we're ready to obey him, like we're one of his servants.*

Shut up, he snarled. *I know what Granddad's up to. You don't have to remind me.*

Then why are we sitting here dithering like a girl? Do what you have to. Be a man.

The sheep bleated in the back of the truck. Inviting him. *We're so easy to do.*

Other Danny whispered, *Remember how you did it at Gundawin?*

His stomach churned. He hadn't eaten today, and that's when other Danny took over. He had to fill the tank, keep himself strong. Scrabbling in his bag, he found the packet of beef jerky he always kept on hand, and some dried fruit. *Can't just eat meat, it only feeds the monster. Fruit is good for you, yeah, that's what everyone says. Drink water so your mind doesn't cloud up. He gets in then.*

He gulped down all that was left in his bottle. There was more in the back of the cab, he'd seen it as he climbed in. He'd grab it when Bert no longer needed it—

No, you're not going to win! Real Danny felt the frantic edge to his thought. He was losing control. The attack on the laundry truck had fed the monster. *Yes, Monster, that was a perfect—*

Don't name him!

'I took her as far as the 95 crossroads at Newman,' Bert was saying. 'It was a few hundred out of my way, but she made it worth my while, if you know what I'm saying.' He winked and made a gun with his hand, giving a conspiratorial grin.

Monster (*Don't name him! Stop it!*) tipped his head and considered Bert. A middle-aged trucker with watery blue eyes and rounded brows that made him look perpetually surprised, spiky iron-grey hair, dropped jowls and the belly of a man who sat down for a living, with little better to do than eat and drink on the way to anywhere.

Janie wouldn't do it with the likes of him.

Wouldn't she? If she was desperate to get away, Monster whispered back.

She's not desperate to get away from me. She's just confused and innocent. No! Stop it! You won't make me hate her too. It's Bert that's lying. You really are a monster—

But the black mist came over his eyes. All he saw was Monster filling him like pulsing blood, beautiful in his perfect rage. It felt so good.

No, no, real Danny moaned.

But when the mist receded and he was back inside his own body, Monster had already used the glass shard he'd taken from the truck and slashed it across Bert's lying throat. The truck was careering off the road, slowing as it bumped over rocks. The truck was crawling now, but one rock was right in front of it, too big, and any moment now, the truck would tip—

Snatching up his backpack, Danny jumped from the truck and rolled away just before the cab's tyre bumped over the sharp-edged rock, and tipped up. It didn't roll, but as the rock ground into its hydraulics, the truck groaned and made roaring sounds, trying to move.

It's gonna blow, Monster warned him. *Get us out of here. Get us safe.*

He ran around to the cab again, climbed up and grabbed the food and water, all of it, and shoved it in Bert's massive pack. He found a knife, and took that, too. Then he put another of his little home-made bombs under the dash, just some petrol in a soft-drink bottle and a wick for a timer. The kind of thing that melted under fierce flame, and forensics would have a hard time discovering. Just an accident, really, that's all this was. Nothing more. Truckers died on the road all the time. He lit the wick. Two minutes and counting.

About to jump out again, he glanced at Bert, throat gaping like a fool's mouth, jaw sagging and eyes staring at nothing. 'I wish you hadn't asked for it,' he whispered, almost in regret. 'You shouldn't have said that about Janie.'

No, he shouldn't, Monster said, in a soft, contented voice. *Lots of people ask for death, don't they, Danny? The stupid ones.*

Yes, real Danny agreed with sorrow as he sprinted back toward the road. *I wish they didn't, but they do.*

The truck blew up a little sooner than he'd planned. Lifted off his feet, he landed face down on sharp red rocks and a patch of thorny scrub.

You'll have to make the next wick a bit longer, Monster said.

He didn't answer Monster, busy working out the logistics of it.

Once back on the 95, he began hitching again. South, yes, she'd gone south. Heading for the Nullarbor Plain and the road leading east. She was going home.

And so was he.

CHAPTER

6

Elly waited for Adam outside the station. The sun beat down, adding pulsing restlessness to the close of day. Shimmering waves of heat rose from the sticky-tar road to the blazing cloudless expanse above. Flocks of sulphur-crested cockatoos and grey and pink galahs took flight from twisted ghost gums, their screeching echoes falling from empty sky to parched ground. It was a lost cry, a lament for so much that could have been—for Macks Lake … and for her. A fascinating and beautiful land gone half arid, half urbanised. She could almost see the thousands of ghost hands reaching down through the millennia, trying to hold on to what was left. A century of farming and romantic transportation by river, now abandoned for cities, jobs and shopping malls.

A life of promise swamped by fear.

Adam was walking toward her. Silver ripples of heat curled around his skin, enveloping him in their tendrils. His body exuded steaming haze.

Just like that, the pieces of childhood friendship she'd convinced herself she could pick up with ease shattered and fell. He was wildness barely contained, a leopard straining on a leash, and it set her heart pounding and warmth blooming all over her skin. She'd never felt so alive, so feminine, yet he'd barely touched her.

When Aunty Hat told her of the family's fears for Adam, Elly had reacted on impulse, wanting to lighten his burden. Dressing in a way she never normally would to shock him, she'd expected him to pick up on her game, to wake from his self-imposed sleep. She'd hoped he'd be in the squad car when she'd driven past it that morning. She'd hoped reminding him of their childhood stunts would remind him of the time when life was filled with promise and excitement. Adam needed an enormous jolt to bring him back to the boy he'd been, and she was the woman to do it.

She had so little time. A week to relive childhood fun with Claudius—and if at the end he put behind him some of the repression of the Jepsons and his stick-in-the-mud Sharon, she'd be satisfied. Anything else was impossible. He'd already lost enough. He needed a woman who'd stay the distance, not one who had to disappear so soon.

What she needed didn't matter. She couldn't let it matter.

Janie, I'm coming for you ...

She closed her eyes, but the vision burned in her mind day and night. Against the darkness was a pleasant, almost handsome face with skin tanned to teak in the outback sun, startling grey eyes and dark wavy hair. A nose broken in one too many fights, and a mouth that lost its generosity in base possessiveness: the only kind of love he'd ever known. Danny Spencer's father had died when he was three. After his mother abandoned him a year later, his grandfather raised him. Jeremiah Spencer, owner of Gundawin, a property of half a million acres rich in uranium, was obscenely rich and highly influential, but knew nothing of love, only ownership. He revelled in playing games with people, even his unstable grandson, and had to win—at any cost.

The last night in Mullalabuk was the recurring nightmare that wouldn't let her go: Danny's hands running down the length of her after he'd dropped his knife, while Mickey and Minnie, her darling pup and kitten, stared sightlessly up at her in dumb reproach.

Blood on her skin, staining her soul.

This is how much I love you, Janie. Can you see? Do you understand?

Revulsion and pain racking her, hating even the name her dead mother gave her because he used it—

'Elly? Sorry I'm late. Paperwork.'

Adam's voice brought her back from the crest of darkness, washing the unwanted hatred fouling her mouth until it was no more than a hovering spectre, waiting its chance to return. Instant healing, just as he'd always done for her without trying. It wasn't hard to smile now.

'Hey, Claudius. Like what you see?' She smoothed a hand over the flame-red duco.

His gaze dropped to the four-seater convertible she'd bought in Broken Hill, then followed the line of her hand and arm to her creamy, cross-strapped sundress, and to her face. 'Oh, yeah,' he said in that soft growling voice, making her senses shiver.

She forced enthusiasm into her voice. 'Great, isn't she? An absolute bargain, too. She was a repossession job.'

He drew closer. 'You don't get Beemers at bargain prices.' He gazed at the beautiful car she'd bought just for him with something near anguish. He wasn't looking at her or talking about her—and most importantly, he wasn't asking questions.

Relieved she'd been able to distract him, she told him how much she'd paid for it.

His mouth dropped open. 'Impossible!'

'The bank just wanted its loan covered.' Laughing, she saw the old magic already at work in him. 'I thought you'd know all about repos, and what bargains you can get.'

'Mmm-hmm, of course, but I'm a father, a cop. I can't go around in a car like this. It's irresponsible.' The words were almost a parody of what his father would have said—what Sharon would have said – as his wistful gaze roamed the smooth-as-satin dash, the sweep of the leather seats.

'Go ahead, Claudius. Touch her.' She opened the passenger door, moving her hand along the seat. 'Soft, isn't it? Feels so good beneath your skin.'

'Hmm.' His hand traced each curve and hollow with exquisite slowness, like a lover's caress, and she smiled. Her wild, reckless, loving Adam still lived and breathed, trying to find his way out from within the hard-nosed cop and the stifled Jepson. 'She's beautiful,' he murmured, almost in silence, as if ashamed to admit so much.

Time for temptation. 'Want to take her for a spin?'

He blew out a sigh, and shook his head. 'I have to pick up Zoe.'

'And she'd hate this car?' she retorted in mock-sympathy. Wondering how he'd answer. Was Zoe his child, or Sharon's?

'She'd love the car, but not you.' He shrugged with obvious regret. 'As I said, she's my self-appointed guard dog against women who look sideways at me.'

She nodded again. 'Memory turned into instinct. She's afraid of losing you, too.'

He turned away. 'She was only nineteen months, but she never got over it. She broke both legs, three ribs, and had massive concussion. She was out of it for three days. The only thing she remembers is the pain, and that Mummy went away.'

'I don't even remember my father.' She fixed her gaze on the shivering mirage in the middle of the road ahead of them. 'I lived on the road with my mother for years, moving every few months. I never let her out of my sight, except when she was at work. She had a boyfriend when I was about eight. I made his life hell until he left.'

He grinned at her. 'Why is it so easy for me to envision that?'

'The same reason I envision those big hands of yours itchin' to get a grip on my red baby's wheel, going at a hot one-ten,' she retorted. 'We're two of a kind, Claudius. We always were.'

He looked away, frowning into that shimmering tar. 'Are we, Elly? Are we still?'

'I think so.' She paused, breathed in a few times before she said it. 'That's how I knew not to come to Sharon and Zack's funeral.'

She could see where the anguish hit him: the solar plexus. 'Thank God someone did,' he muttered. 'The clan made it a wake to remember. I got five offers to take the "burden" of Zoe off my hands.'

She touched his arm. 'How could I not know how you'd feel, after old Abe?'

His face softened with the memories of that golden, innocent summer. She remembered too: he was fifteen and a half, a sulky boy cooped up too long after a bout of pleurisy, needing to run; she was almost eleven, a grieving tomboy who knew every hidden rock, billabong and hollow of the farm, but not how to talk to people. She understood his need to run; he shared her love of wild things, open spaces and adventure, and helped her trust people again. From their first day together, she'd felt the impetuous, rebellious heart trying to break forth from the weight of convention and expectation, just as he felt her grief, and accepted it. For the first and last time, she'd met a kindred spirit. Together they'd forged a bond that surpassed Jepson understanding.

She'd fallen in love with Adam's dog, Abe, the day they'd met— it was the only way she'd come to Adam at first. The Jepsons had sent Abe with Adam to his grandparents' farm when he'd needed to recuperate in the country. Adam's father wasn't prepared to tolerate a howling dog looking for his master.

Then near the end of that summer, Abe had fallen asleep and never woken again.

She'd slipped away from Abe's graveside after a faltering prayer, leaving a silent, stony-faced Adam alone with his grief. That night, she'd watched in silence from her tree as he'd stolen Uncle Adam's tractor and taken it on a mad joyride across the fields, tearing up crops. She'd taken the punishment for him the next day. With all her simple child's heart, her love focused on the boy who understood her as no one else ever had. She'd have done anything for Adam. Anything.

'I'd have welcomed you at the funeral,' he said now, bringing her back to the present.

'No point. You wouldn't have known who I was.' She started the engine. 'So are you taking my red baby for a ride, or are you piking it in that thing?' She wrinkled her nose at the sedate, dark-blue 'family' model sedan. 'Poor henpecked Claudius. My motor-mad mate, whose greatest ambition was to own a Lamborghini, reduced to that.'

★   ★   ★

Henpecked? Adam's nostrils flared; he flung open the back door of his sensible family car, pulled out Zoe's child seat, and secured it in the BMW.

'Get in the passenger seat.'

She obliged with an impudent smile. 'Go for it, Claudius. Burn some rubber.'

A swirl of red dust rose as he flew out of the parking lot. Adrenalin hit him, even at sixty, before he swung the car onto the highway outside town. Then he hit fifth gear and floored the accelerator; he hit sixth, and their heads fell back with the Beemer's surge of smooth, purring power. One-ten; one-twenty; still climbing on a hot, empty road. No guilt or fear. There was no danger to anyone, and none of the guys were on highway patrol.

He laughed with the exhilaration of realising his childhood fantasy. A perfect summer day in a topless red dream machine, warm wind in his hair, riding the highway at a speed no cop should touch unless in pursuit. He glanced at Elly, sharing the moment with someone who understood, and shared his love of fast cars.

Bad mistake.

Her chestnut curls whipped in the wind; reckless laughter illuminated her face. Her dress was the ultimate in feminine temptation, moulded to her curves like a glove by the wind. Dear God, his scrawny little tomboy was all grown up, and everything he'd never known he wanted.

Responsibility. Maturity. Duty. The Jepson mantra was empty, without power, relegated to the back of his mind when he was with her. *Come on, how could a little excitement hurt?*

'Claudius, are you fighting the Mack truck for passage? If you are, let me out! I'll cede you the car, but I'm not ready to die yet.'

Dragging his gaze from her, he jerked the car back to their side of the road.

The truck roared past, mighty horn blasting in their ears, leaving the car shuddering in its wake. He felt his body move in time with it. *Fool!* Two minutes in a dream machine with a woman he hadn't even known dreams were made of until today, and Zoe was almost an orphan.

He performed a U-turn and headed back to town at a sedate pace, self-reproach a lance in his gut. Zoe couldn't afford him taking these risks.

Even so, he could still hear the word *henpecked* chasing itself around in his brain, making him crazy with the need to prove her wrong, to show her he still didn't turn down a dare. Damn Elly for still being able to push his buttons.

He didn't look at her again. Every time he did, he thought and felt things he couldn't afford to, broke rules and managed to make a jerk of himself somehow.

Not somehow. You know exactly how.

Even now he burned with the need to do be wild and crazy in more ways than just driving a car—even a car of his dreams. *Damn it.* Just like all those years ago, she'd corrupted him with a few words, a dare here and there. She was everything he couldn't afford to want—and she'd laugh herself stupid if she knew. As if she'd want a crusty sobersides cop like him—with a child to boot: the daughter of a woman who'd hated her.

'Well, that was fun.' Elly's laughter brought him back from the darkness. 'You rose to the challenge beyond all my pathetic expectations, Claudius. I suppose your wacky sense of humour drove you to impress me with a near-death experience?'

He grinned. 'Henpecked?'

She lifted her hands, palms forward in mock-surrender. 'I take it back. You're insane!'

Dead right, and it felt so damn fantastic. He hadn't realised how long it had been since he'd just had irresponsible fun.

'Claudius, shouldn't you slow down a little? You're doing sixty-five in a forty zone.'

He wasn't ready for the dream to end yet. 'Who's henpecked now?'

She grinned. 'No, my friend, merely aware that we're back in town, and in a school zone, which must be, I believe, your daughter's. I haven't seen any other preschool along here.'

Don't blame yourself. It's not your fault, Adam.

Not waving—drowning. Despite Sharon's dying absolution, he knew whose fault it was that his little girl had no mother, no brother.

Damn it, stop thinking her name!

He hit the brakes, the shot to his heart almost physical. He swung with a screech into the driveway of the preschool, and leaped out of the BMW as if it burned him.

Elly came around the car, laying a hand on his arm. 'Get off the guilt-trip merry-go-round, Claudius. You were having fun. You'd have remembered in a moment or two.'

'Thanks for the comfort, but you don't have kids,' he snapped, pulling his arm away.

'You're right, I don't.' Her voice was filled with odd longing and strange hate, and he felt lousy. But before he could make sense of her mood, it turned again. 'Let me see if I can pick out Zoe.' She peered through the window. Three little girls and two boys sang songs. She pointed to a dainty, angelic child with flyaway silver-blonde hair. 'That's got to be Zoe. She's the image of Sharon.'

His hands made quick fists, but he unclenched them as he regained control. *She doesn't mean to keep saying it*, he reminded himself.

'Stay here. I'll get her.' He stalked into the preschool.

The angst diminished at the touch of a tiny hand in his.

'Hel-lo, Dad-dee!' Zoe always sing-songed her words, with a cute lift on the last syllable. He grinned down at her. An adorable sprite, she had Sharon's blonde hair and angel's face, his green eyes and a mercurial, laughing impishness she must have inherited from somewhere else. She stamped her foot in well-known demand. With a grin, he swung her up on his hip. She gave him a series of hearty, smacking kisses while he signed her out.

Zoe wriggled to the ground at the childproof gate. Adam opened it and, taking his hand again, she skipped outside. 'Ooh, Daddy,' she breathed, staring in bright-eyed fascination at the glowing BMW, the only car in the yard, since most parents picked up their kids long before five-thirty. 'Are we going for a ride in that?'

'You sure are, Zoe.' Elly opened the door for her, smiling.

Zoe's smile died. She shrank behind her father. 'Who's *she*?'

He smothered a grin. Elly was about to meet her nemesis. 'That's Elly, the owner of the car. So if you want a ride, you'd better be nice to her.'

Zoe clutched his leg, sticking her tongue out at Elly. 'I don't like her, an' I don't wanna ride in her stupid car.'

He lifted his daughter's chin, making her face him. 'Zoe, remember your manners.'

Tears filled the green eyes so like his own: angry, insecure, filled with defiance. 'No! She's ugly! I don't like her, an' *I don't wanna ride in her stupid car*!'

His face darkened. 'For that rudeness, you get time out in your room when we get home.'

A gentle voice halted the lecture. 'Would you mind if I talked to her, Claudius?'

When he nodded, Elly dropped to her haunches before Zoe. She didn't smile or try to touch her as she said, 'Hello, Zoe. I'm Elly. I grew up with your daddy—we were like brother and sister. I came to see Daddy, but I also want to be *your* friend. If I spend time with Daddy, we take you with us. I won't take Daddy away from you, Zoe, not now, not ever. And that's a promise.' She held out her pinky finger, curled over.

From behind his leg, Zoe looked into Elly's eyes. So did Adam. They were serious, full of the respect young children crave, but are rarely accorded. Just as thoughtful and serious as Elly, Zoe said, 'Maybe.' And wrapped her pinky around Elly's.

Their linked fingers pumped, once, twice. 'Thank you, Zoe. We'll head for your car, and you can think about it on the way. Would it be all right with you if I come for dinner just for tonight? We could order pizza.'

Zoe's eyes lit up. 'I *love* pizza.'

'A woman of taste, I see.' Elly stepped back. 'Daddy can put you in your seat. I'll sit next to you, so we can have some girl talk. He can be nice and quiet, like a good boy.'

Zoe giggled as Adam strapped her in. 'Be nice and quiet, Daddy. We girls wanna talk.'

Stunned by Zoe's capitulation—or was it a preschooler's test, to see if Elly meant it?—he obeyed his daughter's order without a word.

The girls laughed and sang songs all the way back to the station. Elly taught her a medical nursery rhyme that would help Zoe know what to do if she ever saw others in trouble. They sang it four times, and after the third time, Elly called her Doctor Zoe.

When they reached his car, Zoe decided to go home with Aunt Elly—Annelly, as she'd already begun calling her. She wanted to sing the song again, so she'd be ready to share it with the kids at school tomorrow.

They walked into the three-bedroom bungalow he now called home, Adam carrying the car seat while Zoe put her hand in Elly's. He called the only pizza place in town—one that offered kebabs, too, along with barbecue chickens—and paid extra for them to deliver. The girls demanded a Hawaiian pizza and a supreme for the grown-up, glaring at him in mock-disapproval. When Zoe mentioned her love of the movie *Up*, Elly said she had it on her USB. They could attach it to the TV, and watch it after dinner. They sent Adam to the shop for popcorn and lemonade.

Refusing Elly's dangled keys, he stalked out the door, heading out in silence. He needed time to clear the chaos in his head. In one day, the life he'd treasured since moving here—quiet, predictable, with the security Zoe needed—was going down the gurgler. It was bad enough that she still held the power to turn his life upside down, and damn the consequences—but Zoe had lost enough. Though she couldn't remember her mother or brother, she still had regular nightmares about the accident. *The car's all banged up. I can't breathe! Daddy, help me! Daddy, where are you?*

No, Zoe needed safety, security, continuity and peace. And a father who was hers alone, not riding on Elly's roller coaster. He couldn't let that turbulent magic enmesh itself in Zoe's needing heart. Zoe couldn't afford any more loss. Elly had to go. Tonight.

And if she dies?

The warning on the COPS database blipped back into his memory, and the need to protect Zoe mixed with turbulent shame in his gut. If what had happened to her could make him sick, a seasoned cop with ten years' inner-city experience, what had it done to Elly, on top of all she'd already lost in her life? So much pain, and some of it could be laid at his door. Even the bull that had taken her mother's life had belonged to his family.

Who he put first wasn't up for debate, but he couldn't let his loyalty to Zoe cost Elly her life.

He worried himself sick all the way to the store and back home that she—and Zoe—would be all right.

Back inside the house, he found them alive and safe, playing Ring Around the Rosie.

He watched in silence from the doorway. Holding Zoe's hands, crouched over as she danced, Elly was having just as good a time as Zoe, singing without tune or embarrassment.

If Sharon were here, she'd be singing and dancing with Zoe—and so would Zack.

His throat thickened. All the simple joys Zoe had missed out on, all the life and love and growing Sharon and baby Zack had lost—

'A-tishoo! A-tishoo! We all fall down!'

Woman and child fell to the floor together, Elly's full, flared skirt floating as she fell, exposing long, brown legs in the careless tangle.

His body reacted yet again, his gaze riveted to her. There wasn't a part of her that didn't tease, entice, bind him in her spell. Elly the wild tomboy had called to him irresistibly, heart to heart; the woman did all that, and drove him insane with desire at the same time.

'More, Annelly! More!'

Elly untangled her legs, smoothed down her skirt, rose to her feet and stretched out her hands to Zoe, and they began again. And he kept watching her.

'Hey, Claudius, snap out of it!'

He started, realising she'd seen his gaze fixed on her breasts. He closed his eyes. Oh, man, what a jerk.

Zoe created a welcome diversion. 'Annelly, why do you call Daddy that funny name? His name's Adam.'

'It's a play name.' She sat beside Zoe. 'When we were kids, Daddy named me Elly-May after a girl on television, because I was wild, and loved animals better than people. So I gave him a name. Claudius was a king who couldn't talk properly.'

That dropped her a few points in Zoe's estimation. He watched in amusement as his daughter frowned at Elly, her lower lip sticking out. 'My daddy can talk!'

'Now he can.' She winked at Adam. 'But when he was growing up, he'd stutter—'

Zoe tilted her head. 'What's "stutter"?'

'W-well, s-stuttering is when you take a b-bit longer to s-say a w-word. Your d-daddy did that w-when a pretty girl came near him, because he was scared. I nicknamed him Claudius to tease him.'

Zoe giggled. 'Did pretty girls scare you, Daddy?'

'Yep, they sure did.' He grinned with the memory.

Zoe's head tilted in consideration. 'Annelly's *real* pretty, and you don't talk funny.'

So Elly had gone from ugly to *real* pretty in an hour, and the right-wrongness of that left turbulent confusion churning in his gut. 'I've grown up since then,' he said abruptly. 'I've seen so many pretty girls, it doesn't bother me now.'

The doorbell rang. Zoe yelled, 'Pizza! C'mon, Annelly, let's go get our bestest one!'

'I want to see if you can bring them in all by yourself.'

Zoe puffed up in pride. 'I can. I'm a big girl. I'm nearly five. Watch me, Annelly!'

'I'm watching, sweetie.' Elly smiled as Zoe dashed down the hall. 'She's her daddy's girl, isn't she?'

'Yeah.' Right now, he wished she weren't. The untamed magic that radiated from Elly was already at work on Zoe. When Elly went, he'd be left with a broken-hearted child wanting a mummy. He couldn't take such a monumental risk with his child's heart.

Her laughter faded as she saw the look on his face. Her eyes dulled. 'Well, Claudius? Spit it out. I can see you're dying to lecture me on something.'

She stood before him, chin high, but all he saw was a candle with its flame blown out by the wind; the foster kid waiting for the next round of Jepson disapproval. The girl who'd taken the fall for him dozens of times—but never *from* him, and that thought made him swallow the words burning his tongue. 'Elly, I talked to Aunty Hat,' he said instead. 'Then I looked up Moongallee Creek on the database.'

She turned on him, her eyes glittering like onyx. 'I thought I could trust you. Out of all the men in the world, I thought *you* would respect my wishes, and not violate my privacy, but you're just like all the rest,' she rasped, and turned away.

'Daddy, the man wants his money.' Zoe carried the pizza boxes down the hall, her tongue poking out with concentration. 'Can you see me carryin' the boxes, Annelly? Can you see me?'

'I sure can, sweetie. You're doing a great job!' She wheeled back, her eyes skimming past him to the door down the hall. 'My treat tonight. Don't start without me!'

When she returned to the living room, she wouldn't look at him. 'C'mon, Claudius, I'm starving—'

His hands fell on her shoulders, stopping her flight to the kitchen. 'I wish I could be sorry I intruded on your privacy, but I have a child to protect, and this is a bloody serious matter. I *am* sorry I hurt you, Elly. Let me in. Talk to me!'

Her face remained averted. 'Just tonight. Give me tonight.'

'Stubborn woman,' he growled, relieved at the second chance her words implied. He hated himself for the seesaw of emotions he was letting her put him through, moving from wishing she were gone to being glad as hell she was still here. 'I have four days off, starting Saturday. How does a picnic by the Murray River sound? If it rains before then, we might even catch a glimpse of a paddleboat.'

She rewarded his sacrifice with a radiant smile, filling him with another surge of hotted-up hormones, and a fleeting sense of fun and laughter he hadn't known in years.

'A picnic sounds wonderful. You know, I still treasure the memory of our unorthodox effort in the wilds of Bundanoon after you got your licence, Claudius.'

He laughed, reliving the day in the rolling green hills of the Southern Highlands, eighty miles from his grandparents' farm. The day he'd got his driver's licence, he'd wanted to share his success, do something a little wild and crazy to celebrate it—and he knew only one person who'd understand that feeling. He laughed again at the frolicking innocence of that day, and spat on his hand, just like when they were kids and made a pact to do something crazy. 'Done.'

Her brow lifted. 'I'm still no coward about what's in your mouth, Claudius.' She spat on her hand, and they shook with the solemnity of a vow.

Their eyes met above the clasped hands. Hers were filled with deep, shining wonder. A blush filled her cheek like a rosebud unfurling—and she couldn't tear her gaze from his. Her lips parted. The hand in his trembled.

A superb aura of masculine power—the knowledge of being the man wanted by the woman he desires—pervaded him. All he'd done was touch her hand.

Oh, God, help me. An ineffectual prayer. It was bad enough before, wanting Elly like hell, believing it couldn't happen. Now with the attraction mutual, and violent—for her coffee-coloured eyes held all the hunger for him he knew his must hold for her—he knew his self-control would never last.

Lovers. Him and Elly? It was ridiculous, laughable—and so damn right that his heart filled with strength. It was inconceivable; it was inevitable. It couldn't happen—yet he could no more stop it than he could stop tomorrow coming.

Could his insecure little girl endure Elly's entrance into their lives on a more intimate basis? Zoe liked Elly now, but there was a world of difference between liking Daddy's old friend and tolerating his lover. The roller coaster Elly had brought with her grew fifty feet higher. She was destroying all the serenity and security he'd worked so hard to build here—

Stop lying to yourself. Elly never hurt you; it was always the other way around. Maybe you're bad for her ... and with your track record, you'll probably be bad for her again.

So why did he keep thinking about it? Why couldn't he turn off, move away, avoid her, cut the fantasies dead? He'd done it often enough before.

At that moment she removed her hand from his, her eyes taking on that haunting look of composure, and its practised wrongness struck his soul with chilling force. 'So long as this picnic is more orthodox than the last one. We couldn't get away with that sort of stuff at our age. Even cops can get busted for public indecency, right?'

'True,' he muttered, his heart breaking for her. It seemed he'd even ruined her memory of that day. 'Things might have changed between us since then.'

'Nothing needs to change. We were friends then, we're friends now.' Her mouth formed a restrained half-smile, full of studied serenity. 'I won't be staying long.'

His brow lifted. 'Very effective, Dr Lavender. If you give all your male patients that Mona Lisa look, they'd be too scared of you to try for so much as friendship.'

She choked off the giggle, but her smile widened and her body relaxed. 'Okay, Detective Sergeant Jepson, you win ... for now.'

Relieved he hadn't lost his ability to make her laugh when she threatened to close off on him, he grinned. 'With you, Elly-May, I never expect more than an armed neutrality.'

She looked with peculiar intensity at a watercolour on paper tacked to the wall by a proud Zoe. Her fists clenched and her lovely body became rigid, trembling, but no longer with desire. 'That's more than anyone else gets from me, Claudius. So count yourself lucky.'

Splat. The sound came from the kitchen—and the painful connection turned to laughter.

'Uh-oh. That sounded ominous,' he murmured with a grin.

'Can we eat our pizza now, Annelly? I'm *bery* hungry,' came the complaint from the kitchen. 'And Daddy, I spilleded your pizza on the floor …'

'Yup, looks like your fun's already begun. Welcome to Jepson family life, Elly-May. Join in with us as long as you can stand it.'

Her smile lilted. 'That might be a little longer than you expect, Claudius.'

★ ★ ★

'So the handsome prince took Sleeping Beauty to his castle. They invited everyone in the land to their wedding. And they lived happily ever after.'

Elly closed the book and looked at Zoe, seeing curled golden lashes fanning pale cheeks. No more sleepy calls for 'More, Annelly. Just *one* more story', just a trusting child asleep in her arms, her tiny smile so like Adam's it made her ache. Unexpected tenderness flooded her. Somewhere in the past few hours, this child she hadn't known until today had accomplished what few did: she had made her care. Like father, like daughter. Softly, she lowered Zoe to her pillow.

'Goodnight, little Sleeping Beauty.'

She walked into Adam outside the door. His hands landed on her shoulders, holding her at a slight distance. 'You're spoiling her, you know. One bedtime story is the rule.'

She laughed, to hide the quiver of pleasure rushing through her at his touch. 'How many rules have I broken so far?'

His expression showed awareness of her desire. His hands remained on her, his thumbs caressing her collarbone. 'I've a feelin' you enjoy breakin' rules, Miz Elly.'

'Depends on what they are.' Her tongue ran over her upper lip. 'Some rules exist only in our minds, social taboos that have no meaning. Those I'll always break, with pleasure.'

When he spoke, his voice was low, husky. 'How much pleasure do you think you could stand?'

Though he didn't move, his voice willed her closer. Her breath blew out in a rush. She swayed toward him—

A sigh floated into the hallway, a soft creaking of the bed as Zoe moved. An innocent reminder of all that stood between them.

She stirred, pushing out from under his hands. 'I'd better go.'

He released her. 'I'll walk you to your car.'

She didn't even have to glance at him to know the Sharon Look was back on his face; the look of innate superiority and disapproval of everything she was. She'd lost him so completely fourteen years ago, she hadn't even tried to win him back—her Adam just wasn't there. And it seemed, despite the connection they'd just shared, he still preferred to be gone.

In Elly's prejudiced eyes, slender Sharon of the angelic face and silver-golden hair had never loved *Adam*. She'd set her sights on the second son of the conservative, respectable Jepson family, upper-middle-class lawyers, graziers, school deans and politicians, proud descendants of the English family that crossed the world on a ship in the 1850s. Sharon had taken Adam's loving, adventurous boy's heart and walked all over it. All the qualities Elly had found so lovable in him, Sharon had squashed with a tender, ruthless suppression.

Adam, don't you think it's time you stopped your childish jokes and pranks?

Playing football is for hooligans, not respectable people.

Adam, you're too dirty to hug. You've been out fishing—you don't expect a kiss before you have a shower, do you? You smell like sweat, fish and beer. And those animals …

That Janie's so wild. She's bad for you, Adam. You must stay away from her.

Elly sighed. Perhaps rigid, repressive Sharon had been right for once with the unthinking condemnation she'd never meant for Elly to overhear. And Adam's wife had never been more right than now, three years after her death. This thing arcing between Elly and Adam was crazy. If they gave in to it, Adam's life, maybe even Zoe's, would be in danger. It was better for them both if she packed up and left Macks Lake tonight.

'Good night, Adam.' *And goodbye.* She stepped off the verandah, ready to perform another vanishing act.

An urgent hand pulled her back. 'Elly, don't move!'

Kaltukatjara Community, Great Sandy Desert, Western Australia

'Go back to the road and stay on it. This is our place. You got no permit to come here, or talk to anyone. It's the law.'

A little way from the road, eight sets of dark eyes watched Danny's face in calm challenge, but if he pushed back, the weapons in plain sight would turn on him. Eight men, six of them bigger than him and filled with wiry strength, eyes cold with suspicion.

The town wasn't gated, of course, not in this back-of-beyond place on the Docker River Road on the Western Australia–Northern Territory border. It was barely even a road, just a dusty, blazing-red track with grey-green scrub and straggling trees alongside it, and with houses painted all colours of the rainbow. Poor houses, Danny thought, and substandard humans who'd never get to Perth or Darwin, let alone Sydney. This was as much as they'd ever own. It even smelled poor, just air, dirt and trees. *How dare they lock me out? If they knew the things I've done, that I can destroy this pitiful village with just a phone call …*

'Do you know who I am?' he demanded, hands shaking as he felt Monster crouching behind his quiet veneer, just waiting to leap.

A young man spoke up. 'Yeah, someone who's goin' back onto the road. Now.'

If he didn't care about them, they didn't care about him either. Wind-burned and sore from wandering in temperatures of forty-three degrees Celsius, he'd been trying to get into the community for over an hour. The bloody trucker he'd hitched with for two days entered the town without hassle, bringing food and water to the little store. He'd paid the trucker hundreds to get him in. But though Dave had assured the people Danny was all right, he hadn't got a metre from the road without being stopped by a human barricade with distrust in their eyes. A bloody trucker had been welcomed in, and he, a Spencer of Gundawin, was treated as a common criminal!

Like I said, they're stupid, Monster said softly. *The world's better off without them.*

He thrust his hands into his pockets. He was shaking with the growing need to let Monster loose. He'd controlled it for days now, hundreds of kilometres and half a dozen remote communities. He'd stayed Monster's hand with four words: *Janie wouldn't like it.*

But his sudden sense of certainty that these subhumans had seen Janie, still had Janie here maybe, and were keeping her from him, changed the game. Clarity set his body shaking and brought Monster to the fore.

One last chance, he told Monster. *Just let me ask.*

Monster bowed, and he felt the smile. Giving permission. *I should never have named him!*

'Has a woman been here lately? Her name's Janie Larkins—she's a doctor with the Aboriginal and Islander Medical Commission. I'm offering cash for information.' He held up a wad of notes, surely more than any of them had seen in a lifetime. *Take it, people. Do it. Don't let Monster take over!*

The oldest man there—he looked about a hundred—stepped forward with a younger man's assistance. 'We dunno no Janie Larkins, and we ain't seen a doctor in a year or more.' The effort to say that much wore him out, and the younger men lowered him until he sat on the red powder that was the earth here.

Danny watched him with revulsion. An old man like that was long past his usefulness. Why didn't he drop? Then in the confusion he could run in, find Janie.

A camel wandered past them. With a loud spurting sound, it crapped on the ground, and moved on into the community. A lousy camel could get in, and he, Danny Spencer, was being locked out? The skin of his palms stung as his nails dug in. *Come on, people, I'm giving you a chance to live here. Just bring Janie to me!*

Stupid people don't deserve to live, Monster said, his voice purring. Anticipation brought on the blackness, the blankness taking him over. Locking him in unseen chains, knowing he'd only wake up to find out what Monster had done.

Please, people! Janie wouldn't want you to die! 'Which way did she go after she left?'

The old man on the ground looked up at him and cackled. 'If we ain't never seen her, we can't tell ya which way she went, can we!'

The others laughed. Laughed at *him*.

It's my turn now, Danny. We don't let anyone disrespect us like that. He's just like Granddad, thinking we're nothing but a piece on his chessboard to move around.

Janie, Janie, where are you? Danny cried silently. *Come to me, Janie! He's making me want to fill my hands with blood. Only you quieten the monster inside me …*

I'm not 'the monster', Danny. I'm you, Monster said, soft and smug. *I'm Monster, and I'm all you … you belong to me now.*

No! No, you're not me, and I'll never be yours! JANIE, WHERE ARE YOU?

But she wasn't here, and Monster stepped into him, smooth as blood, hot as the day—

When he came back to himself, no one was dead, and only one man was cut. The others had taken his knife from him, and were poking him back toward the road, armed with knives and spears and a couple of rifles.

The biggest man kicked him in the arse, and when he stumbled, the stupid blackfella snarled, 'Get out, psycho, and don't come back.'

On his knees, he stared up at the man. Monster had retreated somewhere deep inside, licking the wound on his shoulder. Not enough to kill him, just to frighten him. Monster didn't like getting hurt, it made him whimper and hide.

'What did I do?' he whispered, hating to own Monster's acts.

The man who'd spoken held up a phone and pressed *play*.

Danny wanted to throw up when he saw that Monster had tried to stab the helpless old man in the throat.

Don't be angry, Monster whimpered. *He talked to us like Granddad does. I couldn't help it.*

Sick, weary, defeated, Danny headed back to the truck to wait for Dave. But sitting in the cab, he heard a loud whisper: 'We didn't tell him, Mum. Didn't tell him the nice lady's gone.'

A slow smile curved his mouth, and lightened the stain of black on his soul. *Thanks, kid, that was all I needed to know.*

CHAPTER
7

Elly froze as Adam moved with quiet stealth to her car, switching from friend and possible lover to cop mode in seconds. She frowned. Was the BMW a little lower than it ought to be …?

She watched in helpless silence as Adam checked out the car, inside and out, then moved to the footpath, observing the yard, the whole length of the street and the houses either side of his.

It seemed hours before he returned to her. 'All four tyres are slashed. There doesn't appear to be any other damage to the car.'

'Somebody likes me,' she joked, trying to control the tremors working their way out from her pounding heart to her weakened limbs.

He touched her arm and held onto it. 'You're not going anywhere tonight, Elly. From now on you're staying with me. It's obvious you need protection.'

'Because some idiots are jealous of my car?'

His gaze met hers in the darkness, and he spoke very low. 'Danny Spencer escaped from Mackleton minimum security prison sixteen days ago in a prison bombing. He's the major suspect in the bombing and malicious damage to a laundry truck that killed one man and left the other in intensive care, and the murder of another truck driver in the Gibson Desert in Western Australia.'

Danny was out.

With a smothered cry she bolted, stumbling out of her sandals in blind panic, landing sprawled on the gravel driveway.

He lifted her to her feet and led her back to the house, away from the sight of her vandalised car. He sat her down on the sofa, and hauled her close. 'I'm sorry, Elly.' He caressed her back with a soothing hand. 'I put off telling you as long as I could, but with the murder and now this, I had to make it official. Talk to me.'

'No! Don't touch me!' She pushed his arms, trying to break his hold. 'Let me go. If he's here, if he's watching, if he sees you touching me, he'll kill you—he'd even kill Zoe!'

'It's not going to happen.' His voice was so gentle, so kind. 'Talk to me, Elly. I could always help you before, when we were kids.'

'You can't stop him. His sadistic games have begun. If I don't give him what he wants, he terrorises me, laughing from the shadows as my life falls apart.'

'I know about Spencer's fixation with you.' Adam held her in a vice-like grip. 'Until this afternoon, he'd only been traced as far as Mullalabuk in the Kimberley region. To the best of our knowledge he's still in Western Australia. The truck of the dead driver was found just off the 95 Highway at the edge of the Gibson Desert. We're trying to determine if and when he visited the community. We're sending an Aboriginal liaison officer tomorrow to talk to them. Forensics says the truck driver died eight days after Spencer escaped, so that gives us a lead.'

'It doesn't matter,' she panted, still struggling against him. 'He'll find me. The law never stops him. This was the fourth time he broke the Apprehended Violence Order and hurt me, and all he got was thirty days.'

At that his hold softened, allowing her to move away. The implicit understanding in the movement—the freedom of choice he offered—soothed and comforted her.

'We'll get him this time. He'll get twenty years for killing the truck driver.'

'No. He'll get off. He always does.' She paced the room, hating the words that poured from her mouth, but unable to stop them. 'He's a millionaire in his own right, and the only heir of a multi-millionaire cattle baron in the Northern Territory. His grandfather steps in every time the law gets serious, and gets Danny's sentence lowered with the help of an army of psychiatrists who babble about his grandmother's and father's deaths, his mother's desertion, his sad childhood, and promise ongoing treatment. Then he escapes within days with thousands of dollars he shouldn't have, changes his appearance completely, calls in private detectives, and is free to destroy my life again!'

'Like when he killed your dog and cat?' he asked, his voice gentle. Standing near her, but not touching. Protection and caring, but without invading the space she desperately needed right now. 'Is that why you don't have critters any more?'

Her shoulders slumped. Feeling broken. 'Would you?'

He said nothing, just took a step to her, kissing her forehead and moving away again.

'It's not just Mickey and Minnie now,' she whispered. 'A man's dead because of me.'

'Not because of you.' His voice was gentle and hard at once. 'That's Spencer's fault. Don't take the fall for his acts.'

She stepped back. 'A man's dead because I ran away. He's doing this out of frustration and anger because he can't find me. Now he's finally killed a human, Danny's last restraint is gone. He's upgraded from killing animals to human beings because I rejected him.'

He shook his head. 'The bodies of six jackaroos have been found on Gundawin land in the past two weeks. The NT police finally got search warrants on the whole of Spencer's property after the trucker's death. We can't prove it yet, but we believe all six were murdered. Their families suddenly got rich after their disappearances. They must have been paid hundreds of thousands each to not go to the police or the media.'

She stared at him. 'I would have sworn Danny hadn't killed anyone when I knew him – and that's not a hopeful statement, it's a doctor's assessment.'

He shrugged. 'Everything's different now. His status has gone from stalker to murderer. His grandfather, Alicia Florrick and Sigmund Freud couldn't save him. No matter what anyone says or does, he's going down.' He kissed her forehead again. 'I've called in the cavalry. We'll do whatever it takes to stop this creep from getting to you again.'

'Yeah, right—like the cops in Mullalabuk who promised protection? It seemed *protection* meant sending a car once a night. Even after I'd installed a panic button, and used it, they arrived ten minutes after he'd killed my dog and cat, and did *this* to me.' She jerked down the front of her creamy sundress to reveal a scar bisecting her left breast in a jagged *D*.

He took a step back, his gaze fixed on her tortured flesh. 'Bloody hell.'

She covered the scar, shrugging in a pitiful attempt at nonchalance. 'Ugly, isn't it?'

'Ugly doesn't come into it. It's sick! What sort of warped mind brands a human being?'

'The sort whose grandfather buys and sells everything. Jeremiah Spencer told Danny "a woman like me" ought to be thrilled he wants me. Danny refuses to believe I don't feel the same, makes excuses for my every rejection or disappearance. But last time he made sure I'd never forget him—that every time I undress, my first thought will be of him. He wanted to make sure every potential lover I had would know who I belong to.'

Adam murmured, 'A man who loves you won't care about that.'

Her only answer was a withering glance.

A touch soft as cobwebs over her hair. 'Even if he'd branded your face, you'd still be one of the most beautiful women I've seen in a long time, Elly.'

She almost snorted. After Sharon's fragile, silver-gold loveliness, there was no way he could find her curved, earthy looks beautiful. Unexpected proximity and the memories of childhood love were confusing him into an attraction that wouldn't last beyond a week—because before a week passed, she'd be gone, and he'd forget her again.

'Thank you.'

'You don't believe me,' he said, voice flat now.

Unable to say it, she just shook her head. 'I know what I am.'

'I doubt it.' But he changed the subject. 'Why wasn't the attack on you in the Mullalabuk incident sheet?'

'I stitched it myself, and left town once I gave a statement. I knew he'd only get thirty days, with or without this, thanks to Jeremiah Spencer's money and the high-powered barristers on the case.'

Though he didn't touch her, he kept watching her. 'You wanted a shot at a normal life before he found your trail again. And now he's back, all you can think to do is run.'

The insight was unnerving—and the reason for that left her more unsettled. If she'd come to Adam because Aunty Hat had asked her to help him, she'd also come also to prove she'd been wasting her life believing they'd had something special … or to prove that, if it had once been special, it was long over. That it wasn't over—that he could still read her with effortless ease, as he had at the station, and give her space and affection when she needed it—left her floundering amid a sea of uncertainty.

He paced the room, the leopard on the leash returned. She couldn't believe she wanted to smile now, but just watching him threw her back fifteen years, when some Jepson would lecture Adam on his responsibilities in life while he shifted feet, his body jerking with impatience to escape the tethers they tried to put on him.

While Sharon had done a real number on him, she hadn't destroyed him, hadn't managed to turn him into his father. Within half an hour of her arrival today, the real Adam, *her* Adam, had returned, if only in glimpses. It must be killing him, all that unwanted domestication hemming him in, trying to become an acceptable Jepson and failing, as he was now.

All his chained savagery spilled out in pacing feet and four harsh words: 'How did it start?'

Though the memory was anything but funny, she started laughing. 'And isn't it ironic, to quote the song? I saved his life! On my way to the Moongallee Creek clinic, I found a car wreck. I worked for hours to save him, and looked after him at Moongallee Creek clinic until he was transferred to Dubbo Base Hospital. He came back after his release, hanging around every day, telling me he loved me. When I told him I didn't feel the same, he said I was too innocent to know what love was. He kept saying I'd come to love him in time, that he knew I needed him to care for me, to protect me.

'Then he began threatening any man who talked to me—even fellow doctors, patients or relatives of patients. He broke into my office, my house, followed me everywhere—and the police never turned up until he'd gone. When I filed a complaint, he was only taken in overnight. I left Moongallee Creek, contacted my grandmother's cousin, and joined the Aboriginal and Islander Medical Commission. But every place I went, he found me within weeks. The last time, he slit Mickey and Minnie's throats. He couldn't bear that anything had my affection but him. Then he branded me, calling it my eternal wedding ring—he thought it was *romantic*—and kissed me. I whacked the phone over his head, waited for the police, and ran again.

'I've been running from him, from place to place, for almost two years. So many times, I've wished I'd let him die on the road that first day.' She closed her eyes for a moment. 'There goes my Hippocratic Oath. If he was bleeding to death, I wouldn't lift a finger to save him.'

After a long pause, he asked quietly, 'What else did he do to you?'

Her brows lifted. 'What, besides ruining my life, branding my body, destroying my career and dreams for the future, killing my cat and dog, and using his money to continue his warped perversions against me? Oh, and now killing innocent people? Yes, I suppose he could do worse to me … like he did to the trucker. Yeah, I could be dead. I guess I'm lucky.'

He asked it with a fierce note. 'Did he rape you?'

She paced the room, feeling caged. After a few moments, she flung at him, 'Not yet. With his Madonna complex he's afraid to, in case I'm not the pure virgin he needs me to be to take his mother's place. My fear of him keeps reinforcing the virginal stereotype. He wants to worship a mother-goddess—the woman he hates yet desperately needs love from. He's turned me into a deity, and he becomes crazy when I act in any way that reinforces my humanity and shatters his dream. So he approaches me on his knees half the time, then in blind fury when I talk to another man, or remind him of his mother. That's when he *touches* me.' She wheeled to the window. 'My body knows the feel of his hands very well, just as my neck knows the feel of his knife. His grandfather told him their women are Spencer property, like their steers. He believes that's what women want—to be owned by a strong man.'

'Ah, Elly.' He came to her, his eyes heavy with sorrow. 'May I hold you?'

She looked up at him. As if a curtain had lifted in her mind, she hurtled back eighteen years in time, seeing the boy who'd known without words that her world had been shattered by her mother's death, its focus gone, replaced by well-meaning invaders believing they could make her grief go away by giving her a new world, having new things, forcing her to meet new people, making her talk again. Only Adam had known she'd hated to be touched and stroked by outsiders, as though their clumsy words and endless intrusion would ease her loss. But it had always been different with Adam. His touch held a sense of place, of belonging, that no one else's ever had. Only Adam then, and no one since, not even her relatives.

Maybe he still understood.

Almost afraid, she nodded.

He took her in his arms, holding her without compelling her to stay. After a while she sighed, and her head fell to his shoulder. Only then did his hand wander over her hair, so very gentle.

When he spoke, his voice was tight and grim, at odds with the reverential way he held her. 'Whatever it takes to end this loony tune's domination in your life, I'll do it.' A feather-soft kiss on her forehead. 'You're safe with me, Elly—now and always.'

After coming clear across the country to hear those words, she discovered that's what frightened her the most—that he *would* do whatever it took.

She couldn't allow it. She had to go.

This moment might be all she'd get for a long time. She held onto him, sinking into the twined ropes of complicated affection and desire winding around them. 'I can't risk you. He killed a puppy and kitten without a second thought. He killed the trucker. He wouldn't hesitate to hurt you and Zoe.'

A shudder ran through him, but he only repeated what he'd said before. 'You can't blame yourself for the trucker's death, or even your pets'.'

'Who else is there?'

'That's the trap he wants you to fall into, Elly. Trust me, I've seen men like Spencer in my job more than once. This will only end when you show him you're stronger than he is. All abusers are cowards. They like women to cower, to run from them, because it makes them feel powerful. They think inspiring terror is a show of strength, and hope that scaring others hides their own crazy fears from the world. Deep down, they know their women cower and run from them because their behaviour makes them unlovable, so domi-nation becomes a warped second-best for the love they crave. They punish the woman for not loving them, which makes her cower and hate him in private still more. Then when he demands her love she has to lie, and he knows it, which makes him even angrier. As the cycle escalates, the abuser damages her more and more, lost in fury but unable to admit the original fault was his, and too afraid to admit he needs help, because he doesn't want to end up in an institution.'

She tilted her head, thinking it through. After a while, she slowly nodded. He knew her story very well, without her having to say a word. 'I can't risk you and Zoe.'

He shook his head. 'You won't be risking us, Elly. Not now. Every cop in every state and territory in Australia is on the hunt for Spencer now. No matter how wily he is, or what his grandfather pays or who he brings to court, he's going down.'

'He killed Mickey and Minnie because I loved them. Don't you get it?' she snapped, with all the passion of pure fear. 'If he's seen me with you and Zoe, if he slashed my tyres, what he'll do next—' She shuddered.

But again, he shook his head. 'I'm the cop, Elly. This is my territory. I'm telling you, this isn't his MO. He believes his clever tricks make him superior. In his mind, any idiot can slash tyres—and making your car immobile here, at my house, stops you from being alone, which is what he wants most. There's no way it could be him, based on his own behaviour.' When she opened her mouth to argue, he put a finger to her lips. 'Your stuff is at the Rose and Thistle?'

She nodded against his finger.

'I'll get someone from the station to bring it here. You're not going anywhere. There's no arguing on this,' he added, keeping his finger on her open mouth. 'I'm here, Elly. Aren't you lucky? Permanent, personal police protection on tap, free of charge.'

The tenderness in his smile softened the sternness of his face, but it tore at something in her heart, ripping down every barrier she'd tried to erect against him. 'He could burn the house down. He wouldn't think about Zoe not being my child. He'd only think that I'd found a family, and killing you both would leave me alone again, and needing him.'

He pressed his lips to her forehead. 'Let's not go there. Right now, all we've got is slashed tyres. It's not Spencer's style. Like you said, it could be kids jealous of your car. I'll order new tyres for you. Sam the mechanic will get them in if they're not in stock. As for Zoe, I'll send her to my mother in Bowral if the situation escalates.'

'No. I won't do that to her. She's had too many disruptions in her life, and she needs you.' She shook her head, almost unable to cope with the memories lashing at her: living on the move with her mother, home being a tent, or a nearby cheap motel; then, after her mother's death, she'd been shuffled from the Jepsons to her grandmother, and when Nana got sick, to her cousin Kara's family. Every time her life changed, she couldn't help wondering whether she'd been too naughty, too wild, too white or black to become one of them, no matter how she tried. 'Zoe won't suffer for my sake. Like you said, any cop will take my story seriously. I can get help anywhere now.'

He brushed her hand with his. 'But it isn't just any cop you need, is it? You came to Macks Lake. You came to me. You need me.'

Her eyes met his. She had no defences that wouldn't crumble under his gaze, his whispered words and one delicate touch. 'Yes. I came to you.' *I do need you. I'd almost forgotten how much—and it terrifies me.*

'Whatever you want, whatever you need, I'm here.' He brushed her skin once more, and she lost her breath. 'I'll call Rick, ask him to bring your bags from the pub. Your room's second on the left down the hall.'

Her lips parted, dragging in air. She turned away by sheer willpower, fighting for control, but Rick's face came to her mind—the look of fury when she'd seen him through the glass of the conference room, the questions at the pub; the fury leashed, white hot, ready to burst. 'Not Rick,' she whispered. 'He—he—' Frantically searching for words, she could only speak truth. 'He frightens me.'

Adam gave her a long look, then he frowned. 'He knows your case, and is the Aboriginal liaison officer for the area. Will you trust me on this? I know he's intense, but he'd never hurt you. He'll fight for you as nobody else at the station will—well, except me.'

Despite her best will, her head drooped. 'All right.'

She walked down the hall.

'What did he do to scare you?' he asked just as she reached the door of her latest room.

She couldn't look at him, couldn't turn. 'He said—no, it was the way he said it. As if—as if he *knew* me. As if he had a *right* to me.'

She heard the sigh. 'He reminds you of Spencer.'

Her head drooped further, chin almost against her chest. She managed to nod.

Slow, rueful words came. 'He is intense, Elly, and there's a darkness in him—I'm his best friend, and I don't know what it is—but I've never seen him hurt anyone, especially a woman.'

When she didn't answer, he asked the words she'd dreaded. 'Will you trust me on this?'

She nodded again, hating herself for the surrender, but she'd been fighting her loneliness for so many years, and all she felt was tired.

'Thank you.' His voice sounded from right behind her, and she jumped. 'I'm sorry. That was stupid of me.' He picked up her hand and caressed it, so gentle, then he released her. 'I'll secure your car, and call Rick to get your things. You shouldn't be alone tonight.'

'I'm always alone,' she blurted before she could help it—then she closed her eyes. 'I'm sorry. I know you want to help … that …'

'It's all right, Elly. I get it. Stay in your room if you don't want to see Rick. I'll bring your things in when he's gone, tell him you're asleep.' Eyes dark as a night forest, he walked away—and too late, she realised he was using to Rick to put space between them. Considering all she'd put him through today, she couldn't blame him, but as she watched him walk away from her, the haunting repetition of the act hurt her soul. Since he'd left her, it felt as if she'd just watched through windows while others lived, loved, found their belonging place.

Waiting behind closed windows and pulled curtains for Danny Spencer to smash her life again.

Her gaze swung around the old house as the boards creaked. Searching out shadows, seeing in every corner a silhouette of a hand fingering a shearer's knife, lifting to slash—not her tyres this time, but her throat. He'd bombed the prison sixteen days ago. He could be here now.

How many people had he killed, now it had begun?

Danny couldn't have found me this fast. He can't know anything about Adam. I changed cars twice, flew, hitched a ride, changed my hair, my clothes …

Flying to Western Australia on a private charter plane hadn't stopped him last time. Wherever he went, Jeremiah Spencer's bottomless funds loosened people's tongues, except those of the people she'd helped. She could depend on the silence of her people, no matter which clan or tribe they hailed from. She didn't care if it wasn't only from loyalty, but because they hated the repressive authority figures so much: government representatives, cops—or men after their women. Her years with her family and on the run had taught her not to be romantic. And she knew not all Indigenous people were 'her' people. Some of them would give her up for money, or because they resented her 'privileged' background with the Jepsons, and her scholarship.

She sighed, gazing into the night. She would have her tyres replaced, and leave Macks Lake in its dry, dishevelled loveliness, keep Adam and Zoe safe from attack. She wouldn't be able to live with herself if either of them were hurt.

The branding of her body had been a warning. Adam was right about cowardice and his needing power—she recognised all of it in Danny—but the truckie's murder meant his illness was worsening, and he was tiring of her constant flights from him. The unbalanced part of him wanted her caged: to own her, body and soul, or make sure no other man would ever own her. Kiss or kill …

Unbidden, the memory of gentle hands and a tender kiss—the respect it implied—filled her with light and strength. For all his hidden spirit and damaged heart, Adam wouldn't force her to stay in Macks Lake against her will. If she refused his offer, he'd back off, even believing it could kill her. Despite what he'd been through, Adam was man enough to not feel threatened by a woman's strength, or by feeling less than in control.

She had to fight sometime. Somewhere, somehow, this madness had to end. She'd stay with Adam—at least for now—and keep praying for a miracle.

★　★　★

Rick sat in his car outside Adam's house, watching the spare-room window. The room where he'd slept himself more than once, when he'd had a beer too many, or when Zoe had asked him for a sleepover. Now *she* was lying in there.

The friendship was already straining. He knew Adam had lied when he'd said Elly was sleeping—no way would she be able to after the attack on her car.

She was in her room because she didn't want to see him.

Just give me a chance, he'd wanted to shout. Wanted to tap on her window and talk to her. He knew he could change everything with a few words.

But he couldn't risk it. Not yet.

So he waited here, watching the window. Nobody would hurt her on his watch.

He kept writing his plans in a small notebook.

Roadhouse, Outback Way, Northern Territory

Now this was more like it. This lot were very friendly. Over a few free beers, any man would talk to him. No, Janie hadn't been here, but one of the regular truckers had seen her. He hadn't given her a lift (*So he can live*, Monster murmured, but he was getting restless), but he'd seen her struggling with a rattletrap four-wheel drive, and a few truckers had stopped to help. Eventually she'd taken a ride with one of them. Still heading east.

Climbing into the truck he'd bought from Dave, Danny had sent a message to Granddad. *I need maps of Indigenous communities heading east from here.*

He didn't tell Granddad where he was. Implying that the old mongrel knew his grandson's every move increased his sense of power, and would insure he'd send the info.

Half an hour later, just as he'd thought, Granddad sent what he needed. *Change your appearance again, and use the red burner. The police have been here. They'll be tapping all communications since the truck incident. I'll send you my new number.*

I will, Granddad, he wrote back, a slow grin appearing on his face. *Thank you.* Meek and humble. Feeding Granddad's God complex would insure Jeremiah would spill the beans on Janie's current whereabouts as soon as he'd made sure Danny could get there safely.

No, he doesn't know everything, does he? Monster said. *We're as good at games as he is.*

Well, we learned from the best, Danny replied, before realising again he shouldn't be talking to Monster. It only fed the beast.

He looked at the maps Granddad sent. Twenty kilometres east-northeast was another community—and, yes, she'd go there. Amid the positive changes to the town in the past few years was an advertisement for medical professionals. Good.

He put the truck in gear.

CHAPTER

8

The next morning, Elly found Danny Spencer's acts being treated with deadly seriousness by the police for the first time.

Having dropped Zoe at preschool before eight, Adam took Elly to the station and ushered her straight into the senior sergeant's office. Jonas Albright, big, round and dimpled, with twinkling blue eyes and grizzled hair, shook hands with her.

'Elly, I looked up your case after Jepson's call. I have most of the pertinent facts. I gather you don't want to be called Jane any more?'

She shook her head. 'I changed it legally twice.' She flushed. 'Another time wasn't legal—I couldn't afford it to be at the time, since the private detective was close. I bought an identity from a drug addict, but Danny still found me. This is the third time—I only changed it two weeks ago. Elliana Lavender is an Italian woman who lives in the Kimberley, married to an Australian miner. She has a granddaughter of the same name who's close to my age, and has a pretty close resemblance. I paid for the real Elly to go overseas for a few months, in case he tries to buy someone off at the airport or change of name office.'

'If you've done anything illegal, don't tell me. So did you register your new name with the medical registration board?'

She shook her head. 'Only with the Aboriginal and Islander Medical Commission. My uncle—really my grandmother's second cousin, and not a Larkins—is a member of the board. The file's sealed.'

'That should be safe. I'll give 'em a call, make sure it remains sealed.' Albright's mouth twitched. 'Jeremiah Spencer has Chris Bent, the Northern Territory's top barrister, the psychiatrist William Henry and two members of parliament in his pocket. Their latest press release says we need a lot more than circumstantial evidence on the prison bombing before setting up a manhunt for Danny. They're saying he ran in a panic when the explosion happened— that it's part of his mental problem, and he needs treatment, not to be locked away. They even have "proof" that Danny wasn't in the Kimberley at the time of the trucker's death.' He showed Adam and Elly the newspaper item on his screen. The murder was headline news. A dated, time-stamped selfie of a man standing under the *Welcome to Kalgoorlie* sign, more than a thousand kilometres from the Kimberley, dominated the article.

'It does look like him.' Elly looked at the men, more disturbed than she wanted to admit. 'What if he …?'

'Don't forget the Spencer funds—and Danny's the only heir. Jeremiah Spencer could have hired a dozen lookalikes to be in other places for when Danny needs an alibi. And no other inmates skipped after the Mackleton blow.' Adam turned to his superior officer. 'We can call the press, if that's the game, Sarge. Let's give 'em the real story.'

'No media.' Albright's tone was sharp enough to cut. 'If we do, Spencer senior will connect Elly to Macks Lake. Her past with your family is on her record, and her childhood friendship with you wouldn't be hard to discover. So we don't tell anyone Elly's real name. I've put a password on her files. It's for your and my eyes only. You know there've been leaks here—nothing important so far, but we can't risk Elly's case becoming known to anyone else, not with Spencer's contacts. Sydney has assigned two high-ranking detectives to the case, but they can't be here until Monday.'

'That's five days away,' Adam snapped, sounding incredulous.

Albright's hands lifted, and fell. 'All the more reason to keep this case under wraps until we have more help. The rest of the state police are on the hunt for Spencer, but they won't be told your new name, and we'll keep it that way until I receive other instructions from my commanding officers.'

'Rick knows,' Adam said quietly. 'As Aboriginal liaison officer, he has the right, and the access to information networks we don't have.'

Albright nodded. 'You're right. I'll add his name, but that's it.' He patted Elly's hand. 'The fewer people who know who you are, and of your connection to Spencer, the better. Silence can keep you safer than a van of bodyguards.'

Her shoulders sagged. Belief at last—but it felt like sweet poison in her veins, that it had taken a murder to get it. And the thought of Rick taking part in the investigation left a bitter tang in her mouth. 'Thank you, Senior Sergeant Albright.'

The sergeant smiled at her with a fatherly air. 'Control is hard to relinquish, I know, but we won't let you down this time.'

'I—yes. Thank you again, Senior Sergeant Albright.' She wondered if she could ever let go.

The sergeant, stranger to her until that morning, patted her shoulder. 'It will take time. You've been alone with this for too long.' Another gentle pat, tender rather than patronising. 'And call me

Jonas, please. Or Joe—or even Uncle Joe.' He smiled. 'You look rather like my niece, Lily.'

Her mouth opened and closed again, as she fought the urge to cry at his unexpected tenderness. She couldn't remember him, but the long-forgotten hole her father had left in her life bounced back to her memory at the senior sergeant's touch. Could she ever have believed she'd buried the need for a father? What little girl doesn't want her daddy to cuddle her and fight her dragons for her? *Why didn't he want me?*

'Is there reason to believe Spencer's in the state already, Sarge?' Adam asked.

'He was sighted on the Western Australia–Northern Territory border, at an indigenous community – then the next day at the roadhouse on the highway, asking about Indigenous communities. He should still be in upper South Australia or lower Northern Territory, chasing his tail, trying to find the right communities, or to get information from them. There's quite a few communities there, and almost all closed to outsiders unless they have a permit.'

She pulled her permit out of her wallet and handed it to Jonas. 'I know. I—I only went to the closed ones.'

Albright chuckled. 'Of course you know. I didn't mean to imply otherwise. How many clinics did you visit during your journey here?'

'Five.' Why did she say it with apology in her voice, as if she was causing them trouble?

'If you give me the names of the communities, we can send local Aboriginal liaison officers and ask the communities to give confusing signals about north or south, east or west.'

'No need,' she said quietly. 'They're already doing that for me.'

She felt Adam's gaze on her. It was only when pain radiated around her face that she realised she'd sucked in her lips, holding them with her teeth. Her life's vocation of offering help to those in need was also her greatest folly. 'I'm easy to follow.'

'You care, Elly.' Adam touched her shoulder. 'Unless Spencer's miraculously changed his background, he'll get the same response from the Aboriginal people our people did: nothing. They're very loyal to you.'

That strong, stern face, the forest-green eyes lit to a rich masculine beauty when he smiled. Stupid to think of that now—but she'd been without him so long, it was as if she was a starving woman at a feast. She struggled to concentrate on his words. 'Not to me. To our people. To the doctor who helped them for a few days.' She chewed the inside of her mouth, again only releasing it when it hurt. 'If Danny's not in the state, who slashed my tyres?'

'It's unlikely Spencer found your trail this fast, and slashing tyres isn't his MO.' Adam frowned at his boss. 'Could he have bought an accomplice, Sarge?'

'Even if he bought ten accomplices, I doubt he's connected her to Macks Lake yet. An accomplice doesn't fit his MO, either. He doesn't even tell his grandfather his problems. He's so fixated on Elly, he's terrified even his grandfather would take her away from him.' He handed a sheaf of papers to Adam. 'Stationhands believe Danny was the cause of hundreds of killings of animals at Gundawin, almost all female. At fifteen, he became obsessed with a nurse who attended him when he had pneumonia. Jeremiah Spencer paid her off and sent her packing. The woman won't talk, but it's believed Spencer raped her.'

Elly's mouth twisted. 'Of course Jeremiah Spencer paid her. He'll do anything to keep Danny safe until he gets a sane heir for Gundawin.'

'Why doesn't he marry another woman and get his own son?' Adam asked.

'His medical file disappeared long ago, so I can't corroborate this, but Danny told me Jeremiah had mumps after his son was born, and can't have any more children. So Danny's his only hope of getting another heir. Jeremiah offered me a million dollars to marry Danny and have a son.'

'What?'

She shrugged, recounting the incident as matter-of-factly as she could. 'He dislikes my Aboriginal background, and hates most women—Danny says a woman gave Jeremiah mumps—but I'm a reasonably intelligent, fertile female, and since Danny's mental deterioration and previous suicide attempts, Jeremiah's desperate for a sane heir. He said Danny wearies of his toys once he owns them. A year in Danny's bed and he'll forget I exist, unless I try to leave. He said he'd have Danny confined once I gave birth to a son. Gundawin's a third-generation property of half-a-million hectares, rich in uranium, and my son would inherit it all. He said it would be well worth a little sacrifice. He thought I'd be happy about it—an Aboriginal child getting the land back. He couldn't believe it when I turned him down. The eventual price he offered was three million.'

Both men stared at her. Their training helped their mouths stay closed, but two sets of lifted brows and blinking eyes said it all.

'Why doesn't Spencer go for IVF?' Jonas asked after a while. 'It makes no sense. Why not go for his own genetics, if his grandson's are flawed?'

'He's eighty-two,' Elly said quietly. 'Even if he was fertile enough—and that's unlikely since his mumps—his sperm is far more likely to create a child with physical or mental challenges than a younger man's.'

'So no more children. No wonder he keeps on helping Spencer escape,' Adam said slowly. 'But why not just lock him up, and use Danny's sperm with IVF?'

'He doesn't believe in such modern methods. A tech could switch samples, and it wouldn't be *his* great-grandchild.'

Both men looked thoughtful as they nodded.

'But he plays mental games with Danny all the time. He seems to like keeping him unbalanced—I guess it's a control issue. He's the one who damaged Danny.' She shrugged. 'He promised me Danny would be locked up the minute the sex of my foetus was confirmed. Danny wouldn't be able to stand the competition. He'd kill his own child.'

Adam shuddered. 'You've thought it all out.'

'I've had to.' She shrugged, hiding her defensiveness.

'What else have you worked out, Elly?' Jonas asked, his brow furrowed with concern.

She sighed. 'Danny has a passion for the medical fraternity, I suppose because they're the only ones who come close to under-standing the workings of his mind. He had a succession of nurses and psychiatrists in Darwin during his teen years. Jeremiah Spencer paid a mint to try to make Danny normal, but it was too late. Apparently one of his therapists mentioned that a woman's love, a woman to replace the mother he lost, could end the violent streak inside him, and Danny believes it, if Jeremiah doesn't.'

Adam said slowly, 'So when you saved him—'

Her mouth quirked, but she'd never felt less like laughing. 'He thought it was true love.'

'Danny's poured all his dreams of healing and his frustrated lone-liness onto you,' Jonas said.

She shuddered. 'I told him at the start that I didn't love him.' *But I never told him why.* Even if it wouldn't have put Adam in danger, she'd barely admitted the truth to herself in years. She knew she wasn't normal, clinging to a dream that was long gone.

As if hearing her thoughts, Adam took her hand in his, holding it in a strong, warm clasp. 'We'll get him this time.'

She closed her eyes. Could she trust anyone enough to relinquish control over her private torment? But the simple truth was that she had no authority over Danny Spencer. The death of the trucker in Western Australia proved that—and for the first time in so long, she didn't feel alone. 'Thank you, Adam.'

'Anything for you.' His thumb brushed her skin, chasing rational thought from her brain.

Jonas cleared his throat, startling them to attention. 'Is there anything you can tell me about the attack on your car? Do you know anyone in Macks Lake who could dislike you so soon?'

Without proof the Mirakis had damaged her car, she couldn't bring herself to dob them in and drive them out of town again. Fear that they'd be imprisoned without proof, or that Danny would find the Mirakis if she informed on them—and the worry of who might have sent them here, and what they'd do if they found out she was staying with Adam—wove together with her guilt into a tapestry of silence.

'Could it have been some kids, jealous of my car?'

'Vandalism often happens to prestige cars,' Adam said.

'It could also be Mrs Collins who did the deed,' Jonas said. 'She seemed rather put out by Elly's arrival yesterday—though she's usually the victim, not the villain.'

'Oh, gag me,' Adam groaned. 'I wish someone *would* make her a victim, permanently.'

Jonas laughed, and turned to her. 'Since she moved here, Jen Collins has complained about an unbelievable amount of violence, always needing our only detective to investigate. But when Jepson's off shift, the crime rate in Macks Lake seems to drop dramatically. She's visited the station so many times, Mendham handed her an application form to join the service.'

Needing a distraction now—needing to laugh amid all this heaviness—she grinned at Adam. 'So I'm not the only victim of obsession here?'

'The genetic Jepson irresistibility must have rubbed off on you during the years you lived with us,' Adam said, straight-faced.

'Was she the colourful blonde in here yesterday? Big teeth? Looks sort of like a painted bunny?'

With a wicked grin at her apt description, Adam nodded.

Her brows lifted; her head tilted. 'Then you're being stalked again, Claudius. The lady in question is walking through the door.'

He rose to his feet. 'Right, that's it. I'm getting rid of her. All she's seen until now is the polite—' he ignored the choking sounds from his boss '—Detective Sergeant Jepson. Adam's not quite so tactful.' He shut the door on their gusts of laughter.

Jonas got to his feet. 'This I've got to see. The needle-point thrusts of Jen Collins—'

'Versus the battleaxe blows of my tactless Claudius,' she gasped, trying to catch her breath. 'Five bucks says our fancy blonde out there doesn't get a friendly handshake.'

'Done.' Jonas pulled the door open.

In reception, the converted living room/hallway of the original house, the other cops had now arrived—minus Rick, she was relieved to see. Baz, Simon and the female cop, Adele, all had odd, tired grins on their faces as they tried not to watch Adam too obviously. He was leaning aggressively over the counter.

'Slashed tyres?' Mrs Collins drawled, batting her lashes at Adam, not at all intimidated by his hostility. 'Why would I know about that, Adam? Why would I know anything about your *friend*—or is she more than that?'

'It's Detective Sergeant Jepson to you, Mrs Collins,' Adam snapped. 'My private life is none of your business. I won't speak to you again unless you have a legitimate complaint with proof of a crime. I'm not a counselling service for lonely women. Either you know something about the slashing of Miss Lavender's tyres last night or you don't.'

Mrs Collins gave no sign of understanding Adam's brutal words. Long fingers, tipped with violet-pink polish, walked toward his forearm, but he jerked back, hand curling into a fist. Her brows lifted. 'Maybe I know something. Maybe I happened to be driving down your street about eight last night, and noticed someone hanging around her car.'

'If you saw something, why didn't you report it?'

'Because you weren't here,' she said, eyes wide, as if he'd said something very stupid. Leaning over the counter, she gave him a clear view of her cleavage. 'I think my memory needs encouragement. Perhaps over dinner tonight, I might even remember what the perpetrator looked like.'

His eyes filled with sudden pity. 'You'd blackmail me into a date? You can't be so desperate for a man.'

Mrs Collins held his gaze, hers still hungry.

He sighed and shook his head. 'If it's a lover you're after, Mrs Collins, look elsewhere. I'm just not interested in you.'

Jen Collins' jaw dropped. Her eyes narrowed as she snapped it back up. 'Seven at the Drifters' Inn if you want the information. If you don't come, it stays with me.' Her breast heaving, she turned to Elly, who'd just received a five-dollar note from a sheepish Jonas. 'I'd leave Macks Lake if I were you, before real trouble comes. We don't like your kind here.' She turned on her heel and marched out, leaving a cloud of musk in the air.

'Meee-ow,' Baz said, in an obvious attempt to shatter the tense atmosphere. 'And don't it turn her blue eyes green?'

'Because she can't hit first base with Adam.' Simon turned to Elly. 'She probably thinks if she runs you out of town, Adam will get desperate enough to start up with her.'

'Simon's right,' Jonas murmured. 'She's the kind of woman who wouldn't hesitate to blackmail Jepson into a date ... or more.'

Nothing comforted Elly. Stricken, she turned to Adam. 'I'm sorry, Claudius. Looks like your reputation's gone.'

He turned around, but his gaze didn't land on hers. His face was shuttered, locking everyone out. 'It's not your fault.'

Her heart contracted until she could barely breathe. She longed to say, *It's not your fault, either!* But his guilt and regret had been painted in sombre colours by nine years of marriage to a Victorian-minded wife. The boy she'd adored in childhood was still there, locked in battle with his prim and proper Jepson upbringing, and his guilt at the death of his son ... and of Sharon.

It always came back to Sharon.

How she ached to be able to show Adam how unhappy he was in a world where no one took chances, hedged in by what the neighbours thought.

But Danny could be here, watching her now ...

The stained-glass window behind the counter exploded.

'Get down!' Adam dived on her, protecting her with his body as jagged-edged rainbow hues fell over them.

Then eerie silence.

'Get out and check the street!' Jonas barked at Baz and Simon. 'Get car registrations and makes, and bring in witnesses!'

The two constables shucked glass from their uniforms and scrambled outside. Jonas picked up the phone to inform the regional inspector of the attack.

On the floor, Elly locked eyes with Adam, each as breathless as if they'd run a race. His body still covered hers, lying in the most intimate of lover's positions.

'Are you all right?' They spoke at the same time, and laughed.

Then she looked him over, saw the tear in his shirt. 'You're bleeding!'

'It's nothing.' He dismissed her concern with a gentle smile. 'I've had worse than this.'

'Not here—not until I came. I told you I shouldn't stay. I told you what he'd do. I haven't even been in Macks Lake for twenty-four hours, and you're hurt because of me!' She struggled against him. 'It could be Zoe next!'

'I'm a cop, Elly. This is a police station. These things happen, even in sleepy backwaters like Macks Lake. There's no evidence to link the shot to you.'

'Except my slashed tyres, and Mrs Collins' warning!'

His arms tightened. 'Don't go, Elly. Please.' His eyes filled with stark honesty. 'I think you know I have deeper injuries than this little cut on my arm.'

The unspoken words echoed inside her; she knew what he couldn't say. He'd let no one but Zoe into his damaged heart since Sharon and Zack's deaths—but Elly was already there. Like he'd done for her long ago by sharing her wild adventures and tending her bedraggled critters, he was giving her permission to probe his wound, and heal him if she could.

'I—if I can help …'

Her wounded spirit found an echo in the pain in his shadowed eyes. 'You've already helped, more than you know.'

'Then I'll stay,' she whispered.

'Thank you, Elly-May.' His gaze lowered to her mouth. With a little thrill, she felt his hardening body press against hers. He might feel guilty about wanting her, but it didn't change the fact that he did. The need was growing in them both—a hunger that wouldn't abate with denial.

'Elly, if you're all right, could you look at Adele's injury? It might need stitches.'

Jonas's words recalled them to their surroundings. Adam rolled from her just as Rick strode into the station from the back door.

'What's going on?' Rick asked, frowning as he took in the window, Adele's wound and Adam on the floor with Elly.

'Drive-by shooting took out the window,' Jonas said in a terse tone. 'Where were you?'

Rick's frown grew deeper, his eyes on Elly. 'Are you all right?'

Flushing deeper with discomfort, she nodded.

'I was on early calls, remember?' Rick said to his boss. 'Brian Milson from Watkins' Jewellers had a burg this morning. A smash and grab. Kids, by the looks of it—but it's the third this year.'

'A positive criminal outbreak,' Adam quipped, holding his arm up in a vain attempt to stop blood dripping onto the floor. 'Tell Mr Milson I'll go later today. The drive-by outranks it.'

'Get my bag, Claudius. I left it in your trunk.' Elly held Adele's wound as she checked the girl's eyes for pupil response. 'Adele needs stitches, and so do you, by the look of that cut.'

Adam nodded, and strode out to his car.

Rick kept staring at Elly, his brooding gaze unnerving her as she tried to work with her normal efficiency. Then he stepped closer, and she held her breath.

'You might want to be careful ... Elly,' he said, low.

Why did he keep hesitating before saying her name? What did he know?

As she glanced up at him, he nodded. 'Watch what you do, and who you do it in front of. Not everyone here is your friend.'

Fighting the urge to shrink away, she snapped, 'I believe that would be my business, senior constable, and none of yours.'

As if expecting her response, he only shrugged, looking out the window to where Adam was striding back with her medical kit. He turned to Elly, speaking in a low, intense voice. 'Don't set yourself up for a fall. He has nothing to give you. There are others who will do anything to help you, if you'll only look.'

Adele was trying not to stare too obviously at them, but she'd heard every word.

'Mendham, make yourself useful,' Jonas snapped. 'Find the cartridge from the shot and the glass around it, and bag it all for testing. You can clean the glass up, too.'

Rick crossed the room, and wrenched a cupboard open.

Adam came back in carrying Elly's medical kit. 'Has it got everything you need?'

'Yep.' She smiled briefly. 'Got to have the rescue equipment handy.'

She sterilised Adele's gash and anaesthetised it. After probing the wound, she pulled out a sliver of glass with a small pair of tweezers. She stitched the wound and covered it with a clean bandage, then pulled an ampoule, syringe and needle from her bag.

'No,' Adele moaned, cringing. 'I hate needles.'

Elly grinned. 'You don't even drop to the floor for a drive-by shooting, but cry at a tetanus shot? For shame, constable.'

Moments later Adele rubbed her arm, looking sorry for herself. Elly checked the girl's eyes and blood pressure again, trying to ignore the intense interest in her face after hearing Rick's warnings.

'She'll need a day or two off. She has a slight concussion.'

Jonas nodded. 'Mendham can drive her home now.'

'So could Adam. I can look after Elly—if that's her name,' Rick said fiercely.

Everyone looked up, startled.

His boss snapped, 'I suppose Jepson *could* do that—after he's stitched up, to stop the station vehicle's upholstery getting covered in blood—but he won't. Jepson's more than earned the right to be tended when he's injured. And as for Elly, I'm warning you to keep your place—and, obviously, your temper. Unless of course you'd enjoy a transfer to another, smaller, station.'

After a long moment, Rick nodded, then sent a regretful glance at Elly.

Sensing the burning resentment inside him, she flushed and turned away. Within moments, though, as if compelled, she turned back. Adam was staring at Rick, a question in his eyes. Rick met the look with an impassive stare before turning aside to clean the mess of glass.

'Good thing we had a medical professional on hand,' he muttered, loud enough for the entire station to hear it.

'Mendham, get in here now,' Jonas barked.

Rick sighed and walked into the senior sergeant's office, closing the door behind him.

'Line up, Claudius,' Elly ordered, hoping the shaking inside her didn't come through in her voice. Jonas had warned her to keep her name and occupation quiet. Rick seemed to have no such compunction—and now, thanks to the drive-by, her ministrations and his resentful sarcasm and questioning of her name, the whole station knew half the puzzle. Her new name wouldn't mean squat now. She could call herself a nurse if she liked, but a Koori woman medico stuck out like a sore thumb in outback Australia. The bush telegraph would relay the information through the region in hours, and across the outback within weeks.

Wirrah and Lani Miraki. Jen Collins. Rick Mendham. Baz, Simon, Adele. Too many people knew too much about her, too soon. Her cover, tenuous from the start, was in danger of being blown in under a day. Danny was close to Macks Lake, if he wasn't already here. She could feel his shadow over her—the threat of a final showdown. Kiss or kill …

'Detective Jepson, my Genevieve's gone missing again. Please, can you help me find her?'

Adam turned to the public entrance, where a sweet little old lady stood. A grin crossed his face. 'We'll have to use the cuffs on Genevieve soon, Mrs Jenkins.'

The faded eyes, misty with embarrassed tears, shone in gratitude at the gentle joke. 'You'll never need them with her, detective sergeant. Genevieve follows you home every time out of pure love for you.'

Elly grinned, brows lifted in mocking inquiry. 'Another female hopelessly drawn to the irresistible Jepson genetics, I gather?'

'Ever since my first week here,' he informed her solemnly, eyes twinkling. 'The moment she sees me, her eyes light up, and she runs to me—'

'An impressive tale of true love. When's the wedding?'

'—and lets out the biggest moo of joy you ever heard.'

She laughed, taped the bandage down, and rose to her feet. 'Life as a country cop, eh? Sounds like a tonic. Could I help?' she asked Mrs Jenkins. 'I haven't rounded up cows for years—but as Adam will vouch, I'm an avid animal lover.'

'Oh, my dear, thank you so much.'

'We'll come now,' Adam told Mrs Jenkins. He understood Elly's need to escape, to be out in the open air after the stress of the past twelve hours.

Jonas opened his door, and both men emerged. Rick seemed to have been subdued. 'Jepson, we've just had a bloody drive-by shooting, and you want to round up cows?'

The tears in Mrs Jenkins' eyes began to fall.

'No need,' Elly replied quickly. 'I can get the cow for you, Mrs Jenkins. I don't need help.' But her shaking hands belied her words. Adam touched her arm, and she turned away, balling her hands into fists in front of her. *Don't cry. Don't cry.*

'I can go with Elly,' Rick offered. 'I wasn't here to be a witness.'

'I'm fine on my own. I don't need a babysitter.' *And I don't want you.* Her message couldn't be any clearer.

'You need something—or someone,' Rick said softly, and she jumped. She hadn't realised he'd come so close to her. 'Let me in. I'm here for you...Elly.'

Her gaze flew to Adam, begging without meaning to.

'Sarge,' Adam said, his voice soft, 'I can be back in half an hour.'

After a moment, Jonas grumbled, 'Oh, go on, Jepson. Elly, perhaps you can show him how to round up a cow before nightfall for once?'

Grateful for the reprieve from the tension in the station, she packed up her medical kit, trying to smile. 'Thank you, Joe,' she said softly, and was rewarded by the older man's smile. 'I'll do my best.'

Jonas moved closer, waving Rick away. Then he spoke too quietly for anyone else to hear. 'Remember, the drive-by upgrades our standing. They'll fly the city detectives out by morning to investigate, and I'll need your report before then. If your arm's okay, that is.' His eyes twinkled. 'And say hi to Genevieve for me.'

Adam saluted. 'Yes, Sarge.'

'Elly shouldn't be in the open, Sarge,' Rick said from the floor, where he'd returned to cleaning the mess. 'Look at this.'

He held up something she couldn't identify, but everyone in the station turned quiet, looking at it.

'Bloody clever,' Jonas said, still quietly. 'Good work, Mendham. Bag and tag it, and send it to the lab.'

'And Elly?' The worry was clearer now than anything else in Rick's voice, but it only made Elly feel hemmed in.

She squared her jaw. 'I'm going.'

Rick's eyes turned hard and he thrust his own jaw out, but he didn't speak.

'Jepson, take protective measures,' Jonas said, 'and don't leave her alone for a moment.'

Adam crossed to the weapons cupboard, unlocked it, and armed himself. The cupboard relocked, he shepherded Elly and Mrs Jenkins out the door, snatching up the lead rope he kept for Genevieve on his way.

As she left the station, Elly felt the burning of Rick's gaze searing her skin.

The Great Central Road, near Pitjantjatjara Lands, Central Australia

North or south? Where would she go next?

He'd reached the end of the desert highway between Laverton and Yulara—from nowhere to nowhere—a stretch of road covered in shifting sand and red earth under a blazing sky. He'd lived on Vegemite sandwiches—he wasn't eating any meat cooked at the substandard roadhouses on this unsealed, dusty track—and slept curled in the back of the truck. Her smiling face burned in his brain day and night. Which way had she gone? He had to find her before the craving got too strong.

It was too late for another stupid braggart at one roadhouse a few days ago. Lying about his Janie! She wouldn't do it in a filthy truck with the likes of him ...

Would she?

Don't be stupid! She's terrified of it. Wouldn't even look at my body, would she?

She's a woman. All women need a man, Monster said. *She'll find another man soon if we don't find her. And he'll get what we want. She won't wait for us.*

She's not like that, he yelled. *You're so cruel, Monster.*

She's alone and needs care. Monster's voice was soft, beguiling. *You know she does. She's running to someone we don't know. Someone she thinks will look after her.*

Maybe. She's so innocent, he conceded, hating to agree with Monster on anything, but he was right. *We have to find her. Prove to her it's us she needs.*

But the Pitjantjatjara people were the same as the blacks in Western Australia. Janie who? No, no Koori doctors. No one been here in months, except for tourists from the trekking business they'd begun. Single girls on tours, sure, but they'd all been whitefellas or Asians. Try Alice Springs—only a hundred kilometres that way. Pointing northeast.

They're lying to us, Monster said. The danger signals were there, like a little red mist between them, a curtain separating them but growing thinner.

Desperate to hold him in, Danny reached into his bag, scattering money around his feet. 'I'll pay five thousand dollars to anyone who has news of her.'

The women, as one, walked away. The men didn't even blink. When the wind picked up, the kids went running after the money, and held it up at a distance from him, laughing and dancing off with it.

The red mist grew thinner, brighter. Monster brought out his knife, fingering it with slow deliberation.

The men began sharpening throwing spears that had longer blades than his knife. Two men brought out shotguns and watched him, smiling. Every weapon aimed at him.

Monster whispered, *Hire an army of men. Bring them here. Kill the lot of them!*

And now? Danny asked him. *What do we do now?*

You're a Spencer, too important for the likes of these animals. Get Grand-dad to hire some mercenaries later. They don't matter. We need to find Janie before she does the unforgivable—and she will.

Stop it! She will not!

The men with the rifles took a step forward.

Monster made him back off, hatred and fear blending in a potent cocktail in his heart. *Janie's here, or she's been here. She did this to us,* Monster said. *I told you she would.*

No, Danny yelled at him. *You won't take Janie from me! You won't! You take everyone from me!*

I'm the only one here, looking out for you, not like Janie, or those faithless sluts you thought you loved before. I'm still here.

You won't take Janie from me, he shouted again. *She's my princess. She just doesn't know it yet.*

He kept backing away, and turned and ran to the truck before he lost control.

A small boy sat on the shady side of his truck, playing with sticks and rocks, singing a little ditty. About to kick the kid out of the way, Danny noticed a bandage on his leg: grubby and ragged with use, but professionally applied. There was a clinic at this place, but still ...

He reached into his truck, pulling out a bag of sweets he'd bought at the last roadhouse. 'Hey, littlefella.'

The boy looked up, looking reassured by the use of Pidgin. Danny handed him the bag of sweets.

'Got a bad cut there, littlefella,' he remarked, pointing to the bandage.

The boy drew his body up in pride. 'We was fixin' a dingo fence, and I ripped my leg. I got seven stitches!'

'Nice havin' the Koori lady doctor here to help,' Danny remarked casually.

'Yeah. She went in a plane. I wanna go on a plane, one day,' the kid said, a wistful look in his eyes.

'Too bad, eh,' Danny commiserated, heart racing. 'So which way did the plane go?'

The boy pointed north.

Danny thanked the boy and climbed into his truck. He drove out of the community, whistling. Back on the road, he opened his map, searching out Indigenous communities to the north. 'I'm coming to you, Janie. This time, it's forever.'

Last chance, Janie, Monster whispered as the curtain fell between them again.

CHAPTER
9

'Well, that was fun.'

Having returned the errant Genevieve to her anxious owner, Adam and Elly walked across a field toward Mrs Jenkins' boundary fence, their shoes and jeans covered in mud. She watched as Adam swung the rope back and forth, catching it each way.

'I always enjoy a Genevieve chase, getting out in the fresh air and sun. It reminds me of Grandpa's farm.'

'That's what puzzled me about you being so obsessed with becoming a cop, Claudius. You've always been such an outdoors kind of guy. I didn't get the attraction.'

'Too many reruns of *Law and Order* and *21 Jump Street* as a kid, I guess.' He scratched his neck, giving her a sheepish look. 'Car chases, drug busts, shoot-outs with the baddies.'

She grinned. 'And now you're in your *Blue Heelers* phase.'

He chuckled. 'I guess I am—but it's far less exciting here than the show.'

But still you bucked Jepson tradition and expectation. Even Sharon hadn't been able to talk him out of it. His father had bragged he'd become the youngest commissioner in history, but beneath the joke, the sense of parental disappointment had been obvious. If they didn't go into politics or the law, Jepsons owned land—and Adam's brother Jared was to inherit the farm.

'But in Sydney?'

'In Sydney it was fairly exciting. I got to do all I'd dreamed of. I came to Macks Lake for a quiet environment for Zoe. She needed that security, after—' He snapped the rope like a whip. 'Better get you home. We've been forty minutes already. Sarge isn't known for his patience.' After a pause he said, 'After that drive-by, I think I'd better keep that date with Mrs Collins. Her information might be vital to the case.'

'Of course.' She strode to the fence, shaking off his hands when he tried to help her over. 'I can do it myself.'

'Elly, let me help you.'

At his almost exasperated tone, her head whipped back to him, eyes burning. 'You should know I'm no shrinking violet. You spent your life fighting expectation, so stop trying to make me someone I'm not.' She marched to the station's truck on the other side of the highway. The warmth that had begun to bloom inside her as he confided his early dreams withered.

What's the matter with me? It didn't matter how many times she told herself Adam had the right to grieve for his wife, the anger lanced her in sharp stabs with every sentence he left unfinished. He didn't deserve to torture himself over Sharon, who'd reminded her of Elsa from *Frozen*: the ice princess. If Adam's wife had had a heart, Elly had never once seen evidence of it. Why did he love her still, three years after her death?

Why did he ever love her at all? But that was the question she'd never have the guts to ask.

'Elly.'

The hand on her arm, simple as it was, stopped her midstride. Gently, so tender, he turned her to face him.

'I'm sorry. It's not you—you know that. I …' He frowned and shook his head. 'I came here—I wanted nothing to remind me of the past. Now you're here, and it's bringing so much back. Good things I'd almost forgotten … I kept it all buried. But then, when I remember you …'

'It all comes back, good and bad.' She swallowed and closed her eyes. 'I know.'

'If I could just get rid of …' A soft sigh of frustration, then she felt his forehead rest against hers. 'I wish I wasn't part of your bad memories. Don't deny it. I know how much I hurt you.'

When she swallowed and nodded, his skin moved against hers. No longer so alone. Almost afraid, she found his hand, wrapping her fingers around his. 'Not now, Adam. Not this time.'

He reached for her other hand. Barely touching compared to before, but …

'Elly,' he whispered against her cheek. 'I was sleepwalking. You've woken me up, made me feel again. I don't know what to do with this.' A soft admission, lost and sad.

'Me either.'

A long silence while neither moved, only breathing. She expected the silence now, waited for the withdrawal. The ghost between them broke the beauty of the moment. Sharon was a wall fifty feet high, an invisible watchtower between Adam's guilt and his living again. Would she find him somewhere inside, the Adam she'd lost?

'This was why—'

'It's all right, Adam. I know.'

'You can't know,' he whispered, still not moving. Did he too want, need her touch, to feel the connection between them? She was chasing shadows inside him, never knowing the right one to follow. Who would win, the living or the dead?

'I do. It's all right, Adam,' she said again, soft with regret. 'It was there from the start. It's what broke us.' She waited again for his withdrawal, the ice that froze him whenever he thought of her, the unspoken name.

A slow nod, and he still didn't move away from her. She barely breathed lest she shatter their connection, a new bond more delicate than cobwebs.

'I want to fix it, Elly. I really do.'

'I know.' But all the glue in the world couldn't repair the broken pieces of who they'd been. 'We can only go on from here.'

'Only if you stay,' he murmured.

She breathed in, sharp, hard.

'You woke me up.' He bent, moving his cheek against hers, a slow awkward dance of hands and cheek on a cracked road filled with the smell of old mud and cow dung. Nothing else touching. Neither of them daring to move closer. 'You promised you'd stay. You can't let me go back to that—what I was.' He hesitated, and she felt him willing the pain down. He barely breathed the final words. 'So many years, using guns and fast cars and cuffs to feel alive. Then here, nothing—nothing but going through the motions for Zoe. Nobody else could …'

He couldn't say the rest, but she knew. *Only you.* Just as he did for her.

'I didn't know, Elly.'

She longed to ask, just to hear the words after so many years alone, waiting for what would never have happened if she hadn't come here. But it was too big, too frightening to say so soon, so she nodded.

He kept talking, as if to himself. 'All these years. I'd almost forgotten. I wanted to forget. Then you came.'

She knew—oh, how she knew—but she had hardly dared hope *he* would know. A link for a lifetime, a hole the size of the outback without him, without her: fallen, hurting things, accepting less, because it was all they could have. The past fourteen years in silent symphony.

'I thought it would be dead, just a dream that we'd ever find this again,' she whispered.

Another movement of his cheek against hers, his touch warm splendour in a vast, threatening world. 'You came for that. You needed to know if it was—if we were dead.'

Her nod was another caress, drinking it in, all she couldn't have for long. 'But—'

'It's even more.' Closer, still barely touching. 'Part of me wishes it was over.'

'Yes.' *Don't say it. Breathe, just breathe, and let him remember.*

'If—' He shook his head. 'I wish I'd known then.'

She couldn't open her eyes as she said it. 'Before her.'

He stilled. She felt the pain as he spoke. 'It's too late, Elly. I wish to God it wasn't.'

She looked up. Night fell between them with the unspoken name – the shatterer of all they could have been. Adam's broken pieces were so similar to hers, but bore a different name, one he wouldn't speak.

'I always hated triangles. Three angles, and only two match,' she whispered. 'The other's left out.'

A soft, rumbling chuckle. 'You never did make any sense of maths. What about equilateral triangles?'

She smiled. For him. He was right: it was too late. It had been too late the day he met Sharon. Coming here had been an attempt to capture butterflies in a net ruined by holes; all they could have were sweet shadows of the past, and the knowledge made them both ache. Hadn't she always known that, if it could be like this for them, it would also end like this, all undone?

'Even the words for triangles were stupid. *Equilateral. Isosceles.* What idiot makes up names like those, anyway?'

'Nerds,' they answered together, and laughed. Two broken things smiling bravely, remembering when they'd been whole.

'Jonas wanted you back,' she said eventually.

When he didn't answer or move, she opened her fingers, tipped her head back. He dropped her hands, and she returned to the car.

'I'll take you home.' She heard the savage snaps of the tether between his hands as he followed her. 'Baz and Simon can watch outside.'

★   ★   ★

'You left her alone at the house?'

Rick followed Adam into the office. His friend wheeled around, staring at him. He opened his mouth, and closed it. 'Baz and Simon are watching the house,' Adam said.

'It's not enough,' Rick snarled, sick with fear. She meant so much to him already, so damned much. *She needs me.*

'I bought her a portable panic button that calls straight here.'

'That'll help if she's shot!'

Adam frowned. 'Butt out, Rick. Elly needs space when she's overwhelmed.'

'So you think you know her.' Arms folded over his chest, he faced his friend in open challenge. 'Do you really think she hasn't changed in the fourteen years since you ditched her?'

Adam gritted his teeth before answering. 'Why does it matter so much to you? And don't say it's because she's a sister. I haven't seen you obsess over other Aboriginal women who have come in needing help.'

He might have given an honest answer if he thought Adam really wanted to know. Instead, his brows lifted. 'Maybe that's because their cases weren't so bloody desperate, or because I wasn't *locked out* of the cases. As Aboriginal liaison officer for the region, I was the officer in charge—or at least heavily involved.'

Adam conceded the point with a nod. 'I didn't ask for you to be locked out of this one, mate. I'm sorry you are.'

'Did *she*?' He hated that he couldn't talk the case over with Adam as they usually did: sitting here with coffees; sitting at home talking as they watched the footy. But he knew the answer. He'd scared Elly away, not once but twice, with all he felt for her, and she was on the run. From *him*.

Adam fiddled with a pen on his desk. Answer enough.

'I can help,' he murmured, less aggressive now—almost pleading. 'She's my people. Let me in, Adam.'

Adam blew out a hard sigh. 'I wish I could, mate—you know that. But it's not my call.'

'Talk to her. I know I can help.'

'I did,' Adam said quietly. 'You're not helping with all your demands, mate, or by implying that Elly isn't her real name in an open office. She's already dealing with Spencer. You have to back off, give her space.'

He knew Adam was right. But it wasn't the same. Not even Adam understood. He *was* frightening Elly away, and she was the only one with the right to push him out of her case—or let him in. He had to put a lock on his tongue. He'd tried and tried, but he was obsessed. He knew it and she knew it. If he could make her understand …

I can. There's only one way.

Not yet. I have to wait for the right time. Then she'll understand all I can't say.

He felt his eyes turn hard and cold, looking through his friend. It was obvious what he needed to do, and nobody could stop him. He turned for the door.

'Don't go to her,' Adam said softly. 'Your intensity frightens her, mate. She needs quiet and space and gentle handling when she's this freaked out. You have no idea what she's been through – even before Spencer began stalking her.'

For a moment, the situation hung on a knife's point, his defiance and his need; friends divided in a way he'd never foreseen. Both thinking the same: *You can't have her. She's mine.*

Then Rick spoke, just as softly as Adam had. 'She'll need a friend when you hurt her.'

'I won't—'

'You will. You know it, and I know it. Even she knows it. The guilt colours everything you do. You have no right to Elly until you can forget your wife.'

Adam clenched his teeth again. 'I said butt out, mate.'

He turned his head, looking at Adam over his shoulder with burning eyes. 'Will you marry her … *mate*? Will you commit to her, give her the family she needs? Because if you can't, then *you're* the one who should butt out.'

'How do you know what she needs?' Adam snapped. 'You met her less than two days ago, and you're acting like a bloody expert.'

But he saw right through his friend for the first time. 'Tell me I'm wrong. Tell me you're not thinking of the good Elly is doing for *you*, for Zoe, and damning the consequences for her when she's left alone again.'

Silence met his accusations. Guilt, suffering, loss and a dozen other emotions crossed Adam's face: an admission without a word.

Rick looked right into that pain, knowing there was something more important this time.

'Haven't the Jepsons done enough damage to her? Let her go, mate. Let her walk away, and find a life without you.'

Without waiting for an answer he left Adam's office, knowing he was right. Elly deserved the commitment his friend could never give her until he laid his unquiet ghost to rest.

★ ★ ★

Adam wanted to punch his mate's lights out. Hating Rick for the first time, because he'd held up a mirror to his soul, and to Elly's deepest need.

She's not here for protection. She's here for you.

All the wrongs he'd done her years ago, he was doing all over again. Reverting to the boy who'd never fit in with his family, he was reaching for the vivid life, the sense of belonging he'd only known with Elly, without counting the cost—not to him, but to her.

He ached to have a second chance with her, but for his own sake. Breaking his promises to her, and to his dead wife. Hating himself for only *thinking* of stopping it. He knew he wouldn't, because he needed her. Now three words screamed inside him, released like ugly birds: *What about Elly?*

What a mess. What a damn freaking beautiful mess. If the situation wasn't breaking Elly now, it soon would be. He couldn't give her what they both knew she needed, because the soft presence of his dead wife wouldn't leave him in peace.

Please, Adam, swear to me. It's all I ask of you.

It had seemed little enough to vow at the time. Now it was like the glass that had fallen over his body today: multicoloured, and sharp enough to draw blood. It left the darkest part of him exposed, and willing to ruin the best friend he'd ever had to save himself. Not waving, drowning, and only Elly could pull him out. But at what cost?

It's not fair, Sharon, it's not bloody fair.

★ ★ ★

'Annelly, can we get more pizza tonight?'

Elly smiled at the hopeful little angel's face, mischief dancing in her green eyes. 'Sorry, little one. Before Daddy went to pick you up, he told me about the rules around here. That means a good dinner.' As Zoe's face fell, she leaned down to whisper, 'I bought fresh peas and chicken, and I'll make oven fries, too. Want to help me shell the peas? You can play boats with the shells in a bowl when we're done.'

Zoe's eyes lit up. She helped Elly with childish enthusiasm and gleeful laughter. Once the peas were shelled, she dived into a cupboard, retrieved an enormous bowl, and created a pool both inside it and on the floor around Elly's feet.

'That's a novel way of entertaining her. Most people use the TV.'

Elly turned to find Adam behind her. She caught her breath. He wore jeans that moulded to his legs and a black T-shirt with white letters across it that read *I'm Not Normal*. His skin was a deep bronze from his time in the relentless Australian sun. He was so much like the boy she'd lost that she ached.

'I think I've spent too much time in remote areas.' She kept her voice light, trying to will her heart to stop pounding. 'The kids who don't have PlayStations or Xboxes have novel ideas about entertainment. Besides, I like having her here with me. She makes me smile.' She looked him over again, knowing her eyes held the hunger she didn't know how to hide. 'Great outfit, Claudius, but the bunny lady will hardly be impressed.'

He shrugged. 'That's the point. I want her to be unimpressed. She's not getting the message any other way.'

She laughed. 'Poor Mrs Collins. I wonder if any guys have taken so little care about their appearance for me.'

His eyes darkened as he looked her over. 'I doubt it.'

A wild blush filled her face. Her blood pounded with the needs vying in her: to keep him safe, and to keep her distance. To love his body, just once. But there was a new distance between them since he'd dropped her home this morning, and she didn't know how to bridge it, or even if she ought to.

'Look, Daddy, I got a pool! Annelly maked me a pool! Wanna play boats?'

As Adam dropped to his haunches to play with Zoe, the phone rang down the hall.

'You play with her. I'll get it.' Elly bolted to the old-fashioned green wall phone that went with the old house, panelled walls and second-hand furniture Adam had bought with the place.

'Hello?'

'Harlot!'

The harsh whisper, with that awful warped tone of the electronically scrambled voice, made her gasp.

'Delilah. Jezebel. Dark-skinned whore. We don't like women like you in our town.'

'Who is this?' she demanded, willing away the twisting knife. *You'll never be one of us.*

'I hear there was an accident at the police station today. Detective Sergeant Jepson and Constable Dobbins were injured. Leave Macks

Lake before someone really gets hurt. Find one of your own men, and stay away from ours.'

She dropped the phone. It bounced against the wall as she covered her mouth with a hand.

'Elly?'

Blindly she turned from Adam to the wall, huddling against it.

'Who was that?'

When she remained averted, and silent, he snapped, 'What did they say?'

'An obscene phone call.' She tried to laugh. 'These nuts follow me everywhere. I attract 'em like magnets.'

'Elly.' His tone of voice told her he was in no mood to laugh away her problems.

'They called me a harlot, Jezebel, a dark-skinned whore. They said to get out of town before someone else got hurt.' She couldn't make herself say the rest.

'Male or female?' he said, sounding official. Still the distance: *her* Adam would have known not to push. But this man—

She shrugged. 'I couldn't tell. They used one of those voice-scrambler things. It had Private Caller on the ID.'

He hung up the receiver, still bouncing against the wall. 'I can still get it traced. Do you think it was him?'

'It could have been.' She shivered. 'He uses those old-fashioned words—whore, strumpet, harlot—like his grandfather. If he thinks I'm with you—'

'He could be trying to scare you, pretending to judge you to get you out of town, and get you alone.' Adam's curse, too soft for Zoe to hear, ripped the warmth of the summer night. 'That's it. I'm not going. You and Zoe can't be left alone.'

She nodded, sighing. 'I don't think I could stand to be alone tonight.'

He lifted her face. 'You're not alone, Elly. I'm with you. Remember that.'

One touch, a hand on her face, and the air around them stilled.

She used the tip of her tongue to moisten her dry lips, hoping he wouldn't see the pulse pounding in her throat.

He let out a quiet groan, watching the motion. 'Elly, don't do this to me. We're not kids now.'

Something in her died with his words. 'So I'm doing this. I'm forcing you.'

'I didn't mean that.'

She looked at him. 'Didn't you? I think you did. Who talked to you today? Who made you guilty? Who made you remember?' She'd expected it, the freezing of him. Cold as the grave she was in, his turbulent ghost.

'Sailing, sailing, sailing on the sea … gunna catch a fish, and make a wish, for my daddy and me!' Zoe's lilting voice hovered in the air, sweet and childish, shattering all that was and wasn't there.

He sighed. 'Oh, damn it.'

She only nodded. So much unsaid between them: a black hole that could only close with a name. But it wasn't her name to speak.

His eyes burned. 'You wouldn't stay in Macks Lake even if we caught him.'

'You wouldn't want me to.'

'You have to stop. It's no good for either of us.'

'So it's me again. *I* have to stop. This is all *my* fault.' Bitterness filled her. 'The bad girl corrupting the good Jepson. It's that black and white—literally.'

'No, damn it, it isn't like that, and you know it. Stop the wilful misinterpretations.'

Her whole body stiffened. 'Sorry, Uncle Stephen.'

His eyes blazed. 'I am not my father!'

With shaking shoulders, sick to her stomach, she gave a pitiful attempt at a shrug. 'Aren't you? Isn't that what you're trying to be now?'

'Stop it,' he hissed, his eyes still smouldering. 'You're trying to distance me.'

She laughed, a sad and bitter thing. 'Just following your lead, detective sergeant.'

'I'm not—'

'Lie to yourself if you want. I treasure what we used to be too much to lie to you.'

The flame burned out, leaving his eyes hollow. 'Used to be. So you're putting an end to it.'

'As I said, I'm just following your lead. I'm accepting this is what you want. If you'd stop putting the blame on me for your fears, I'd be grateful.'

He stilled, searching her face. Another moment of dancing on a blade-edge of recognition; then it died. 'You're here for my protection and help, and I'm helping you for the sake of old friendship. Let's leave it at that.'

She looked away. 'I think I should go back to the Rose and Thistle.'

'You said you wouldn't leave. You promised.'

'But you never promised me anything, did you?' She pressed her lips together to keep herself from saying any more, but the truth tumbled out anyway. 'I can't go on this seesaw with you, up one moment, down the next.'

'So now it's my fault,' he said. 'You come back into my life, change me and expect me not to be confused? You expect me to know what I feel in less than two days. You're my childhood friend one moment, then the next you look at me like you'd die to have me.'

And though he couched it as half-sarcastic insult, he'd spoken the reality of all her dreams like a release of rushing water from a swollen dam.

'I would,' she said, not daring to look at him. 'I *would* die to have you, even if it's only once.'

'Damn it, don't talk to me like that, or I'll do something we'll both regret.' But he didn't move, didn't turn away.

'You might regret it. I won't.' She'd gone as far as she dared. Looking up at last, she saw him fighting his need. Wishing, hoping, he'd drop his barriers, take that step, move that inch.

'Learn.' The want and the forbidden warred in eyes. 'You'd better back off now, or believe me, you'll sure as hell regret it later.'

'So you know my mind—or is it yours?' she taunted. 'Worried what the relatives and friends will think? It's a big risk, being with me—and risks are something you haven't been good at in the past.'

'I don't give a damn about your Aboriginal background, if that's what you mean. But take this as a warning—I'm no damn good at relationships, or with women.'

Her brows furrowed at the revelation flung at her like a gauntlet. 'But you were married for nine years.'

'Yeah, I was, wasn't I.' It wasn't a question. His eyes cold as a winter sea, he punched numbers into his phone. 'Hey, Rick, Elly had a threatening phone call. I have to interview Mrs Collins, and Elly shouldn't be alone ... Yeah. Thanks, mate, I owe you one.' He didn't look at her as he hung up.

'Rick?' she whispered, a brick falling in her stomach. Her heart hurt with its pounding. 'You called *Rick* to stay with me?'

'You don't know him.' He still wouldn't look at her. Yes, he knew he'd just done the unforgivable. 'I know he's intense, but Rick will take care of you.'

'You gave me no choice,' she said slowly. 'I told you I wanted him off the case. I *told* you he scares me!'

'It's best for you. He's one of your people.'

The pain was too familiar. 'Aren't you … one of mine?' she asked with a sad little catch in her voice.

'You shouldn't have to ask. You know I am. I always was.'

'Not while Sharon was alive to stop you.'

He lifted her face, hands gentle, his eyes blazing. 'Stop it. Stop talking about her. Don't think about her. Don't say her name!'

Something inside her cringed beneath the force of his unhealed emotion.

Moments later his bedroom door closed with a quiet click that told a stronger story than a mighty crash. The dead were still living.

'Annelly, I think something's burning, and I'm *bery* hungry.'

She returned to Zoe, leaving Adam alone with his ghosts.

CHAPTER
10

'Uncle Rick!'

Laughing, Rick caught the flying blur in his arms as he came through the front door, lifting her onto his hip. Zoe snuggled into Rick's strong brown neck, arms around him tight enough to choke. 'Let's play Barbies. Daddy got me the tea-party set he promised!'

'Thanks, Daddy.' Rick's face was one big comical grimace. 'I think Daddy needs to buy a Ken dolly for me.'

'Yeah!' Zoe cried. 'I'll tell Daddy, and then we can play *all the time*! Our dollies can get married, just like us!'

'Yay!' Rick's face softened as Zoe gave his cheek a smacking kiss.

Elly smiled. Somehow his relationship with the little girl eased her fears. If a four-year-old wasn't intimidated by him, if he could play Barbies with a small, motherless girl, then he couldn't be as frightening as she'd thought. 'It looks like Zoe has a hero.'

'Fiancé, thank you,' he corrected her, dark eyes twinkling. 'We're getting married when she's sixteen, just like Ariel and Eric in *The Little Mermaid*.'

'Uncle Rick's my *boyfriend*,' Zoe informed her smugly. 'He looks *just* like Prince Eric!'

'You're right, Zoe. He is like Prince Eric, with darker eyes.' Hoping she was wrong about Adam's best friend, Elly grinned. 'Congratulations, brother. You've found yourself a wife.'

A friendly remark, with no guile, yet Rick's smile faded. 'I'm glad you think so … sister.' His voice was even, his gaze unemotional, but still she felt all he was holding inside.

'Zoe's waiting for you,' she said, turning away. She had files to read on the people she needed to visit tomorrow.

After he'd played Barbies with Zoe to her heart's content and read her stories until she was blissfully asleep, he cornered Elly in the kitchen.

'So tell me about the threatening call tonight, Jane Ann Larkins.'

She dropped a plate as she whirled to face him. 'How—?'

He picked up the shards of the broken plate. 'Oh, come on.'

'The network,' she said, voice flat.

He shrugged. 'It wasn't hard. Ain't that many Koori lady doctors around. I called your people in La Perouse, identifying myself, and they told me their worries.' His glance at her was cool, accusing. 'They're glad to know you're alive, by the way.'

Her eyes flashed. 'How dare you pry into my private life! Did you tell them where I was?'

He dropped the shards into the trash, then turned to her. 'I know more about you than you think. You've held off from your people since you landed on their doorstep. You don't know our rules. You're playing whitefella beneath the skin.' His burning gaze blistered her. 'You patch our people's cuts, but don't tell them your name. Your grandmother is still wondering what she's done to deserve your leaving without trace after years of care and support. You play on the loyalty you know our people will give, but give none yourself.'

Her eyes narrowed. 'You know nothing about me.'

'I know a lot more than you think,' he said in a way that left her shaking with uncertainty.

'What, because of our shared heritage?'

He touched her chin, fingers curving around it. 'You don't believe that can happen?'

Her eyes blazed as she pulled out of his hold. 'Don't touch me. I didn't give you permission to touch me.'

His hand fell slowly.

'Like I said, you know nothing of me, personally.' More disturbed by his words than she wanted to admit, she mumbled, 'I wanted to protect my family. If he goes to them ...'

His brow lifted. 'You mean Danny Spencer, Janie?'

She shuddered. 'Don't call me that. I'm Elly now.'

'I'll call you Elly if you promise to stop shutting me out.' He didn't touch her, but stepped closer. 'You turn to whitefellas for help when I'm right here. Look at me, Janie, and understand the truth. I'll do whatever it takes to help you. That's why I became an outback cop. It's why I came to Macks Lake in the first place. I'm here for you. Give me the loyalty. Don't turn to the wrong man.'

'The wrong man?' She used her coldest tone, the barrier that brought most men to a stammering halt.

But Rick didn't even hesitate. 'A man so drowned in guilt he can't see you beyond childhood memories. A man so locked in the past he has no future to give you beyond a few hours in bed,' he retorted, finding her most vulnerable spot with unerring accuracy. 'Don't turn your back on your own people, Elly. I'm here for you.'

'You don't know me. You only met me yesterday.' She pushed him away with a hard laugh. 'A similar heritage gives you nothing. I didn't even know of my Aboriginal background until I was fifteen. My mother never told me, and the Jepsons sure as hell didn't.

I thought my father was from Italy, and my mum never once told me where she was from.'

'When you found out the truth, did you hide it?'

She didn't answer.

'Exactly. Stop trying to bluff me, Elly. You're Koori, heart and soul, just like me.'

'You're not Koori, you're Paakantyi.'

'Semantics. It's just a name for the area we come from, but we both are what we are. You wouldn't be helping our people out here otherwise. Just like I'm out here as a cop.' He sighed, but kept his distance. 'Look, Adam's the best mate I've ever had. He's a great guy—one of the best—but he'll never be yours until he can stop torturing himself over his wife and son's deaths. You're a beautiful, special woman—too special to wait for disappointment.'

Was he speaking from a racial perspective, or did something more elemental, dark and primitive lurk beneath his veiled warning?

'Tell me what's going on, Elly. Trust me,' he said very quietly, eyes sincere. So handsome, so masculine, yet all she felt was dread. He'd keep digging until he knew the truth … and his digging could leave someone dead.

'No,' she said, just as quiet, just as sincere. 'I don't want you. I don't need you.'

He sighed. 'One day you'll regret saying all this. One day, you're going to love me.'

They were the same words Danny had used the first time she'd rejected him, and panic filled her. 'It's time you left,' she hissed.

'Yes, it is.'

They whirled around. Adam stood in the doorway, legs splayed, arms folded, face grim and cold as he watched them. He looked like he wanted Rick to leave—in an ambulance. He moved forward and put a casual arm on the kitchen counter, a barrier between her and Rick.

'I'm here now, mate. Thanks so much for coming.'

Rick stood his ground for a moment. Then he took a slow step back, a challenge in his eyes. 'You're welcome.' Said with the same sarcastic politeness with which Adam had thanked him.

Elly hated herself. What was it about her? She'd said and done nothing to encourage Rick in any way, yet she was coming between friends.

'We got the trace back on the call tonight. It came from a burner phone bought months ago in Mildura. Mildura police interviewed the owner of the store this afternoon. He doesn't remember the buyer, but records show they paid cash,' Adam informed them in a tight voice, before Rick reached the door. 'And you were right about the shot, Rick. It was a steel ball, but shot from a BB gun. Sydney says Spencer can't be here, so both the shot and the tyre slashing are being dismissed as a kid's prank. Backup's still not scheduled to arrive until Monday.'

Elly frowned at Adam. 'Weren't you with Mrs Collins?'

He shrugged. 'I lasted an hour. If she had information for us, she wasn't giving it away.'

'What was she giving away?' Rick murmured.

Adam looked at Elly, and she knew he'd seen it, the little flinch she tried so hard to hide. 'Nothing I was tempted to take.'

'Not for her want of trying, I'll bet.'

He shrugged. 'I learned something tonight: there's things you can't force or change, no matter how hard you want it—or don't want it. Some things just are.'

Their eyes locked.

'Thanks for coming, Rick,' he murmured, his gaze still on Elly. 'I appreciate it. See you in the morning.'

Rick held his ground, but spoke gently. 'Elly, please, just think about what I said.'

'I will.' She was still looking at Adam, quiet hunger rising inside her once more. 'Thank you for coming, Rick.'

Rick stalked out in silence, closing the door behind him with care.

'So you gained nothing?' she asked, still staring at Adam. Unable to look away. 'Has she got an alibi for either incident?'

He shrugged. 'She left the station just before the shot. She was alone in her car. But a few witnesses have stated they saw her car at least eight blocks from the station when they heard the shot.'

'Could she have done it?'

'It'll be hard to pin on her. She's never owned a firearm. Apart from the litany of false complaints she's made since I came here, all she has is a couple of speeding tickets. Her methods are nagging and emotional blackmail. She hasn't come to my house, or done more than try to gain my attention at the station or the grocery store.'

She sighed, feeling torn.

'There's something you haven't told me.'

'No,' she answered far too quickly, shutting him out.

He moved closer, tilting up her face, as Rick had done a minute ago, but she felt no disdain now, no furious rejection, only a wild sort of helplessness.

'Are you attracted to Rick?'

The lovely feeling died. She jerked her head away from his hand, her voice cold as a winter night. 'What business is it of yours?'

A pause pregnant with a hundred unspoken thoughts. 'Can't old friends ask personal questions of each other?'

'Be a hypocrite if you want. I don't have to play along.'

'Fine,' he conceded. 'You know the truth anyway. I'm jealous as hell. You're driving me crazy, and seeing other men touching you, or coming near you—even a top guy like Rick—brings on a primitive urge to ram my fist down his throat. Is that what you want to hear?'

Her defiance died. A hand lifted, reaching for the air at her waist again, before she forced it to fall. When she answered him, her voice was cold and flat. 'No. Another crazy, possessive man is the last thing I need right now.'

Her deliberate comparison shocked him; she saw his anger fade. 'I'm not Spencer. If you like Rick, I'll back off.' He trailed a finger over her cheek and her lips parted on a rush of air—a rush of wanting. 'I just want the truth, darlin',' he whispered. 'Talk to me.'

With the touch, and the endearment he'd never used before, she could no longer fight the truth. 'You know the answer already. I didn't ask him to be taken off the case because I like him.' She sighed. 'Rick's a handsome man. I'd have to be dead not to see that. But when he touches me, it's—it's just not there for me.'

'He was very close to you when I got here. What did he do to you?'

'He called me Jane Larkins,' she whispered. 'Jane Ann Larkins. He knew me.'

'It's all on your case file, Elle,' he said softly. 'So tell me, what really scared you? What does he know about you that I don't?'

Elle. The cutting of her nickname was an intimate act he hadn't done since he met Sharon. 'The seesaw,' she reminded him, just as softly. 'You're confusing me, Adam. Are you the cop, the friend or the lover now?'

'I'm bloody confused myself, but I know one thing. We belong together,' he said, voice rough. 'We've always belonged together. Even while we were apart, sometimes I'd think of you, and I felt you there with me.'

When you were with Sharon. She didn't say the name, didn't dare to. 'I never felt you.'

'Never?' he whispered, moving closer.

'Never. I wish I had. I tried, but—'

'She was there.'

Elly almost gasped, for his voice had lost the harshness; he wasn't locking her out when speaking of his wife. 'Yes.'

He bent, moving his cheek against hers, his bristle scratching. A memory to hold onto when she was gone, when she was alone.

'You never left me, Elle. A part of you was always with me. Even when it made life too bloody hard, I couldn't let go of you.'

And she always knew it. That's why she destroyed us. They stood holding each other, and she wondered when she'd put her arms around his waist.

'I wish you'd been with me,' she said, not knowing which admission was safer, only that this one wouldn't make him lock the door on her.

'I don't understand why you don't hate me.'

The answer was too big and terrifying to admit, even to herself. *This moment* was too big and terrifying, when she knew the future as clearly as if she was a seer. So she broke it.

'I hate you for leaving me with Rick tonight.'

'What did you tell him?' And there he was, Adam the cop, jealous-as-hell Adam, not her Adam, her Claudius, who broke her heart every time she glimpsed him.

She almost laughed. 'You came home not five minutes after he brought up my name. Do you think I told him my life story?'

'What *did he say*?'

She shrugged. 'He talked to my family.' *He said I'm going to love him … he warned me off believing in you.*

He swore, and she reared away from him, feeling as defensive as if he'd accused her.

'It wasn't through any wish of mine! I don't want them to know about this. Danny knows where they live. If he thought the family knew anything, he'd slash his way through them to find me. I wouldn't have come to *you* if I thought he knew about you and Zoe!'

His eyes softened. 'How long has it been, Elle?'

Confused by his return to the manner of the boy she'd adored, she frowned savagely. 'Don't talk in riddles. Say what you mean.'

'How soon after you realised how dangerous Spencer was did you start isolating yourself to save the people you love?'

That he understood why she'd isolated herself where Rick had only accused her of abandoning her family hurt as much as it was a sweet relief. Yes, Adam still knew her—no matter how much she wished he didn't.

'I changed phones the next day, and haven't contacted anyone since.'

'And he put the chains around you. No wonder he's convinced you love him. You've done everything he wanted.'

'Running doesn't exactly denote love.'

'I wasn't criticising you, just giving you a cop's perspective. By isolating yourself, you're playing right into his hands,' he said, still tender—but it was as if a door had been opened in a long-dark place; the light he poured on her sent blinding pain through her head. She closed her eyes, rubbing her temples.

'Stop it.' It was a plea. 'I left you alone.'

'All right,' he said quietly. 'I'll call Sarge.' He hesitated. 'Rick should be part of the case, since he already knows so much. He's an excellent cop, and a good man. I swear he won't hurt you, Elle. He only wants to protect you. We need all the help we can get right now.'

Even with her eyes closed, she felt him willing her to say yes. Adam had always been a bulldog when he believed something was right. There was little to do but give in.

'All right,' she said, tired of fighting. 'Just don't leave me alone with him. I'll go to bed.'

She looked up, and then she didn't want to go. She could stand there all night, looking into his eyes, filled with the tang of out-lawed desire. So much hunger in a single look.

'Good night,' she whispered.

CHAPTER
11

Adam was caught: snared by her, inside the expression in her eyes. So long since—no, he'd *never* seen this, the beautiful helplessness of a woman trapped inside her desire for him. He'd never known it could happen for him, least of all with the girl who'd been the other half of him all those years ago. His Elly, who was still all he couldn't be, but would give anything to become.

Had this always been inside two grubby, defiant children playing in the bush? Had they been blind to all they could have had?

With unsated hunger burning his gut, and lingering shards of hot jealousy filling his brain, he had little will left to resist. His hand trailed in delicate possession down her jaw, butterfly fingertips over her throat and shoulder. 'Good night, Elly.'

Her tiny gasp flashed into his body at the speed of light. The last shreds of jealousy disappeared. Her yearning was his. Her need was his. Her taboo no less compelling than his: her memories of rejection equalling his burden of guilt, his sworn vow. Elly wouldn't stay while Spencer remained alive. She'd never risk his life, or Zoe's. How could he think of endangering his beautiful daughter, when there was a murderer on the loose? Could he? Would Elly stay with him, even if he stopped Spencer?

The impossible choice. Heart and soul, he was bound to her—and if he'd almost forgotten it once, he never would again. Janie and Adam, Elly-May and Claudius—the love always half-forbidden, the call from heart to heart defiant, inextinguishable. And as adults—

You are what you are. You'll destroy her, just as you destroyed—

He turned away, the fury and need tearing his heart, gut, loins apart. 'Go to bed, or I'm going to do something very stupid.'

He felt the wild, sweet call of her heart grow cold with despair. After an interminable silence, her gaze fell. She nodded, and walked into her room without looking back. Would that moment ever come again? He couldn't go to her, he couldn't tell her—

A scream tore the heavy curtain of silence, shearing it into jagged slices. *'Adam!'*

'Elly?' He bolted to her room and kicked the door open. Checking her over first, he saw she was unmolested, but she was pale, her eyes wide. With an unsteady hand, she pointed to the half-open window. On the top pane, in dripping red letters, were the words:

BLACK SLUT

He tore out the front door. A pale sedan was screeching around the corner, its true colour impossible to name in the deep darkness of an unlit country night, its plates obscured by mud.

He ran back inside. Elly stood where he left her, still transfixed by the macabre decoration. As he snapped the blind shut he heard a high-pitched gasp and swung around. 'What is it?'

One hand on her chest, she pointed at the mirror on the 1920s-era dressing table that had come with the house. The sticky trickle of red dribbling down the mirror's slightly dusty surface was not paint.

As if hypnotised, she moved to the dressing table, fingers stretching to the foreign substance. He gently drew her out of the room. 'Don't touch anything. I need to collect evidence.'

She turned away. And then he saw the tremors start.

He forgot he was a cop. He forgot about calling the station, or getting his kit out of the car to sweep and print the room. 'Ah, Elle.' He dragged her against him, loving the feel of her against his skin, the earthy, natural essence of woman that radiated from her. 'You're not alone. I'm here.'

She snatched him close, breathing into his shoulder. Tears dropped onto his skin. Then she moved away so fast she almost fell into the wall.

'I–I'm okay.' She scrubbed her cheeks with the back of her hand. 'Go call Jonas.' When he resisted, she added, 'Please, Adam. I'll be fine in a minute.'

'Elly, don't—'

But she'd turned away, unwilling to fully share her burdens, even this fear. She still needed to learn trust.

Sighing, he pulled out his phone, dialled his boss's number, and described the incident to the sarge. 'Jen Collins has a light-coloured sedan,' he reported grimly. 'I think I saw a Toyota symbol on the boot.'

'Many people own light-coloured Toyotas around here, including Mendham.'

'He just left.' He stilled, feeling the unwanted suspicion coming down the line. 'We're only hurting ourselves by leaving him out of this. Elly's given permission to let him back in.'

'Good,' Sarge said grimly. 'We need some good news. The situation is already getting out of control. Whoever this is, they're bloody clever. Everything could either be an accident or a kid's prank. They're not doing anything threatening enough to warrant backup, or to prove Spencer's in the area. In fact, we know he isn't. A white man asking questions about an Indigenous doctor was reported to be in Pitjantjatjara lands, and his acts were crazy enough for it to be Spencer.'

'So who the hell is doing this?'

'We'll get them,' Sarge promised, voice hard and dark. 'As we thought, Sydney's dismissing the drive-by as a prank, because of the BB gun — and so would we, but for the other incidents. Sydney's got the usual amount of problems to deal with there, so they won't act until they know Spencer's close to here. Suits from Sydney will arrive Monday, so collect the evidence in Elly's room and take shots for them.'

Knowing his boss had more to say, Adam waited in silence.

'You know what I have to say, Jepson. From Monday, you're out. Your relationship with Elly puts your objectivity in question. She needs you. So stick with her day and night until we find out who's targeting her. If anything comes up, we'll contact you.' A little pause. 'Correction: *I'll* contact you. Take orders from CIB, or me, or Mendham when it comes to his area of expertise. Make your reports to me, or Albertson at CIB. If anyone else—anyone at all—contacts you, play dumb and give me the details.'

'Got it.' The irony wasn't laughable. Days and nights with Elly, the one woman he couldn't resist, ignore—or have.

'Just look after Elly.'

Adam hung up, the words ringing in his head.

He found her in the kitchen, finishing the dishes, a Sphinx-like calm hovering around her.

'Are you okay? Pretty scary thing to happen.'

A little shrug of her shoulders.

'Think that's blood on your mirror?'

She shook her head, emptying the sink, taking up a tea towel.

'I'll do that.' He reached for the tea towel, but she snatched it back, wiping each piece of crockery with meticulous care.

He let her go. In a life where nothing was under her control, she could do dishes.

'Spencer was reported to be in Pitjantjatjara lands yesterday, six hundred miles southwest of Ayer's Rock. Apparently a kid you'd stitched up told him you'd headed north in a light plane.'

'Uluru.' Her quiet answer showed no sign of emotion. 'Ayer's Rock reverted to its real name in the 1980s.'

Relieved she was speaking, even if she'd given no acknowledgement of what he'd said, he replied, 'Sorry, keeper of the Indigenous flame.'

Her eyes flashed. 'I believe in truth, not in hiding it behind prettily packaged words and terms. It's a habit I picked up from my people, even if the Jepsons ignore it!'

'Okay. Sorry. Where did you go after Uluru?' he said, to get them back on track.

'I went north. Then I hitched a ride to Charleville in Queensland, flew to Sydney, and caught a train to Broken Hill. Then I bought the car, and came here. And yes, I stopped at the Koori communities on the road here, so he can trace me. Satisfied, Detective Sergeant Jepson?'

And just like that, her walls were back in place. He repressed a sigh. 'I'll collect evidence from your room.'

A few minutes later, she came into the spare room and stood at a distance, watching him work.

Crawling from under the dresser, he held up a spatula with a gloved hand. 'I'll send this for testing, but I'm certain it's fake blood. The capsule was left outside the window.' Switching on his phone torch, he opened the window again and showed her. 'You can't sleep here tonight, Elly. We'll dust the room tomorrow, but I doubt we'll find any prints but ours.'

'They left the capsule as a warning,' she stated, in a flat voice. 'Next time it will be real.'

'The blood at the station was real.'

When guilt turned her eyes to pools of pain, he wanted to kick himself for opening his big mouth. 'Whoever's doing this knows the law—but it isn't Spencer,' he said more softly. 'We know that much. Looks like they never entered the room. They painted the words back to front, and squirted the fake blood from outside. See the traces of it along the carpet? So we can't even get 'em for break and enter, just malicious damage—and that's if we're lucky. Again, most judges would treat it as a kid's prank. Almost everything so far has been pranks that would be dismissed in court, maybe with community service.'

'Slashing my tyres wasn't a prank,' she argued. 'And surely shooting out the station window was an attack against the police. Two of you were injured.'

'A BB-gun shot is teenage territory. A kid would probably get a suspended sentence for it. And the tyres—any judge would rule it as the act of a jealous kid. Unless we find a connection between the three incidents, proving otherwise won't be easy.' He sighed. 'If someone wants you out of town, they're being bloody clever about it.'

Her face still held that unusual hardness, the determination. Her foot was back out the door already. 'Well, they've got what they want. I'll go tomorrow.'

'Why are you giving in to them? Do you imagine the danger will disappear with you, since there's little chance of this being Spencer?'

She looked at him, defiant. 'Yes. I do. So do you, or you wouldn't be dismissing the pranks for my sake, to make me think there's no real danger.'

Damn her for still knowing him so well. 'And what happens when you're on that lonely stretch of highway between here and Broken Hill or Echuca, with no one to help you for miles?'

'Let him kill me. At least you and Zoe will be safe!'

He closed his eyes, hearing the truth in her words: she loved him still. She even loved his child. Sharon's child. 'How the hell do I live with letting you die alone?'

'Ssh. You'll wake Zoe,' she whispered harshly.

'Answer me, Elly, damn it,' he growled. 'How do I live with your death?'

'Like you did last time. Just forget I exist!'

He reared back. 'I never forgot you, Elly!'

'Yes, that was obvious from the day you met Sharon. Talk's cheap, Claudius, but actions reap. I'm going.'

'So you want me to bury another person I care about?'

She put a finger to his lips, but her face remained hard. Determined. 'You don't want to bother, don't. Just send my body back to my people in Sydney, and forget me all over again. After all, they're *my* people, aren't they? Like you said. They might even tend my grave.'

'I never forgot you. I never wanted to leave you. I've never had a friend like you, before or since.' He dragged her against him. 'Dear God, Elly, don't you know how much I missed you? Don't you know I never stopped caring—that I still care now? I buried your memory because it hurt too damn much to be without you.'

She stilled as he stiffened. But she didn't speak, so he was forced to go on.

'The hole in me was miles wide. I was a fool to let them—let her—' He stopped, but he knew she'd hear it, the taboo, the name he couldn't say aloud. 'If you run, this time I'll follow you. This time I *will* protect you. You got that?'

She shuddered against him. 'Can't you understand? He's already killed one man. I couldn't bear it if he hurt you.' She gave him a brave smile. 'And Zoe's our first priority. I can't put her in danger any more than you can.'

'Elly—' He groaned under the weight of an anguish that seemed never to end, no matter how much he wanted to change it. 'I'll send her to Mum's. There's too much danger here.'

She looked stricken. 'No! I won't let her lose her security! She's only in danger if I stay.'

He shook his head. 'She's been wanting to see her nanna for months. We do a Skype call with Mum every Tuesday and Friday. They're dying to spend time together. I'll call Mum tomorrow, and give Bowral police a heads-up.'

'You know you can't do that. Jonas said it would put everyone in danger.' She put up a hand when he was about to argue. 'I'll leave tomorrow, if my car's ready.' And she walked away.

He found her on the old sofa with a throw and a cushion, her face composed. 'You can't sleep alone. If whoever this is can knock over your room while we're home, and shoot out the station window without a trace, you're a sitting duck here.'

With startling suddenness, she lost it. 'Stop it! I left you alone!'

'But you're not safe alone.'

'I haven't been safe since the day I met Danny Spencer! And I'm used to being alone.' Her voice grew softer with every word. 'I've been *alone* most of my life.'

Tenderness, and the need to make it up to her, flooded him at the admission. 'Elly, you'll never know how sorry I am for leaving you like I did. I should have called you, asked you to come for visits, or met you in the city.'

She lifted her face from the cushion. Her expression was vivid and radiant with fury, taking his breath away with her savage, burning beauty. 'So now you're the god of all creation? Do I look like a failure, or a weakling who needs a strong man to protect her? I didn't just survive without you. I got a scholarship on my brains, not through an Aboriginal charitable scheme. I worked like a dog, and was in the top ten every year. I got seven offers to join a special-ist city practice. Not bad for wild little Janie Larkins, who they said wouldn't amount to anything! I should thank you for forgetting me. You taught me a vital lesson: love doesn't last, and friendships are forgotten—but I can make it on my own. Yes, I loved you. I still love you, but I don't need you to save me.'

About to snap, withdraw—anything to cover the hurt her speech evoked—he had a sudden series of visions. One after the other, they came to him.

A child whose father had deserted her and whose mother's death threw her into a new world and family, feeling the charity child in a prim-and-proper upper-middle-class environment. Saying the words *I can make it on my own*, trying to survive.

A grieving tomboy sitting alone in their tree, deserted by her best friend, repeating the words every night, trying to convince herself of their truth as he made a life without her. *I don't need him. I can make it on my own.*

A wild country girl sent to her city relatives, an alien in a new culture, welcome, cared for, but having no one familiar or loved to talk to. Repeating the words again as she tried to fit into a new life and family, a whole new world. *I'm fine. I can do this.*

A strong, beautiful woman, chased by a psychopath intent on stealing her to fulfil his dreams. Repeating her litany as she ran from another town, another potential family, a place she might finally find peace.

In every vision, she was alone.

No wonder she'd thrown herself into his arms that first day. In isolating herself to save family and friends from Spencer's violence, she'd been starved of the simple gift of human touch.

His poor wild child. The Elly-May he'd loved so deeply was dying—a flickering flame buffeted by constant storms; a transplanted flower wilting for lack of attention. If he let her down now, she might never live again.

He hauled her into his arms and carried her to his room.

She struggled against him. 'Adam, put me down! Where are you taking me? If you think I want to go to bed with you now, you need your head read!'

'Ssh.' He laid her on the bed. 'You're safe with me, Elle. Tonight, and always. As much as I want to make love to you, it's not what you need now. You need to feel safe—that someone cares for you. Sleep, darlin'. I'll be right here if you need me.'

A little silence, then she startled him with her mumble. 'I don't want to sleep in her bed.'

'It isn't,' he replied, his voice harsh. 'She had her own bed ... and her own room.'

'I—really?' she whispered.

He nodded, trying to banish the memories of degradation that still bit deep. 'I wouldn't lie to you. She never slept in this bed with me. So go to sleep.'

'You don't have to do this.'

In her words, her voice, were the years of loneliness she was trying so hard to hide. It banished the visions of his private humiliation as nothing else could. His heart constricting, he pulled her close, marvelling at how right it felt to have her in his arms. 'Ah, Elle,' he whispered. 'How long has it been since someone gave to you, held you, without wanting something in return?'

'Don't.' She moved back, a plea in her eyes, drawn from the loving heart she kept so shielded from everyone else, even as it called to his as it always had. 'Don't let me depend on you. I'm too close, want too much. If—' Another hesitation, then she said it. 'If I fall in love with you, it could kill us both. And Zoe.'

His heart overflowed. That was his Elly-May: she always refused to compromise. *Isn't it already too late … for both of us?* Tangled up in each other's souls, so damn lost without each other. If he lost her again, he'd fall down so bloody far he doubted he'd ever climb out.

'Trust me, Elle.'

In a stretch of quiet, filled only with the delicate night symphony of crickets, she nodded.

Gathering up some pyjamas, he handed her the shirt and, taking the bottoms, went into the bathroom to change.

When he returned, his heart started slamming in erratic rhythm against his ribs. The shirt that once covered his skin now caressed hers. It felt as intimate as a lover's kiss. Her long honey legs, smooth and bare, lay in a tangle on his sheets.

This night was going to kill him.

'Adam.' Her voice sounded as strangled as his throat felt. 'Put on a shirt.' Her gaze fixed on his bare chest and stomach. A dusky rose flush crept over her cheek and throat, staining her shoulders and breasts under the open neck of his pyjama shirt.

The honesty of her desire for him was humbling. He drew a ragged breath, fighting for control. She'd been attacked since arriving here. Tonight she needed a love that transcended the physical. She needed to know she could trust him with her secrets, with her body—with her very life. He pulled out a T-shirt from his drawer, yanking it over his head.

'Better?' he asked hoarsely.

She gave a wavering smile. 'No, but it's safer.' She still couldn't drag her gaze from him.

What was he that she, who could have almost any man, could want him? 'It's going to happen.' His words were croaked, rough, far from sensuous or confident as sharp lumps formed in his throat.

'I know,' she whispered, soft as a brush of her lips on his, lush as a promise. Her eyes looked into his with the defiant courage, the integrity so characteristic of her. 'Don't use me, Adam. Don't make love with me if you still love her. Don't touch me if you believe the things the Jepsons thought of me. I may not have much in the way of social status, but I deserve better than that from you.'

'Much better than that.' He lay beside her, facing her. His shaking hands brushed her hair from her face as he tried to dredge up the right words. The damage his wife and family had done to Elly was unforgivable, as was his forgetting her. Yet here she was, giving him a second chance, one he didn't deserve. *Where along the line did I change? When did courage and truth become less important than peace and quiet?* 'You still don't know what you mean to me, do you?'

'What was it about her that makes her so unforgettable?' She whispered the words, as if afraid to say them out loud. 'Why does being with another woman fill you with such guilt, three years later?'

Even with sheathed claws, she tore him to shreds, dredging up a truth he still wanted to hide. *Not any other woman. It was always you she was terrified of.* He opened his mouth to say it—and the tired whisper came to him again.

I know I wasn't the wife you wanted me to be, Adam, but I tried so hard to make you happy. Please, it's all I ask of you.

The memory of Sharon's dying hour filled him with conflicted loyalties. Elly might deserve the truth, but Sharon hadn't deserved death. Nor had his baby son. And his wife's final request—and her secret—still lashed at his heart with the relentless ferocity of a cyclone.

'It's all right, Adam. It's enough that you're here with me now,' she said quietly, breaking into his inner darkness with painful understanding.

There was a long silence so deep, so profound, he wondered if she'd fallen asleep. Then a warm rush of air touched his throat.

'I didn't mind it so much, being the alien among the Jepsons when you were there. But then you were gone—and something in me died. I didn't know who or what I was without you. I couldn't make myself care any more.'

The lump filled his throat, threatening to cut off his air supply. 'I know.' Oh, how he knew. 'It was the same for me.'

'But you left me behind.' A whisper he barely heard.

'I had no choice. I'd made a vow.' Unable to help himself, he buried his face in her hair, inhaling her scent, taking her warmth in through his pores. He hadn't realised how cold he'd been. Thirteen years as a half-man, walking in the shadows of life, not quite dead, never truly alive. 'It's one of a hundred regrets in my life, but hurting you is at the top of the list. I didn't know how much I'd lost until you came back. When I lost you, I lost myself too.'

Two days with Elly made him see the truth—he was back. She'd woven her spell over him, and he was alive again. He didn't want to question why she loved him. They needed each other. It was as simple, and as complex, as that.

She burrowed herself in his arms. 'And now?'

'Mum and Jared know you're with me. They'll keep the secret, but said to tell you they're glad you're safe.' He added, 'They care about you, you know. They always did. They just find it hard to show it. It's the way they are.'

After a few moments, she softened against him. 'It seems like years since I slept.'

He dragged her even closer. 'Say good night, Elly.'

'Good night.' She snuggled tight against him and yawned. 'Don't leave me, Adam.'

Gathering the ragged ends of his self-control together, he moved his too-obvious state of arousal away from her thigh, and brushed his mouth over her cheek. 'I'll be here when you wake up.'

Even breathing answered him. Her clean scent of powder, shampoo and sensuous woman surrounded him like a benediction as he, too, slipped into the deep sleep that had eluded him for so many years. He held her through the night, and dreamed of running barefoot on his grandfather's farm, hunting for critters, and skinny-dipping in waterholes—

And of a madman with a shearer's knife hacking off his baby's golden hair, branding her fair skin.

Harts Range Airstrip, Plenty Highway, near Alice Springs

With a pounding heart, Danny watched the plane land. This was it, a yellow Cessna with the right registration painted on the tail. Even in the dry, pulsing heat, he could feel the closeness of her on his tongue, could feel her skin in his mouth. Redemption. An ordinary life with an extraordinary woman. It was all ahead for them ...

Janie, where are you now? Are you as alone as me? Does your heart hurt like mine?

Of course not, Monster snarled. He was getting angrier by the hour. *She doesn't love us, Danny, not the way we love her.*

You know nothing. Go away, he yelled back. *You aren't me, and you love nobody but yourself.*

Who are you yelling at, me or Granddad? Monster taunted. *Remember how he used to use that razor to slash—*

The yellow Cessna turned into its hangar, and Danny strode over, blocking out the voice of sinful sweetness. He didn't need reminders: the itch was physical now, constantly curling his hands over an imaginary knife. Finding Janie was as imperative as his next breath. He couldn't bear Monster's company any longer. He didn't want to become—

I am you, Monster's whisper came spinning from the blackness behind, a Frisbee he had to catch, because if he didn't, someone else might.

You will never be me. And Janie will come home with me. You wait and see. The relief of the temporary control was like cool water in this parched red land, so close to the only place he'd ever called home.

Oh, we'll see, my dear, Monster said, spinning again in the darkness. *We will.*

He hated it when Monster aligned them, like wheels on the same truck.

As soon as he was in the semidarkness of the hangar he pulled off his reflective sunglasses, revealing brown eyes with dyed black lashes, nothing like the description on the radio. 'G'day, mate,' he called when he saw the pilot climb down from the cockpit. Holding in the anger that put Monster in the light.

Yes, he's young and handsome, tall, broad shouldered and blond ... Janie might have liked this one, unlike Bert.

Monster had read his insecurities with unerring accuracy. How such an uneducated nothing did that, Danny couldn't guess.

The pilot grinned. 'G'day, mate, how's it hanging?'

Danny hated that saying—so crude—but made himself give the requisite answer. 'A bit to the left.'

The pilot laughed. 'What can I do you for?'

He doesn't mean he wants to do me, he put in before Monster could take offence. *It's just a saying, which you'd know if you weren't so busy being angry all the time. Get an education!*

You're educated enough for both of us, Monster answered, *and I don't see it's made you very happy. Or overly decisive,* he added, with meaning.

He got to the point before Monster could find a reason to attack. 'I'll pay you ten thousand dollars to fly me to wherever you took Dr Larkins the other week.'

The man tilted his head. 'I don't know any Dr Larkins. Sorry, mate, you'll have to ask someone else.'

'Pretty Koori woman, this tall, with—' He stopped before he said 'long, black hair' since he'd heard from the last trucker that Janie had cut and coloured her hair. He didn't mind, he understood they'd both need to hide when this was done.

The pilot's smile faded with the mention of 'Koori', and Danny knew he'd made a fatal error. Yes, the pilot was looking through the beard he'd dyed dark, the hair he'd dyed black and permed the other day. He must have heard about the manhunt on the radio. But there was no mention of Janie being Koori on the radio. Political correctness and all that.

Janie warned him against us, Monster said. Voice too close, he was coming out of the darkness.

Danny felt his hands start to shake. He had to establish control. Any weakness now, and Monster would take over. And he'd begun to suspect Monster didn't want him to find Janie at all. He didn't like women, just like Granddad.

Had Granddad somehow implanted Monster in his brain?

But as he watched, the pilot's hand left his pocket, and moved around his back. He was probably texting the police station only a few miles off.

Control the situation, now. He whipped out his pistol, pointing it at the pilot's heart. 'I think you do know her. I think you flew her somewhere,' he said quietly. 'Put that phone down. Now, please.' He straightened his elbows as he took full aim.

The pilot dropped the phone, his face a bit less pretty, white and twisted with fear, sweat trickling down it. He wanted to take a photo with his iPhone to show Janie he wasn't so good-looking as she'd thought, but he couldn't drop the pistol.

He heard the slight bleeping sound of the sent message.

'Get back in the cockpit, please,' he said, smiling. A real man laughed in the face of danger. Women liked real men, strong men who could control any situation. 'I have eight bullets in this. Any tricks and I'll shoot the tyres first, and have plenty left over to make . you die in slow agony.'

The pilot tripped over the stairs as he ran into the plane.

One step behind, Danny helped him up as he fell.

'Th–thank you,' the pilot stammered, hands shaking. Not good. He had to fly the plane.

'What's your name?' he asked in a friendly tone.

'T–Trevor,' the man whispered.

'I don't want to hurt you, Trevor.' He held in the desire to call him 'T–Trevor'. 'I won't kill you if you do as I say.'

It was true. He wouldn't. He could leave any dirty work he hated to Monster. And sadly, since he'd texted the cops—or someone—Trevor had made death inevitable. Why couldn't people just do the right thing?

He went on, voice gentle. 'Just take me to where you left Dr Larkins—that's all I ask. Oh, and no communication with the tower—none at all. That includes turning on the radio.'

When the pilot hesitated, he said, 'I don't want to shoot any-thing, Trevor. I'm a patient man—but I might get angry, and hit the wrong place.' He pointed to the radio switch. Waited.

Trevor flipped it off.

'Good,' he purred. Yes, he was in control. No need at all for Monster to step forward. 'Now where did you fly my friend?'

After a long moment, Trevor stuttered, 'Ch–Charleville.'

Oh, how good it felt. Things were as they should be now. He directed operations while lesser folk obeyed, and Monster kept quiet. Yes, it was a good day. 'Then take me to an airport an hour's drive from Charleville. East-southeast all the way, I believe. No more hesitating, or I might think you're waiting for the police to arrive, and I just might panic.'

Three minutes, and they were in the air. Just as they took off, he heard the faint wail of police sirens. Turning his head, he saw the all-terrain vehicle arriving, lights flashing.

'No turning any way but east-southeast,' he said gently to Trevor. 'Not if you want to live.'

The man's hair was plastered to his skull. Not so pretty now, a dun shade. His eyes were bugging from his head, and his lips sucked into a thin line.

Monster pulled out his iPhone and took a picture of T–Trevor to show Janie. Just in case.   ᴗ

CHAPTER
12

The dawn light sent searching fingertips through the eastern window, and Elly opened her eyes to a rose-gold world. A gentle awakening, unfurling like flower petals, filling her heart and spirit. Adam's heart beat beneath her hair. She'd never known this, the simple happiness of having someone holding her, someone who cared for her. Bliss so delicate, a yearning so ethereal she dared not name it, whispered inside her soul.

This is how much I love you, Janie …

A scar that went deeper than her skin. An innocent puppy and kitten dead, because of her, and now two men were dead.

The exquisite rapture shattered. Danny's closeness crawled beneath her skin. If he discovered her with Adam, he'd do much more than carve a possessive brand on Adam's skin.

A Jepson family picture sat in pride of place beside the bed; the only photo Adam had with his son. Sharon held Zack, Zoe sat on Adam's lap.

This is belonging. And you don't. You never will.

She slipped out of bed, dressed in silence and left the house, always the quiet shadow she'd become over the past two years. She vaulted the fence, bolted to a paddock, and crossed it in a strong, steady run—but she'd learned long ago she couldn't outrun her memories, or the terror that stalked her wherever she went.

In the middle of a paddock, she fell to her knees. *Oh, God, please keep Adam and Zoe safe!*

Then she got up and kept running.

★　★　★

When she returned half an hour later, a hoarse demand assailed her. 'Where the hell have you been?'

She blinked at a pale, blazing-eyed Adam, half-dressed and fully furious. 'Running.'

'Why didn't you take your phone or text me, let me know?'

'You were asleep. I thought I'd be back before you woke up. I never take my phone on a run.'

Terrified she was a target, even here, he dragged her into the house. 'You can't do that.'

'Don't tell me what to do.'

'Elly, you're being stalked by a lunatic, armed and bloody dangerous. He could kill you!'

'You think I don't know that? I've had his knife at my throat, and my *breast*. But I can't live my life in fear. He's taken everything else—I can't even do follow-up treatments at the places I visit. All I have left is my morning run—I won't let you take it from me!'

'I was worried sick he had you.' He held her up against his chest, holding her so tight she could feel the pounding of his heart. 'When I woke up and you weren't in the house—'

Wouldn't she have felt the same in his place? Tenderness flooded her now. 'I'm sorry,' she murmured against his shoulder. 'I should have texted you.'

'Damn straight. Don't scare me like that again, hear me?'

'I won't.' She smiled and moved away with slow deliberation, terrified he'd see how needy a simple hug made her. 'I'm fine,' she said, hearing the huskiness and hating it. 'But never being alone drives me crazy. I needed space to think.'

'So long as it wasn't thinking about leaving Macks Lake.' He spoke in a voice of fierce protectiveness that melted her resolutions like chocolate in summer heat. 'What's that?' He pointed at the bag she held.

Here it came, the fight. She spoke lightly. 'Restocks for my kit.'

'What was open at six am?' he asked.

'Dr Schumacher's house.' Hating what was to come, she made herself say it. 'I made arrangements to do a clinic run at Kutringal today. The pilot from the Aboriginal and Islander Medical Commission comes in at nine at the airstrip. Have my tyres been replaced yet?'

He stared at her in disbelief. 'You can't go to Kutringal, or any Aboriginal town in the region! By openly visiting a Koori community, even one a hundred and fifty kilometres away, you might as well call Spencer to tell him where you are!'

Her temper flared. 'These people need help. I'm going to Kutringal today, whether you like it or not.'

'And you'll visit the local hospital too, I suppose? Why not take an ad in the paper? *Koori doctor available to help anyone in need. Just don't call me Janie!*'

Teeth gritted, she repeated, 'I'm going to Kutringal. These people haven't seen a health professional except the fly-in nurse in almost a year.'

He frowned. 'Why hasn't Dr Schumacher been?'

'He has an unstable, painful arrhythmia that escalates when he's stressed, and flying scares him. He's only done it all these years because there was no one else.' She waited, but when he didn't answer, she looked at him, a quiet challenge in her eyes. 'Would you refuse to attend a murder scene if someone threatened you, Claudius?'

'Somehow I knew you'd turn it round to me.' He pulled a wry face. 'Yes, your car's ready. We'll take my car to get yours, then head to the airstrip.'

'We? Aren't you working today?'

'You are my work from now on.' His grin was crooked, rueful. 'So I will take care of you, whether you like it or not.'

Like it? She averted her face from the sight of him, fierce, protective, half-naked. Hating what he did to her, because the treasured emotions would soon become just another hurtful memory she couldn't outrun. 'Bodyguard duties in the police service? That's unusual, isn't it?'

'I'm off the case because of our past. I could just do other work, but because of the potential for danger to me as well, Sarge has put me on paid leave. I've been ordered to stay with you night and day. You're our only concrete link to Spencer. He's following your trail all right. Another body was found last night at the western edge of Pitjantjatjara lands. His throat was slashed. He's been ID'd by the owner of the roadhouse on the Gibson Desert Road. He gave a woman a ride in his truck from Mullalabuk to the highway near Mount Magnet.'

She felt the colour drain from her face. 'Peter?'

'Can you give us a surname?' He all but jumped on her for the information.

'Davidson,' she croaked. 'Peter died for giving me a lift?'

'Not exactly.' His voice was grim. 'The man bragged he got it on with you. He said you did it in the cab of his truck. He told anyone who'd listen, apparently.'

'Poor Peter liked to brag. He didn't have anything much else.' A tear trickled down her cheek. 'Killed for a harmless lie.'

He reached for her, but she broke away. 'I need a shower—and if you want to catch that flight with me, you'd better haul your daughter out of bed and into preschool.'

'We have to go to the station first, give evidence and our statements.' He gave her a penetrating look. 'I'll get your clothes.'

Another reminder of last night, and the danger she'd put him in. Her stomach tightened. 'I need a long skirt and covering top, and a hat. The heat could be a killer out there.'

He pulled on rubber gloves before he entered her room, back in cop mode again—the side that distanced him from her. She sighed, reaching for her waist to twist the curls no longer there. She refused to look at him as he emerged from her room with a skirt, a top and her underwear.

'I had you picked as more of a lace and satin girl.'

From man to cop, repressed Jepson to Sharon's widower to her Adam—did he even know which he was? From aching with loneliness to fierce sexual need in seconds, and then a love so pure it was a warm, sweet light in her darkened world.

If Danny sees what Adam does to me, he'll kill him.

She plucked her plain cotton underclothes from his hand, taking care not to touch him. 'The me you've seen the past few days, or the me you knew as a kid? I haven't changed much since then.'

'I'm not sure about that. You still surprise me every time.'

She closed the bathroom door in his face, and leaned against the tiled wall, shaking. The trucker was dead. Peter was dead. She had to keep her distance.

★ ★ ★

Two and a half hours later, she released a sigh as the small plane lifted off the bumpy red outback runway into the blazing sky. 'I love flying. It feels like nothing else exists.'

'The "nothing exists" being Spencer?'

Her mouth quirked. 'You know me.'

'Better than probably anyone else. You don't give much away.'

The hurt his remark invoked jolted through her. 'Then why am I going to Kutringal?'

'I didn't mean you're selfish.' His answer held a sense of care, of choosing each word before he spoke. It was a barrier that hadn't been between them as kids, and this time it wasn't because of Sharon. After they'd given their statements about the attack last night, Jonas had taken Adam aside, telling him something that had made the friend and cop mingle. 'You never stop giving, even to people you don't know. But you hide your heart. You don't let others know what you're thinking or feeling.'

She looked out the window, squinting at the bright morning sun in a glittering sky. 'I haven't met all that many people who are interested in what I think, or feel.'

His hand covered hers, lifting it inside his palm. 'Any time you want me, I'm here.'

When he spoke like that, she ached with the need to hold that light and warmth inside her—

But Danny's face, pleasant enough, almost handsome, with beautiful grey eyes made ugly by desperation, appeared in her mind, a wall between them. As did Sharon's beautiful, heartless face.

'Thank you, Claudius. I'll remember that.' She smiled and withdrew her hand.

Kutringal lay in the middle of nowhere on the western side of the Darling River. Dust and grit, red earth and straggling scrub, with a creek running through it that filled only after a dumping rain. One hundred and eighty-eight residents, mostly young families and the elderly. Most young, single people were long gone, to cities, or working on huge properties, or in prison.

As was the case with the other communities she'd visited, the welcome given to her was reserved. With the help of Adam and the pilot she set up a rough clinic, using a small tarpaulin stretched out on poles from the plane to give the illusion of privacy. For confidential matters she used the plane itself, keeping the windows and blinds closed, enduring its sauna-like atmosphere with the cheerful calm that soothed her patients' embarrassment at exposing their weaknesses and intimate problems to a young woman not yet thirty.

Warned by the Aboriginal and Islander Medical Commission about the conditions here, she'd brought an extended kit with immunisation shots, insulin and vitamins, her gynaecological kit, and all the eye, ear, nose and throat equipment and medications she could get from Dr Schumacher at short notice.

It took six hours to attend everyone in the community. The pilot, a trained paramedic, used syringes to wash eye infections with saline solutions, bandaged injuries and handed out pills. Adam, who had an updated first-aid certificate, sorted out the most urgent cases. After that he became her usher, showing the next patient in, providing glasses of water to the patients from the fifty-litre tank of bottled water they'd bought in town, fixing shelter for the patients with a spare tarpaulin cover when the arid heat threatened them with dehydration.

To her relief, most people here spoke English and Pidgin as well as their own language. She listened carefully, watching for cues on how to cause the least offence, picking up key terms in their language and using them to gain trust and respect.

'Four with hypoglycaemia,' she informed the pilot, after drawing up blood for further tests than the finger-prick kit allowed. 'Can you get the information leaflets on diabetes and the insulin kits? The local teacher or the fly-in nurse can explain the routine again, if they forget later. The boy with suspicious headaches probably just needs glasses, but we'll take him back to the hospital with us to get him checked out. There are general vitamin deficiencies. They've planted a new orchard over there, so ask them if they want the vegetable seedlings to add to it, and the Kakadu plum seedlings. The ground's fertile enough since the rain, and it's optimal time now, with more wet weather on its way.'

The pilot handed out the necessary information, insulin kits, vitamins and seedlings. Elly showed people how to self-inject vitamins and insulin, and handed out info on the relevant Aboriginal health organisation to contact for further help.

She accepted the elder's offer of a late lunch with a smile. She returned to pack up as the people moved to their homes—a mix of trailers, pre-fab houses and mia-mias, traditional wood and bark housing—to begin the meal. In deference to the visitors, it would be conducted outside, a community event.

Adam watched her clean up, an inscrutable look on his face. 'That was incredible.'

'As in incredibly boring and hot?' she teased, wiping the perspiration from her brow.

'No. Just incredible. You love this life, don't you?'

Her shrug was defensive, a cover for her shyness. 'I didn't become a doctor to get a flashy office in the city.'

'You could have, though.'

His observation, filled with admiration and belief, warmed her right through. 'This is what it's all about for me. Knowing I make a difference to the lives of people out here makes me feel complete in a way treating people with hundreds of other doctors in the vicinity to choose from never could.'

'If you'd gone into a specialist city practice you'd have a home, a steady income.' He added abruptly, 'You'd never have met Spencer.'

'I take the bad with the good. My heart, my spirit, is whole. It's enough.'

'More than enough,' he guessed, touching her face. 'You were born for this life. You make a difference. I understand now why you insisted on coming today.'

'Thank you.' She nestled her cheek against his hand for a moment, revelling in his pride in her. 'Like you were born to be a cop.'

'Maybe.' He turned aside to pack up the tarpaulins. She turned to the water dispenser, wishing she knew what was bothering him. For once, it didn't feel like it was connected to Sharon.

Lunch was a simple affair, meat buried on coals and slow baked, onion and hot damper with the wild honey called sugarbag, bush potatoes and cups of tea made from a campfire billy.

Adam wolfed down the potatoes, bread and honey, but hesitated over the meat. 'What's this?' he asked her after the first bite. 'Tastes like lamb, but—'

'Kangaroo,' she mumbled, eating her portion with relish.

He almost dropped the plate, his face showing his revulsion. 'I'm eating our national symbol and one of the world's most beautiful animals?'

She grinned, her mouth full, and didn't speak again until she'd swallowed. 'Yep. Hunted especially for our visit, I suspect.'

He recoiled. 'I can't eat this. It's indecent.'

A brow rose as her smile faded. 'Indecent?' she drawled. 'Always the Jepson. You don't object to the slaughter of six-week-old calves for veal, or buying a chicken that had three months of life crammed in a cage in unsanitary conditions, but a decently hunted adult kangaroo is a problem for you? Before you despise this offering—and it's quite an honour, since these people don't hunt very often—make sure your double standards aren't hanging out. Just because you buy meat packaged in a supermarket doesn't mean the animal lived or died well. At least this one had the life it was meant to live before it got to us.'

After a long moment, he lifted the meat to his mouth again. 'Tastes like lamb,' he repeated. 'It has a subtle flavour.'

She rewarded him with a glimmering smile. 'No fat or cholesterol, either.'

Grinning, mouth full again, he touched her cheek with his index finger. 'Thanks for putting up with me.'

Her heart softened with tenderness. The man had a gift of making her melt.

If I fall in love with you, it could kill us both.

With a brief sting of regret for the normal happiness she'd probably never know, she turned to the woman beside her, asking about her life.

After lunch the elder, Minyenbarra, came to them, thanking them in English for their time, for her care. Elly replied in a fumbling attempt at his language, making the thin old man smile and hold out his hand. She shook it in grave courtesy.

Seeing Adam hulking behind Elly, the elder's wife, Mirimi, asked in Pidgin, 'So is this your man?'

Without thinking, and withering with embarrassment, Elly turned to Adam. He moved to stand beside her and took her hand in his, almost aggressive in his protection.

Mirimi laughed. 'Does he know what he just did?'

Her head lowered, Elly shook her head. 'Please don't.'

'Look at me, girl,' Mirimi said quietly.

Compelled, Elly obeyed—and whatever the elder's wife saw there satisfied her.

'He made the statement.'

'Please don't,' she repeated, but the elder's wife said a few quick words to the group of women behind her, and they scattered to their homes.

When they returned, Minyenbarra touched their linked hands. He looked at her, and spoke in Pidgin. 'Don't play with this one. He cares—maybe too much. He's hurting.'

Her head drooped. 'It's not a game to me either, uncle.'

'We all know that. Wasn't sure you knew it, too.' He turned to Adam, his watery gaze both stern and questioning, and spoke in English. 'She's a good woman. Look after her.'

Looking lost, Adam nodded.

The women handed Elly a basket, two mats of dried and dyed grass, woven in circular fashion, and a traditional dot-painted digging stick. The men gave Adam a ceremonial spear, the spoon-shaped woomera needed to send the spear true to its target, a boomerang and a fishing net.

Struggling to hold in the tears, Elly received her gifts with quiet thanks.

Adam asked her for the local words of gratitude and spoke them.

The pilot, Mike, received his gifts last.

When Mike left to start the plane, Elly started packing her kit. From the corner of her eye she saw the elder approach Adam, speaking in a voice as gnarled as his fingers.

'She's a good woman,' she heard him say again. 'Alone too long, though. Needs more care than she'll show you. The strong ones do.'

She could barely keep the tears from her eyes. What was it—the people or this day, the anniversary of the day he'd met Sharon? He probably didn't even remember, but for her, this was a day of quiet mourning. The day she'd lost him.

Now, thanks to Jonas and the people of Kutringal, the day was reborn for her. But if Adam knew what they'd just done …

She watched Adam smile, obviously touched by the solemnity of the old man's simple words. 'That's why I'm here.'

'Don't let her down, boy, because she'll never let you down. She's that kind.'

'I know.' As she struggled against fresh tears, Adam lowered his head, much as she'd done. 'I swear to you I won't, sir.'

Minyenbarra put a hand on his shoulder and smiled. 'I believe you. Come and visit us next time she comes. You'll be welcome.'

Adam put his hand over the elder's, smiling, but Elly could almost feel the lump in his throat. The lack of a father's affection was something else they had in common. A workaholic lawyer, Stephen Jepson had never tolerated his wife, Susan, even hugging her sons in his presence. *Stop making sissies of them,* he'd say in his harsh way. *It's past time they became men.*

Funny how she'd forgotten that until now.

She got into the back of the plane with Scott, the boy with suspicious headaches, as well as his mother and one of the hypoglycaemic women. Adam had to sit in the front to balance the plane. The trip home consisted of treating her patients, talking to them in quiet mix of languages she knew he couldn't follow. She could see he was burning to ask what the little ceremony had been about, but she couldn't face it yet. The day had changed too much for her, turning established pain on its head, bringing unexpected gifts. Unlocking something she'd rather have kept inside her heart, unacknowledged.

★　★　★

Adam went home alone, taking their gifts with him. Elly had accompanied her patients to the small hospital in Macks Lake, remaining with them through the night. On evening shift, Simon took the station pager and offered to stay with her, to allow Adam to take Zoe home instead of arranging for a sitter. After the attacks at his own home, he couldn't risk his daughter to a teenager.

The house remained unmolested while Elly wasn't in it, but once Zoe was asleep, it felt cold and empty, as it had before Elly landed like a comet back into his world. Too tired to accept Rick's offer of watching the cricket over dinner, Adam found himself prowling the house, knowing he'd rather tackle the problems that came with the sunshine of her laughing, giving presence in his life than endure another day alone.

Simon dropped her home at six-thirty the next morning. She came in the door holding an envelope. Her eyes had heavy shadows beneath them, but her smile was cheerful. 'Sorry I'm late. I delivered a baby while I was there, a man came in with a broken leg from a motorbike accident on his farm, and a child with a spiked temp came in about three. It's been a hectic night.'

And you've put a spotlight on yourself for Danny Spencer to see. But the words were as hurtful as they were useless; she couldn't be anything but what she was, and though he needed her to be safe, he didn't want to change a single thing about her.

'How are the others we took in?'

'Scott's fine. We're sending him to Dubbo base hospital for a CT scan this afternoon, but Dr Schumacher agrees that he probably needs strong glasses. They'll be on their way back to Kutringal by tomorrow. The fly-in nurse will go with them.'

'What about the diabetic woman?'

'She's unstable at present, but that's to be expected. Once we have her on a diet and insulin plan, she should stabilise.' She held out the envelope with a grin. 'I found this under the door. Got a dark rendezvous on for tonight, Claudius?'

He grinned as he sniffed the envelope. 'No perfume, my imaginative Elly-May.' He opened it and, as he read, his brow twitched.

Watch out for Janie Larkins. She's lying about her name, and she's not as good as she acts. She got off on grog one day and killed a patient.

'What the hell—' He held out the note to her. 'Who knows your real name here?'

She took the note. He watched her face as she read it. She was a good actress; her face gave nothing away. 'Oops. Looks like my dark secret's caught up with me,' she said with a light laugh, returning the note to his hand. 'You're the D, Claudius. You'd better investigate, see if I need that cell you threatened me with.'

His frown deepened. 'If someone else knows who you are, we'd better find them before Spencer does.'

She grinned. 'Unnecessary, my worrisome Claudius. They gave *you* the note, not the media. We're still safe, for today at least.'

She knew who'd written the note, he'd stake his life on it, but she didn't want to talk. If he helped her to relax, though … 'Then how about that picnic? It's a perfect day.'

Her tired face lit. 'Sounds just what I need. A long drive in my red baby, and a lazy picnic with you and Zoe.'

He hesitated. 'It's Friday. If you want peace, we can drop Zoe at preschool.'

Her eyes widened in indignation. 'Picnics, paddleboats and fun without Zoe? Never!'

His heart turned to mush. He forgot about interrogating her. He hadn't even realised the test he'd given her until she'd aced it. She'd kept her promise not to take a small, insecure child's daddy away. A promise most adults would dismiss without problem, she refused to break.

Because she'd been that child. Elly understood his daughter, as even he did not. Last night, Zoe had asked at least ten times when Annelly was coming home. 'I miss her,' she'd sighed. He'd had to restrain himself from saying, *So do I.*

She'd make a great mother.

Oh, hell. He wanted the whole package: dedicated doctor, reckless, stubborn, feisty woman. She accepted him—all of him—as no one ever had. With Elly, he never felt inadequate. No changes necessary. She even loved his daughter—the child of a woman who'd openly disliked her.

He wanted to make her laugh when she was suffering. Making the shadows in her eyes vanish was more important to him than having her in his bed. She was much more to him than the quiet woman or the Koori doctor everyone else saw. After a thirteen-year emptiness in his life, she was still the best friend he'd ever had. And he loved her. He didn't know if this love was what it should be, or if he could give her what she needed, but he did know he'd never tire of her in a lifetime. No amount of guilt would change that.

Despite the danger, more than his untamed streak had resurfaced. He was alive again. His wild child filled his heart to overflowing with simple joys he'd almost forgotten existed. She even made his desire for her a joyful thing … and her returned craving for him was pure magic. For the first time he wasn't merely a cop, or a Jepson, he was her best friend, just as he was hers—and she wanted him.

The shadows of emptiness were fading to white.

As if reading his mind, she looked him up and down, taking in the slim-fit jeans and simple dark green T-shirt. 'No wonder the bunny lady's got it bad for you, Claudius. You're a hot babe.'

The pounding beat of his heart filled his ears. 'Look who's talking.'

'You think so?' Looking surprised, she glanced at the marked and grubby cheesecloth skirt and white long-sleeved top she'd worn to Kutringal the day before. 'I wouldn't describe this outfit I have on now as anything approaching hot.'

'You'd make me hot if you wore a sack.'

'You're not alone.' With a tiny sound of distress she wrapped her arms around his neck, and brushed her mouth over his. 'Please, Adam. I've got to know, if only once.'

His final shreds of resistance falling in a screaming heap, he returned her caress, no more than a hesitation, so damn afraid of the rejection to follow. But she whimpered against his mouth, holding on to him as if she were falling down.

Aching to slam his mouth against hers with all the pent-up hunger in him since his first sight of her three days before, he was about to do just that, when he remembered her face as she showed him the scar Spencer had left on her; defiant, pain hidden, so sure of his rejection. And he remembered the violence she'd seen too much of in the past two years.

Another tender brushing of mouths. It physically hurt his whole body as he waited for her to take the lead, but it was—hell, 'beautiful' seemed such an overdone word for the glory of what they were together. Another soft whimper, and her fingers wound in his hair as she pulled him down. Begging or demanding—he didn't care. She wanted him, his Elly wanted him.

The second woman he'd kissed in thirteen years, and God knows, he had no confidence in his technique, but when he deepened the kiss at last her arms tightened around his neck and her mouth opened as if she were made for the purpose of kissing him. Her whimpers of desire filled his throat and touched his heart; her body moved against his in heady arousal. She slipped her hands under his shirt, curling her fingers in his chest hair, dragging her nails down his back, not so much drinking him in as gulping him down. When he pushed her against the wall, one of her legs hooked around his, dragging him as close to her as he could be without being inside her. And all the while their mouths were locked, tongues meshed in a kiss that was deep, scorching hot and animal wild. They were devouring each other, starving for more—

And he'd never been happier in his life. At thirty-three, at last he'd discovered real passion. So blinded for so long … if only he'd realised what had always been between him and Elly, right from the start. A meeting of minds, and glory of body, heart and spirit as true, right and perfect as the dishevelled red-ochre glory of the outback after a storm.

Childhood mates, best friends, confidantes—and, at last, lovers. Janie and Adam; Elly-May and Claudius. Her yearning was his. Her need was his. To hell with taboos. At least for now.

'Whoa,' she murmured when they finally parted, giving him a dazed and unsteady version of her brilliant smile. 'Now that's what I call a kiss, Jepson. If you'd done that to me years ago, you could have won every argument we had without saying a word.'

He grinned, the joy she always inspired in him filling his heart and gut. She'd never know what those words meant to him. He kissed her throat, and felt her tiny purr against his mouth. 'Elly, you're driving me insane,' he muttered, hand moving to her breast.

She arched into his hand. 'Oh, Adam, don't stop.'

The thrill of her mindless desire kickstarted a pounding beat of intense need. He took her hand from his back, kissing the soft flesh of her palm and inner wrist. 'Let's go.' He opened his bedroom door.

'Daddy!' Zoe's sing-song voice filled the air. 'I'm wakey!'

He groaned, burying his face against Elly's throat. She tried to pull away, but he restrained her. 'I'm here with Aunt Elly, Zoe,' he called, his voice hoarse.

Zoe skipped down the hall until she noticed them, and skidded to a halt. 'Why're you hugging Annelly?'

'Because I want to,' he replied without defence or apology, testing uncharted waters with his daughter. 'You want to hug her, too?'

Suspicion and jealousy filled Zoe's green eyes, along with haunting fear. It slugged him in the guts. Sharon had always looked like that when he brought up Elly's name. And for the first time, he wondered if it had been something deeper than simple prejudice.

'We're going on a picnic by the river to look for paddleboats today,' Elly said with a smile. 'Want to skip preschool and come with us?'

A grin spread over Zoe's features, and she ran into their arms. Adam swung her onto his hip, and she kissed Elly. 'You can hug Daddy if you want, Annelly, 'cause you're my friend.'

'Thank you, Zoe.' She blinked, hard and fast. 'I don't have a daddy, so your daddy hugs me if I need one.'

'I will too!' Zoe hugged her tighter, with another smacking kiss.

She took Zoe from him, holding her tight, covering her little face in kisses. 'You've made me all better.'

'Sometimes Aunt Elly needs lots of kisses, Zoe,' he said softly, his gaze lingering on Elly, loving the traces of the passion they'd shared still in her face. 'Can I do that, too?'

'You said I was your best girl, Daddy!'

The pain in her baby voice alerted him. Turning, he saw the tears puddled up in Zoe's sweet eyes.

'You said you don't wanna kiss no girls but me!'

'That's right, Zoe. I was so tired this morning, and a bit sad, and your daddy kissed me better—but if you don't like it, it won't happen again.' Elly's answer was all gentle acceptance for the child's feelings. In the long silence, she lifted her pinky. 'Remember, Zoe? I do,' she said. 'I love your daddy, but I love you too.'

Then Zoe lifted her pinky, and they renewed the pinky promise. In the gesture, Adam saw the farewell he couldn't stand. *I can't lose you again, Elly. Not now.*

'I—it's okay, Annelly—you don't have a d–daddy, so you can share mine if you want, 'cause you won't take him off m–me,' Zoe hiccuped.

'Never. He's your daddy forever.' With a final pump of their linked pinky fingers, she kissed Zoe's cheek, nose and hair. 'Thank you for sharing him, sweetie. You'll have him all to yourself again in a few days.'

The dark image of two dead bodies, dumped for carrion in the vast Australian desert, created a bleak aura between them. Ugly. Insuring the farewell, and he wanted to punch something, someone.

Elly stepped out of the group cuddle. 'I need a shower.'

He nodded. 'I'll pack the food, and get Zoe ready.'

She offered him a weak smile. 'I'll get a plastic cover for your stitches from my kit, so you can swim.'

Adam dressed Zoe, responding to her bright chatter on automatic pilot. He understood Elly's withdrawal only too well. Danny Spencer's ugly acts were as tangible a barrier between them as the memory of Sharon and Zack's deaths. She wouldn't allow herself any form of a normal life while that mad dog hunted her. She'd loaded those deaths onto her overburdened conscience. They were two of a kind, all right—because he could do nothing about clearing her of her burdens until he could find out how to work a similar miracle for himself.

Despite their recent passion, he felt the doubt in her ready withdrawal. She still couldn't trust him not to hurt her ... and given his track record, he couldn't trust himself.

But neither of them could afford to trust anyone else.

Grimly, he went to call Sarge about their trip, and to request one of the station's two satellite phones.

Charleville, Far Western Queensland

Serenity was such a wondrous feeling. Breathing it in, he took a minute to just enjoy the precious moments. One step closer to Janie.

I told you we'd feel better, Monster said. *He had to go.*

Danny looked at the body of the pilot, the handsome face twisted in terror, slack mouthed and stupid in death.

You wouldn't like him so much now, Janie, Monster commented.

No! No! She's going to be so upset with me! Funny how the scream was so loud it filled his entire body, but didn't make a sound. *Janie, Janie, I'm sorry. Please come and save me!*

I'll save you, Danny. I'm here. I'm always here.

No! Granddad put you inside me. You're a spy. You're here to keep Janie away from me!

I'm the only one who loves you, Danny.

Shut up! I'm not listening to you any more!

He'd already taken T–Trevor's car keys. He hopped out of the plane and took the Fiat out of the hangar—now this was a more appropriate ride for him than trucks—before he locked the hangar. The ride wouldn't last—someone in the tower or office would want to know why T–Trevor hadn't signed out after landing—but even an hour or two was precious. He'd have time to sell the car with the new ID Granddad said was waiting for him at Charleville post office, and buy a new car. A few more precious hours he had to waste, when he could be finding Janie.

Granddad knows, Monster said. *We need to make him tell us.*

He'd called Granddad on the plane. He said she'd headed south. Last known whereabouts in Broken Hill. *Sure, Granddad, I believe you. You know exactly where she is—and if you don't tell me soon, Monster's going to tell you something you really don't want to hear.*

I'm going to tell him anyway, Monster said. *Trying to control us this way!*

T–Trevor had sworn he hadn't hit on Janie, that she was just a ride—but who'd believe that? Married men had eyes, were as sleazy as any other when it came to pretty women—and by the end, T–Trevor would have said anything to stay alive.

The world was a cleaner place without men like that. Women were safer. Janie was safer.

South of here, Broken Hill was calling him. He felt it, her presence there. And from there—

Granddad knew.

Granddad would tell him soon. He just had to hold on, be obedient just a little longer.

CHAPTER
13

The hour-long drive south to the river bend was uneventful. Handing Adam the car keys, Elly pushed the passenger seat as far back as possible and slept through Zoe's excited chatter until he pulled up at the cool, grassy stretch beside the river, a popular spot for picnics and camping.

The mighty Murray was a sad sight compared to its heyday. Drought, damming, farmers' irrigation licences and industrialisation upriver had taken its toll. Yet it was still beautiful—a wide, fast-flowing slipstream of cool water shaded by eucalypts and willows, still deep enough after hard rain for the river's famous paddleboats. The scent of red earth, scrub and eucalyptus filled him with a sense of peace, as it had from the day he'd discovered this spot. Despite being born in Sydney, he'd be happy to spend his life in Macks Lake.

'We're due for more rain tonight or tomorrow, but we won't see any paddleboats today.'

'It's lovely, even without them,' Elly breathed, her eyes aglow. 'Can we swim?'

He pointed south. 'The river's too fast for Zoe, but there's a billabong down that way a bit, hiding in the ring of gums and willows.'

Without self-consciousness, she stripped off her white dress to reveal a modest yellow tankini. 'Last one in's a rotten egg!' After putting on Zoe's floaties and covering them both in sunscreen and zinc for their noses, she grabbed Zoe's hand and dashed off to the billabong at the river's edge.

An image flashed into his brain: two sated bodies, naked and sheened with sweat, eating a lazy picnic before reaching for each other again—

'Coming, Claudius?' The faint cry was sweet and mocking as a kookaburra's call. He was beginning to love that stupid nickname. He stripped off his shirt and bolted after them.

After an hour of playing piggy-in-the-middle and Marco Polo, and tossing Zoe between them, they left the green stillness of the pool and returned to the picnic basket.

A slight shadow slithered into oblivion behind the low branch of a tall eucalyptus tree before his trained peripheral vision could decipher it. It was probably a kookaburra or a koala, but a niggling sense of unease lingered. Since the attack on Elly's car, he'd begun looking for shapes in shadows, meaning in the slightest movement.

Australian law didn't allow cops to carry weapons outside shift, and he sure as hell wasn't going to register one at home with an impressionable four-year-old to bring up. Violence was part of his life at work, but never would be at home. But now he wished Sarge had offered a pistol, along with the satellite phone. Sure, the pranks so far didn't warrant armed protection, but the thought of this jerk terrifying Elly into leaving town—and then do what to her, when she was alone?—filled his soul with an overwhelming violence.

Elly looked so tired, so vulnerable. He didn't want to spoil the day for her. If she wanted to relax, he'd make certain she would.

After lunch, Zoe fell asleep under the shade of the tree he always came to, the mighty red rivergum stretching the biggest of its boughs over his fair-skinned daughter—but when the sun changed position he scooped Zoe and the blanket up in his arms, and carried her to another tree about twenty feet away that had the best shade when the sun turned, so she could sleep undisturbed. He put a sun umbrella up and over her for further protection. She sighed and flipped onto her tummy, cuddling her favourite stuffed toy, Kev the Koala, which she called Cammy.

'So what happened at Kutringal yesterday?' he asked Elly as he lay beside her on the blanket under the larger tree. 'What were the presents for?'

She twisted her head around, her lip caught between her teeth. 'They gave us all gifts. It was their way of thanking us for our care.'

'Elly.' He lifted a brow. 'What was the other thing? It felt— solemn, somehow.'

'Are you sure you want to know?'

He grinned to hide the sudden trepidation. 'Why do I get the feeling this is something that'll scare me?'

She didn't smile back. 'It might,' she conceded quietly, 'but I won't hold you to it.'

He frowned, intrigued now. 'What did Mirimi say?'

Her gaze fell. 'She—she asked if you were my man.'

'And?'

'You answered her question for me.' Her fingers were twisting around each other now. 'In our culture, if you're playing around, you do it in private. If you take a woman's hand before the whole clan, you've made a public statement.'

The connection hit him then. 'When he laid his hand over ours … Did Minyenbarra marry us, Elly?'

'Only in a spiritual way. It only becomes legal if we both acknowledge it, and send for the relevant papers. He's a registered celebrant.' Her worried gaze roamed his face. 'When Minyenbarra told you to take care of me—'

'My answer was like a vow.' He looked at her, frowning still. 'Why did you let him do it?'

Turning to look out over the water, she shrugged. 'It was a bit of fun, right?'

'No. So … we're married,' he murmured, trying to take in the shock.

'Like I said, it's not legal, and it doesn't ever have to be. Because we didn't give the obligatory thirty-three days' notice, the marriage was spiritual only. If we ask him to send in the papers to the relevant authorities, in thirty-three days, he'll send us papers to sign. He'll only send them in if we sign and return them to him. Then, according to Australian law, we'll be husband and wife.'

His gaze locked with hers. 'So I'm your husband, if you want me. Do you, Elly? Did you claim me as your husband?'

Her lower lip pulled into her mouth for a moment before she spoke. 'I won't ask Minyenbarra to send the papers, Adam. You've given me enough.'

She was stating a simple truth. But which truth did she believe— that this stalker would soon run her out of town, that Danny Spencer would kill her? Or that, like every other Jepson but Aunty Hat, he'd want to get rid of her as soon as he could without looking bad in the eyes of his community?

'Did you claim me, darlin'?' he asked again, trailing a finger down her cheek.

Her eyes closed. Something like a hiccup came from her throat. 'You know I did,' she whispered. 'Just this once.'

A haunting echo of her words this morning. He felt their farewell coming. Over before they'd begun.

'What if I claim you back? What if we make this real?'

She shivered, but didn't answer. They both knew she didn't have to. She still didn't believe, and he couldn't blame her.

So he took the conversation into less dangerous territory. 'Tell me about your life since we lost contact.'

'What's to say?'

'A lot, I think. If you trust me enough to tell me.' He didn't make it a question.

Lying beside him, he felt her tiny shrug. 'I went to Nana's a few weeks after your wedding. Being my weird self, I didn't fit in there, either, although I know they love me. My second or third cousin—I can never work it out, her grandfather's my nana's cousin—anyway, Kara and I are good friends. We were born two months apart, and she's a nurse, so we have a lot in common. But a few others in the family thought my uncertainty about our culture and a family I'd never known meant I was ashamed of my Koori heritage. I copped a few lectures on Koori pride.'

He watched the play of emotions across her face. Tiredness had opened her to him in a way he hadn't seen since she'd returned to his life. 'Aren't you? Proud, I mean?'

'I don't see the point. If my parents weren't who they were I wouldn't be alive. Why be proud, or ashamed, of what I had no hand in? Princess or pauper, Caucasian or Koori, I'm me.' She frowned. 'Mum never told me about her background. I've since found out she was a Stolen Child, taken from her family in Narrabri and put in a religious foster home for no good reason in the late sixties. She had fair skin like her dad's family, and the religious people thought she could pass for a white person. They might have meant well, but they never understood what it meant to be taken away from her family. Mum never got over it. See, Dad got to stay with his family—and then after having my brother and me, he left Mum, like she didn't matter. Looking back, I realise she was pretty bitter about that—and about his taking my brother. I went to Narrabri once, but there was none of Mum's family left in the area. I guess I'll never know why she hid my heritage from me.'

'It must have been hard for her, losing husband and son at once, if she was a foster kid,' he said quietly. 'Have you ever tried to look for your brother?'

She nodded, sighing. 'I don't want to talk about it.'

Guessing at what she'd been about to say, Adam changed the subject. 'Do you like the Indigenous part of you? I thought you'd feel stronger about it, considering the life you've chosen.'

'I do. I like being part of one of the longest continuing cultures on earth. I'm glad to see my people fighting to keep our heritage.'

'Is that why you joined the Aboriginal and Islander Medical Commission?'

'No. I joined for the confidentiality Uncle George—Kara's father—promised.' Her eyes turned sombre. 'I joined the Flying Doctors so I could treat anyone in need.'

'That sounds like the Elly-May I remember. You love helping out. You have to be needed.'

She relaxed, laughing. 'Two of a kind, Claudius.'

He grinned, acknowledging it. 'It surprised me when you told me you were a doctor. I always envisioned you becoming a vet. It was all you ever talked about when we were kids.'

She rolled over to pluck a stalk of wild grass, and tickled his face with it, like she had when they were kids. But this time its effect wasn't amused tolerance. He struggled to concentrate on her words.

'Living in the city changed me, seeing so many sick people instead of critters to tend. Nana talked me into medicine, and I'm glad she did. I signed on with the Flying Doctors, and found my passion. Treating my people, learning from them as I help, I'm discovering my heritage, my spirit. I love the bush, and bush people. I love the diversity of bush medicine, the innovative spirit of working here. I've delivered six babies on isolated farms. I've operated on an opal miner trapped down a broken mine shaft while I was suspended by ropes. I've answered calls to villages and towns, road accidents, even a train derailment. But it's just as well I didn't get into medicine for a Lamborghini, because I'll never earn enough.'

'Don't the Aboriginal and Islander Medical Commission pay well?'

'Most of that was with the Flying Doctors.' The smile faded. 'Uncle George—Kara's dad—sends me cash every month, in an envelope. I text him my latest address with a burner phone, and I only send to the burner I bought Uncle George. Danny found me last time through a banking transaction in Western Australia.'

'Computer tap, or a rat in the bank?'

'A well-paid rat is my guess. Danny carries a mountain of cash in his sack. I suppose he and Jeremiah change their burner phones weekly, like Uncle George and I do. Anyway, I withdrew everything I had from my account the day I left WA. I've been living off it ever since.' She turned onto her side. 'Tell me about your life.'

He made himself laugh, knowing her confidences were at an end for now, and it was her turn to probe. 'You know it all, Elly-May. It's all been pretty boring and predictable.'

'Even in the SRG?'

He looked at the ring of trees lining the river. 'Classified. I can tell you about policing in a general way, but the SRG's out of bounds. I thought you meant my family life.'

A long hesitation, and he knew that whatever she was about to say, he wouldn't like it.

'How did you really cope with the accident?'

His body turned tight and hard with the memory, but it was only fair—he'd probed her pain. 'Take old Abe's death, and multiply by about a hundred.' His heart pounded in a strange release he hadn't expected. He'd hidden this for so long. But Elly wasn't trying to fix his life for him, and somehow that made it easier. 'How could I cope with what I didn't know? The family was right. I shouldn't have kept Zoe. I wouldn't change my life, even for her. Policing was the only thing I was good at. If I'd stayed home with her, I'd have gone right over the edge.'

Gentle hands soothed his shoulders. 'Zoe's fine, Adam.'

'Not then she wasn't. She had two years of night terrors, and instead of being there for her, I made it worse by diving headfirst into all the riskiest cases. I don't know why—diversion, dulling the memories, or trying to kill myself—but Zoe deserved a lot better than she got. Being shot changed my life for the better—and hers.'

Her laugh broke into his black mood of self-recrimination. 'That sounds like my Claudius. Only a maniac like you could be grateful for taking a slug in the chest.'

He grinned at her, glad to leave his past behind. 'We're a pair of wild ones. Two of a kind.'

'I'm not grateful for my life-altering incident.' She rolled away and sat up, her face turned to the shining brown-green river. 'It's warping me, Adam. My life's consumed by where he is now, how he'll feel about what I do. How he'll react.'

'We'll get him, Elly.' He sat up.

A soft rustling came from high above and a light rain of ghost-gum leaves drifted around them. A phalanx of pink galahs flew out of the tree, bright against a blazing blue sky, their screeches fading. Lizards scattered from the base of the tree, bolting to the reedy ground near the river's edge. He smiled at her relaxed body, hand caressing the grass and weeds in absent absorption. She was in her milieu here, belonging to the natural world around her. How had she coped, living in Sydney all those years?

She shivered. 'Sometimes I think I'd give my life for one normal day. A day when I don't wonder if he'll find me. What he'll do to me.'

Feeling unsettled, but not understanding why, he wrapped his arms around her waist, pulling her back against him until she rested on his chest. 'You'll have it, I swear—more than just a day. I won't let him get to you. I won't let him hurt you again.'

She twisted around, gazing at him with fierce intensity. 'Even if you could promise that—and we both know you can't—I don't think I know how to be normal any more.'

Dear God, how that hurt. All the more so because he understood. 'You were never normal, Elly.' When she stiffened, he caressed her damp curls. 'Outstanding, amazing, incredible, yes—but never normal.' He cupped her face in a hand. 'You have an amazing power to give laughter, love and healing to animals or people. You've done that for me twice—and both times, in less than three days. That's your magic for me. You make me love life, open my eyes to its possibilities and its beauty. Don't underestimate it, or lose it. Your looks—and your job—are the least of your gifts.'

The pain in her eyes died. She smiled, luminous through the sheen of budding tears. 'Thank you, Claudius. You've always known how to make me believe in myself.'

'And you've always known how to make me laugh, and be happy in the moment,' he murmured. 'Until you came, I'd forgotten there was more to life than being a cop and bringing up Zoe. I'd almost forgotten I was a man.'

'If this morning was any indication, you're a man all right, in perfect working order.' She flashed him a sweet, mischievous smile, desire hidden in its depths, but she didn't move. She left her hands on his shoulders, giving him the choice.

Just this once, she'd said. She wouldn't ask again. The next move was his.

'I'm not sure,' he said, slow and mischievous. 'I might need some more practice. Just to be sure.' And moving closer still, he kissed her.

When her tongue explored the cavern of his mouth with tender aggression, he made a low, growling sound of pleasure. Her palms and fingers drank in the rough warmth of him from shoulder to thigh in a dragging touch of unashamed need.

'I've wanted to do that for so many years,' she sighed.

He pushed down the straps of her top, letting her breasts spill into his hands—but she made a tiny sound of distress, trying to cover herself.

'Elly, don't hide. The scar makes no difference to me, except for hating the pain you suffered. Your breasts are still beautiful. *You're* beautiful. You're my wife—mine. I claim you,' he whispered, acknowledging the words he'd wanted to say from the moment she'd told him about their 'wedding'. Feeling the kick at a subliminal level. *Don't forget me, Adam. Don't forget your promise.* But even Sharon's ghost had no hold over him when Elly was in his arms.

She gave a tiny gasp, and looked into his eyes with devastating honesty. 'Don't say that unless you mean it, Adam. Please don't. You—you've always meant more to me than anyone I've ever known.'

Past and present melded with her words, beauty and suffering, and he searched for the right words. 'You're in my veins, Elly. Don't you know that? You always have been. They couldn't get you out of here'—he touched his chest—'no matter what they said or did. Even when I'd have given anything to forget you, just to shut them up, just for peace, I couldn't not love you. You're the only person who ever knew me, all of me.' He looked into her eyes, her beautiful, disbelieving eyes, and then he knew what to say. Sharon's face came and went in his mind, in fading reproach. Nothing he did could hurt Sharon now—but his power to hurt Elly left him humbled. 'If you'll give me the number to call, I'll ask Minyenbarra to send in the papers.'

'Adam ...' Her eyes closed, and tears trickled into her hair.

'Don't cry, baby,' he whispered, kissing her cheek, her forehead.

She opened her eyes again, and his heart stuttered at the shimmering joy in them. 'Even when you were gone, when you were with her, no other man could ever touch me here.' She touched her chest too. 'I waited for you.'

Unbearable light filled places in his soul that had been dark for too long. She couldn't have told him her feelings more clearly with the time-honoured three words. Elly was his. Only his.

Now wasn't the time for passion, much as he ached for it. She needed to know he was hers, too—that he would wait for her, as long as it took. So he pushed her straps back up to cover her, kissing every inch of her skin with tender reverence. Even so, she writhed beneath him, crooning his name. His heart filled with joy: the exaltation of a man arousing his woman. He'd never known it could be like this. Never in his thirty-three years had a woman given him all of herself, no reservation, no hesitation or holding back.

When she tugged his shorts down, he came back to earth with a thud. 'We can't, Elle.' He kissed her once, twice, glancing at the other rug.

She gave a whimpering protest and locked her arms around his neck, tugging him down to her. 'I want to make love so much,' she whispered.

Above them, a bough of the massive eucalyptus creaked and swung in the gentle breeze. Slivers of bark fell to the ground, landing in her hair. It suited her, his lovely wild thing. With a smile, he brushed the tumbled chips out of the curls on her face, drinking in the sight of her rumpled, sexy confusion. 'So do I. You don't know how much. But Zoe might wake up.'

She bit her lip and took long, unsteady breaths. Her hands trailed down his arms, pulled him down to kiss his throat. 'Sorry. I forgot.'

He groaned and smiled at the same time.

Cockatoos and rosellas took squawking flight to the wide expanse around them. A pair of frill-necked lizards performed their strange two-legged run toward the river. It felt right being here with her. No wonder he'd loved coming here from the first. He'd been reliving his and Elly's childhood memories with Zoe, trying to make her less like Sharon, and more like Elly.

It was only then he realised the depth of all he'd done, and hadn't done. Forgetting Elly had been on the surface only: he'd spent all these years looking for echoes of her, while refusing to break his word to Sharon.

Or that's what he'd half-believed. The truth was deeper. Since Sharon's death, he'd been terrified to look Elly up in case she was married, in love, in a relationship—happy without him. That she was still his Elly—down to changing her name to the one he'd given her—showed him she'd never forgotten, never stopped loving him.

Thank God, oh thank God she came to me.

'Tonight,' he whispered.

To his surprise, Elly buried her face in the shoulder she'd pulled down.

He felt his heart jerk. 'You don't want to?' Damn it, he thought he'd scaled the barriers she'd put up against him. Or was it a case of history repeating itself?

'You know I do.' Her answer was muffled against his throat. 'When you touch me, all I can think of is how much I want to make love to you.'

'Is that bad?' he teased, feeling the thrill clear to his toes at her husky confession.

She looked up, and it wasn't the woman's eyes; it wasn't the woman's voice speaking. Echoes of his wild child rang inside his soul with every word she spoke. 'You left me. You were the only friend I had, the only person who I truly believed cared about me. But you didn't even say goodbye. Even at your wedding, you forgot to say goodbye to me.'

He closed his eyes, hating the pain that never lessened, never went away. How could he be angry with her for fearing he'd desert her, when he already had? How could he doubt her when every time she mentioned it, it showed him how much he meant to her? 'Elly, I was just a boy. We were playmates, soul mates even, but you were a little kid. I barely knew what you looked like. But I'm a man now. I couldn't forget you if I tried. I've never been the kind of man who plays around with women.'

'I know,' she said softly, still the hurting child.

'Then you know being with you now is a gigantic leap for me. I meant what I said when I offered to call Minyenbarra—but we have more than the two of us to consider. If you'll give me time, a month or two, I know Zoe will love to have you—'

A harsh crack sounded right above them. 'That was a gunshot!'

A queer, creaking groan came, just before another shot. Twigs and small branches cascaded around them—and Adam put the signs together with seconds to spare. Jumping to his feet, pulling Elly with him, he bolted for Zoe, shouting, '*Run!*'

Just as he snatched Zoe into his arms, the bough fell with a resounding crash. More debris showered father and daughter as he kept rolling them away, scratching arms, legs, faces until they were out of range. Zoe screamed, burying her face in Adam's neck. He caressed her hair with a shaking hand.

A whimper snapped his eyes open. Elly lay sprawled beneath the furthest of the branches spreading from the bough. Jagged scratches ran up her skin from thigh to shoulder, and across her face from her fast-swelling lip to her temple. Her head lay at an odd angle where a branch pushed it.

He jumped back to his feet. 'Elly!'

'Daddy,' Zoe sobbed, hanging onto his leg. 'Daddy, don't leave me!'

It was only then he realised he'd put Zoe down to go to Elly. Lifting Zoe back to his hip, he ran over. 'Elly. Elly!' She didn't move, and he held off, terrified he'd hurt her. His first-aid knowledge, always current, felt completely inadequate for the injuries she'd sustained.

The remnants of the crushed satellite phone lay in pieces under the fallen bough.

Her medical kit; she took it everywhere. She'd packed it in the car this morning. It was like an extension of her body.

Carrying Zoe, he ran to the car—but he could see the kit wasn't on the backseat. It wasn't in the trunk, or under the passenger seat. The kit was gone, the satellite phone dead, and his and Elly's phones were both out of range. He grabbed them just in case he found enough spotty reception somewhere here, and ran back to Elly, still prone beside the branch.

He put Zoe down beside him. 'Sweetheart, Aunt Elly's hurt,' he said over her repeated wails to pick her up. 'I have to make her better. Can you help me?'

Gulping down hiccups, Zoe glanced at Elly, and fear filled her eyes. She fell to her knees beside Elly. 'Annelly …?'

He cleared branches from Elly's inert body, fear chilling his heart. Tyres slashed, shot at, threatening phone calls—and now this. How would she be when she woke?

If she woke …

Stop it.

When he caught the maniac doing this, he'd squeeze the life out of him with his bare hands.

You're the one who put her in danger today. You've failed her, even as a cop. You ought to have known this would happen. They're still here, with a bloody gun, and you have nothing.

With careful fingers, he opened her eyes. She had slow-reacting pupils, but they weren't uneven, which meant possible concussion, but no brain damage. He pressed around her head—a big lump at the back told him why she had concussion. The bleeding was sluggish. With extreme caution he moved her, fingering her spine, feeling no undue swelling or cracks.

A moan rumbled through his questing hands as he sought to find anything else broken or bleeding. With exquisite tenderness, he caressed her tangled curls. 'Elly, don't give up now. Come on, darlin', please wake up!'

Calming down at last, Zoe saw what he was doing, and made a mewing sound of distress. 'Annelly, Annelly, wake up. Wake up! Look, here's your bag!' Before he could stop her, Zoe threw the medical kit on Elly. It must have been near him the whole time. How had his little girl noticed and he hadn't? 'Make her better, Daddy!'

Another moan of pain. Elly stirred, one hand feebly pushing the bag off her body.

Zoe opened it, scrabbling inside. 'Wake up, Annelly. Look, here's a Band-Aid!' After throwing a small shower of Band-Aids over them both, his little girl fell on Elly, wetting her face with tears. 'Don't go 'way like Mummy and Zacky. Wake *up! Wake up!'* She shook Elly hard. 'Wake up and tell me what hurts, Annelly! I'll put a Band-Aid on it!'

Adam watched Zoe tugging at Elly, too distressed to pull her off. He'd shown her pictures of Sharon and Zack, of course, and talked of how they hadn't wanted to go away—but he'd never dreamed she'd taken it so far inside herself. At four, his baby girl understood death too well—this had probably awakened her patchy memories of the accident—and she'd extended her fear of being left alone from him to Elly.

Which meant the thing he'd feared most had already occurred. Zoe was under Elly's spell; she'd fallen as fast and hard as he had all those years ago. Like father, like daughter—and the frenzy of worry in Zoe's eyes as she bent over Elly's form was more eloquent than her simple words. 'Annelly, oh, please wake up! Put Band-Aids on her, Daddy. Make her better! *Please!'*

Elly's eyes opened with the little girl's sobs. 'Mmm … Zoe?'

With a glad cry, Zoe fell on Elly's breast. 'Annelly, Annelly, you waked up! Good girl!' She kissed Elly's face with salt-wet lips. 'I got you some Band-Aids.'

'Thank you, sweetie.' Her voice was a cracked whisper. 'I'm sure they'll make me all better real soon.'

What the hell was he *doing*? Standing around watching a tender moment, when the maniac could shoot again at any time? He hauled his daughter up. 'Zoe, wait, sweetheart. She might have a sore back.'

Elly wriggled fingers and toes, moved her arms and legs, and gave him a slow, reassuring smile. 'All in one piece,' she reported in a stronger voice, reaching out to hug Zoe. 'No numbness or double vision, nothing broken. Just scratches, a fat lip and a fatter headache.

Stupid tree.' With a half-smile she held out an arm, the other still holding Zoe close. 'Want to come feel for yourself?'

'Zoe, let go of Aunt Elly, and run to the car.'

His voice came out harsher than he'd intended. When she obeyed, looking frightened, he hauled Elly up in his arms. 'We have to get out of here. Whoever did this might start again.'

The sweet teasing faded from her eyes. 'You mean this wasn't an accident?'

'You don't remember the shots?' he asked, with a flicked glance at Zoe, who hadn't gone far, and was watching them, wide eyed.

She frowned and carefully nodded. 'Right.' When she spoke again, her voice cracked and broke like the tree branch. 'I'm so sorry, Adam.'

He sat her in the passenger seat and saw Zoe safely into her car-seat before he answered with two soft, brief kisses. She winced.

'I hurt you. I'm sorry.' He traced the purpling swell on her lip with a gentle finger.

'I'm not.' She smiled crookedly, not using the bruised side. 'I have years of fantasies about you to catch up on.'

Even injured, she knew how to make him feel so damn glad he was a man.

'What's fantasties, Daddy?' An interested voice piped up from the backseat, a voice holding no resentment or underlying fear about the kiss she'd just witnessed. Whether that was a good or bad thing right now he didn't know.

'Oops,' Elly whispered.

He grinned. 'I'll leave that one to you, Annelly. Stay here. Bring the roof up, and shut the windows. I'll scout the area.' He started the keyless ignition.

She frowned. 'Where's the phone you brought?'

'Crushed,' he said tersely. 'Our phones are out of range.'

'How did they know we'd come here?'

That was the question he'd asked himself. 'I've come here dozens of times with Zoe.'

'But how could they possibly know which tree we'd sit under?'

'I always come to that tree. Zoe's fair, and it has the most shade. No other tree had branches as big as the one that fell.'

As he'd expected, the light left her eyes. 'So ... you think this is about you this time?'

He nodded. At this moment he'd do anything to lighten her burden of terror and guilt. 'I'm sorry, Elle. I need to think about being less predictable now, obviously.'

Her face only grew darker. 'Nothing happened to you here until I came.' She turned to bring Zoe to the front of the car, as she brought up the roof. 'Let's put Band-Aids on each other, while Daddy does his policeman thing,' she said to the little girl.

'I'll bring your kit back.' He ran back to the picnic site. When he returned to the car, he opened the kit, grabbed tweezers and a scalpel, and a few specimen jars and plastic bags. He glanced at Elly, and saw the too-calm knowledge in her eyes. 'I need the passcode for your phone.'

She frowned at him. He mimed clicking with a camera, and she told him, even more calm than she'd been seconds ago. The quiet screamed her intention. She was going to run for his sake and Zoe's, and he didn't know how he could stop her.

'Back soon,' he said, because there was nothing else to say. Stupid, inadequate. How did he make her want to stay?

Putting the rest of the medical equipment on the driver's seat, she pulled Zoe onto her lap. 'Look at this, Zoe! Loads of Elsa and Anna Band-Aids right here, and a special cream that'll make you all better.'

'I'll put the cream on you, too,' Zoe said solemnly, and as he returned to the glade, Adam heard his daughter give Elly a big, smacking kiss. It unlocked something in his brain he couldn't take the time to identify now.

Once I make Elly safe, then I'll work on making her want to stay. In Macks Lake. With me.

Closer to the tree, he unlocked both phones and turned on the cameras. He took hundreds of shots of the entire scene. Ten feet long, two feet thick and rotten more than halfway through, the bough would have fallen sooner or later, but two bullets had made it fall earlier.

Looking up, he turned hot, then cold. There was a rope hanging from above the broken-off branch. The shots had come from directly above the branch—which meant the shooter didn't have to be a good shot, only a good climber.

This case only became more and more insane.

Though he'd known it since he heard the gunshots, he saw the truth with new eyes. Someone who'd known his favourite haunt had prepared for this attack in advance. All they'd have to do today was follow them long enough to know where they were going, speed to get here ahead of them, climb the tree and wait. When he and Elly had laid out the picnic beneath his usual tree and gone to swim, whoever had attacked them had climbed up, waited for them to return, shot down the branch, and moved up to a higher branch well out of sight.

They were probably still up there now, laughing at him.

None of this made sense. Why go to all this trouble? Why not just shoot them all?

The slashed tyres. The drive-by with a BB gun. Painting Elly's window. The ridiculous letter. Now this. And though the attacks were escalating, and people had been injured, not one of the attacks had killed anyone. Even the madness of these attacks felt—purposeful. Like something rehearsed.

His instincts switched on and glowed. *It's something to do with Spencer. He's not here—that's been established.*

Was Jeremiah Spencer behind this? What had Elly said? *He'll do anything to keep Danny alive and free until he has a sane, legal heir for Gundawin.*

Has he paid people to attack us now, when his barristers can prove Danny was nowhere near Macks Lake? All of this does just enough damage to make Elly decide to leave Macks Lake, before Danny gets here. Then whoever he's sent here can take her quietly, without fuss, and present her to Danny.

He used the zoom feature on Elly's camera-phone to look up the tree, but there was no sign of anyone in the thick foliage—especially with the thick grey clouds rolling in from the south, turning the day dark before its time.

Whoever this was had to be someone who knew Adam well—or had come here with him before. Grimly, he accepted the few candidates, putting it together with the information leak at the station. Evidence would be hard to find if the perp was a cop, but Adam was an expert.

This couldn't have been Rick; his friend was the sanest guy he knew. But still …

He used the tweezers to pick up smaller pieces of the bough and the bullets with their casings, and dumped them in Elly's little ziplock bags. Almost no chance there'd be fingerprints on them, but DNA had been found in the weirdest of places before.

He hoped they'd find something incriminating. But even with Spencer's upgrade to murder, it would take weeks to get the results.

Before he left, he looked up at the tree one more time, almost hearing the mocking laughter. Their stalker had been with them again, and he'd ignored the signs because he'd been too focused on what he wanted from Elly. Exactly as Rick had told him he was. Dear God, he'd been so bloody selfish with Elly. Even now that her life was in danger, he'd forgotten protocol for a kiss.

Never again.

After searching the glade for signs of movement or how the stalker had arrived there, he returned to the car. He composed an email to Sarge and attached the pictures. But he still had no signal, and the email didn't send. Why hadn't he realised how vulnerable they'd be out here?

He was too damn accustomed to the conveniences as a city cop, and too unused to danger here in Macks Lake. *I won't make that mistake again.* First thing back in town, he'd buy a high-speed mobile Wi-Fi device to take wherever they went, a personal satellite phone, and a dozen burner phones if he had to.

'I've collected all the evidence I could find,' he told her. 'I got the bullets and casings. Shoe heels left gouge marks in the branch. I took photos. The size could be either an average male or a tall female. Looks like the whole area's been cleared of branches before we got here. I can't see any recent signs of another car. I'm guessing they got here by boat, but traces are impossible to find. As soon as we're back, I'll call Sarge. Simon and Baz can get whatever evidence they can to send to the nearest forensics lab.'

'How did they make it up a tree that size?' She cuddled Zoe on her lap.

'There aren't any low branches, no sign of a ladder in the vicinity, nothing but the rope. I'm guessing they climbed up.' Despite the solemn look on Zoe's face as she swiped half a tube of antiseptic cream over Elly's cheeks, mouth and nose like it was zinc cream, putting Elsa and Anna Band-Aids wherever she saw a scrape, any lingering urge to laugh at the comic decoration died when he saw the stricken look in Elly's eyes.

'I warned you.'

'It can't be him. He couldn't possibly have got to Macks Lake, found out about this place so fast, and set it up in time with absolutely no evidence left behind. We'd know he was here.'

Her face only hardened. 'We should go.'

'We'll get him, Elly.' Wishing his reassurance hadn't sounded like a broken record, he reached for her, but she shrank from his touch. He took Zoe from her instead.

As he strapped Zoe into her car seat, he spoke in a gentle tone. 'Elly, I'm the detective. I'm telling you Spencer *couldn't* have got here in time, let alone found out about my favourite picnic area and the tree I always go do. He was in northern Pitjantjatjara lands only a few days ago, still asking about you. He doesn't know where you are yet. This has to be someone else. Something to do with me, or my past as a cop.'

'Yet nothing happened to you before I came. That's the truth,' she whispered, the shaking not just in her voice this time. 'You know Danny may not be working alone.'

So she'd made the connection to Jeremiah as well. 'I'm taking you to the hospital,' he said to distract her. When she would have refused, he added, 'I'd like Zoe checked out as well.'

As he'd expected, it stopped her argument. The fear in her eyes proved that the love between the two people he cared about most was already mutual.

Then Elly looked around at the picnic ground one final time, and gasped. 'Oh, no!' She ran from the car. 'Get a towel, or a blanket, quickly!'

He knew that tone too well, and it rocketed him back fifteen years in time. As he reached for the spare blanket, he smiled to reassure Zoe, who looked scared. 'It's okay, Zoe. Remember Aunt Elly told you we had play-names for each other?' Zoe nodded, eyes solemn. 'I named her Elly-May after a girl on TV, because she was always rescuing animals and bringing them home. I think she's found one for us to take home and look after.'

Zoe's eyes grew enormous with excitement. 'Can we, Daddy? Can we have a pet?'

With a pang, he realised that, in avoiding the more poignant of his childhood memories and honouring Sharon's beliefs about animals belonging outdoors, he had let Zoe miss out on one of life's greatest joys. 'If we can't keep this one, we'll get you one soon. Would you like a puppy, or a kitten?'

'*Claudius! I need you!*'

He undid the straps and swung Zoe back up on his hip. 'We can talk about it later.' And, blanket slung over his shoulder, he strode to where Elly was struggling to reassure an injured, panicking bird—a mallee fowl, he thought.

'Quickly, put the blanket over her head. She's hysterical—her nest was crushed with the branch fall. No eggs survived. The poor thing will grieve. Is there a local WIRES house, or a representative vet in town?'

He nodded. 'Lorne Wallace is the best.' He gently put the blanket over the bird's head, the way she'd taught him years ago.

Elly didn't even look at him, her attention on the bird. 'There's an empty box in the boot. She needs to be calm on the trip in, or she could die of shock. She won't be calm if someone's holding her.' She frowned at him. 'Why are you still here? Hurry, Claudius!'

Despite the lingering danger, he felt a little thrill as he ran back to the car. Catapulted to another time, another life, when he lived half the summer in the wild with her, in the northern part of Sutton Forest, always Elly's helper, never angry or embarrassed to be the little girl's gofer, and never happier than when, dirty and bedraggled, they brought the injured creatures to the farm to tend.

Despite the fear and the peril she'd brought with her, he was happier, more alive than he'd been in years. This couldn't be the end for them. He wouldn't let it be.

It took a while to get the terrified bird into the box, and calm the poor creature enough for it to rest. Elly sat in the back seat beside Zoe, holding the box.

He strapped Zoe, who was all wide-eyed interest and excitement, back into her seat.

Adam struggled to hide his thoughts as he started the car without a problem. Whoever had attacked them wanted them to get back in one piece. Whoever this nutcase was, they had one goal in mind: to make Elly leave town.

But this prank had gone too far. The fallen branch could have killed them both. Spencer wouldn't be happy with that—and neither would Sydney. The casings were definitely from a pistol this time.

He flicked a glance at Elly as he drove off. Zoe was firing soft questions at her about the bird's care, and she answered with unending patience. When his eyes met hers in the rear-vision mirror, she mouthed, *A future vet?* Even with the little joke, she looked so stressed, so tired—and so resolute. How long had it been since she'd had a day when she didn't look behind her, move on in the night, run for her life?

'We need to talk.'

She gave a swift glance to a wide-eyed Zoe. 'Not now.'

*   *   *

It was long past nightfall by the time they turned into their street. They'd all been checked out by the local doctor, and Lorne Wallace had taken in the wild bird. By the time he'd pulled into his driveway, Adam could almost see the bags packed in Elly's head.

But when they walked inside the front door, Zoe said, in a voice that shook, 'Annelly, can you sleep wif me tonight? I think I'm gonna have a bad dream.'

After a moment Elly answered, tender and loving. 'You know what, Zoe? I think I might have a bad dream, too. I'd love to sleep with you.'

Relief flooded him, even as Zoe's eyes grew wide. 'Do grown-ups have bad dreams?'

'I do, when I have a sore head.' Elly touched the back of her head. 'How about we try to put nice thoughts in our minds, so the bad dreams go away? I've got some special happy bathtime stories to tell.' At Zoe's eager assent, she led his daughter to the bathroom. 'A long, long time ago, before most people walked on the earth, in a time called the Dreaming ...'

During bath, dinner and bed, she told Zoe the happiest stories from the Dreamtime to distract her from the terror behind them. Was it also to remind him of the differences between them, as he'd done to her with his talk of Rick?

Glancing into the bedroom, he saw Zoe snuggled into Elly, listening to every word of yet another story, her eyes fixed on the warm, mysterious face with the uncomplicated adoration only a child can give—and sharp lumps filled his throat again. Elly's eyes were full of love as she gazed at Sharon's child. Such an easy image, seeing them as mother and daughter, and a house filled with dogs and cats and other damaged critters, laughter, singing, dancing and pea boats.

Then Elly's eyes met his, and the image, delicate as porcelain, shattered. The blossom of trust, always tenuous, had been annihilated with the crushed picnic basket. Their minds held the same question: What if that branch had fallen on Zoe?

If he'd lost his precious little girl—

What if I'd lost Elly?

His body turned hot and cold, imagining the world—his world—without Elly. A rush of sourness filled his throat. Not again. Never again. Not having her in his life at all was better than knowing he could only visit her grave. He had to know she was alive, somewhere—even if she was with another man. He couldn't contemplate the thought of no laughing, giving Elly-May in the world.

He heard Zoe's last words as she drifted into sleep: 'Annelly, can we make banana pancakes in the morning? The ones with smiley faces you promised me?'

The hesitation was telling before she answered, her eyes meeting Adam's. 'Of course, sweetie.' The look was a plea, asking him to take Zoe away after breakfast, leaving her free to run.

He shook his head. He wouldn't, *couldn't,* do it. He'd never leave her alone again—not ever, not if he could stop it. He'd take a bullet before leaving her to Spencer's questionable mercies.

But she closed her eyes, shutting him out.

Grimly, he called Sarge to tell him of the day's events, and the loss of the satellite phone. Sarge said he'd be around in half an hour.

While he waited, Adam secured the house. To save her from Spencer, or whoever this nutcase was, he had to remain one hundred per cent cop. No more touching her. No making love. Only God knew how he would manage it, but her life might depend on his skills as a detective—and on his keeping whatever shreds of objectivity he had left.

When he returned to the bedroom, Zoe was sound asleep. Elly's eyes were also closed, but her lashes fluttered too fast. It was a ploy to avoid the talk he'd threatened—he knew it just as he'd known it the first day. He murmured, 'Sarge is on his way.'

With a little sigh, she opened her eyes and climbed out of bed, obviously stiff and sore. 'I can't leave Zoe for long. I promised.'

'You need more painkillers, and a whole night's sleep,' he said quietly, touching the lump at the back of her head. 'You were unconscious for almost four minutes.'

'Ow. Back off, Claudius. Even bandaged, that hurts.' She managed a weak smile. 'You worry too much, my long-lost friend. You forget—I'd barely slept all night. My body was just catching up on shut-eye.'

Yes, she was distancing him in a dozen subtle ways. Now wasn't the time to push her. She was staying until tomorrow. At this point, it was all he could expect.

Broken Hill, Far West New South Wales

'There's still no word as to the whereabouts of prison escapee Danny Spencer, who has allegedly killed three men and wounded four others on an outback rampage from the Gibson Desert to the Nullarbor Plain. Until now, the police have concentrated their efforts on Alice Springs and Kalgoorlie, where there have been scattered sightings of Spencer. Police Superintendent Graves reiterates that, should you see Spencer, do not approach him, but call the police hotline. He is to be considered armed and extremely dangerous.'

They gave a description of Danny, including his education.

So the cops had found T–trevor's body.

Thanks, Granddad, he thought, smiling. His current driver wouldn't connect him to any rampage, given his complete change of looks—including the re-breaking and setting of his nose, and the chemical peel he'd had done after Charleville, thanks to the deregistered surgeon Granddad had sent to him on an isolated property he'd bought outside of Cobar. The professional makeup job covered the bruising beautifully, now the swelling had gone down. And he'd been quiet the entire trip, allowing no erratic behaviour from Monster. He hadn't answered any of Monster's accusations or taunts. He was quite proud of himself.

'That guy sounds like a real worry,' his lift, Darren, said.

'I reckon,' Danny replied, in a broad outback accent. 'Nut-job should be in lockup.'

Why are you letting him talk about us like that? Why are you talking about us like that?

Shut up, you idiot, he answered. *Do you want us to be caught?*

So far Granddad was texting him with every move the cops made, and what Granddad didn't know he made sure all Australia could hear on the radio, thanks to the press releases he sent to the media. Wily old bastard would pull out all the stops to keep him safe—at least until he'd got Janie pregnant, and there was another heir to carry on the Spencer name.

He knew Granddad's plans for him afterward, too.

Granddad would free him from one place after another, until Janie gave Granddad a boy. No way was he telling the crazy old money-grubber, so proud of the bloody Spencer name, that his last and only heir had had a vasectomy last year—not until he had Janie, and was safe.

It ought to be fun torturing him for years with his only hope.

Yeah, he'd learned to play the game from the best. With half a dozen words, he'd destroy the crazy old bastard. As if he'd hand old Jeremiah another child for him to isolate and turn into a replica of himself.

At a roadhouse on the Silver City Highway outside Broken Hill, Danny thanked Darren for the lift and said he was heading southeast now. He hopped out of the car and, in the bathroom, pulled out his last change of clothing. He'd message Granddad via his third lawyer, the shady one, for more clothes, hair dye and contact lenses. Now he wore respectable jeans and a long-sleeved checked shirt. He had fair skin from the chemical peel, an almost straight nose, brown eyes behind thick glasses shaded by a battered Akubra, and red hair. He'd even dusted his whiskers with henna. No cop would give him more than a cursory glance now.

He'd find an internet café in town first thing. He never used the 4G on his burner phones. It was too easy to trace. Granddad's coded emails sent to an anonymous email address via another anonymous address would tell him what to do next to avoid capture. He'd be long gone before anyone could trace him. From the chat among truckers and farmers in the roadhouse for a drink, he learned about the roadblocks set up on every entry to Broken Hill, the outback town made famous by iron ore and silver mines.

I told you we had to keep this lift alive, he told Monster, with some smugness, struggling to remember the guy's name. *We're too close now to kill anyone.*

You don't think she's under police protection by now? You don't think she's running from us the way Alix did, and Michelle did before her?

Shut up! She's not like them!

Isn't she?

You sound just like him. Like Granddad!

Take that back!

I won't. You hate everyone, just like he does. You want to kill everyone!

That shut Monster up for a little while, long enough for him to hop on the back of a sheep transporter and ride the last mile into town hiding amid the sheep. He knew Janie had been here. He could feel even the ghost of her presence fill him with light and hope and love. She was smart enough to vanish without trace if she wanted to. That she left a trail for him to follow told him she loved him, even if she didn't know it yet. She was too smart to not know how to hide her traces, if she really wanted to be rid of him.

So innocent. How she needed him to protect her.

You think she's still innocent?

Shut up, you stupid idiot! You are *Granddad, trying to get us put in an asylum!*

Yeah, it worked again. He knew the way to shut Monster's stupid mouth now.

His plan hinged on the tradition of trust prevailing in country towns … and luck was with him again. Acting on the information he'd gleaned from the local paper, he headed for the Catholic church.

It was open, still and silent, dark but for a hundred lit candles representing the prayers of the faithful for their recently deceased priest. Nauseous, a little fearful of all this spiritual stuff, he rushed through to the presbytery. A quick twist with a piece of wire and he was inside. 'Goodbye Danny Spencer, refugee from the law.' He chuckled as he slipped into the late Father McGillicuddy's spare robes. 'G'day Father O'Dowd, who's come early from Armidale to take confession from the faithful in the area, including the Aboriginal towns and settlements.'

So, back to the same question: north or south? Which way did Janie go?

Skirting the town on a tourist minibus, he noticed the road-blocks were heavier on the road south. Excellent. He hopped off the bus at the next stop, and headed south. The cops that hailed him to chat accepted easily that he was doing a little tour before conducting the service for Father McGillicuddy.

Peter, a garrulous Catholic, stopped to pick up Father O'Dowd from the side of the road heading south. He didn't even question why the good father had no car, but Danny was soon half-crazy trying to answer questions about confession, Mass and Catholic funeral arrangements.

Ten minutes later, after stopping on the pretence of needing a toilet break, Peter was knocked out, tied, gagged and in the trunk.

Two minutes. That's all we need, Monster whispered. *You know you want to.*

Danny sighed in regret. The twitch—Monster's lust to kill—was a heartbeat beginning to pulse inside him, too. Janie would like Peter. But Janie wasn't here, and her tenderness couldn't hold him back, not with Monster creeping closer all the time, growing bigger—

We can't kill him with so many cops around. They'll know it's us.

That held Monster back, but for how long, he didn't know.

Given no choice but to hurry, he took the massive risk of using the net on his phone to look up Catholic confessions, and the rituals expected by the flock. All the way to the next town, he practised the words. Somehow that soothed Monster, too. He even began chanting with him, harmony to his symphony. It felt good, like he wasn't alone.

So why do we need Janie? Remind me, Monster whispered.

He drove on with dogged determination, but he was beginning to wonder himself.

All the Aboriginal towns on the southern road had cops at their entry and were closed to everyone, even ministers of religion. And beneath his smiling acceptance of the necessary precautions, his blood grew hot and thick, his mind pounding. So Janie had been and gone— again. She had to be with cops somewhere—some bigger town—for these cops to be so bloody-minded about letting even priests in.

He drove off sedately enough, but Monster was a slow scream in his head.

Faithless harlot … she did this to us.

He was coming closer and closer, bigger and stronger, chaining them together, in their mind. When was the last time he'd disagreed with Monster, really, not just yelling to shut him up?

Janie! I need you!

'Where would she go on this godforsaken road?' He pulled out a road map, scanning the names of towns in the local area, which, here, was a thousand-kilometre radius. 'Griffith. Mildura. Hay. Moama. Macks Lake—'

Hold on, Danny. Where have we heard that name?

He crashed his head against the wheel, but no answer came.

So he called Granddad. 'What's in Macks Lake? What have I forgotten?'

A slow, almost purring sound of approval. 'Good lad, Daniel. I knew you'd work it out, given time. Dr Larkins' foster cousin moved there, a widower with a child. He was with the federal police, but is now in the regulars. A Detective Sergeant Adam Jepson with the Macks Lake police service. She's staying with him—in a separate room, of course.'

That was it! Of course! 'Thanks, Granddad. I'm grateful for your faith,' he said humbly.

'Everything is already in place for you, Daniel. I'll text you the numbers of the people I have placed in town. They're waiting for your call. Write them down—'

'And destroy the phone, yes, I know, thank you Granddad,' he said, returning to the meek tone Granddad liked from everyone. Any hint of attitude and Granddad would turn off the tap of money and information.

'Just marry the girl, and get her pregnant,' Granddad snapped.

'Of course, sir.' Danny thanked him again, played the good, subservient grandson, grateful for the opportunity to be clever, instead of having everything handed to him. Then his face broke into a disbelieving grin. He'd found Janie at last.

About time, Monster grumbled. *Now let's go to Macks Lake, and we'll see who's right, and who's a slut.*

CHAPTER
14

Adam jerked awake with the first soft tap at his window. He padded over and pulled the curtain back a crack. The face he saw in the muted hues of sunrise didn't surprise him. With a nod toward the kitchen door, he exchanged pyjamas for shorts and a T-shirt. Strange how he'd missed Elly's presence in his bed, though she'd only slept with him once.

On his way to the kitchen, he peeked into Zoe's room.

Having been given strong painkillers last night, she was out for the count, her body curled in a ball, holding Zoe in the cradle of her arms. His daughter's head lay on her breast. Feeling all the force of what might have been—what ought to have been, had he not married Sharon—he gently closed the door again. No anchor, no chains pulling him under, and he thanked God once more that Elly had returned to his life.

He let Rick in the back door, and turned on the coffee machine while Rick closed the door to the dining area and hall. He didn't need to ask to what he owed the honour of the early visit.

Rick turned to him, speaking in a low voice. 'How is she? Is Zoe okay?'

The second question softened him. Rick's fierceness was an imperfect cover for his deep loyalty to those he cared about—and he wondered whether they'd remained unmolested last night because Rick had watched the house. He refused to think of the other option. 'You're still engaged—but I'm sure she'll expect a dozen kisses better, Prince Eric.' They chuckled, dispelling the tension sure to return with his next words. To put it off, he made two coffees, and handed one to the friend he wanted like hell to trust.

'Elly has concussion, and—'

Rick frowned, his eyes hard. 'You can't let her leave. She'd be a sitting duck out there.'

'I know,' he snapped. 'I've been thinking about it half the night. She only stayed this long because Zoe asked her to sleep in her bed, and she promised to make her pancakes.'

'Thank God for Zoe.' Rick sipped his coffee, but his frown grew deeper. 'Look through her luggage while she's cooking. Take the one thing she couldn't bear to leave behind.'

The insight took him aback. He swallowed a swig of his coffee to give himself a minute to think about it—about why it disturbed him that Rick, a born detective, would think about that, and he hadn't. 'Such as?'

The suspicion he couldn't quite dispel must have been in his tone, for Rick stiffened. 'You know her better than I do, of course. It's just a suggestion.' The words were calm enough, but some defensiveness simmered beneath. 'It's obvious she came here because of her memories of you. If she's sentimental enough to seek out her childhood friend, she's sentimental enough to have hung on to an item, a picture of her mother, or one of you. Or maybe she has a toy from her childhood?'

Damn clever. 'That would be just like Elly.' Yeah, she was bound to have something precious in her suitcase, or more likely some photos stuffed in the zipped pocket of her medical kit. She was certainly attached at the hip to the thing. Searching her bags might not be a kosher thing to do, but it would keep her safe—and that was all he could afford to care about right now. 'I'll do it.'

A sound came from down the hall. Rick drained his coffee at a gulp. 'I'd better go.'

Adam shook his head, listening. 'By the sounds, it's Zoe. Elly had enough painkillers to sleep in until ten, at least. Stay for a bit, mate. I need to talk to you about what we're going to do about Zoe.' His eyes twinkled. 'And I'm a coward. Zoe was pretty scared yesterday. She wouldn't forgive me if she found out you left without giving her those kisses to make her better.'

Rick laughed, his body relaxing. He turned as the door opened, and held out his arms with a smile as a delighted Zoe leaped at him.

★ ★ ★

'We've found another body.'

Jonas's words sent a lightning bolt of shock through Elly, adding to the pain in her head, which had barely lessened overnight. Adam had brought her to the station as soon as she woke, well after ten, and had ushered her straight into the senior sergeant's office.

Adam held her hand; his voice was grim. 'Where?'

'In a hangar in Charleville, Queensland. A Trevor Hammersmith. Apparently he flew you to Charleville just over two weeks ago, Elly. Is that right?'

She sagged in her chair, filled with despair and loathing. 'Yes, he did.'

'We think he flew Spencer there under duress. After he killed Hammersmith, Spencer somehow reached Broken Hill and slipped through the roadblocks.' Jonas spread a newspaper before them. 'We haven't yet caught Jeremiah Spencer contacting Danny, but with the availability of burner phones, and his unlimited funds to hire people to pass messages, it's all too easy. We know he must be keeping Spencer up to date on our operation.' His kind face was creased with concern. 'The deaths are escalating, and every killing increases Spencer's sense of infallibility and power. Unless he's killed anyone we've not yet found, his blood lust must be screaming by now. According to his former psychiatrist, the thrill of killing has probably become a sexual replacement for him. He thinks Spencer will be impotent until he's killed someone.'

Her voice shook, but she forced the words out. 'So he'll kill someone as soon as he gets here, before he sees me. He'll need to, to feel like a man.'

She felt the shudder rip through Adam, but neither man denied what she'd said.

'We have to be ready for him,' Jonas said.

'He'll go straight to the hospital,' she said, flat. 'He will have looked up the town by now, and he knows that's where I'll be. You need to transfer as many patients out of there as you can, and cancel outpatient treatment. Send them to a private clinic for now.'

'We don't have one here,' Adam said quietly. 'This is a town of six thousand people, including the outlying areas. The hospital is all we have.'

'Then send as many as you can home, or get the ambulances and the RFDS to transport as many as possible to the Mildura Base Hospital, or Goulburn Valley Health Hospital, Shepparton, or even Adelaide or Melbourne.' She sighed. 'I'll talk to Dr Schumacher about setting up a home clinic—it will only be for the next few days.' She shot Adam a defiant look, but he only smiled.

When she'd woken, she'd gone to her kit, and found two things missing: her mother's picture, the only one she had, and a photo of her with Adam. She'd been thirteen and he, almost eighteen. They'd caught three big trout, and come home so covered in muck that Aunt Irene had insisted on their having an outdoor shower before coming into the house. Adam had negotiated with his grandmother: photos for showers. They'd been so damn proud of their catch. Fish and chips for everyone that night. It was one of her best memories of Adam's grandparents.

Damn him, he knew she wouldn't leave town until she had the pictures back.

The twin emotions of fury and a small, sneaking gladness roiling in her stomach, she pulled her hand out of his. 'Have any outsiders been seen at the Indigenous communities nearby over the past few days?'

'Only a priest for confessional yesterday,' Jonas replied. 'He goes every month.'

'Whoever shot that branch down on us yesterday didn't want us dead.' Adam's words were hard. 'They left the car unmolested this time. They want Elly out of town—alone and isolated. I suspect it's Jeremiah Spencer's work, hiring people to run Elly out of town before Spencer junior gets here. Someone will be waiting for her car, and they'll take her.'

Jonas nodded. 'Well thought out, Jepson. We'll need a list of suspects, so we can check their financials.'

She shuddered, but kept quiet, glancing at Adam. He looked so grim and angry as he discussed the manhunt. *How does he do it? How can he switch off like that?* Just like at the picnic: one moment, he was the lover she'd always dreamed of, confirming their marriage; the next, he was prowling the area with her phone and medical equipment as if she didn't exist.

I do the same with my job, and my animals. Another way in which they were matched.

She started back to the present as she heard the senior sergeant say her name. 'Sorry?'

Jonas was looking at her, his gentle eyes determined. 'You're holding back on us, Elly. Rumours about your past, especially the story about you drinking and killing a patient, are flying around town. If you know who wrote the note, your loyalty is commendable, but it's very foolish to keep their secret if it's hampering our progress in the case.'

She fidgeted with the denim of her skirt, looking at it as if it held the secrets to life. But there was no choice now. 'There was a pilot at a big cattle station who drank on duty, and when he was flying an injured jackaroo to the Moongallee Creek Base, he was inebriated enough to endanger every life on that plane. I had to report it. He was dismissed, and his wife, a cook on the property, left with him. He lost his pilot's licence. They live in Macks Lake now, or somewhere nearby. I saw them my first day in town. I didn't think they saw me.'

Adam grimaced. 'They wouldn't have to, Elly. Once you took care of that boy and the others in the hospital, the grapevine would make sure the whole town knows who you are.'

Jonas tapped a pen on the desk. 'Their names?'

'Wirrah and Lani Miraki,' she mumbled. 'I don't know what she's doing now, but he's a stockman and ringer.'

Jonas's brows rose. 'From pilot to sheep shearer. He must be fairly upset.'

'They are upset. I heard them talking about it. But I can't believe they'd try to kill me.'

'Tribal loyalty is a romantic notion,' Jonas said dryly, 'but don't count on it to protect you, Elly. One thing I've discovered in my time out here is that Aboriginal people have much the same prejudices as anyone else, and hurt and kill each other with as much enthusiasm as any other people, with all the same excuses for their behaviour.'

'I wasn't speaking on any so-called "tribal" level, Jonas,' Elly said, flushing. 'I'm a doctor, trained to make assessments of others. The Mirakis resent my part in losing jobs that were quite prestigious and paid well. I'm sure they wrote the note. They might have made the threatening call to frighten me into leaving town, and set the rumours going, but the tree incident, the gunshot at the station, and the painted window at Adam's house just aren't like them.'

'Why?' Adam asked.

'Wirrah's brother, who worked with them on the property, is in prison. He got fifteen years under the "one punch" law, when he put another ringer in a coma. He's had a rough time, been hospitalised twice in the year he's been inside. Wirrah's terrified of ending up in prison. I just can't see him doing anything that would result in more than a caution.'

Adam nodded. 'That makes sense. I'll look into the Mirakis, check out their alibis.' After a moment, he added, 'Sarge, it seems too coincidental, their being here.'

'I was going to say the same,' Jonas agreed. 'We'll look into their financials, and that of their new boss.'

She had to say it. 'Jonas, Rick warned me about trusting whitefellas, even Adam. He—' She hesitated. Cop loyalties ran as deep as Indigenous ones.

The paternal pat on her hand startled her. 'I know, Elly. His interest in you is too obvious to miss.' He sighed. 'Has he tried to touch you, or instigate a relationship?'

'Both … I think.' When both men lifted their brows at her hesitant qualification, she fumbled to explain. 'He confuses me, really. He hasn't pushed the touching, but his obvious resentment that I'm close to Adam, and his possessiveness of a stranger makes me nervous around him, even though he seems to want to protect me.' She shuddered. 'He keeps pushing me to trust him, to let him in, but his intensity frightens me.'

Adam's hand gripped hers. She jerked away from him and paced the office, feeling trapped. What was it about her that created such fixation in men? 'I didn't encourage him,' she flung at Jonas, unsure if she wanted to convince him, or herself.

'I know, Elly,' he replied gently.

Adam watched her with worry in his eyes. 'He's spoken to me, as well. He basically said she needs a man who understands her. He said, friend or not, he'd do grievous bodily harm to me if I hurt her.'

When her eyes flashed, Jonas shrugged. 'Are you surprised, Elly? The level of feeling between you and Jepson is obvious. Mendham isn't the only one who dislikes the notion of you forming a relationship. Jen Collins was in the vicinity at the time of the gunshot and the tyre slashing.'

'So was Rick, and Elly found the painted message and fake blood within five minutes of his leaving my house the other night.' Adam rubbed his unshaven jaw in frustration. 'But it isn't like him, Sarge, you know that. This is totally out of character. He's one hundred per cent cop, and proud of his work as an Aboriginal liaison officer. He'd see such attacks as letting down his people—both cop and Aboriginal.'

'You're right, Jepson, but his pursuit of Elly is also out of character.' Jonas sighed. 'I don't want it to be him, either, but he must be taken into account. The BB shot and the picnic attack weren't pranks, though they've been made to look so.'

'Rick would cut off his arms before risking injury to his cowork-
ers, or letting down his people—and if he loves Elly, why would he
frighten her? He's not Spencer!'

Adam's passionate belief in his friend calmed Elly's fears, because
she knew *he* would cut off his arms before risking injury to her. So
she began to think with distance, and saw the truth.

Slowly, she said, 'Rick—his intensity reminds me of Danny,
yes—but it's not the same. I can't see him risking injury to Adam,
or to Zoe—he adores her. I don't think he'd hurt me.'

When Adam flashed her a grateful smile, she knew she'd done
the right thing. She might not yet believe in Rick, but Adam did,
and it was enough for her.

★ ★ ★

'It's obvious his feelings for you run deep—and that's out of character for him, to dive in so fast. You know that, Jepson.'

Adam watched his boss's frown deepen as he said, 'He's too smart
to believe Elly would like him more if he scared her, Sarge.'

'Yet still he's doing it,' Sarge said slowly. 'And he's been taking time off for headaches the past few days. That's also out of
character—and he's been to that picnic place with you.'

'Macks Lake is a small town. Everyone takes an interest in each
other. A thousand people could have found out where I go for picnics, just through someone passing us on the road.'

'True, but still ... you know how hard he takes things. Remember what he was like after Teri left town?'

Adam sighed, remembering the mess of grief he'd pulled Rick
out of after his beautiful, faithless girlfriend skipped town with his
electrical appliances and an itinerant shearer. 'Yeah, I do. But he
was on shift yesterday—'

'As you said yourself, Jepson, most of the attack was set in advance—and he went home before lunch with one of his headaches.'

Something in his chest jerked. 'No. I'm telling you, he wouldn't hurt Zoe, or Elly. I can't believe he'd hurt me, either.'

Sarge said nothing, and Adam felt his boss's unspoken doubt in an uncomfortable mirror of his own unwanted suspicion. 'He can climb like a cat,' he mumbled. 'He got Zoe's kite out of a gum tree that size a few weeks back, at the same picnic site. But I still can't— no, I *won't* believe he'd put Zoe at risk. I just can't. He loves her. He's family to us both.'

Sarge picked up the phone, punching numbers. 'The way we're handling this case isn't working. It's time to get full backup. It's best for Elly. We haven't been able to hide the fact that she's here. An Indigenous female doctor in the country's so rare, people will remember her and talk about her to anyone who asks.' Sarge spoke into the phone. 'Sir? It's Senior Sergeant Albright at Macks Lake. Re the Danny Spencer case, we need reinforcements now. We've had another attack on Dr Lavender, and her property. We suspect Jeremiah Spencer is paying our suspects to create diversions, and we have an officer who's behaving—well, erratically. Our Aboriginal liaison officer, Senior Constable Mendham. The situation's beyond us. Great. I heard … Does he? So do I, sir … I agree, I was about to put it to Dr Lavender. Thank you, sir.'

Sarge looked at Adam as he hung up the phone. 'Commander Albertson wants Elly to go into hiding today, before our reinforcements arrive.'

'I agree, Sarge,' he replied with relief so palpable it almost hurt.

Sarge nodded. 'Good. We'll hide Elly's car in my garage, and she can head to Alfie's shack out on the Murray tonight—'

'How does my going into hiding help anything now?' Elly asked, meekly enough, but Adam could feel the anger taking her over.

'Too many people already know I'm here. If Danny comes and I'm not here, he'll attack others to get me to come back.'

Sarge shook his head. 'Albertson believes that with enough reinforcements, we can take him in quietly, and I agree.'

'Well, I don't. I know him. You'll be risking innocent lives unnecessarily.'

'Why isn't your life innocent?' he asked quietly, and saw her blink. 'Why is your life worth less than anyone else's? Are you responsible for Spencer's mania? Did you ever encourage his violence?'

She rolled her eyes. 'Of course I'm not, and of course I didn't, but ...'

'But?' he asked, when she couldn't finish. 'Well?'

'Don't confuse the issue, Adam. I–I just *know* this is wrong. I have to be here when he arrives, or he'll hurt someone else, take someone hostage. You don't know ...'

'No, I guess I don't. I'm just a cop,' he said dryly, and saw her flush. 'I don't know much about hostage situations with unstable people. Cops don't deal with situations like this on a regular basis, and don't have protocols in place for possible hostage situations.'

She blushed still more, and bit her lip. 'You don't know Danny,' she said, too softly.

Sarge spoke. 'Elly, your presence will only escalate the situation. We've done this before. Your presence will make him hope he can get what he wants, and get away with it. Your being here will only make things worse.'

'Then talk to *me* about it before you tell me what to do. Don't take over my life as if I'm not here. Don't make plans for me without discussing it with me.' She leaned over the desk. 'I'm tired of running. I'm sick of asking "how high?" when Danny Spencer, a Jepson or anyone else tells me to jump. He doesn't own me, and neither do you.'

Adam stood up, taking hold of her arms. 'Elly—'

'And neither do you.' She shook him off. 'I'm not a victim, a target or a case to solve. Thanks to him I've lost my job, my home, my family and friends, even my *name*. I won't let you take my choices away from me, too.' Her eyes filled with unexpected tears, but she kept her chin high. 'I thought you would understand that.'

'You know I do. I don't want this, either. Do you think we'd push you into this if we had a choice?' He rubbed his jaw. 'But we're a country station with few resources and no allotted safe houses, and everyone knows each other's business. The city cops coming in don't know the area, or anything about Spencer apart from reports. If we do our best to ensure your safety, we're free to concentrate on the case without worrying you'll end up dead.' He rubbed his forehead. Then he looked at her. 'I thought you were starting to trust me.'

The blood drained from her face. She turned away, staring out the window through the blinds, as if longing to be out there. 'I want my photos back.'

'Of course.' He moved up behind her, but backed off when his words made her jump. 'I'm sorry, Elly. I should have known it was a mistake. Forgive me?'

She nodded. 'It's been a long time. Maybe we don't know each other that well anymore.'

'Don't say that. I was stupid, selfish. I wanted to stop you leaving me.'

Her answer felt like inevitability. 'I have to go, sooner or later.'

'Later,' he whispered. 'Much, much later, Elle. Please.' Even softer, he said, 'I talked to the family this morning while you were in the shower—both your family and mine—and talked them into disappearing for a bit.'

She whirled around to face him. 'No. No!'

He made his smile gentle, understanding. 'Not the way you think. Mum, Jared and I have bought sixteen cabins on a nine-day cruise to New Zealand, leaving tonight. Zoe will be in a cabin with Mum, and there's a kids' club on board. She's so excited to be going on a boat with Nanna and her cousins, she's not even thinking about being without me. She's booked on an early afternoon flight to Sydney with Rick.' When she looked up in alarm, he shook his head. 'Rick is the only man I'd trust with my daughter. He offered to take her, and see the family safely off before flying back tomorrow. He's the only one she'd go with besides me, and he knows I won't leave you. So he asked Zoe if he could take her. While I packed for her, he bought her a bluebird ring. She's wanted one for six months. She says it's their engagement ring.'

She stared at him, eyes lost, blank.

'Hey. I spent thousands to see our families safe, in a way that makes everyone happy. My four-year-old thinks she's engaged. So smile, woman.'

After a moment, she did. 'Yes. Um, that's funny. Thank you.'

'I'm sorry we can't go with them on the cruise,' he went on, 'but …'

'I wouldn't go anyway.' She wheeled away again. 'I'm sorry I ever came here.'

I'm not.

She turned her head, looking at him as though she'd heard his thought.

'I'm sorry if you don't like the plan, Elly,' Sarge broke in, 'but Jepson's right. We can't afford to divide resources to keep an eye on you and your families. This way they're safe, and you will be too.' He tried to smile, but it wavered. 'We have to put you where Spencer and his grandfather's paid people won't find you. This shack is the closest thing to a safe house we have. Only Jepson and I know of it. Alfie was my cousin. He left the shack to me.'

'All right. I'll do what you want.' But she sounded exhausted. Lost.

Adam gently pushed her back into the chair. Crouching before her, he took her face in his hands. 'Trust me, Elle. I'll make sure you get the life you want.' His thumbs caressed the lower lip she hadn't realised she was biting, pulling it out from her self-inflicted punishment. 'You're going to make that more sore. If I were sick, I'd let you treat me without argument. I'm the cop—let me take care of you, and our families, and take you where you'll be safe. I swear this nightmare will end. If I have to kill Spencer myself to set you free from him, I'll do it.'

Tears glistened on her lashes. 'All right.'

'Thank you.' He gathered her against him. 'Thank you for trusting me. I'll do everything I can to keep you free and safe.'

A hushed sound, choked and hurting. She nodded against his chest.

He lifted her chin, and kissed her cheek. 'I swear I won't let you down this time.'

'Sorry, Sarge.' Baz's head popped around the door. 'Forensics found no traces of the attack at the picnic area except the rope. It's good Adam got the evidence he did—someone destroyed the rest before we got there. They burned the branch. The storm cleared all other signs out.'

'Where was Mrs Collins?'

'She says she was at home with a migraine. She saw the doctor for it last night. Dr Schumacher confirmed that.' Baz hesitated. 'She has no form, Sarge. Anyway, how would a woman do the weirdo's trick with the tree?'

'As easily as a man, South,' Sarge replied dryly. 'We're not discounting anyone at this point. Check out a Lani and Wirrah Miraki.' He asked Elly to spell the names. 'Find out when they arrived in town, and if they have alibis for the times of all the attacks on Elly.'

'Right-o, Sarge.'

'Call Simon and Adele in. It's time you all knew what's going on.'

Baz flicked a glance at Elly, nodded, and disappeared.

Adam frowned, still holding her close. 'I'd hoped we'd keep this under wraps until the reinforcements come and Elly's out of here.'

'That's what will happen. You two will leave now. The only way into the shack is by a dirt track. Take the four-wheel drive and cross the river by boat. Herb left his aluminium dinghy tied up on the jetty. I saw it two weeks back. It looked pretty stout to me, if rather old. It's time to let everyone know the whole situation. They want to help you any way they can, and until the city reinforcements arrive, they're all we have. And if you go while I'm still talking to them, they can't know where you've gone to tell anyone—or follow you.'

Elly broke away from Adam's hold. 'I'll go, but I'm so tired of being alone—'

Sarge smiled at her. 'The super would nail my hide to the wall if I let you go to the bathroom alone right now. I think we could talk Jepson here into bodyguard duty. In fact, I don't think we could prise him away from you with a crowbar.'

'Damn straight.' Adam looked into her eyes. He'd lost the battle with his guilt. He was alive, and he couldn't keep living as though he were apologising for that. *Any woman but her* ... the trouble with his promise to Sharon was that he didn't want any other woman— and he'd begun to suspect Sharon had known that when she'd asked it of him. 'I'm coming with you, Elle, whether you want me or not.'

But Elly smiled, and it was like the sun coming out on a cold, dark day. 'Yes, Jonas,' she murmured. 'I'll go with Adam.'

Silver City Highway, near the Sturt Highway Turnoff, Far Southwest NSW

So radio silence had finally happened. The police had shut down the media.

They knew he was close, then.

They're too late, Monster murmured, and Danny felt the smile in his voice. *Granddad's done us proud this time.*

Danny smiled too. *Yes, he has.*

Four packages delivered to him by different truckers over the past two days, off the highway, two handovers happening during a locust storm so thick police would have had trouble seeing anyone on the main highway, let alone on the little forest road to the side. He had all he needed—all but one thing: a way in to Macks Lake. Police were manning every road in, and as he passed the river, he saw police boats stopping every watercraft, searching it.

The 4G reception tanked out here, so he called Granddad's new-est burner. 'I need a map of the Macks Lake region. I need a way in.'

'You'll have it in an hour. Just get the girl pregnant,' Granddad snapped, and hung up. Old codger was getting really antsy if he had to keep repeating himself.

Minutes later, a text came through with a detailed map of the region—and Danny smiled. *Here it is, Monster.*

Oh, yeah, Monster said, admiring the beauty of it, the simple solution. *We're in.*

CHAPTER
15

From the moment he'd landed in Sydney with Zoe, Rick had felt the presence of his watchers.

He'd met Adam's mother, brother and other sundry relatives, then seen Zoe safely into the collective Jepson bosom. When Zoe introduced him as her fiancé, he'd barely been able to keep in the laughter—but the Jepsons weren't as tight as he'd expected. They'd soon laughed, too, and were too busy asking after Adam to care about Rick's role in Zoe's life.

'You're his best friend, and Zoe loves you. Thank you for caring for my family,' Susan Jepson had said, and invited him to a family dinner before they boarded the ship.

After dinner, he'd met Elly's father's family. Through the network, he'd discovered Shirley Larkins' mother's family had moved from Narrabri to a remote community in far northwestern New South Wales, a place that demanded a permit to get in, but Elly didn't know about that yet.

That'll be a nice surprise for her, he thought. Something that would help them bond when he got back. He'd go with her to meet them.

Elly's Sydney relatives were so frantic to hear about her they didn't even ask who he was. Dot Larkins, Elly's grandmother, cried in his arms for a few seconds before pushing him off, frowning at him and swearing she never cried, like it was his fault. If she could see the future—when he brought Elly back to them—she'd cry, all right. For now, he enjoyed being brought into her family for a few hours.

One girl in particular—Elly's cousin and close friend, Kara—kept looking at him, head tilted, eyes filled with interest. Something about her made his heart beat faster. She asked him a few questions that were too close to the bone for his comfort. What did she know, or suspect?

Once he'd seen everyone off, and promised to be there for Zoe when she got back, he'd gone to the hotel he'd booked. Waking at 5am, he'd headed straight to Bankstown Airport, and caught the small police plane back to Macks Lake.

Yeah, he felt the presence there, too. His followers had reached home ahead of him.

He drove into a neat driveway about a kilometre from Adam's house—the shared driveway of a battleaxe block with two houses on it, one neater and well kept, the other with dead patches of grass and drooping flowers, dirt on the windowsills and spiderwebs on the verandah, and a general air of neglect. The house hadn't been used in a year, yet he felt the presence of watchers here, too—but they didn't know what he knew. They hadn't had the time to do their homework as thoroughly as he had.

He was ready for this. Time to put the plan into action, and damn the consequences.

He walked around to the back of the front house, calling, 'Hey, Jen, how's things?'

* * *

'Wow. Sarge wasn't exaggerating when he called this place rustic.' Mouth turned down, Adam surveyed their temporary home. 'The question is, will it stay up through the night?'

In the half-light filtered by a dense crop of old-growth eucalypts and mist from the nearby river, a shack barely stood on the loamy grounds, half-sagging on the trees behind it. Made of spotted gum logs, the wood's natural red had darkened with time and savage weather to dirt-encrusted auburn-black. The creamy white boles of the trees surrounding the house, with their peeling bark, gave rise to their nickname: ghost gums. In the dawn they looked downright scary. After the attack at the picnic site, the swaying branches, the scent of rotting wood and mould and the river's rushing was a threat in itself.

The whole place looked, sounded, even smelled of fear.

The door squeaked like a warning as it swung on rusted hinges. Filthy windows carried shadows in the dirt patterns. A crude fireplace filled one corner and housed a blackened pot hanging from a rusted hook. There was a half-collapsed bed covered only by a ragged blanket scattered with animal droppings in another corner. No tables or chairs, no floor but the dirt and a large fluffy rug that might once have been white, also covered in filth, animal droppings and dead insects. No running water, no bathroom facilities.

After a two-hour drive east to cross the Victorian border, an hour back west, sleeping the night in the car, and a forty-five-minute drive on a rutted road barely fit for mountain goats, Adam had already let her down. 'It feels like Tolkien's Old Forest, closing in on us,' he muttered, feeling ashamed and embarrassed to bring her here. 'I'm sorry, Elly. If we need to stay longer than a day or two, we can find better—'

'Some of the places I've stayed in the past year or so were on par with this.' She surveyed the shack with a little smile, wise and mysterious in the muted light of the cabin. 'It's lovely, in a rustic way. All it needs is a clean-up. It's right against the river, too. We'll have total peace, and somewhere to swim.'

'Thanks for trying to make the best of things, but this place is a mess. There's no heating, no light, no running water or bathroom facilities. It's unfit for a woman to live in.'

She picked up the rug and dragged it outside to beat the dirt out of it with an ancient broom she found in a corner. Between sneezes, she replied, 'Hey, cut it out, Claudius. We're lucky to have a river nearby for water and bathing, and for fish. When I was in the desert, I had to collect dew on leaves and in bark cups to drink.' She batted off his hands as he tried to take over the task, smiling even though her eyes were streaming from the dust. 'You forget, I'm an outback doctor. I'm used to heat and dust. I can cook on a fire, light a lantern, and use the bush for bathroom purposes. Don't worry about me. Go and set up the protective perimeter with all that equipment Jonas gave you while I clean up here.'

Although he'd known her since her wild, sleep-in-the-mud childhood, her cheerfulness left him in a state of wonder. He checked out their surroundings, imagining if it were his mother here, or his grandmother—or Sharon…

A sudden image flashed in his brain: Sharon, grey faced, with cracked, purple lips and dried blood in her golden hair, dying in agony. They both knew she wouldn't have been in the accident but for his negligence, yet she made no accusations, laid no blame. She'd even absolved him. She'd only asked two things of him. One was to bring up Zoe as she herself would have. *Love our baby, Adam. She'll need you, with her mummy gone.*

The other promise he refused to think about. He'd already lost the fight. He'd been forgetting his vow to Sharon from the moment Elly walked into the station.

No, it was more than that. Rebelling against the life he'd known wasn't right for him, but without Elly, he'd been a sleepwalker with a gun and badge. He'd done what he could, but it was never enough. With Elly, it was always enough. *He* was enough—and he didn't want to walk in the shadows of what others wanted for him anymore.

When he returned from securing the perimeter, the shack looked cleaner. The windows had been wiped enough to let light in, and to see out; the dirt floor looked packed down. Elly came around from the river, covered in dust—the colour of her tumbled curls muted and her denim shorts and singlet top turned a shade darker than her skin. She was barefoot, and humming to herself. The blanket was slung over her shoulder. After beating it with the same ancient broom, she hung it over a tree branch to air beside the rug. As he watched, she brought out the picnic basket and filled a pot with river water, poured liquid soap in, and began washing both rug and blanket. The wonder of her—he was fifteen again, and learning how he wanted to live from a scrawny ten-year-old up a tree. Learning about true belonging through her love and acceptance, and through her bedraggled critters. When he'd nicknamed her Elly-May Clampett, she'd retaliated with Claudius, and in doing so, they'd created a world of their own.

He'd been drowning ever since he'd left it, left her. Never again.

Noticing him watching her, she smiled. 'We can only use this water for cleaning. Don't wash your hands in it until we've boiled it, and only drink the bottled water. There've been bouts of blue-green algae in the region. We don't know what miraculous or misanthropic microbes this section of the river hoards. We don't want to start our romantic wilderness trek with a bout of gastroenteritis.' She chuckled. 'It's good we brought plenty of drinking water with us. But we can boil this if we decide to rig up the outdoor shower.'

Something inside him burned with pride. That was his Elly. She didn't complain though her life wasn't her own, had never been completely her own. She laughed in the face of the kind of adversity that would send most women into fits of tears or silent defeat. He knew from experience how many people ended up giving in to their stalker's demands—and wound up another statistic of violent abuse at the hands of a man (or woman) unable to handle real life with the object of their fantasy. He'd learned years ago that no human could ever live up to unbalanced dreams of perfect happiness.

Elly compromised, but never backed down. She'd fought Spencer, Rick, Sarge, even him. She'd taken them all on and remained undefeated.

Even this adventure didn't bow her. When they'd found Alfie's dinghy half-sunk just before sunrise that morning, she'd laughed and said, 'Well, it's better to know now, rather than when we're midstream with our food supply!' Sleeping in the front seat of the car, she assured him she'd slept in worse places: 'Remember the muddy creek bed at Uncle Adam's farm?' When he'd battled the rutted track to the cabin, she'd hung on and sung, 'We're on the road to nowhere!' When they had to hide the car, and carry or drag their supplies for the last few kilometres, returning twice for more, she'd hoisted them on her shoulders and gone ahead of him.

Stalked by a lunatic, her life torn apart by murder attempts, pranks and threats, sent into hiding with barely more than a change of underwear, she'd made a hovel livable and a shower from questionable river water—and she did it all with her head held high and an unconquered smile.

She was right about this place, too. He looked again, this time seeing bush and cabin in the shining glow of a summer morning, and her honey skin bathed in the dappled light filtering through the ring of ghost gums. This was Elly's natural element—and after so many years, it welcomed him home as if he'd never been away.

They drank tea from a thermos, sitting on the banks of the river, paddling their feet in the coolness of rushing waters. Sensing her need for space, he didn't touch her, didn't speak. She glanced at him, and smiled.

He cupped river water in his palms and splashed his face. *The bush equivalent of a cold shower*, he thought wryly, letting it splash over his shorts. It didn't work. He doubted immersing himself in the entire river would. Man, he felt like a virgin again: so fumblingly eager to touch her he couldn't think straight.

The sound of a boat's motor coming towards them made his cop's instinct kick him right up the backside. 'Elly, get back in the cabin,' he commanded in a whisper, pulling his gun from the picnic basket.

'No.'

He swung around to frown at her. 'Elly, how can I protect you if you won't—'

'Who'll protect you?' she muttered, eyes flashing. 'I'll hide in the shrub. Don't worry, none of this shrub is dangerous.' She disappeared into the bushes while he packed up the picnic basket, throwing it into the cabin before he moved behind a tree, gun in hand.

The motor cut as the boat rounded the bend in the river.

He glanced at her, hidden in the shrub. She was watching the river with intent eyes, a branch in her hand, ready to strike.

He turned back to the river, pride burning in his heart. She was beside him all the way. Never had there been a greater contrast between the two women in his life than at this moment. If he could have forced her to come here at all, Sharon would have relied on him, hiding in the cabin, too scared of the bush around her to use it for camouflage. Once, he'd thought being the protector of his woman would make him feel strong. But the deaths of Sharon and Zack had taught him the price of failure. All he felt in the face of Elly's determination to help him was arrogant gladness. He hadn't realised how long he'd carried his burdens alone.

The boat passed them, carrying only a couple of fishermen. Light-headed with relief, Adam shrank back so they wouldn't see him.

'Whew.' Elly laughed, emerging from the scrub. 'Just as well we didn't light a fire.'

He didn't yet have the heart to tell her they wouldn't be lighting a fire at all. 'We need to rig up a net with leaves and branches to hid our presence from passing boaties. We can tie it to a tree, and undo it when we want to swim.'

'Clever, Claudius. One would think you'd taken women into hiding in the bush twenty times before.'

'Who says I haven't?'

The sudden vulnerability in her eyes ended the joke. 'Don't say that. I couldn't stand it if you'd shared this with anyone but me. This is our life, Claudius, our world.'

Ah, hell. 'You know I haven't,' he said quietly. 'This is just you and me, us. I don't know of another woman who'd want to share this with me, or do anything but cry or demand I fix it up for their comfort.'

She frowned. 'I'm not them. I'm not her.'

He almost choked, admitting it. 'I know, and I'm glad of it. I don't want you to be anyone but yourself.'

She walked to him, wrapping her arms around his waist, breathing in the sweat and dirt on his skin. Kissing his sweaty shoulder, his dirt-dusted throat. 'I'm happy out here, because this is us. Out here, you're mine.'

The lump in his throat became the size of a football, cutting off his breath. He kissed her cheek, her jaw, his hands on her hips holding her without pressure. The rightness, the beauty—Janie and Adam; Elly-May and Claudius—a day to pretend they had all the time in the world.

He knew as well as she did that a day or two was probably all they'd have before Spencer got here—but the thought of this being it for them made him rebel. *No! It isn't fair.* The thought of a life-time with Elly was so right he couldn't question it. The vow he'd made Sharon was wrong, *wrong*. She was gone, and he was sick of living a half-life. The only time he'd ever truly felt alive was when he was with Elly. But how could he stop her from leaving him for good, once all this was finished?

'Let's get that net done,' she murmured, her voice husky, as if she'd heard his thoughts.

They moved silently as she found leaves and branches while he rigged the net and hooks.

'I'm hungry,' he said after they'd set up the net.

'We have cold food, but we have a few potatoes and some butter. We can catch fish and cook chips, just like when we were kids,' she suggested, with a glimmering smile.

With some sadness, he shook his head. 'The smoke would be seen for miles. People hereabouts know of Alfie's death.'

'So ends our camping fun.' She pouted. 'No warm showers. Not even coffee at breakfast.'

'There's a dozen iced coffees in the pack from Sarge's wife—the strong brand,' he said, wanting to make up for it somehow, 'and a half-dozen bottles of iced tea.' When she didn't answer, he said softly, 'We're here, Elle. Let's make the best of it.'

Her eyes softened and she smiled. 'I plan to.' A promise.

The satellite phone rang. With a quick smile of apology, he walked away to answer. 'Sarge? What's the latest?'

'You get there safely?'

'Yep. Elly cleaned the cabin while I secured the perimeter, including rigging a leaf net to cover us from the river. We almost had some visitors—only fishermen.'

'Good thinking.'

'What's the latest?'

'The Mirakis appear clean, but their alibis for the incidents are a bit shaky. Our visit scared any defiance out of them. If they did anything, they won't admit it, or do any more from now on, I think—but they only came here a month ago, having been recom-mended for their positions at Longa Station by Will Sanderson, their former employer at Griffin Station.'

'The one who sacked Miraki for drinking on the job?'

'Exactly. We're looking into it, checking Sanderson's bank accounts. I've got a feeling you were right. This has the hallmarks of Jeremiah Spencer. He'll stop at nothing to keep Danny safe, until he gets a sane heir.

'Both Jen Collins and Mendham are under surveillance by two of the best undercover teams in Sydney,' Sarge went on. 'Teams well known to you, I believe.'

'Hall and Brady, Levitz and Barlow?'

Sarge laughed. 'They're the ones. Levitz and Barlow picked up Mendham's trail at Circular Quay, and flew to Macks Lake ahead of him. When they saw Elly's photo, Hall and Brady said to tell you you're a lucky bastard. Brady said if you get bored, he'd swap duties with pleasure.'

'I'll bet he did,' he murmured, watching Elly beating the whitish rug again with the old broom, seeing dust and heaven knows what flying in every direction. 'Tell him when it snows in the Nullarbor, I'll think about a swap.'

'Jen Collins has gone quiet,' Sarge said. 'The Mirakis seem subdued for now; we can't trace them to the picnic-ground attack. Baz and Simon interviewed Mrs Collins' neighbors. They ID'd Mendham as having visited her more than once in the past few days.'

He shut his eyes. 'I'd have staked my life on it not being Rick. No—it can't be. I won't believe it. I trusted him with my daughter!'

'Zoe's safe, Jepson. Levitz and Barlow confirmed it.'

'I didn't mean it that way. Do you think I'd have left Zoe with him if I wasn't one hundred per cent convinced that he was with us?'

Sarge sighed. 'I know—but collusion between Mendham and Collins is a possibility we can't ignore. When I asked him about it, he laughed, and said they've begun dating. Said he'd keep her away from you permanently. We can't argue with that, and he knows it.'

'He's protecting Elly, Sarge—proving he cares for her. That I can easily believe. He's giving Elly a chance to see him as he is.'

'I believe that, too—as much as I believe Elly won't see it. She's that type of woman.'

'What type is that?' he snapped.

'Come on, Jepson,' Sarge snapped back, 'you know what I mean, you more than anyone. Elly's that rare creature who doesn't see any other man apart from the one she wants. Utterly faithful and devoted for life.' His boss let that sit for a moment before he went on. 'Congratulations, Jepson. You're a bloody lucky man.'

Feeling proud and glad and lousy all at once, he muttered, 'I know.'

'If I can give you one piece of advice?'

He sighed. 'I think I already know it, but go ahead.'

'Becoming intimate before the case is closed will put you both at risk.' Sarge spoke as if he had a frog in his throat—thick and awkward. Aussie men didn't talk about *emotional stuff*.

But there it was. He'd known it, didn't want to hear it, even now he had. But the words went round and round in his head, like those stupid dance lessons he'd had at school where he had to pick a girl to dance with. Round and round with an unwanted partner. He didn't answer.

When Sarge went on, it was with a wary note. 'You know what I'm saying. Your judgment's already clouded. Put what distance you can between you, for both your sakes. You're in too deep as it is.' A little pause. 'I know it's hard, Jepson, but it's for her safety as well as your own.'

Sarge was right, he'd lost his objectivity. To protect Elly, he had to find it again—and keep his hands off her. That was the first rule of a good cop.

But how the hell was he going to do it? If he made love to Elly, he put her in danger. If he held off, she'd misinterpret his restraint, believe he'd rejected her, and shield her heart so effectively she'd never let him—maybe not any man—near her again.

The damage he'd done to her never seemed to end.

'Right.' One word, but it jerked like a puppet pulled sideways. 'Thanks for that.'

His boss didn't apologise, or say goodbye, just quietly hung up.

The mists of the morning burned out by eleven, leaving the day cloudless and hot. The rains of the previous day and night might never have existed. Adam caught Elly's longing glances outside as they worked to make the cabin habitable, but she made no complaint until the food was away, the bed made, and everything as clean as it could be. Then she fell onto the picnic blanket with a luxurious sigh. 'I'm sweaty, gritty and aching in places I didn't know I had.'

He cocked his head toward the river. 'Want to wash all the grit away?'

Her face lit. 'Do we have anything to swim in?'

'The river. See it there?'

She pushed him, with a laugh. 'Clothes, Claudius. I forgot to pack my swimmers.'

He had, but with the recent conversation and its aftermath still doing the do-si-do in his head, he wasn't going to tell her, and break the mood.

'So, you wanna do it?' She looked into his eyes, an impish challenge. 'We've done it once before.'

Hold off for now. Don't touch Elly until the case is closed.

'We were seventeen and thirteen then.' The day he'd got his driver's licence, he'd driven straight down to his grandparents' farm. Straight to Elly, wanting to celebrate – and her dare had become one of his sweetest memories. He'd barely even looked at her; she'd been a little girl then. But now, everything had changed. The vision of slipping buck-naked into the river with her grabbed hold of him and wouldn't let go. 'Just a pair of kids,' he said, voice rough.

'Yes,' she said softly. 'We were. But wasn't it fun?'

Adam, please—any woman but her.

No, Sharon. I couldn't be what you wanted then, and I can't be now.

Yet the anchor was back, made heavier with Sarge's caution, weighing him down.

He fumbled to reply. 'You go in. I'd better, um, check in with Sarge, see what's doing.'

The light left her eyes. 'Don't worry. I'll rig up the outdoor shower instead. Have we got any facecloths? I hope there's not too many microbes in the water. I can't afford to get sick. So many people depend on my work, and—'

Ah, hell, she was retreating as he'd feared she would … and he couldn't stand it. No matter what he'd promised, he couldn't lie to her, or hurt her again. 'Elly, no.' He grabbed her as she passed him. 'I'm not rejecting you, darlin', I swear it.'

She wouldn't look up. 'It's all right,' she murmured, a catch in her voice. 'I understand. The case has to come first. Catching Danny's the top priority.'

Though everything she said was right and understanding, he felt her leaving him in her mind, and his panic grew. 'You're not a case, Elle, not to me.'

She shrugged. 'You're a cop. It's what you do; your entire life apart from Zoe. You're helping me, and I'm interfering with that. I'm sorry. I won't ask again.' Her hands pleated the edge of her shorts, dust falling all around her bare feet. 'If I could stop it, I would, but no matter how hard I try—and I've tried so hard through the years—the way I feel about you never changes.'

The job and the responsibility that had for too long been a burden crumbled, leaving him stripped bare. 'Ah, Elly, how can I be anything but a man when you talk to me like that?'

'You're doing better than me,' she murmured, standing stiff. Refusing to look up. 'I just keep making a fool of myself, throwing myself at you.'

'Elly, look at me.'

She shook her head. 'You need to give your report.'

'I lied,' he said. 'I was afraid. But I'm not now. Look at me, Elly.'

'I *can't*,' she cried, twisting her arms out of his gentle hold. 'Every time I look at you I forget Danny, the case, everything but how much I want you.'

Ah hell, the raw honesty of her, his lovely untamed thing: no prevarication, no fear, just this shimmering desire for him that knew no bounds. 'Do you think it's any different for me? But if I lose what objectivity I have left, I put you in danger. I have to stay focused to keep you alive.' He pulled her against him. 'It's only for a few days. When Spencer's put away, I'm all yours, for as long as you want me.'

She only shivered in answer, and in it, he felt the farewell.

'I'm *all* yours,' he repeated softly, trying to make her believe it.

She just shook her head. 'Don't make promises you can't keep. If she isn't with us now, she will be later. The moment you see her picture—or Zoe—again.'

How well she knew him—but this time the pain in his heart was for Elly. 'Maybe so, Elle, but it was always the same with you. She tried and tried to get rid of you, but I couldn't let go.' He pulled out his wallet. 'Remember when I took this?'

She looked at the photo, and a little smile curved her mouth. 'I was so mad at you that day.'

'You didn't come out of the tree for hours, and you kicked me every time I tried to come up to you. So I took this photo of your grumpy face, with your foot out, ready to kick me again.' He chuckled. 'I have no doubt I deserved it, but what did I do?'

'You said you were going to the school dance with Sarah McLeish.' Her rueful look, her dusty face, was so beautiful in its honesty it made him ache. 'I was so angry, because you never thought to ask me.'

'Stupid jerk,' he muttered. 'I didn't mean to hurt you.'

'I knew that. I was only eleven—the whole school would have laughed at you if you'd taken me, and I knew it, but ...' She lifted a shoulder and turned away, staring at the net hiding the river from them. 'I just wanted you to ask. I wanted to dance with you so much.'

He wanted to kick the boy he'd been for causing the pain beneath her words. For missing all that he could have had for a lifetime, if he'd only looked at her, waited for her. 'You were like my little sister then. My best friend. I only saw what I needed in you, Elle. I didn't know.'

'I know.' She nodded, trying to smile—giving him absolution. That was how much he meant to her—how much he'd always meant to her.

'Come here,' he whispered, holding out his arms.

She bit her lip, her eyes bright, and stepped into them.

He hummed as they waltzed around the patch of dirt and weeds, dust falling from their sweaty, gritty bodies, and he felt her hidden laughter. 'You sing then,' he retorted to her silent mockery.

She only moved closer, putting her arms around his neck, changing the waltz to a slow dance. He wrapped his arms around her waist. Her head rested on his shoulder. He stopped humming. The symphony of crickets, birdcalls and the rushing river was all the music they needed.

'Now I know why,' she whispered.

He nodded. Their first dance could only ever have been out here in the wild. The rightness of it was too strong to question or deny, everything that had always been there and always would be, bigger for its being unspoken. Right and perfect.

'I wish I'd known that day,' he murmured, the photo still clutched in his hand.

'You might have been seen as creepy if you did.' Her voice was full of laughter.

He swatted her butt, and she laughed again. He drew her closer as they moved over lumps of dirt and clumps of dried grass in bare feet. In the heat, they both shivered.

'I think I was afraid of even looking at that door, let alone opening it,' he said quietly. 'What it would lead to.'

'What it could mean,' she agreed. 'That's why I couldn't say anything. If I'd lost you …'

He heard it in her voice, the first bit of faith. Thank God he'd kept that picture. Seeing it, she'd recognised she *hadn't* lost him. 'All those years, I tried to forget. To be what they wanted.'

Her hand ran up his back. 'To fit into their ordinary world.'

He nodded. 'I thought it was me, that I was wrong, a broken puzzle piece.'

'That's what they thought. What I thought about me, too.' Her fingers strummed against his spine, and the hard thrill of it ran through him. 'You learn to survive.'

Survival. The perfect word for it. 'Was it better with your family?'

She sighed. 'Yes and no.'

The rest remained there, hovering between them: the belonging that was neither Jepson nor Larkins, nor even cultural, but Adam and Janie alone.

I should never have walked away from you.

I should never have married Sharon.

He didn't say it again. He didn't have to.

She spoke as if she'd heard his thoughts. 'It wasn't the time, Adam.'

'Is it now?' Dear God, the longing in his voice. The wounds that just wouldn't heal without her. *Don't leave me, Elle. I don't know who I am without you.*

She touched his face—not even a caress, but leaving her hand on his cheek, as she looked up at him. 'Yes. It's time.' Her eyes were forgiveness and hope and love, no doubt or question, just certainty. Then her finger whispered across his mouth. 'Tomorrow we are who we've chosen to become, we return to that world. But we still have today, here. For now, we have us.' Watching him, she slipped free a button, two, exposing warm brown cleavage. Another, and his tortured gaze saw breasts free of restraint, warm and soft and ready to fill his hands.

Then she stood naked and proud before him. 'I claim you as my husband, Adam Jepson. Take your clothes off.'

He was helpless to do anything but obey.

She was already at the net, and he could only follow. After unhooking the net from the ghost gum, they waded into the water, diving under, then coming up out of the cool green depths.

'Adam...' Her voice was strained, her gaze riveted to his body. Huntress turned prey. Janie and Adam. Inevitability.

'Dear God, Elly, you're beautiful,' he said, as overcome as she was.

She blushed, staining all the way to her breasts. 'It always hurts me when other men say that. But you ...'

With a thrill of male arrogance for the desire she couldn't hide, he tipped his head back, beckoning to her. 'Come.'

She rose like Venus from her shell, robbing him of breath. Her hand moved into his, her eyes serious. He led her into the reed-filled shallows and sank down among them, pulling her close. She straddled him, drinking in his skin with her palms and fingers.

'I've dreamed of this for years—touching you,' she whispered. 'It was always you.'

He touched her face—only her face—and she trembled. In everything spoken and unspoken, he knew how much this meant to her. How much *he* meant to her. He knew, but couldn't understand. Why him, when she could have so many men?

'Elly—' His tongue tripped over itself. 'You know how much I care about you, that I want to—'

A finger to his lips hushed his faltering speech as she gave him the brave, reckless smile that hurt him so much. 'Today, tonight, we say what we want to say, and we make love. Tomorrow there's no regrets, no guilt or shame. We'll be the best of friends, just like we always were. No regrets.'

His heart constricted at the look in her eyes. The antithesis of pale, angelic, afraid-of-life Sharon, who'd dictated every action by what the family would think, what the neighbours would say, how it looked to others ... how she'd face everyone tomorrow. She'd never even thought to take a risk in her life. She'd never known how to think outside her prim little boxed-in world. The ordinary world. The Jepson world.

No wonder Sharon had been so terrified of Elly.

Elly could never belong in the ordinary world—then or now. Her heritage was the least of who she was. Living her life in avid curiosity and joyful adventure, loving him without demand or request from child to woman, she'd taught him to live again without even trying, not once but twice. It made him want to play the knight for her, to risk his life to save hers, to give her the whole damn world on a platter—and risk the most intimate secret he kept.

Tonight he'd take a tigress by the tail. For one night he'd live, and take the consequences when they came.

★   ★   ★

Rick didn't need to part the curtains to know his city minders still watched every move he made; their presence crawled beneath his skin. Once his brothers in arms, they'd become the enemy, just as they'd been during his childhood in Broken Hill.

How he'd burned with the injustice of it back then. If his people caused any trouble, the media reported ABORIGINES RIOT, or MORE ABORIGINAL PROBLEMS—and people in town talked of 'the Aboriginal problem' for days and weeks. Lately the unwanted spotlight focused on MEN OF MIDDLE-EASTERN APPEAR-ANCE; 'the Muslim problem' screamed the headlines. But when the gubbas did it, it wasn't WHITE MAN ON RAMPAGE WITH A GUN, or WHITE MEN RIOT. Racial accountability became individual accountability for those of northern European descent. Which was why he'd never thought of becoming anything but a cop. The more who took on the system to balance the scales of justice, the better.

Five days ago, he was a respected member of Macks Lake cops, Aboriginal liaison officer for the region, running a local youth group and basketball team—one of the good guys. Then he'd seen Elly's lovely, laughing face, cracking jokes to hide the terror … and he *knew* her, knew what she needed as even Adam did not.

He knew what he had to do now. He was ready. Everything was in place. He had to go on with it now. There was no turning back.

CHAPTER
16

The words of absolution on her lips faltered as Adam showed her his naked need. Her eyes came alive with joy.

He kissed her gently, mindful of her bruised lip, but, impatient with his restraint, she broke his barriers with a gentle touch of her tongue on the roof of his mouth. Their mouths meshed, bodies slipping against each other as they pulled closer in tearing hunger. Her legs locked around his hips and her hands were everywhere, tender yet urgent as they played over his skin, arousing him so bad he couldn't think. Wanting to take her then and there, in the slippery coolness of the river. Almost did—then he thought, *This is Elly.* In the past, he'd been too thoughtless with her. He couldn't let their first time be so selfish.

'Let's go inside,' he murmured in her ear.

She pulled back with a hand over her breast, covering the branding she'd received at the hands of a madman. Her gesture, the self-hate and belief she'd only disappoint him, had never hurt him more.

'Elly, don't hide from me. Your scar doesn't turn me off any more than I think my scar would for you.' His hands parted his chest hair to reveal a small but almost lethal welt, the eternal legacy of his brush with death.

Her eyes darkened at the sight. Then she leaned forward to kiss the scar, slow and tender.

'Mmm. Good idea.' He moved along the whole warped line of her scar with slow, intimate kisses.

'Oh, Adam, th–thank you …'

He smiled at her, the sheen of tears in her eyes luminous, joyful. 'My pleasure entirely, I assure you, ma'am.'

Her hands fell from his body, her legs from his waist. She stood and held out her hand, a warrior queen from the Dreamtime. 'Come inside, Adam.'

Suddenly he felt clumsy, inept, a fumbling youth asked to bed a goddess. Could she find him anything but inadequate? 'I don't have protection, Elly. I didn't have time—' He clicked his tongue, and told the truth. 'I was too bloody embarrassed to start fresh gossip about us in Macks Lake, and there was no time to go anywhere else.'

'So?' Her smile was beauty and shadow, joy and pain. 'Can you believe the thought of having *your* child would be unwelcome to me?'

The raw honesty of her answer left him speechless.

She held out her hand. 'Claudius,' she said softly, one word blending past and present, woman and child, best friend and lover. 'Come inside.'

The shadows lengthened as they entered the cabin. She struck a match and lit the old kerosene lamp hanging from a nail. 'The bed's broken. It'll never hold our combined weight.'

'We can't risk it anyway—it might squeak.'

She giggled, and the image of a goddess splintered. She was real, a warm, living woman—a woman who wanted him. 'And that would bother you?'

He hated to remind her. 'We have to listen for outside sounds, Elle.'

Her smile faded. 'It's good I cleaned the rug, then. It should be dry by now.' She walked out, and came back in with the blanket and rug. 'Clean and dry.'

He lifted the broken door, securing it against the frame with the picnic hamper. Then he lay with her, taking her in his arms. She searched his eyes, sensing his inner turmoil. 'What is it?'

Was he man enough to say it, or too much of a man to admit it? Oh, damn, this was awkward and beautiful, raw and terrifying. He dragged in a breath. 'It's been a long time for me.'

Then he remembered all his fears and doubts about her staying with him in Macks Lake, and the only solution he could come up with. 'I brought you something.' Without waiting for her to ask why the hell he'd bring it up now, he reached into his jeans pocket. 'I'm sorry. I didn't have time to get a box, or wrap it.' He held it out to her, thrusting it at her like a schoolboy handing his first date a corsage.

She looked down and her eyes widened, her mouth falling open. 'Is this—what—?'

'Yes. It's Grandma's wedding ring. She left it to me.' Before she could answer, or reject it, he blurted, 'You said we could do what we want tonight. I want to give this to you.'

She didn't look up. 'Did … she …?'

'Grandma never said so, but I know she wanted you to have it. She left you a letter, saying how much she loved you, how sorry she was to send you away,' he said, aware that he was babbling, but he had to stop her from finishing the question. One mention of his wife's name now might break him—and then he'd break her. 'I've kept both of them for years, waiting to give them to you.'

Her mouth twitched as she looked up at him, eyes brimming with laughter. 'And you chose to give it to me when we're both naked?'

He saw the idiocy of it now. He should have taken her out to dinner, ordered wine, given her flowers—anything but this. 'I'm so stupid. I'm sorry, Elly, I—'

'No. It's perfect,' she whispered. 'There couldn't be a better time and way. It's us.' And she smiled at him, luminous with joy. 'It's Elly and Claudius.'

Relief flooded him; he'd got something right for her. 'Yes, it is. See?' He tilted the ring so she could read the engraving on the inside: *Elly and Claudius.*

Tears spilled over. 'I–I …' She held up her right hand.

He shook his head and, lifting her left hand, slipped the ring onto the third finger. So right, so perfect, Elly wearing nothing but the ring he'd given her. 'I had it sized and engraved yesterday when you were sleeping.' He'd paid double for Milson to get the job done in under an hour. Unable to tell her he'd left her with Rick while she slept, he kissed her. 'I called Minyenbarra yesterday. The papers will be at home when we get back, and we're going to sign them. I had to look up the number, since you wouldn't give it to me.' He said it with awkward defiance. Sixteen again, and so afraid of rejection, even now when she lay naked in his arms. *Stay with me, Elle. Please don't go.*

'Well, you didn't give me back my photos,' she mock-sniped, tears spilling from eyes as bright as the sun.

She filled his life with joy and laughter, even at this moment. He buried his face in her neck. 'That's my Elly.'

She hugged him tight. 'Yes, it's me. Can we *please* stop talking now?' she begged. 'I don't know about you, but I've waited half a lifetime for this, and I keep thinking the stupid phone will ring any moment and stop us.'

Caught halfway between coughing and laughter, he lifted his head and kissed her with all the desire consuming him. She responded with sweet fire, her mouth devouring his. She lifted his hands to her breasts with a whimper of need, crooning in a smoky-soft voice. He slowly lifted her body higher, exploring her with his mouth and tongue until he reached the taut, dusky nipples. He drew one into his mouth, suckling, abrading its tip with his tongue.

She writhed against him, crying out, 'Oh, Adam, that's so beautiful!'

'Claudius,' he rasped, wanting to hear her cry out the nickname with passion.

'Claudius …' She murmured words in a soft, purring language he didn't know. The music in rain, the song of an angel—a torrent of joyful pleasure from the woman he'd always want above any other.

He laid her down, nipping the skin of her ribs and belly, his hands exploring, his confidence soaring at her whimpering little cries and her body's instinctive arch up to meet his hands and mouth.

'Translation, please?'

She watched him touch and kiss her body, her eyes filled with such emotion it warmed the still-cold places in his soul. 'I'll tell you tomorrow, if you still want to know. Tonight I can say and do what I want.'

And he no longer had to ask. Craving to say the words *stay with me, Elly. Never leave me.* As terrified as she was, because if this hour was inevitability, so was tomorrow's parting.

'Oh? I guess it's time to retaliate, then …' He kissed her hands in tender reverence, but when tears shone in her eyes, he moved up her arms, and then down her body, slow, intimate. She cried out, curving into his hands and mouth wherever he kissed her. He loved her with hands and lips and tongue until she cried out, 'Claudius,' and her body convulsed in release.

The scent of her, warm and womanly and drenched in unashamed sexuality … he shuddered, then kissed her and laid his body on hers, joining them—

He stiffened, his mind reeling in shock as he encountered the barrier he'd never expected to find. 'Elly?' he gasped, his mind reverting to another night like this, with a dread-filled sinking in the pit of his stomach.

She bit her lip, trying to smile even in her pain. 'I'll be fine in a minute.'

'Are you hurting much?' he asked, preparing to withdraw.

'Don't,' she cried, holding him inside her, his lovely wild thing. 'It's not hurting much. I'll be fine in a minute.'

'Why?' Everything he wanted to ask came down to that one question.

'No spiritual or emotional why to it. Just one of life's choices.' She smiled at him. 'On that first skinny-dip in the wilds of Bunda-noon the day you got your licence, you never even looked at me. But I couldn't look away.'

He didn't know what to do with that. 'But that was fifteen years ago. You were a kid!'

She kissed him. 'I've never felt like that about any man since.' She trailed her hand down his body and he groaned, fighting for control. 'I've dated a lot of men, but it was never like this. I even tried to go this far once or twice, but I couldn't do it. They weren't you.'

His fear was thrown aside. In this most intimate position, her words filled his heart with the same arrogant gladness he saw on her face. She'd chosen him to be her first lover. Not just any man, she wanted *him*, Adam. She'd waited years for him.

Confirmation of all she'd left unsaid came to him on quiet feet. No woman waited so long for a man, unless—

If I fall in love with you …

He held her gaze, compelling her. 'There was never an *if* for you, was there?'

Even here and now, she lifted her chin, undefeated. 'Are you sure you want to know?'

For answer, he picked up her left hand, caressing the wedding ring. More inevitability, despite everything that had pulled them apart in the past, and still pulled them apart now. This ring was supposed to be there, damn it, and put there by him.

'Was there an *if*, my Elly?'

She shook her head. Show no fear; take no prisoners. She'd even tell him the truth during her pain in this most intimate act.

She waited half a lifetime for me. She loves me. How stupid to be so surprised by it, when he'd known all along nobody would ever love him the way Elly did.

Dragging in slow breaths, giving her time to adjust—or was it he who needed to take it slowly?—he felt her move, taking him deep inside her. He heard her gasp, and even a man as ignorant of female pleasure as he was couldn't miss it.

'Adam …'

He moved further inside her, filling her, and though she flinched, desire made her eyes stay open.

'Yes, oh, yes,' she whispered, adding a torrent of words in her other language: words of need, of joy; crying aloud in pleasure. She began to move with him, her hands and lips caressing his body, giving as much as she gained. Sweet, fast loving that left them slicked in sweat. And when he found release as intense as the love they'd created, she'd already found completion, her velvet softness contracting all around him in the exquisite aftershocks of her second climax.

And still, the silence around them was broken only by the symphony of crickets and birds.

He buried his face in her hair, revelling in all they were. Then he rolled over, taking her with him so she lay on top of him. He caressed her face and back with an unsteady hand.

'Adam?' The word was uncertain.

He should have known she would sense the change, feel his pain. He kissed her flushed, damp cheek, trailing his lips to her mouth. 'Not you, darlin'. You've never hurt me in your life.'

She turned her face away from his kiss. 'It's her.' Her voice was flat, pain underlining the name she now feared to bring up.

After a moment, he nodded. If he didn't say it now, he'd lose her; and for the first time the choice between the two women in his life was easy. 'She never enjoyed this. That's why we had separate beds. Until tonight—until you—I thought I was the problem. You know what they say: there's no frigid women, only bad lovers.'

The uncertainty faded. 'Oh.' Her face softened. 'Well, we both know I can't give you any comparisons; but if you're a bad lover, Claudius, heaven help me if I ever meet a magnificent one. It might kill me.'

He laughed and kissed her, feeling as if he'd conquered the world. 'How are you feeling?'

She smiled down at him. 'Smug. Happier than I've ever been. Wanting to repeat it as soon as possible.'

He laughed again, nuzzling her neck. Then he gently put her aside and went to the corner, wetting a towel in the washbowl to clean the smear of blood from her thighs. 'Are you sore at all?'

She smiled at him in tender gratitude. 'Was she in a bad way?' she asked, surprising him again with her insight.

His mouth quirked, but he felt no desire to smile. 'She locked herself in the bathroom. She didn't let me touch her for five days, and then only because she wanted to get pregnant. We only ever did it when it was peak time for conception—once a month, and by the end of the first year I hated touching her. She never enjoyed sex once in our whole married life ... and neither did I.'

Why that made Elly laugh, he didn't know. 'I hope you don't expect a similar response from me. I'm a little bit uncomfortable, but I don't have the slightest urge to scream, or hide from you. If that's normal virginal behaviour, I'm glad I wasn't the average virgin.' Grabbing the towel from him, she threw it aside. 'I waited fifteen years for tonight. So if you think this is the end, think again, buster. I want more.'

He burst out laughing, but grimaced as she shushed him, her eyes alight with mischief. 'I should have known. Why wouldn't this be different to any other experience I've had? You're not like any woman I've ever known.'

Her hands caressed his chest, her lips moved from his throat to shoulder to stomach, warm and soft and full of life-affirming passion. 'I want to make love to you this time. Show me, Adam. Teach me how to make you happy.'

'You already have, more than you'll ever know.' He lifted her back up to him and kissed her. 'You'll never need lessons when it comes to making me happy, Elle. I think you were born knowing how to give me everything I want, everything I need. But you have something you can teach me.'

He saw understanding in her eyes. '*Guwi ngaya, yanada warriwul djanaba dali nguwing,*' she whispered in the rippling tongue of her grandmother's people, the Eora.

'What does that mean?'

She gave him a mysterious smile, a sweet blend of child and woman, light and shadow, past and present. 'You'll just have to trust me on that.'

She taught him the words filled with ancient beauty as she loved his body, touching and kissing him with a fervour that left him weak, sated, shaking—aroused again too fast, but it was never too soon for her. With Elly, he never had to ask, or hope, or dread. She was with him all the way.

This was the wedding night they'd been cheated of years ago— by Jepson expectation; by his meeting Sharon—but more than anything else, he and Elly had been cheated by his blindness.

He lit a lantern as darkness fell around them. Making sure that the light remained only inside the cabin by blocking the window with the black plastic he'd brought. He listened again for outside sounds, as he had the whole time.

'I have another fantasy,' he said lazily, to distract her from what he was doing. Protecting her and making her happy entwined in a double rope. His joy and responsibility in one.

'Hmm?' The sleepy look in her eyes, so sated and joyful, filled him with more happiness. '*Another* one? How many years have you been storing all these up?'

He chuckled and, returning to the rug, played with her breasts. Their instant response to his touch fascinated him. 'I've only had this one since our picnic.'

'A sexual fantasy about a picnic?' She blinked, looking doubtful. 'What does it involve?'

'We have all we need. Naked bodies, covered in sweat—' he licked a trail of perspiration from the underside of her breast as he spoke '—and food.' He grabbed the picnic hamper.

Her eyes filled with laughing trepidation. 'This fantasy of yours doesn't involve whipped cream or warm chocolate, does it?'

One brow lifted. 'You always did have a better imagination than me. Now, my idea was just to eat before making love again, but if adventure is what you want ...' He held up a jar of honey, grinning. 'The bush equivalent of body paint.'

She backed off, looking shy, doubtful—and yet intrigued. 'Um, Claudius? I'm not sure I'm that adventurous yet.'

His fear of rejection a thing of the past, he poured a tiny drop on her belly. 'Think about it. Getting sticky and messy, and all the cleaning up ...' He ran his tongue over the honey.

Though she made the purring sound he was fast becoming addicted to, she shook her head. 'No, let me.' But she only smeared a drop on his nose, and softly kissed it off. Another smear on his lips, and then, with slow, brushing kisses, she shared the taste with him. Then her eyes darkened, and she leaned forward; his forehead met hers, and they just stood there, holding each other. Hands moving only in soft, tickling motions on each other's backs.

'Much better,' he agreed unsteadily. 'You always know what to do, Elle.'

★   ★   ★

In the deep night, exhausted yet unable to sleep, Adam watched the beautiful mystery lying asleep in his arms. Elly had done nothing but give to him from the day they'd met—and tonight she'd given him the ultimate gift.

Lying in her arms, tired and replete, he felt the stirring of change. A calm rebellion against the life he no longer wanted, a hatred of the burdens he'd long wanted to shuck. Maybe at last the pain from his unsatisfying marriage, and the guilt over Sharon's and Zack's deaths would no longer guide every decision he made for himself and Zoe.

His gaze turned inward, to three years ago, as he said the words he should have said then.

Goodbye, Sharon. I loved you, but I won't do as you asked. You were wrong to try to hold me inside your world, when you knew I was unhappy. You were wrong about Elly. She's the best thing to ever come into my life. I can't doubt that any more. I won't regret that I've broken my promise, when I would never have asked it of you.

At last he'd found the key to the peace of mind and heart he'd craved so long. Just as Elly had done for him half a lifetime ago, she'd known how to find him, locked as he'd been in his self-imposed prison, and in years of perfect friendship, in trusting him with her life, in one night of loving, she'd handed him the key to escape.

Elly loved him without borders, without reproach or guilt, regrets or shame; no lectures, restrictions or conditions. The weight chained to his heart snapped and fell to his feet. The only woman he wanted had shown him that he was more than man enough for her. His own personal miracle. In this tumbledown shack, hiding from a madman, he'd at last found the way to forgive himself for the past, because Elly had shown him how.

He could only hope he could do the same for her—and that she'd stay long enough to let him. It would take a lifetime.

Silver City Highway, north of Macks Lake

A couple of local cops were the only impediment that 'Father' Danny met at the outskirts of Macks Lake, probably because he'd bypassed the main roadblock outside town.

The forest trail marked on the map Granddad had sent him had indeed been unmanned. They probably didn't even know about it—but Granddad had been preparing for Janie's eventual flight here months before Danny had even thought of it.

Naturally, Monster said, with some dryness. *As if he'd tell us without our begging for it, or making a deal with us to get what he wants. We'll show him.*

Yes, we will, Danny promised him. *It's almost time, my friend, fear not.*

I fear nothing, Danny. Haven't you learned that yet?

Except being hurt, Danny thought, but didn't say. It would only make him angry, and they needed to have clarity now.

A slim, dark-haired cop strode to the car. 'G'day, Father.' He identified himself as a lapsed Catholic by his guilty inability to meet Danny's eyes. 'Coming for Mass?'

Danny took the maximum risk, revelling in it. 'You'd know if you came to church now and then, constable.'

Sure enough, the cop flushed.

'Why on earth are you out here? Why is there another road-block after the last? Is it necessary? You poor things, it's thirty-eight degrees.'

A call came over the two-way radio in the police car. 'Macks Lake Station to Unit 2, do you read me?' The older man coming toward them turned back.

The young man, little more than a boy, shifted from foot to foot. 'Sorry, Father, we can't give information.'

No, Monster, put your hand away. We have to play it clever now. Danny sighed in relief when Monster dropped his hand from the knife in the centre console. 'I can certainly understand that, constable. I can't even repeat what's told me in confidence under oath in court.'

The boy muttered, 'That's in the confessional.'

Glad he'd studied up on Catholic rites and beliefs, he said, 'I con-sider anything you tell me sacred, constable.' After twenty seconds of silence, he prodded. 'You seem troubled about this matter. If I can help?'

With a half-scared, half-thrilled look, and a guilty smile of antic-ipation, the boy leaned forward—and then he seemed to see the collar anew, and drew back. 'I'm sorry, um, Father, I can't speak.'

The 'um' gave it all away—as did the hand behind his back. And Danny was glad he'd prepared for this moment in advance. *Quietly, Monster.* And he put the car in first gear. *Ready.*

A weak thump came from the boot of the car. Danny blinked, surprised and rather grateful his captive was still alive. Brian—or was it Peter? —hadn't done anything to hurt him, after all.

In the meantime, Monster had taken the knife out of the console. The fat cop came running—

But in a flash of sunlight, the knife went soft as butter into the boy's gut. The boy doubled over, gasping, and fell to the ground. Monster took a second to admire his handiwork, the lovely, lovely blood, the joy and power of it, then, with a screech of tyres, Danny roared off, skidding across the road before straightening the car.

He felt no fear. He'd bet the fat, wheezing cop hadn't taken a shot at real people in his career. He'd go for the tyres, and would miss.

Yep. Exactly, Monster said, checking in the rear-vision mirror. Happy, sated with the stabbing, while Danny felt that rare thing, an erection.

Now we know exactly where Janie will come.

Another map Granddad had sent last night showed him the way to the hospital.

It's time, Janie, he and Monster thought, in harmony at last.

CHAPTER
17

Elly awoke to the early daylight song of birds and a cool place on the rug beside her where warmth and a loving arm had been. A kookaburra laughed nearby.

She'd heard men lost interest once they'd had the woman they lusted after. Even though Adam had mentioned making their marriage legal, he'd spoken no words of love, given no promises for the future.

It's best if he doesn't.

Today was the barrier she hadn't been able to pass in so long. She no longer knew how to plan for the future. So if today was all she had, she'd take it—and run.

She found him just inside the perimeter. Barefoot and with mussed hair, clad only in jeans, he was using the station's second satellite phone. A rush of pleasure flowed through her, watching him. She became caught in the play of his profile, the quirk of his lips, the intent seriousness of his eyes contrasted with the mussed dark hair, how his hand was shoved in his pocket, jingling coins as he concentrated. The stern cop had disappeared. He looked like a boy again; the boy she'd loved for so many years. He looked *alive* again. No traces of 'Old Sobersides' in his face. Adam, *her* Adam, was back.

If there was such a thing as morning-after etiquette, she'd never learned it. All she could do was stare at him, aching to have him again despite a slight tenderness inside. This might be it for them, their last day.

As if sensing her presence, he turned and smiled at her. A relaxed, happy smile: warm, intimate, welcoming, different from the sexually charged grimaces he'd sent her way the past few days. He gestured to her with his free hand.

She ran to him, wrapping her arm around his waist and burrowing her face in his shoulder. She nibbled his skin in the way she'd learned drove him crazy.

'Uh-huh. Got that. Yeah, Sarge, I—*Elly*,' he hissed, covering the mobile with his hand, 'not now. Elly, come on, stop that.'

She laughed up at him, seeing the huge grin covering his face. 'Make me.' She began to pull off her clothes as her teeth continued to nibble his chest.

'Yeah, Sarge. I, uh … yeah, that's good …' His voice had an anguished quality, gaze locked on Elly's busy hands and mouth. 'What about, um … yeah, Mrs Collins. Yeah, that's her name. What's she up to—*Elly!*'

Her hand slipped into his open jeans; her tongue dipped in and out of his navel. 'Hmmm?' she purred. 'Is there a problem?'

His jeans fell to the ground, and he was naked beneath, completely aroused.

'Yeah. Yeah, well, you know Baz. Thanks, Sarge. I'll call later … um … Elly needs me now.' His words were so fast they were almost incoherent. He disconnected, threw the phone into the car, stepped out of his jeans and lifted her in his arms, carrying her back to the cabin.

'So you like to play games, huh, doc?' he growled, laying her on the rug, nibbling exquisite places in retaliation.

'Oh, yeah,' she gasped, wriggling as he brought a pleasure to her body she hadn't ever known to dream about. 'You can play that one all day.'

'You like this game?' he murmured against her hip. 'And I thought I was torturing you.'

'Call me masochistic, but I *love* this game ... mmm ... cops and doctors.'

'Since we both have a fixation with cuffs, we could try them again, in a different way.' His brows lifted mockingly.

She laughed. 'I can hardly wait.'

'It's pretty hot in here.' His eyes asked the question.

Joy filled her. Claudius was here with her. 'I could do with another swim.'

Grinning, he grabbed her hand, and they bolted to the cool, slippery sensuality of the river.

★   ★   ★

Sitting astride him after, legs still wrapped around his hips, she murmured, 'I think something's biting my toe.'

'You want to get out?'

She shook her head, smiling. 'So what's the update?'

He sighed. 'Rick's on his rostered days off, and appears to be going his own way. The Mirakis are minding their own business, or so Baz says, but they have to leave Longa Station if their boss asks them to. Mrs Collins is hiding in her house behind closed curtains. No one's seen her since last night.'

'Did the roadblocks turn anything up?'

'Only a priest on the road yesterday, two towns north of Macks Lake.' He grinned. 'Sarge said Baz is suspicious of his nearness to us, but Baz has this love-to-hate-'em attitude about religious people of any denomination. I don't know what they did to him, but he's a rabid agnostic, atheist—whatever.'

She frowned. 'Didn't Jonas mention a priest visiting the Indigenous towns the other day? Isn't that a little suspicious?'

'No, it's part of country life. We don't have a Catholic priest here, just one Anglican minister and a few smaller denominations. Plenty of smaller outback towns don't, these days. It's not much use in some places. Farmers can't take every Saturday off for confession and Sunday for mass. So once a month a priest from Broken Hill or Mildura visits here, stopping at the little towns and communities on the way, giving Mass, listening to confessions. I'll check up when he last came, just in case. You never know. It could end up being an important lead.'

In a few words, he was gone again—her sweet, giving lover vanished, and the cop took his place. Though she knew it was for her sake, it still hurt that he had a name, a place to belong, a settled job, a family, and she had nothing. The things she'd wanted all her life, a simple sense of belonging she'd only ever had with him, and he'd already taken it away.

'I wonder if the Flying Doctors will take me back? I left without giving notice.'

He frowned. 'Remind me what town were you based in?'

'Moongallee Creek.'

'That's five hundred kilometres from here.'

'So the boy still likes maps.' She laughed. 'Four hundred and sixty-three, to be exact.' She rose from his lap to put space between them.

'You're leaving Macks Lake.' It was almost an accusation.

She shrugged lightly. 'Well, it was never a permanent thing moving here, Claudius; it was always just a visit. This is your town, not mine.'

'Then what is it we've got here, Elly? Did you use me to get experience? Was I just some one-night thing for you?'

'Wasn't that what I was for you?' she shot back, hurt by his sudden ferocity. 'Come on, be honest. Would you have brought *her* here to this shack and made love to her? You made it clear where I stand. One night was all I'd get, and I took it.'

He lifted her left hand. 'Right, I made it so clear you'd only get one night by giving you a ring, and calling Minyenbarra? It wasn't me who's made it clear from the start that it was never going to last.'

She narrowed her eyes. 'I always knew better than to ask for anything more than this. Anything beyond one night would bring the fury of the whole Jepson clan down on your head for bringing home a blackfella!'

'You do my family a disservice, believing they think so little of you, or judge you on your background. And even if they did, I don't give a damn.' His eyes flashed hot with an intensity of fury she'd never seen in him. 'That's always been *your* hang-up, not mine.'

'The skidmarks you left behind when you left my life made that clear!'

He sighed. 'I'll apologise for that for the rest of our lives if you want, but again—and listen to me this time—*the problem was mine. It had nothing to do with how I felt—how I still feel—about you.*' He wrapped his fingers around her arms, dipping his head so she had to look into his eyes. 'I'm not the one always comparing you to her—you are. Are you saying a king-sized bed in a five-star hotel would have made yesterday better? Or a ceremony in a church? I had all that the first time around, and look what I got! I bloody cherish giving you that ring, and having our own private marriage, both at Kutringal and here, because you and I were always apart from the ordinary world. I cherish *us*, and everything we have. But if you want all the trimmings to prove it, fine. A king-size bed in a five-star hotel, with room service and a Sydney Harbour view, after a big wedding with both sides of the family there—will that do? If that's what it'll take for you to see I respect you more than any woman I've ever known, you'll have it. I'll call every Jepson in the phone book to tell them we're together if you want, and invite them to the wedding. I'll turn us into what everyone else is, if you want it—if it'll stop you from turning the most beautiful experience of my life into a dirty one-night stand!'

She sat abruptly in the water too shocked to take it all in.

He held her shoulders. 'This was *not* a one-night stand to me, Elle. *You* could never be that to me. No matter what happens, no matter what you decide, I want you to be in my life, my future.'

Stunned, she could only say, 'Oh.' Then, 'How?'

He hesitated. 'Do you remember the one passion I had when we were kids besides cops and fast cars?'

She smiled at that. 'Of course. Planes.'

He nodded. 'It's something I never got around to trying, but I still want to.' His eyes searched hers. 'My time as a cop's run out. I'm not enjoying the life any more. I've been burning out for years. By the time I was shot, all I wanted was to resign and find a new life, but I was stuck, I still needed to make sure Zoe had security.' He smiled at her. 'Then you came to Macks Lake, and I discovered what I want to do with the rest of my life.'

She frowned. 'In what way?'

'We flew to Kutringal.' He paused. 'I think I was of some use to you there.'

She nodded, as the pieces began falling into place.

'I've got three months of long service leave owed to me. I could quit the service and take a couple of months to update my advanced first-aid certificate and get my pilot's licence. I thought—if you'd consider staying—we could apply to start a Flying Doctor base in Macks Lake in the disused wing of the hospital. The area's desperate for extra medical help, as you must have noticed. Dr Schumacher's sixty-three, with a heart condition, and run off his feet. He could take the town for another couple of years, and we could handle the outlying areas and Aboriginal communities.'

'We can't start a base, Adam. They're all in cities and big regional towns. It takes years, and we'd need a lot of funding. But ... we could start a clinic, offering flying services to outlying areas,' she said slowly.

'So—do you like the idea?'

She looked out over the shining expanse of river in the direction of Macks Lake, realising that, in five short days, she'd grown to love the little town. 'You know how to tap into my dreams, don't you, Claudius? Being a doctor in remote areas, caring for those with little medical access, has been my dream since I began medical school. We could apply to the Aboriginal and Torres Strait Islander Commission for some funding, but it's going to be hard.'

'But will you think about it?'

The question was so tentative, so unsure, she wanted to kick Sharon's butt for destroying his confidence. How could she have Adam, have his love, and want to change him? Yet ...

'Of course I'll think about it. To have my dream come true with *you*—how could I not want it? Did—did you really mean it?' She lifted her left hand, still bearing his grandmother's ring, which shone in the filtered sunlight like a promise of forever she'd never been able to see before.

She gasped when he pulled her back to him, hard and fast, and kissed her. 'I told you, I don't play games with women. How could I ever just fool around with you—*you* more than any woman? How could you believe I would? Last night, I made a commitment to you.' He looked into her eyes, and again she saw the haunting uncertainty. 'I thought—hoped—you did, too.'

★ ★ ★

'Your family would hate it.'

'I disagree. Anyway, even if you *are* right, I told you that doesn't bother me.' Adam frowned, sensing something deeper than her words implied. 'What did they do to make you think they'd hate the idea us being together?'

She shrugged, looking out over the water again. 'I did it to myself. On your wedding night, I took off with your best man.'

He gasped. 'Greg? He never said a word. Damn it, I'd have killed him! You were just a kid, and he—'

'A kid who passed for eighteen at the nightclub and hotel room he took me to. Didn't you look at me once that day, and see I *wasn't* a kid anymore? No—you only had eyes for her.' Her shoulders slumped. 'I didn't care what happened after you went. So when that guy hit on me, I went with him. I thought, *At least he sees me, he wants to be with me ...*'

Dear God. She hadn't even known Greg's name. His poor wild child. Lonely, heartbroken Elly, leaping at Greg's advances like the child she still was. Desperate for someone, anyone to care, she'd taken off with a stranger because he'd left her, too immersed in his happiness to see his little friend's pain. So absorbed in his dreams of a life and woman that would never materialise, he'd left the best friend he'd ever known so completely and utterly alone. Worse,

he'd never even noticed. He'd deserved the consequences his blindness had brought … in more ways than one.

He caressed her back, trying to defuse the grief she hadn't yet put
behind her after so many years. 'What happened then?'

She shuddered. 'I hated it when he kissed me. When he tried
to touch me, I told him I was fifteen, that he'd lose his job in the
police force if he had sex with an underage kid. He dropped me
outside your grandparents' farm, and bolted. It was three in the
morning.'

*After your wedding, she sat in her tree, pining for you so badly we feared
for her.*

He drew her head to his chest. 'Then what happened?'

She hiccuped. 'A couple of weeks later your grandparents told
me about my Aboriginal family. They said they were sending me
to Sydney to—to find another friend.'

Oh, yeah, he just bet they did—and he bet he knew who'd led
the chorus. He could hear his father's gleeful words: *Is she pregnant?
She's so wild! It's in the blood, you know. Thank God we got Adam out of
her way!* He could see it all: the lack of understanding, the unthinking bigotry poured over a confused little girl who'd just lost her
best friend.

He even understood why she'd remained a virgin so long. At
least she'd proved the truth to one Jepson.

Guilt at realising why she'd driven herself to success the past
twelve years hit him like a brick. 'Ah, Elly.' He sighed, caressing
her wet curls. 'You were so scared I'd judge you for taking off with
Greg, you wouldn't let Aunty Hat call me. That's why you waited
so long to come to me, isn't it?'

She shook her head, looking lost. 'You weren't mine any more.
You belonged to her, and she wouldn't even let us be friends.'

'Why didn't you come … later?'

'I didn't know if there was a point. I kept in touch through Aunty Hat. I wanted to come, but Aunty Hat said you'd gone into a world of your own, full of grief and guilt. I could hardly bear it when she told me about the shooting, and I couldn't come to you. Danny was stalking me by then, and I couldn't risk his hurting you or Zoe. But the last time I called, Aunty Hat said you'd retreated so far from life that Zoe would suffer. Danny was in prison. You lived at the other end of the country from where he was. So I came, hoping I could help.'

He nodded. 'Aunty Hat was right. I felt like I was dead, only going through the motions for Zoe's sake. Then you came, and hit my life like a comet for a second time. Aunty Hat knew what she was doing.' He sighed. 'No one else could have done for me what you have.'

'I'm glad I could help, for a little while.' She looked out over the river.

'It doesn't have to be this way, darlin',' he said huskily. 'You're running away again, and for what?'

She only stared at him. 'What else can I do?'

'Stay with me, Elle,' he whispered. 'Start the clinic here with me. Give us a chance, Elle. Just stay.'

After another hiccup, she turned her face once more, looking at the water, glimmering grey-green with the sunlight filtering through the trees. 'I feel as if you've handed me all my dreams in an hour—but we both know everything in my life's on hold until Danny's out of it forever. Until that's guaranteed, I can't make any promises, and with Zoe to protect, neither can you.'

He heard the farewell in her voice, and she was right—he couldn't endanger Zoe. Neither could he push what he wanted on Elly until he was sure he could give her the life—and be the husband—she deserved. Until he knew what *she* wanted. 'Tell me what you want, Elle. Not the work dreams, I get that. What do *you* want?'

She couldn't look at him, but her fingers moved through his hair. Looking at her, he wondered if she knew what she wanted, or if she'd dared to dream beyond giving to others for the last decade or more. She'd run for so long, she didn't know what else to do.

Then she looked at him, and he knew the answer.

He'd been her only dream.

Dear God, he'd never even begun to hope he could be so loved by any woman—but he had been for more than half his life, and not just by any woman, but one extraordinary woman who knew him, inside and out. If only …

'You still don't trust me. Why?' he asked before he knew he was going to. 'What have I left undone?'

Her wet hair sprayed him as she turned around, eyes touched by uncertainty, so haunting he knew the time had come.

'Go on. Just say it, Elle. Get it out there.'

She gathered her resolution over long seconds where she bit her top lip, frowned and blinked. Looked at him. 'Say her name, Adam.'

He almost smiled. *One step ahead of her at last.* He'd been waiting all morning for this. 'Why?' He made his voice rough, angry, to convince her he needed healing—needed *her.* 'What will that achieve for you?'

'Nothing for me, Adam. It's for you.' She spoke with an almost shining clarity, at odds with the fear in her eyes. 'You have to leave her behind, say goodbye. Then you'll finally start to heal, and *live.*'

'This isn't living?' He swept his hand between them, indicating their intimacy.

'This was you and me, saying the farewell we didn't get last time. Maybe it was you stepping forward, too—but you'll yank back sooner or later, because you're still chained to her. You're afraid to let go of her,' she said quietly, eyes hurting him with their courage—not for her, for him. 'Have you been to her grave, Adam?

Have you left flowers, talked to her, told her it's time you moved on, for Zoe's sake and yours? Until you do, you'll take her with you no matter where you go. You'll feel her with you wherever you are. You'll always be her widower.'

He saw the truth she'd been holding in the whole time she'd been here. And he faced it with rage in his heart so strong it contained the whole world—not at Elly, not even at Sharon; because that damned abyss he'd just climbed out of was so close, and they both knew it.

And yet, knowing this would come, he walked into that chasm. 'You think it's love that ties me to her? You're wrong. I stopped loving her years ago, long before Zoe was born.' He looked into her disbelieving eyes, and nodded. 'But I was responsible for their deaths. I was so busy avoiding her that I avoided my kids, too—and when Zoe got a high fever, and Sharon called me to take them to the hospital, I was too busy getting useless info from some junkie's pimp that I told her I'd meet her there. And the drunk driver hit her on the way, killing Zack instantly, and Sharon was gone before the next morning.'

Elly was so still he was tempted to tap her hand to force her to breathe again. 'That's a lot to walk away from,' she said at last.

He nodded. 'But I'll do it,' he said evenly, 'if you do the same.'

'Let go of you?' A whole world of sadness in her question; oh, yeah, she'd known what he'd do, what he'd demand. Or she thought she'd known.

And until last night, she'd have been right.

'No.' Still quiet and even, as he held her chin in his hand. 'Let go of Spencer, Elle. Walk out of the cage he's put you in, leave his chains behind you, or you'll feel *him* with you no matter where you are. You'll always be his victim.'

She drew in a breath, and choked on it. Tears pooled in her eyes as he fought to breathe.

He patted her back. 'If you don't, you'll face him over and over at the same disadvantage. Bullies are cowards at heart,' he repeated as she kept coughing.

When she finally got control again, she stared at him with resentful eyes. 'This must rank as the weirdest post-coital conversation in history. We're still *naked*, for heaven's sake.'

He shrugged. 'We're weird, Elle. We always were. So, I'll go first.' He faced her anger, almost but not quite smiling. 'I said goodbye to Sharon last night, made my peace. She was wrong in thinking you're bad for me. I finally understand that she was putting her own fears on me in making me promise never to find you.' He kissed her, so softly. 'Come with me to her grave, and Zack's, if you like, but you're right. I owe her and Zack better than that. But though I'll always hold part of them with me, I'm no longer her widower. I'm ready to move on. Are you?'

She was still staring at him. 'When did this become about me?'

He almost laughed at her confusion and resentment. 'We're two of a kind, so ready to rattle each other's cages, but so afraid to even look at our own.' When she still wouldn't say it, he continued, though reluctantly: 'I wasn't afraid to let her go, Elle. I wanted to, but that last day—before she died—Sharon apologised for being a bad wife, as she put it, and told me why. A friend of the family had abused her from nine to twelve, and it made her what she was: afraid of everything in life, and terrified deep down that, if she wasn't perfect, he'd come back and hurt her again. Sex was the least of it, and the worst, if that makes sense. Even she couldn't sort it out, and going for help was never an option, when she'd never even told her parents. Her abuser threatened to kill them, and she'd believed it.'

Elly closed her eyes. 'Oh, the poor child,' she whispered, and he felt her kinship with the woman who'd been her enemy for so long. 'I wish I'd known ...'

'She didn't even want to tell me, but the relief and peace on her face, when she had—I was glad she told me.'

'I understand now,' she said softly. 'It's the same reason, for me. With Danny,' she clarified when his confusion must have shown on his face. 'Every time he hurts me, I see the lost child his grandfather abused. He has old cuts all over him, you know—whip marks. I asked him about it when I was treating him, and he said, "I needed to become a man, and stop crying for my mother." He said it so *casually*. He told me his mother left when he was four.'

Now, at last, her acts made sense. He ought to have realised all along that Danny was another injured critter to her, and she hated that she couldn't heal him. 'It's not the same, Elle. Sharon didn't kill anyone. If she had, I'd have had her committed, for her safety and that of others.'

Silence greeted his words. How his Elly had always hated cages— almost as much as she hated her limitations. That she couldn't heal everyone and everything that suffered. At last she said, 'I'm getting cold.'

Too late he remembered how many times she'd been to the police, how many times they'd let her down. 'You know what I want now. I'll let you think about it.' He kissed her cheek and stood. 'I'd better check in with Sarge. Anything could've happened in the past few hours.'

The phone was ringing as they reached the cabin. 'Sarge?'

'Well, it's about bloody time you answered. I've been calling for almost an hour!'

Seeing Elly had followed him in, he shot her a grimace as he answered, 'Sorry, Sarge.'

'Thank God you've finally answered. Where the hell have you been? I told you to stay near the damn phone!'

He sobered. 'What is it? What's wrong?'

'A priest got through the roadblock this morning. When Simon refused to give him information, the priest stabbed him and drove straight to the hospital, demanding to see Elly.'

That bloody priest. 'Simon? How is he? Is he alive?'

Elly gasped, and began pulling on her clothes.

Sarge's silence told him something was very, very wrong. 'Come on, Sarge—just tell me if he's alive!'

'He is—for now,' Sarge said tersely, 'But he needs surgery.'

'Where's Dr Schumacher?' More silence, and he saw the reflection of his own fear in Elly's frantic shoe lacing, her search for her medical kit. 'Sarge? Where's Dr Schumacher?'

When he spoke, Sarge's voice was sombre. 'When he realised Elly wasn't in town, Spencer set a homemade bomb off in the hospital carpark, killing one woman and injuring six people. Then he took Dr Schumacher hostage. Spencer's waiting for Elly in the hallway to the OR with a suicide vest on and a gun to Dr Schumacher's head.'

CHAPTER
18

'Oh, my God.' Adam almost dropped the phone.

Elly snatched it from him. 'Hi, Jonas? What happened?' She stiff-ened when Jonas filled her in. 'Call every hospital or clinic in the region. We'll need whoever they can send.'

'There's a massive pileup on the Midwestern Highway. One car's on fire, with two people trapped in it, one a baby. I don't know how long it will be before they *can* send anyone.'

And she knew that this was the reason he'd called, though he wouldn't say it. 'Okay. Send someone with a boat. It's quicker, and every minute counts. Send the bush fire brigades and any available paramedics while we're on the way.'

'You can't come here, Elly,' Jonas protested, but it was weak.

'You know as well as I do that I'm the only chance those peo-ple have. I have to make him let go of Schumacher, if nothing else. Those people need one of us.' She disconnected and turned to Adam. 'I have to go back. The Flying Doctors are caught up in a massive accident and fire on the Midwestern Highway.' There was a look of blank horror on his averted face. 'I should have left town days ago. I knew he was insane enough to do something like this.'

At last he looked at her. But his eyes were dead, his body stiff. 'I'd better get dressed.'

She flushed and left the cabin. He'd made her feel like a dismissed hooker.

He had his jeans on when he came out of the cabin. 'Sarge is sending his brother-in-law Henry with the car and boat—every available officer's needed to negotiate with Spencer, though I'm the only one in the area with hostage negotiation training. Others are on their way, but it'll be at least two hours. This time we'll take the straight road back. It doesn't matter who follows us.'

She nodded, refusing to allow herself the luxury of tears. Her presence had put his friends and the townspeople in danger. If those people at the hospital lost their lives, including young Simon, then Jane Larkins, a doctor dedicated to saving life, would be as guilty of the deaths as if she'd set the bomb.

'I should never have come here.'

'Stop saying that. This is not your fault.' He slammed his fist against the doorframe so hard he punched a hole through the rotting wood and ripped his skin. 'I'm no better than Spencer. I put the entire town in danger so I could be alone with you.'

Two of a kind, all right—but this time, the consequences weren't his burden to bear. She snatched back the anguish of the guilt she'd brought on him. 'If I hadn't been here, you wouldn't have had the choice to make.'

'Elly, love, don't do this to yourself.' He tried to take her in his arms, but she shrank back. 'Spencer's the insane one. You can't keep taking the flak for what he does.'

'I can if it's true. By coming here, I put the entire town in danger!'

'I'm a cop, Elly. I knew the danger when I took you into my house … even before that, when I looked up the case. I could have told you to go, but I didn't.'

'No, you couldn't. Not after you found out what happened to me. Guilt and pity clouded your judgement, and I played on that, because I wanted you.' She looked down, but said it anyway, because she had to, just once in her life. 'Because I wanted one happy week with you. I've always been in love with you, Adam.'

He reached for her. 'Elle—'

'He can take me,' she whispered. 'I swear I'll leave this time.'

'God damn it, no!' He gripped her shoulders hard; his face was stern, unyielding. 'For Pete's sake, don't offer that up front.'

She looked at him. The moment of love had passed, and now she felt dead inside. 'We'd better go out. The boat will be here soon.'

'You don't believe me. I'm the trained negotiator, Elly! If he takes you now, he'll—'

'Kill me?' she whispered.

He paled. 'Don't say that.'

She looked at him as if for the last time. 'One of us has to. I'm the one who came here and damned the consequences.'

'Please, Elly, don't do this. *This is not your fault!*'

She kept her face averted.

'Listen to me. I've taken part in negotiations in over twenty sieges and hostage situations. This is all wrong! You do it this way, and no one wins. He'll keep Schumacher to strengthen his power over you—and what he does to you before he kills you won't be pretty. These nutcases are always completely self-absorbed, eager to punish the object of their obsession for what they see as crimes against them. He'll kill you, and it'll be all for nothing. He'll just move onto the next woman, and ruin her life, too.'

She looked at him, swaying a little, but her eyes remained resolute. 'At least it won't be you, or Zoe. That's all I can do.'

He dragged her against him, breathing hard. 'Listen to me. *What he's done is not your fault.* You can't give your life to him!'

She pushed him away. 'I–I've got to—' She barely made it four steps before she started retching.

She felt warm, strong hands holding her up. He waited until she'd purged, then he pulled her against him, sitting against the outer wall of the cabin, rocking her. 'Oh, baby, what he's done to you … what we *all* did. How long has it been since something happened that you didn't take the blame for? Didn't accept the punishment?'

She just looked at him, barely comprehending his words.

'You're leaving,' he murmured. 'You were always going to run, even after we made love.'

She turned away, her heart tearing itself into shreds. 'I always knew we could go nowhere.'

A short silence. 'You're wrong. Neither of us are one-night type of people.'

'I had to be.' She said it hard, and said it straight. 'If Danny gets me, he'll rape me. I couldn't let him be my first.'

'So you chose me over a psychopath. How bloody flattering,' he muttered, hard and bitter.

'No!' she cried. 'I told you I love you, and I meant it! Danny, Rick, Simon, my patients and the men at medical school—all of them only saw what I look like, what I could earn, what Dr Jane Larkins could do for them. But you—you *know* me, you love me. You made my first time everything I could have hoped for.' She smiled at him, knowing this would be her last chance to say it. 'No shame, no guilt and no regrets. You're the love of my life.'

But as ever, he'd seen beneath her words to the truth. 'Oh, bloody hell. *This* was why yesterday and this morning happened. You're still planning to do it. You're going to give yourself to Spencer.'

When she couldn't look at him, he snapped, 'To hell with no regrets! We have something incredible, something I've never known before or will again. You brought me back to life. You made Zoe love you. You said you'd think about the Flying Doctor idea. I gave you my grandmother's ring. You say you love me. Now, because he shows up, you're walking out on us?' His voice cracked. 'Damn it to hell, no! This is all wrong! Why the hell did you come here, make me love you again? Why did you make Zoe love you? Did you ever think there was a chance for us?'

'A chance?' Her head shot up. 'A chance for us? If I made you think that, it was more than you gave me!'

'Really?' he snapped, lifting the hand that bore his grandmother's ring.

'All right, I never thought there was a chance for us until then. Until we came here, whenever we talked, you thought of her. When you kissed me, you compared me to her. When you touched me, you wished she'd have responded like me.'

He whitened. 'That's not true!'

'Isn't it? Then tell me, would you have offered her the same deal you offered me this morning? Set up a base, be my lover, but I don't know about the future? Would you have offered that to her?'

'Damn you. I never said that. I gave you a ring. I called Minyenbarra. I even said I'd invite every bloody Jepson in the phone book to our wedding. You're the one clinging to your belief that I don't care, that I'll leave again because I did *when I was twenty years old*. You might forgive it, but you're never going to forget. You've made me like everyone else who's hurt you. So you return to my life, make me love you again, make Zoe want a mummy—and then you leave us anyway, even after I change my entire world for you. And you even convince yourself you're bloody noble as you do it.'

She closed her eyes. Was he right?

'You say you came to help me—but all you've done to me is what I did to you.' When she shook her head, he snarled, 'Yeah, you are. You're walking out on a little girl who lost her mother. At least I can say I was too young to see the damage I'd done. Can you? As revenge goes, it's pretty damn thorough, isn't it?'

She stared at him, unable to answer. Feeling the truth of his accusation dig into her bones. 'She'll forget me,' she said at last, fumbling with the words. Wanting to believe it.

'As you forgot your father, who left you when you were even younger? As you forgot me?'

The last shred of self-righteousness inside her withered. 'Adam—'

'Don't say it. What you do to me is one thing, but I won't absolve you for what you're doing to my daughter. You think I'm cruel for what I did to you? At least I've tried my damnedest to make up for it! *I'm* not planning to walk out on a little kid who loves and needs me. You say I'm the love of your life, that you came to help, but by leaving, you'll make Zoe think everyone she loves disappears from her life, just like—'

'Sharon?' she snapped, glad of the excuse to be hard and angry.

'I was going to say, just like *you* believe everyone has always done and will always do to you. You'll damage a four-year-old to protect yourself from happiness, in case it hurts later.'

The argument died in her again.

'Coward,' he flung at her. 'You'll risk your life, but you won't risk *living*. You'll run away just like you did at ten, at fifteen. What's your excuse this time?'

She felt her eyes glaze over as she faced the most unpalatable truth of all. 'I suppose that I have no faith in myself. That I don't believe I deserve happiness. That I don't deserve you, and Zoe. All I can do is save you now, and walk away.' When he would have spoken she lifted a hand, gave him a quick smile. 'Please, I have a lot to face today. Can we leave it there, Claudius? I–I need to think.'

He nodded, but lifted her left hand. 'You might want to take the ring off. Spencer won't like it.' He kept watching her, eyes as flat and angry as she'd felt, and she deserved his anger. 'You can always put it on your right hand, to remind you of Grandma. She's safe, isn't she—because she's dead. She can't threaten you with a love you're too afraid to accept.' Throwing the words she'd used about Sharon right back at her.

She flushed as she put the ring on her other hand. She'd done it now. It was well and truly over.

★　★　★

When she heard the sound of a motorboat, she returned to the cabin. 'The boat's almost here. Could you call for an update on my patients? I need to know what I'm up against, so I can prepare. Your hospital doesn't exactly have new millennium technology, you know. Kinda back in the eighties.'

After long moments of a silence that hurt them both, he went outside, punching numbers into the satellite phone.

She stood alone in the cabin, its rustic beauty haunting her soul. Her gaze fell to the rug. The smear of blood whispered what she'd lost—something far more than her virginity. In a sudden feverish need, she grabbed the washbowl, soap and towel. Falling to her knees, she scrubbed at the spot, feeling like Lady Macbeth with all the force of strange, comic tragedy.

A shadow fell across the floor. She knew he was watching her, but couldn't make herself stop scrubbing. 'It's gone.'

'Yes.' She rinsed the towel, lifted the basin and walked past him. She threw the water over a patch of wild dandelions. 'There you go, all gone. End of discussion, end of guilt. Nothing happened. Just old friends, like always.'

He watched her still, tight and brooding. 'No. Elly—'

She bit down hard on her lip. 'Don't, old friend. I hate autopsies. Gruesome things that pull apart the past and don't help the future.'

'I was going to say that Sarge called again. Simon's situation is critical,' he said bluntly. 'One of the men in the bombing died half an hour ago.'

Turning cold to the marrow, she left the cabin without a backward glance.

His footsteps crunched on fallen gum leaves as he came to stand beside her at the river, where she watched for the boat. She turned to him and saw blackness and pain surrounding him like an aura, and hated that she'd been the one to put it there. She'd never expected to mean so much to him—that her leaving would be anything but a relief.

Hands in pockets, voice rough, he said, 'Spencer is allowing firemen and paramedics to work on the victims on the proviso that you come ASAP. The Flying Doctors have contacted Dubbo Base Hospital, but they've got a major multiple MVA at Hay that's blocking the highway. The hospitals at Broken Hill and Mildura are sending doctors and nurses, but there's only one qualified surgeon coming. The others are all tied up in the accident, stabilising patients before transfer.'

Unable to look at him, trapped by guilt every way she looked, she turned back to the river. 'I'm not a surgeon, but surgery was my best practical stint. I did a year in the OR during my residency, and I had plenty of hands-on experience with the RFDS.'

'Sarge had already evacuated more than half the patients in the hospital, but a few critical patients couldn't be moved without doctors to attend them. The Specialist Response Group team is getting nowhere negotiating with Spencer. He's holding Schumacher in front of him, with the wall at his back. And he rigged a dead man's switch on the bomb vest.'

'I knew they'd get nowhere,' she said quietly. 'The major part of his mental illness centres on distrusting everyone in the world but the one he's fixated on.'

'I get it. I was wrong. You told me so.'

She sighed. 'Don't bother. I know you want to make me look at you again, so you can begin your persuasion tactics. You're a trained negotiator, and I've worked with enough resistant patients to know the tricks.'

'All right. Then I'll tell you the truth. You can't help anyone by giving in to his demands. He'll only take more hostages later, kill more people every time he suspects you of anything, and blame the deaths on your suspected infidelity. You'll have given your life to him for nothing.'

Not for nothing. For you, and Zoe. She squinted out over the water, refusing to feel, or to answer the concern in his tone for her. 'The boat's coming.'

She stepped into the water, getting wet to the knees as she slung her bag into the boat. Jonas's brother-in-law Henry reached down to her, lifting her over the side.

Alone in the bow, she faced forward. She held herself apart from the men's terse conversation, cloaking herself in the isolation that had been her protection since childhood, and bracing herself for what must come. The daughter of endless generations of nomads in a harsh, fragile, beautiful and unforgiving land, she knew there must sometimes be a sacrifice of one to save many.

It was time.

CHAPTER
19

The ride to the hospital was tense and silent. When they got to the car, Adam told Henry to go home before slamming the portable siren on the roof and driving north like a maniac, careening around anyone in his way. Rows of parked vehicles pointed the way to the hospital: fire trucks, ambulances, the media; the cars of terrified relatives of the injured, desperately waiting for help.

At the hospital, Elly leaped from the car and found herself before an unbroken line of cops, fire fighters and paramedics. Jonas took her arm, leading her to the door.

'What's the latest, Jonas?'

'We lost another one.' His voice was terse. 'Two are still serious, one critical. The paramedics and firemen are doing all they can. A team is on the way from the Mildura Base Hospital.'

'Simon?' Adam asked.

'Stable for now, thank the lord. The nurses outdid themselves with some patches and a machine of some sort.'

Elly sighed. One piece of good news, at least. 'Is everything ready for surgery? Is everyone prepped?'

'A nurse told me two of the critical passengers have head wounds, the serious patient has a compound fracture of his thigh that's still bleeding, and severe concussion. One's stable enough to wait. They have a nurse specialling her.'

She kept heading for the doors, so fast Jonas had trouble keeping up. 'Where is he?'

'Outside the operating rooms.'

She nodded. 'Are the team bringing surgical equipment? There won't be enough sterile packs, saline solutions or blood. I'll need—'

The doors opened for her as she started to run through.

Rick stood in the doorway of the ER wearing a flak jacket and helmet, his face set hard. His gun was cocked and ready to shoot. 'Elly, come with me.'

'Don't be a fool, Mendham. Those people need her help,' Jonas snapped. 'Let Elly go. You can fix any problems you have with her later.'

Rick gave his boss a hard look. 'I'm the only one with a hope of getting through to Spencer and protecting Elly at the same time.'

Adam stepped forward. 'Rick, let Elly pass. A dozen lives depend on her now, and I have to negotiate with Spencer.'

'Not you—me. Elly, put these on.' Rick picked up another flak jacket and a helmet, and tossed them at her. 'I'm not letting my sister walk into a life and death situation without me.'

Elly blinked. Something in the way he'd said it … She shook her head. She had to remain focused on the hours of surgery ahead. 'Rick, please, you have to let me go.'

Rick tossed her an odd smile. 'That's what you always said when I held you too long when we were kids. "Ricky-jim, let me go! You're squashing me!"'

A collective gasp came from all around, but Rick looked only at Elly, who was gaping at him. 'Do you remember me now, Janie-jan?'

The long-forgotten nickname made the odd sense of almost terrifying protectiveness she'd felt from Rick from the first day click at last. Looking at his dark, handsome face, the resemblance became clear, days too late. And she *remembered*. Her mouth opened and closed, making helpless sounds. At last she croaked, 'Ricky-jim? M–my *brother* Ricky?'

'At last she remembers me. I've been dropping hints for days, but would you listen?' He shook his head with a wistful smile.

She threw her arms around him, amazed, afraid to let go in case he vanished. Loving her real name for the first time in a long time, because she'd found the one person with the right to use it. 'But how? Why didn't you *tell* me?'

'Would you have listened?' He laughed at her when she bit her lip. 'We'll talk later, Janie-jan,' he said softly. 'We've got work to do.'

'Ricky … oh, Ricky-jim …'

'Flak jacket, Janie,' he said softly. 'Obey big brother now. We can hug all you want later.'

Caught between laughter, panic and tears, she kissed his cheek and obeyed him; but when he moved away, she stepped with him. Unable to let him go, even for a second. *My brother…*

With a little smile, Rick looked at Adam and Jonas, who were both still staring. 'Sorry to keep my relationship to Elly quiet until now, Sarge, but I'm sure you get why I did.' He glanced at Adam. 'I know you have more experience than me, but Spencer will accept my authority without feeling threatened. He'll accept that she came here to me, not you. It'll keep her safer if you stay out of it. I just need ten minutes.'

Adam closed his mouth, and tilted his head. 'Why?'

'You'll see.'

Slowly, Adam nodded. 'We're going to talk after this, mate.'

Rick punched his shoulder. 'You'd better be wanting to ask me a question … mate.'

Adam thumped Rick's shoulder in return, and they grinned at each other.

The other cops stepped back. If it was the rule to keep family away from hostage situations, Rick was right: he was the only one with any chance of talking Danny Spencer down without arousing the manic jealousy that led him to kill.

'Ready,' Elly said. Amazed, thrilled, almost unable to believe it—she'd all but forgotten anyone else was there, even Adam. The strangest, most beautiful miracle of her life: the brother who'd vanished when she was three years old had returned to her at the moment she needed him the most. Ready to protect her to the death. *My brother. My family.*

Rick clipped the helmet onto her head and took her hand. Still not quite believing he wouldn't vanish if she let go, she clung to him.

'Adam, stay out here,' Rick tossed over his shoulder. 'The way you look at her is too obvious. The rest of you, keep six feet back.'

He led Elly into the heart of the small hospital, murmuring soft instructions all the way.

A scream split the air the moment they reached the hallway to the OR. 'Let her go! She's *mine!*'

A man in priest's robes stood at the end of the double row of chairs leading to the swinging doors of the hospital's two operating rooms. In his late twenties, now red haired, the deep teak skin somehow fairer, with startling grey eyes, his nose reset—Danny seemed to be someone else, apart from those eyes, and a mouth that lost its generosity in possessiveness. But this time his mouth didn't curl in the slow, cruel smile of ownership, but turned down in fury. He held Dr Schumacher around the neck in front of him, a gun aimed at the older man's head, a remote detonator with a dead-man's switch held between two fingers of the arm holding the doctor.

'I said let her go, copper pig, or I'll blow this place to bits! She's *mine*!'

When she'd have pulled away to save him, Rick held her tighter. He smiled at the madman and nodded, keeping his other hand, the one with the cocked gun in it, behind him. 'Hello, Danny, isn't it? I'm Janie's big brother, Rick.'

That stopped Danny halfway down Suspicion Street. He peered at Rick, then Elly. He blinked, shook his head, stared again. For the first time, she understood what was in Danny's mind. The resemblance was strong enough to make her want to kick herself. She, who'd been looking for her brother all her life, had never even considered Rick's sense of possessive protectiveness as being family oriented.

'She doesn't have a brother,' Danny croaked at last.

'Our father took me away when I was five. Janie was three. Then Dad died. I lost my family, just like you did. Like Janie did. We've only just found each other again.' Rick took a step forward. Releasing Elly's hand, he fished two folded documents from his pocket.

'What are you doing?' Danny barked.

After another step, Rick bent down, placing the documents a metre from Danny. Then he stepped back. 'See for yourself.'

Danny jerked Dr Schumacher around, keeping the rifle trained on the old man's head. 'Pick them up, and show them to me.' He bent at the knees as the doctor collected the papers, keeping himself hidden behind his captive.

Danny scanned the birth certificates. When he looked up, his gaze was strangely hollow. 'All right.' He seemed arrested by the news, not even looking at Elly. 'Why are you showing me these? What do you want?'

Rick looked puzzled. 'What do you mean, what do I want? I want the same thing you'd want if Janie was your sister.'

Danny blinked. Frowned, eyes clouding with confusion. 'But she's not my sister.'

'No.' Rick kept his voice smooth, moving his hidden hand a little. Elly saw her brother's gun enter his pocket. 'She's *my* sister, my only family, and you frightened her. I need to protect her.'

'I'd never hurt her!' Danny's expression turned wild. 'You're not her brother. You're a copper pig. This is a mock-up. You—'

'No, Danny.'

Danny's head swung around to Elly, eyes hungry and despairing. Wanting to believe with a child's fear and hope.

'It's true,' she said. 'Do you remember I told you while you were trapped in the car that I lost my father and brother when I was little, like you lost your parents?'

Slowly, Danny nodded. Licking his lips, so lost and insecure, but his hands held true to the gun and the remote of the homemade bombs covering his body.

'Look at him, Danny. Look at our faces. Rick is my brother.' She hugged Rick's arm, and followed the instructions her brother had given her as they walked through the hospital. 'I came to him when you frightened me.'

Danny's eyes unfocused, widening with suspicion and disbelief. 'N–no … Granddad told me you came to that other guy, the one with the kid …'

'Why would I come for a foster brother, when my *real* brother was here? I was only three when he left. I'd forgotten him—but Rick remembered me. He contacted me through the Aboriginal and Islander Medical Commission a few weeks ago. Rick asked me to come to him; it was a coincidence that Adam was here at all. It's Rick I ran to.'

'But … Granddad said you stayed with the other guy …'

Softly, Rick said, 'And your granddad has never lied to you or hurt you, has he, Danny?'

Danny stared at him, eyes becoming unfocussed.

Rick nudged her, and she said the next thing. 'I came to Rick because he's my brother, because he wants to protect me.'

'*I'll* protect you,' Danny said in pathetic eagerness, eyes alight, a pitiful echo of Zoe's excitement when Elly had told her about the picnic. An insane child distracted by an unspoken promise, while wearing an armoury strong enough to kill hundreds. 'I wouldn't frighten you!'

A subtle squeeze told her to keep quiet. She squeezed back.

'Janie loved that puppy and kitten you hurt.' Rick spoke in a gentle but stern manner.

Danny blinked. 'A dog and cat?' He laughed, as if it was the last thing he'd expected to hear. 'Animals are on earth to serve us. You don't *love* them. They'd fulfilled their purpose—I'd come for her. We were together.'

'Do you know anything about our family?' Rick asked quietly. 'Our mother taught us symbiosis with animals. I believe that. *Janie* believes that. She takes after our mum.'

Shaken, Elly stared at Rick. How did he remember so much that she didn't?

'You don't know Janie,' Danny scoffed, but now his body shook. The rifle moved with it. Dr Schumacher's eyes turned watery with terror. 'You've only been with her a few days. I've known her two years!'

'I'm her family. Of course I know her. She always loved animals, even when she was very little. If you found your mother again, would you remember things about her, Danny?' Rick asked, so gentle he was almost crooning. 'After your grandfather ran her off Gundawin, she missed you so much. Wouldn't you spend all the time talking to her, finding out what she loves?'

'*My grandfather did not run that slut off Gundawin!*' Spencer screamed, sweat beading on his forehead, finger on the remote shaking. 'She ran off with a stationhand and forgot me!'

'It's not true.' From his other pocket, Rick pulled out a letter. 'Your mother never had another man, Danny. This is a copy of one of a thousand letters she wrote you. Your grandfather burned most of them, but she never stopped writing. The housekeeper at Gundawin—Mrs Rowntree, is it?—kept a few of your mother's letters back, and sent them to me to give you.'

As Danny's mouth fell open, Rick said gently, 'Your mother's on her way here right now, Danny. She'd do anything to see you, to be with you again.'

Elly had to hold in her own stare of amazement. Rick—*my brother*—hadn't just worked on his negotiation skills, he'd prepared for this day with a thoroughness that touched her. He'd told her the truth from the start: he'd do anything to protect her. He must have come to Macks Lake to wait for her. For the first time in a lifetime, the void in her filled—she had someone to truly belong to. Brother and sister, blood and history—and a man's love she never had to question. Someone who brought out a love in her that would never frighten her again. Someone she could trust with her life.

'Your mother's on her way, Danny,' Rick said again, when Danny didn't answer.

'I don't want anything from her!'

Rick sighed gently. 'I haven't seen my mother since I was five. I know that if she were still alive, I'd do anything to see her again. I wouldn't want to die wondering if she loved me, *missed* me. I'd want to know why she didn't want me, if she did leave.' A quiet, thoughtful answer, and if it mirrored all Danny's pain, it was also exactly her thoughts about her father. Rick was more than her brother: he was the mirror of all she'd felt in her life.

Don't let me lose my brother now I've found him. Please.

Danny's jaw dropped further. His tortured gaze fixed on Rick with the kind of haunting doubt she'd known since childhood: *Why didn't my runaway parent take me?* Rick was leading everyone in the corridor down an emotional path, but Danny most of all. Piece by piece, he was pulling down Danny's paranoid defences, weakening his resistance. Her brother was a master at instinctive negotiation. Worried sick for her patients, she could only hope Rick could bring this to an end soon.

'Once you've read these, we should talk.' Rick held out the letters. 'I'm the head of the Larkins family. Talk to me first. Let Janie help the people in the OR.'

'You're still a cop.' Quick as lightning, Danny's expression darkened; he held the gun to Dr Schumacher's head. 'She's *mine*. Janie, come to me, and this doctor can help everyone.'

'Danny, I've met your mother—Lorena,' Rick said quietly. 'Your grandfather kept her away from you all these years, but she'd like to meet you.' From his pocket, he held up one more thing: a photo. 'She's outside the hospital now, waiting for you.'

'Stop it! Stop it! Granddad didn't—' Danny's eyes unfocused, turning inward. 'He … he wouldn't …' Moments passed agonisingly slow, while Danny worked it out. Looking back to a life that had led him to this moment, with a dozen guns trained on him.

At last he spoke. 'Mama …?'

'She'll be here any moment. She's coming for you.' Words soft as a dream, filled with meaning.

Danny closed his eyes. Then, just like elastic snapping, he woke up, turned to Elly. He kept his gun aimed at Dr Schumacher's head as dozen guns trained on him. 'I don't know her. I don't need her. Come to me, Janie.'

Elly's head lifted. No matter how many guns they aimed at him, none of these other people mattered. Rick had done all he could. He wouldn't risk Dr Schumacher's life, and nobody else had a hope of talking him down. This was her fight—it was time to put into practice the instructions Rick had whispered to her on the walk down the corridor.

She made herself answer, willing the pounding in her heart to slow. 'I don't like men who hurt people, Danny. I don't like *you* when you do things like this.'

Danny's face mottled. 'Come to me, and the nice doctor can save lives!' He jerked the thin old man by the neck, making him gasp in pain and terror.

She refused to move. 'He's not a surgeon, Danny. If these people die when I could have saved them, I'll never forgive you, will *never* love you—and that's something you can't control with a gun or a bomb.'

'You won't have to,' he answered, with a little oblique smile— and she knew what he had planned. It made perfect sense to a man who believed Romeo and Juliet was a true story—and deep down, it was what she'd expected since he'd killed her puppy and kitten.

All abusers are cowards, deep down … hiding their crazy fears from the world …

Her head lifted. 'No, Danny. I won't let you touch me. Not after what you did to me last time, what you did to all those people on the way here. I'm not a whore to be used that way. You have blood on your hands.'

'It's your fault. You weren't there!'

Jonas gasped, 'Elly, you're breaking all the rules of—'

'Let her go, Sarge,' Rick murmured to his boss. 'She knows him. She knows what she's doing.'

Another murmur came from far behind, soft as a breath. How she heard it she didn't know. Maybe he didn't even speak it aloud. 'Remember what he is, Elle.'

She sighed in tension and relief. Adam knew it was vital to remain in the background, but he was here. If Danny sniffed out the slightest hint of anything beyond a kid's history between them, someone would die. Adam trusted her to get this right.

Her eyes trained on her foe, she took a step towards him. Hundreds of lives in the balance, and Adam's words made sense. *Remember what he is: all abusers are cowards.* 'You don't scare me anymore, Danny.'

'I'm tired of these games you play with me, Janie,' Danny snarled, finger tightening on that remote. 'I'll punish you if you keep talking like that.'

Elly, be careful!

She felt the cry in Adam's head, felt his fear for her, but she willed him to remain quiet. Her concentration had to stay on Danny, or this would escalate into a bloodbath. She already had enough injured people on her conscience.

'Punish me for telling the truth, Danny—or for not being scared of you anymore?'

Danny blinked. 'Stop it! You went away with that copper pig, the one with the kid! *He's* not your brother! *That's* not the truth. You can't talk to me without respect!' He gave Dr Schumacher a vicious shove, pushing him to his knees and forcing the rifle into his mouth. The poor man sagged in fear, his eyes begging her to help him.

'She went with me, Danny,' Rick said softly. 'Do you think I'd trust my precious sister to anyone but me?'

Danny threw him a wild glance. 'No. The people Granddad sent to Longa Station said she was with the other guy.'

'The Mirakis are liars,' Rick said, harder now. 'They want to see Janie hurt. Your granddad should never have sent people like them here, people who want revenge on her.'

'Granddad ...' One foot began to twitch. 'They're better than the other one. All she can say is my Janie's a slut! I hate her!'

'No, Mrs Collins isn't nice,' Rick agreed without surprise. 'Your granddad should have sent nicer people to help you.'

'Granddad! *He* doesn't care about anything but—' Sudden anger took over his face. 'Stop it! He's lying to us, Danny! We're in control here!'

Elly watched Danny's face changing as the more dangerous personality she'd only glimpsed when he'd slit her pets' throats came to the fore. What was the procedure for dealing with this?

'What's your name?' Rick asked softly. 'The one who's taking over?'

Danny blinked, eyes clearing. 'No! Don't talk to him. Leave him out of this, or everyone will end up dead!'

'Because he has his finger on the dead-man's switch, and the pistol?'

Danny nodded, eyes frantic.

'He's slipping out, Danny.' Rick didn't move, barely seemed to breathe as he spoke. 'He's coming closer all the time, isn't he? You've tried so hard to control him, but he's here now.'

Another nod, big-eyed, lips sucked in.

'What's his name?'

Like a child in the dark, Danny whispered, 'Monster. Don't make him angry ... please ...' Both feet twitched now.

'It's when you're alone he's at his worst, isn't it?'

When Danny nodded yet again, Rick took one small, careful step forward. 'You can do this, Danny. You can win. You're not alone.'

'That's why I came! I can't do it without Janie! She's the only one who makes Monster go to sleep.' Danny lifted the switch, his eyes different. Confident. 'No, she doesn't. Is she stopping me now? I'm the strong one here. I know what to do.'

'Do you, Monster?' Elly started walking toward Danny. 'You think you're in control by hurting people? I don't like it when you scare people, and hurt them. And you won't hurt me. Danny's a good person. He won't let you hurt me.'

'I hurt you the last time you defied me!' he screamed.

'What, you mean this?' She pushed the shirt aside to reveal the scar, ignoring the fury boiling in her brother's stance as he saw it. 'It changed my life, Monster, but not the way you think. I'm not scared any more. I won't run. I saved Danny's life, worked night and day to help you both stay alive. *Both of you love me.* You won't use me to get revenge on your mother.'

'Shut up!' he screamed, in a frenzy. 'Don't talk about that filthy harlot. I'm gonna do you over like the slut you are, and then you're gonna die.'

'Is your mother a harlot? Can you prove that? Or is that what your granddad told you? And how can you call me a slut? I didn't leave you when you were hurt and needed me.'

Danny blinked, his expression filled with too-bright confusion, personalities competing in his eyes. 'I don't know! *I don't know!*' He jerked Dr Schumacher by the hair. 'You need to know who's a man!'

Elly shook her head. 'I could never love or respect a man who enjoys hurting people.'

'A real man has to show a woman who's in control!'

'Your grandfather was wrong. That's why he was never happy, Danny,' she said softly. 'He hurt women because he couldn't make them love him. Monster's making the same mistake as your grand-dad always has. I don't want a boss. I want a man I can give my whole heart to, a man I can respect.'

Still he held the gun on the doctor, but his breathing was uneven. 'I can't stop it until you help me, Janie! If you want to save people, you have to make Monster go away!'

Poor, warped Danny. 'I'm not qualified to make Monster go—and he's breaking all the oaths I took to save life. I could never stay with you until you get help.'

'You will save me!' Danny made gibbering sounds, and then the fierce, bright-eyed Monster took over. 'I'll make you do it. *Get out here, Jepson!*'

A slight commotion, and Adam was beside her in a flak jacket and helmet, a gun cocked and ready in his hand, his gaze trained on Danny. 'I'm here.'

Elly felt her knees buckle. *No*, her mind cried. *Not you, Adam. Not you!*

Rick held her up. 'Stay strong,' he whispered. Slowly, she nodded.

Adam pushed her aside, mouthing something to Rick, who nodded and moved back.

After one small, shaking step, she couldn't go further. Rick drew her backward, holding her hand. She clung to her brother as Adam spoke, quiet and sincere.

'Danny, if you do this, it will destroy any chance of making Janie love you.'

'Shut up!' He kept the gun poised by the doctor's mouth, but pointed the remote at Adam. 'That woman said Janie's done it with you.'

She heard laughter in Adam's voice. 'What does Jen Collins know? She's angry and jealous because she has a crush on me, and I rejected her. You know Janie, Danny. Men fall in love with her because she's so giving and strong, but she's so innocent. All she ever wanted was a brother, not a lover.'

Danny's eyes swung to Elly, then back to Adam, frowning as he thought about it. 'She said Janie's been spending all her time with you!'

'Of course she has—and with Rick. We're all a family. We love each other.' As Danny's face turned dark, Adam lowered his gun, and went on as if he'd said nothing wrong. 'We've been like brother and sister since we were kids. She came to my wedding. My wife knew her.'

'Y–your wife?' Danny faltered, his gaze swinging back and forth as if watching an invisible tennis match. 'But she's dead.'

Adam nodded, his whole bearing taut. 'Yes, but I still love my wife. Janie knows that. All she wanted in coming here was the love and protection of her brothers.'

Elly had to force herself to show no emotion when Danny's gaze swung to her. She only nodded. Danny turned back to Adam, ferreting out the truth.

Adam nodded. 'Would you like to see my wife?' Putting his pistol on the ground, he fished out his wallet slowly showing Danny every move he made. He held up a family picture, the only one with little Zack. 'This is my Sharon, and my children, Zoe and Zack. Aren't they beautiful?'

'Janie knows?' Danny couldn't stop staring at the picture. His voice veered between disbelief and hope. His balance, never strong, was wavering. 'She knows you love your wife?'

'Of course. She's always known.' He folded the photo back into his wallet. 'I know how it feels to lose the only woman I'll ever love, Danny,' he said in a tone of quiet conviction. 'No one can hope to understand that the way we do. Others, they see a beautiful, wonderful woman like Janie, and don't believe any man can love her as I do—like a best friend, or brother.'

A momentary veering back to suspicion. 'She has a brother.' Danny tilted his head at Rick.

'Now she does. The whole time I knew her, she didn't. She's only just found Rick again. He's my closest friend here. We've all become family.' His voice turned indulgent. 'Would you like to see Janie as she was when I first met her, when she was eleven?'

One side of Danny's mouth quirked up. He nodded.

He fished out the other photo from his wallet, showing it to Danny. 'Look at her. Up her tree, just like always. That's where I met her. She didn't trust anyone. She only came down to pat my dog.'

Danny chuckled and nodded, startling the distant onlookers. 'That's Janie. She finds it hard to trust any man, because her father and brother left her.'

The words shook Elly to her core. Was she so transparent even a madman could see her clearly? Rick's hand tightened on hers, saying what she needed to hear without words. *Your life has changed, Janie.* She gulped down the familiar sense of abandonment, clinging to Rick's hand in return. But the seesawing of her emotions made it hard to concentrate on ending this situation.

'You're so right, Danny. She was always running away, or pushing people away. Look at her here, with her foot out. She was kicking me that day, because she was so angry with me. Scrawny wild little thing she was, always disappearing. It took ages for her to say more than "hi" to me. We eventually became best friends, which is why she came to my wedding. Why she came here when she was scared. Who else could take care of her but her brothers? Someone here has been hurting Janie. They hit her with a tree branch, slashed her tyres and called her a slut. Look at her lip, all swollen.'

Danny stared at Elly's mouth, his face turning tight with fury.

'Do you think Rick would trust any other man with her but me, and vice versa? You and I know we have to protect our women. I kept Janie safe and pure for the right man.'

He took another step closer as Danny's defiance and fury began to crumble, and turned to amazement and hope. Then his face darkened again, and Elly could see the character called Monster taking over.

'You were hiding her from us!'

Adam nodded. 'Of course I was. I thought it was you hurting her. But you weren't even here. It was Jen Collins, the Mirakis—the people your grandfather paid attacked her, Danny. He paid them to hurt her, and terrify her.'

'Granddad,' Danny snarled, his eyes hardening. 'He doesn't want us, just another boy to own and screw over.'

'I'll only talk to you, Danny.' Adam kept his gaze on Danny. 'Monster doesn't know Janie. Only you do. Only you will look after Janie.'

As she watched, Danny's fury melted and more hope came; with it, the other personality retreated. Though Adam was no psychiatrist, his negotiation skills were working. He was keeping Danny happy, the key to restraining the other personality.

'I will,' Danny said eagerly. 'If she stops running away! I can't stop him when she makes him angry. She has to obey.'

Adam made a clicking sound with his tongue. 'Janie has a habit of running away when she's sad or scared. Don't take it personally. She wouldn't have saved your life if she didn't care, would she?'

'She said she doesn't love me!' Danny's voice was a wail, a child falling into a nightmare. As the negative emotions came forward, the other personality stepped up. His finger tightened on the trigger of his remote, just a notch, and Elly held her breath. The nasty little boy who took pleasure in creating havoc and death was coming back, his focus all on Adam.

'Can men ever work women out, Danny?' Adam put a subtle emphasis on the name. 'No means yes to them, and yes means no—but Janie isn't like that. She ran because you really scared her last time. Cutting her made her think you never loved her at all.'

'But—but it was a sign of love. She knows it means I love her!'

'Who believes cutting a woman means love—Danny or Monster? Or Granddad?' he asked, very softly. 'Because Janie doesn't know it. It hurt and terrified her.'

'*What?*'

Uncertainty filled the crazed eyes—and, as Elly's lungs refused to work, Adam put the killing blow together.

He spoke very softly now. 'Janie lost her parents very young, like you did, Danny. She lived on the road until she was ten, then she moved around from family to family. She grew up feeling lonely and unloved. So she doesn't always know when someone loves her, or if they're using her. Janie seems so strong, but beneath that, she really needs stability and love. A man who won't frighten her, or offer her less than the home and family she deserves. Right now she thinks you don't love her—that you just want the doctor, or the beautiful woman, not the real Janie.'

Abracadabra. The lust and fury left Danny's eyes as they swivelled to Elly, with that sickening gaze of hope. 'Janie, you know I love you … don't you?'

She only had a minute. Keeping her gaze trained on the suicide vest, she hoped to God she was right in what she saw, because hundreds of lives depended on it. She felt Adam willing her to say the right words. Rick squeezed her hand, a brother's faith. *You can do it.*

'When you hurt me, when you called me those nasty names, it felt just like the people who hurt me when I was a child. When you hurt my little fur-babies, I thought, *He hates me …*'

Adam stepped back as they watched Danny overtake Monster. The gun and remote in his hands slipped an inch. 'Oh, Janie, Janie—'

Her head lowered. She peered at him from under half-closed lashes. 'I run away when I feel scared or unloved. I can't help it.'

Danny's whole face softened; his hands loosened still more. 'Janie,' he whispered with cloying adoration. 'You'll never feel unloved again. We'll be together forever!'

She repressed a shudder, and even managed to smile at him. She could almost hear Adam and Rick's thoughts, *Drop your weapons, Spencer. Drop your weapons …*

A nurse ran from the direction of the ER, and whispered a few urgent words in Jonas's ear. Elly closed her eyes, silently begging, *Don't say it …*

'Elly, one man's situation has become critical. He's haemorrhaging.'

Danny's eyes took on the fierce glitter again, and his finger tightened on the dead-man's switch. Monster was here. 'Yeah, *Elly.* He's gonna die if you don't do something. So come to us, *Janie*, and we'll let the nice doctor go. He's the only chance he has.'

She took a deep breath, let go of Rick's hand and walked to Danny.

'Elly, don't go to him. He'll kill you!'

She looked right through Adam, her eyes distant, as if their shared past, their night and morning of love never existed, then she turned back to Danny. 'Let him go,' she commanded as she reached Danny's side. 'I won't come to you until he's safe. Until you put down the remote.'

But as Danny released the old man, he grabbed Elly, making sure her body covered his from the aim of the police guns. Dr Schumacher stumbled away without a backward glance.

Cocking the rifle, holding the remote still, he dragged her into his free arm, pointing the muzzle at the back of her head, both personalities merging for a moment of triumph. 'I knew you'd come to me, Janie. We belong together. So kiss me, baby. And then we'll die together.'

She said quietly, 'I won't kiss you until the remote's gone, Danny. There are small children in this hospital. They're as young as we were when we lost our families. It wouldn't be fair.'

A slow blink, as his personalities balanced on a knife's point.

She dropped her head to his shoulder. 'Please, be my Danny now,' she murmured, gentle and meek. 'I know you'll give me my last wish. I could love a man who would save children. The gun is for us.'

With a long sigh he moved slightly away from her and, keeping the gun trained on her, he switched off the remote and put it carefully down on a plastic chair to his left. 'Janie …?'

Her eyes filled with true gratitude. 'Thank you, Danny. A real man knows when to give.' She stepped back into his arms.

'Kiss me, baby,' Danny whispered.

She obeyed him without hesitation, her left arm hooking around his neck, her right hand fumbling in her jeans pocket beneath the flak jacket, as Danny's finger tightened on the trigger.

The horrible kiss went on, Danny's free hand roaming her body. She heard him growling low in his throat, growing slowly angrier as the kiss didn't arouse him.

It's almost time—wait, just wait.

Behind her, she heard Rick whisper, 'Dive tackle. Now.'

No, Ricky, Adam, please! I can't lose you! She kissed Danny in desperation—but she'd failed; Monster came out to play with Danny's anger. And then, as Adam and Rick dived at Danny, Monster turned the rifle.

Adam dropped like a stone at Elly's feet.

A glance showed blood pooling, rather than pumping, out— thank God. It wasn't the carotid artery, probably the jugular vein. His life was still in danger, but he wouldn't die soon. Rick rolled onto Adam's body to protect him from a second shot, hands going to the wound.

'Get off him,' Danny roared. 'I don't want to hurt you.' He looked at Elly, and she knew her kiss hadn't fooled him—and shooting Adam had aroused him. 'I'll do you now, Janie. Your boyfriend's gonna die just before we do.'

With narrowed eyes, she looked only at Danny, spoke only to Danny. 'You let Monster out so you don't have to take responsibility for hurting my friend. But you *are* Monster. And he disgusts me.'

'I'm in control here!' He bent back for the dead-man's switch.

She whipped out the scalpel she'd hidden in her jeans pocket, taken from her kit on the way into town. Its honed edge glittered in the ward lights as she slashed through the shoulder of the home-made suicide vest and into his right arm. Cutting into tendon and nerves, rendering the arm useless.

Danny gasped as suddenly nerveless fingers dropped his weapon, his whole arm shaking. Pleading eyes looked at her, a child to its mother. 'Janie, no … not you …'

Weary, sad, hopeless, she whispered, 'You *are* Monster.' And she pushed the knife into the other arm, same movement.

He gasped and swayed, both arms useless. 'No … not you, Janie. Not you … there's nobody else who cares … nobody …'

'Danny, my darling, please don't say that. I'm here.'

His hands hanging at his side, dripping blood, Danny choked, staring past Elly in disbelief. A middle-aged woman, with startling blue eyes behind glasses, thin and somehow ragged despite her neat clothing and greying hair pulled back in a ponytail, stepped forward from among the police.

'Danny, I've missed you so much. My beloved boy.'

Danny visibly shook, either from the wounds or the shock of seeing his mother again at this critical time.

Elly dropped to the floor beside Rick, who was holding Adam's wound. She pulled off her flak jacket and handed it to him. 'Pressure bandage, Ricky, but be careful. Don't block his breathing.'

The police moved in as Rick used the flak jacket to bear gentle weight onto the wound. He looked up at the officers, shaking his head. He mouthed, 'Ricochets. Hold off.'

'Mendham's right,' Jonas said, just as softly.

Still the police kept their armoury of weapons trained on Danny, ready for a chance that wouldn't hurt anyone in the room.

Danny kept staring at the woman moving toward him. 'I don't know you! Go away!'

The woman smiled and softly sang, 'Incy-wincy spider climbed up the water spout ...'

Danny seemed mesmerised. As she continued to sing, he swayed side to side, mouthing the words, fingers twitching, attempting but failing to create the shapes of the nursery rhyme. Blood dripped to the floor from both sides of his body.

When the song finished, the woman said, 'Do you remember we sang that together every night? You wouldn't go to sleep without it. Did your grandfather sing it to you after he forced me away from Gundawin?'

Blinking hard and fast, Danny came back to the present. 'You left me. You *left me*!'

'No, Danny,' came the woman's answer, gentle and firm. 'Your grandfather hated me, as he hates all women. Because he'd lost your father, he wanted you to himself.'

'You're lying,' Danny said, but his voice shook.

'If you want me to say I'm lying, I will, but I don't think it will make you feel any better. He hurt you, didn't he? Just as he hurt me. Did he brand you with his whip, too?' She pulled back her sleeves, showing a multitude of white, crisscrossing scars.

His mouth hung open. He tried to move his arms, but they were useless. After a few moments, he nodded. 'Prove this isn't a trap,' he rasped. 'Prove you're my mother.'

The woman held out a photo. 'Here we are, darling, the day you rode your first horse on Gundawin. Do you remember that day? Your grandfather threw you on. You were so scared, you cried for me. So I rode a horse beside you, and we held hands the whole time.'

He whispered, 'And Granddad was so angry. Said you were making a sissy of me.'

'But I didn't care what he said. You're my precious boy, and I protected you, just as your father would have. Just as I will now,' Lorena Spencer said, quiet but full of love.

Danny stood transfixed. He didn't even notice that Elly was at his feet, working with Rick to save Adam's life. She heard the gentle flow of words from above her without really registering them.

'Did he force you to kill animals when he was angry, like he tried to with your father? Or did he kill them all, and tell everyone it was you doing it?'

The corridor was silent. Police held their guns and waited for a chance. Rick's hands grew slick with Adam's blood, while Elly held Adam's throat at either side of the wound to slow the blood flow.

'He blamed your father for his violence, too,' Lorena's voice said gently. 'Your father left Gundawin at twenty—and he met me in Melbourne four years later. I was an only child. I wanted to have an extended family. It took two years, but I convinced Neil to make peace with his father after you were born. It's the greatest regret of my life.'

Danny's eyes started to close. 'Go on,' he said, in an uneven voice.

'Jeremiah ran me off Gundawin before I could take you with me. I wanted you to be safe from him.'

Danny seemed to have forgotten Elly existed. The child forever seeking approval, battering at the gate of belonging, belief and love without restrictions, had found it opened at last. For the first time, the door to Danny Spencer's nightmare life was opening.

'I left Gundawin three years ago ...' The question was beyond plaintive: he was imploring now.

Hurry, Elly begged Lorena Spencer in silence. *Adam doesn't have long.*

'Your grandfather had one of his crony's companies hire me, then he accused me of embezzlement. I served three years. I was released a week ago, thanks to evidence given at the parole hearing by Senior Constable Mendham. Then he brought me here to wait for you. I never stole a cent from that man, Danny. And I'm not anything else he's accused me of being.' She sighed. 'I've been alone for twenty-five years, longing for you every day. Your grandfather made me suffer all these years for not being the kind of faithless woman he expected me to be.'

'You're here,' Danny whispered.

'I am. I came for you, Danny. I've always loved you, and I always will. No matter what. You're my beloved boy, my son.'

Elly felt her hands slipping in the blood pooling around them. This was it. If Lorena couldn't connect to Danny, Adam would die.

'What are you doing?' Danny demanded, when Lorena stood in front of him, arms open.

'Waiting,' Lorena said simply. 'You've been forced into too many things, Danny. I'm aching to hold you, but you tell me what you want.'

His eyes clouded over and his lip quivered. 'Mama.' He pronounced it as a small child would; with love, need, confusion, fury.

Lorena stepped up to Danny, put her arms around him, around the bloodied shoulders, and held them, creating a makeshift pressure bandage. 'I've dreamed of this moment for twenty-five years.' She stood up on tiptoe, kissed his cheek and mouth, so gently. 'I'm sorry I couldn't save you from him, my darling. I'm sorry I couldn't come to you before. But I'll never leave you now we're together. Never. No matter what.'

The crowd in the corridor held its breath. None dared move, or make a sound.

Elly looked at Rick. Then she turned to Schumacher, who was sitting in a plastic seat in front of the OR doors, staring in disbelief at the mad tableau before them all. *Gurney. Stat.*

He got up in shaky silence and went through the well-oiled swinging doors.

Danny lowered his head until it rested on his mother's shoulder. 'Mama.' A world of suffering in a single word, all that Jeremiah Spencer had conditioned him not to say, not to want.

Lorena touched his face. 'Darling Danny. Beautiful Danny. Mama's here, Mama's here.'

The sobs began, forced from his very soul: the torment that could never be erased.

Jonas stepped forward. 'Come on, son, your mother and I can look after your wounds.'

Danny blinked. 'Janie ...'

Lorena Spencer pressed his wounds with her hands. She said, 'Come, my darling, I'll fix your wound. She doesn't love you as I do. We don't need her. She's not worthy of you.'

Surrounded by police, Danny left with his mother without a single glance at Elly.

CHAPTER
20

For a second Elly just looked at the half-empty room. The blood on the ground, on the chairs, was the only evidence that her worst nightmare had been real.

The blood on her hands, on Rick's hands, was the evidence that it wasn't over yet.

'Where's that damn gurney? I need a sterile bandage, now!'

Two orderlies burst through the OR doors, accompanied by a nurse. On Elly's count, they got Adam on a board and lifted him onto the trolley. 'Keep holding the wound, Ricky, all the way into the OR. We've got to stop the bleeding as soon as possible.' She looked up at the paramedics crowding around. 'Tell triage to get the OR fully prepped, stat! Keep the other patients stable until I can get to them. Are the doctors here?'

'Within the half-hour,' Dr Schumacher reported tersely as he came through a side door, gloved and gowned.

She nodded. 'Let's go. Keep holding the wound until someone takes over in the OR, Ricky.' She put her hands on top of Rick's as his slipped, slick with blood, keeping her thumbs pushed above and below the wound to slow the pulsing. She pushed Rick's hands back together, showing him how to cup them over with fingers holding stronger. 'Dr Schumacher, assess the other patients. Operate on the less critical ones in the ER. *Run!*' she snarled as he dithered. 'I know you've been to hell and back today, but it's over! Get inside and operate before someone dies. If you can't, stabilise and prep the patients for the Flying Doctors to transfer, and keep the ORs clear for the critical patients. Do it *now*!'

The shaking doctor nodded, and ran for the emergency room.

The wailing of arriving emergency services vehicles sounded outside. Nurses and ward assistants bolted out to help the arriving doctors and nurses carry out the vital equipment they'd brought with them.

Rick straddled Adam's body on the gurney, holding the wound closed with the pillowed part of the flak jacket as they ran for the operating room. One of the hospital staff brought Elly an opened sterile bandage when she asked again. With no time to clean her hands, she said to Rick, 'Take the jacket off on my three. One, two, three.' He pulled the jacket off and after a glance, she applied the bandage across the wound. 'Take it, Ricky, hold it just like this, with softer pressure than the jacket. The bleeding has slowed a little.'

He nodded, and took over.

'Don't die, Adam,' she whispered, tears streaming down her face as she kept applying pressure either side of the wound, keeping together his fragile hold on life. 'I'll do anything, pay any price, if you don't die.' But looking at him, she knew the price had already been paid, the sacrifice made.

She should have known it would end like this.

The OR was ready when the trolley crashed through the swinging doors.

'This man has a grazed jugular vein. Apply a clean pressure bandage to his throat while I scrub.'

The anaesthetist took the pressure from Rick, pressing the wound with gentle urgency while the scrub nurse unrolled another bandage, and another inserted a cannula into Adam's vein.

'We've got it from here, officer,' the nurse said. 'Thank you.'

With a nod and a bloodied hand extended to Elly—quickly dropped when she shook her head, still scrubbing her hands—Rick left the room.

'Is the bullet still in?' the anaesthetist asked Elly.

'I couldn't feel it. He turned side-on just before it hit. I think it grazed the vein and passed through. Nurse, can you take off my helmet?' Having washed her hands once, she coated her hands again with antiseptic solution, scrubbing to the elbow while one nurse removed the helmet and held out a gown, and another covered her head and face with a cap and surgical mask.

'BP ninety on fifty, diastolic weak. Pulse one-oh-two and thready,' the scout nurse called.

'I can't feel hardness in the throat,' the anaesthetist reported. 'There's no puncture mark, only a long graze, and the nick. I think you're right. The bullet passed by the vein, barely grazing it, and passed out again. A lot of the blood's coming from the injury to the oesophagus rather than the vein.'

Elly sighed. 'Thank God. Has the bleeding slowed yet?'

'I think so.' The anaesthetist's eyes crinkled above the surgical mask as he smiled at her. 'I'm Rod Cummings.'

'Jane Larkins.' She gazed at Adam's still form. 'But I answer to Elly.'

'The Jane Larkins who disappeared from Moongallee Creek?'

Elly nodded. 'Pack the base and crown of the neck in ice. Got a line in yet?' she rapped at the scout nurse, who nodded and ran out the door to call for ice. 'Use normal saline with an iron infusion until he's stabilised, and the EPO's here. He's B negative. Dubbo and Broken Hill are probably empty from the MVA, and ten to one we don't have anything but O and A positive in store. Let's do what we can. Thank God it wasn't the carotid, or we'd lose him.' She sighed. 'What I wouldn't give for some Oxycyte, or whatever it's called now.'

'Bloody red tape,' Rod muttered, referring to the legislation holding back the entry of perfluorochemicals—the life-saving non-blood fluids—into Australia. 'It'd be a gift for doctors in isolated regions at times like this. Will you graft the graze?'

She nodded, calling for the appropriate equipment in a harsh tone to hide the wobble of fear. 'Prepare his inner thigh for graft. Clean the wound around Dr Cumming's fingers without losing pressure,' she instructed the scrub nurse. 'If only we were in Sydney!'

'A laser and harmonic scalpel, and it's over in half an hour.' Rod shrugged, eyes still crinkled with a smile. 'But we make a difference here, even if sometimes we use damned bush medicine, with twenty-year-old equipment and tactics.'

Her eyes smiled back at him. All the outback doctors she'd met had the same work ethic and belief. 'Let's concentrate on the equipment and the patient we have.' She was proud of herself for calling Adam 'the patient', as if her heart weren't pounding and her stomach sick with terror. She was Adam's only chance now, and she had to be one hundred per cent doctor. 'Suction to that blood! What's the BP?'

'Ninety on forty-five, pulse one-ten.'

Come on, Claudius, live! Fight! 'Increase the drip rate to sixteen. Let's expand what blood he has. Why the hell don't we have a cell salvage machine here, or blood patches?'

'The machine is being used on the young cop, and he also used all the patches we had,' the scrub nurse said. 'He wouldn't stabilise.'

Simon. Another reason for guilt. Refusing to give in to it until she'd saved Adam, she turned to Rod. 'Did you bring any?'

He nodded. 'Not as many as we need, because the MVA happened first. I'll call Stone, see what's free, but they had to be used on those waiting for surgery.'

She nodded, sighing. 'Where's the damn ice?'

The scout nurse bolted to the door, took the ice packs from a ward assistant and applied them through sterile pads.

'Can't we slow his pulse?' Elly snapped as the ice packs took only minimal effect. 'For God's sake, lower his temperature by ten degrees to buy some time! Every minute's precious.'

Rod injected the IV, and the blood slowed to a sluggish pump. The sweat breaking Adam's brow slowed.

She sighed. 'Clean and suction. Anesthetise the wound before I tie it.'

'Why? He's totally out,' Rod replied, looking puzzled. 'He's doped enough to sleep till tomorrow.'

Impatient with the nurse's slowness, she swabbed the wound herself. 'He woke up during his appendectomy, fully anesthetised.'

Rod frowned. 'You know this guy. You know his blood type. I can see the fear in your eyes. You care about him.'

She held in all the words tumbling to her tongue, saying only, 'He's a childhood friend.'

'Then you know the drill! You shouldn't be here!'

'Schumacher was kidnapped and held at gunpoint today. He has a heart condition. He isn't qualified or up to anything but the minor injuries. Martin's working on the brain haemorrhage, and

Stone has enough to do with those in the ER. Adam's better off with me than bleeding to death while he waits in line!' Not giving Rod any more time to argue, she worked with furious speed on the vein graft, making meticulous tiny cuts, salvaging what blood Adam had left while she grafted the nick, tying up the blood vessels and rejoining them with minimal blood loss.

★ ★ ★

'You were right,' Rod said quietly an hour and a half later. 'You've done it, and in bush record time. This guy will live. A fine job in a bloody difficult area, Elly. I don't know anyone who could've done a better graft on a jugular graze.'

Elly drew in ragged breaths, limp and drained, as the nurse wiped sweat from her brow. 'Thanks. I try.'

'You *try*? Hell, girl, you'd have made a bloody fine surgeon! That's as damned near a perfect job as any I've seen in any of the city teaching hospitals, and I've seen plenty. What are you doing hiding out here in no-man's land?'

Drenched in perspiration from the effort of being detached, she wiped an errant curl away from her forehead. 'Working with my heart. I'm a Koori girl. I love the bush, and treating my people.'

'I'm telling you, you've missed your vocation,' Rod insisted, watching her close the wound. 'Poetry in motion, Elly. This guy will barely have a scar.'

No. I'm the one who'll be scarred by what happened to him today. She looked down at Adam, so cold and grey. Her heart constricted.

'Doctor, Detective Jepson's retained blood will arrive from police headquarters in two hours,' the nurse called.

Elly shook her head. 'That time's passed. Keep it back in case he needs it later. Right now his blood needs to stay thin until the graft strengthens. Finish up, and get him to recovery ward,' she ordered the nurse. 'Give him more EPO in four hours, and IV antibiotics for three days. The last thing he needs is an infection. We'll see to the young cop now.'

With a last glance at Adam's drawn face, she left the operating rooms for the ER, experiencing the rush of exhilaration she always felt at the end of a life-and-death situation, but tinged with added poignancy. If she'd put his life in danger, she'd just given him another chance at life.

The next six hours in theatre, operating on patient after patient, exhausted her. Simon was the hardest. Seeing him so pale and still, she remembered the teasing boy she'd met, but she pushed the thought away—guilt would only destroy her ability. The cell salvage machine had saved his life already—she only had to operate and clean the mess.

Praise God for that.

It was deep night by the time she left the OR on quivering legs, her eyes dry and stinging, her head pounding, but feeling something approaching peace. She'd done all she could to repair the damage she'd helped create. The haemorrhaging man from the car-park attack was still critical, but he'd live—and the others would live without permanent injury. That was all she could ask.

Jonas waited outside the ER, his kind eyes filled with compassion. 'Come with me now, Elly. We'll take your statement.'

She stumbled as she followed him out, but Rick was there. His arm moved around her waist. 'Lean on me, Janie-jan.'

Fighting tears of exhaustion, she put her head on her brother's shoulder, letting him lead her out. 'I forgot you, but I never stopped missing you, Ricky,' she whispered.

'You'll never have the chance to miss me again.' He caressed her sweaty hair, holding her in the fierce protectiveness she at last understood, and welcomed.

At the station, Rick insisted on their giving statements together. The senior sergeant allowed his request. His questions for them were almost identical anyway—apart from the first one. 'Why didn't you tell me about your relationship to Elly, Mendham?'

Rick lifted his brows. 'You know why. You pulled Adam off the case as soon as you knew they were friends. We needed all the police power we could get. And after a year of working on it, I had everything prepared.'

'You could have included us,' Jonas barked.

Rick shook his head. 'Not likely, Sarge. I came to Macks Lake for one reason—to save my sister.' He smiled at Elly. 'I didn't remember you either; I was adopted at five by the Mendhams. But one day I was processing a case, and the name Larkins came up. It struck a chord in me. After a few weeks of checking out why, I asked my mother about it. She'd already told me I was adopted when I was eighteen—but now she said I'd cried for Janie-jan for six months after I came to them, and insisted on being called Ricky-jim. Eventually she told me the whole truth—that our dad had sold me to them, and disappeared.' He laughed. 'No wonder she freaked out when I applied to become a cop.'

Disturbed more deeply than her exhaustion could show, she took his hand. 'He *sold* you?'

Rick nodded. 'The Mendhams lost five babies, and one living daughter. They wanted a son. I don't know how our father heard of them, or how he arranged the adoption unless Mum signed the papers. I've been looking into it, but there's some irregularities, and I had to put your case first.' When she squeezed his hand in mute commiseration, he shrugged. 'I applied for my birth certificate—and under the pretence of it being part of the investigation, I got yours, too. When I did your background check, I found out about Adam. I talked to his brother Jared, and his great-aunt Harriet about the case. They both told me how much he meant to you. I reckoned you'd show up sooner or later, so I applied to come here.'

'You did more than that,' Jonas remarked, writing it all down. 'A lot more, I'd say, son, considering you knew that Jen Collins and the Mirakis had been paid by Jeremiah Spencer. And bringing Lorena Spencer here was absolute genius.'

'Yes, it was. Lorena Spencer's loss was probably a central trigger to Danny's mental problems. She was central, critical,' Elly said softly, squeezing Rick's hand.

'And nobody even thought of it but you,' Jonas added. 'Excellent work, Mendham.'

Rick shrugged again, face flushed. 'I had a year to prepare for this, and it seemed nobody was looking into Jeremiah Spencer's acts. The killing of animals had been going on long before Danny was old enough to have done it, and half-a-dozen jackaroos disappeared after Danny left. Their families suddenly had their debts paid off—as did the Mirakis and Jen Collins. And the case against Lorena Spencer was too thin. Her former boss had miraculously cleared all her debts, and the judge in the case had a new apartment on Magnetic Island. Once they both knew I was looking into how they managed that with money they hadn't had before the Spencer case—and that I'd sent copies of all the information to the anti-corruption commission—they quit their jobs and disappeared. After that, getting Lorena out of prison was easy.'

Elly stared at him in wonder. 'Jeremiah Spencer offered me up to three million to have Danny's baby and give it to him. I can't believe he didn't try to bribe you.'

Rick grinned. 'An anonymous third party offered me a hundred thousand dollars to back off the case. I sent a recording of the phone call to the commission, again on the understanding that they wouldn't move against the old man until Spencer junior was in custody. Then he threatened me—again through an anonymous source—but I was clean enough not to need to worry.'

'Did he threaten your life?' Elly murmured, head tilted. Rick's shrug was answer enough. 'You risked your life for me.'

'You're my sister,' he answered. 'Don't tell me you wouldn't have done the same for me. I won't believe you.'

Elly sighed and put her head on his shoulder.

'You did this all on your own.' Jonas was staring at him in awe. 'Son, are you interested in becoming a detective? We could use two here—especially lately.'

'Maybe.' Rick laughed. 'I did have a lot of help, though—remember the network, Sarge. I had access to workers on Longa Station, Gundawin, and here in town, through the mob. Everywhere Elly went, I visited on my days off, and the mob talked to me once I identified myself both as Elly's brother, and an Aboriginal liaison officer.'

'Ricky,' she whispered. 'You did all this, and I treated you like garbage.'

'Our dad left us both with trust issues,' he said softly, sounding peaceful. 'I knew who you were, or I might have suspected you too. Just don't do it again, little sis.'

She tried to laugh, but a sob came out. He hugged her. 'I told you you'd love me one day, didn't I? Okay, it took saving your life to do it, but I said I'd do anything to save you.'

Then she did laugh, hugging him back. 'Yeah, yeah, big brother, I owe you. I get it.'

'I get why you didn't tell me about your relationship,' Jonas said, 'but why not call us in?'

'Our only hope was surprise, once the city cops took over—and it was obvious they would, sooner or later, given Spencer senior's influence, and his manipulation of the media. So I kept quiet on everything

I knew. When Elly's trail finally seemed to be leading here, I used my RDOs to get Lorena Spencer out of prison before Elly arrived. I'd bought a small place only a few weeks before that, so I put Lorena in it.' He grinned. 'It wasn't quite coincidence that the house was on a battleaxe block behind Jen Collins' house. During all those dodgy headaches I had, I watched every move she and the Mirakis made.' He pushed some papers he'd brought from his desk over to the senior sergeant. 'Check these out, Sarge. She isn't who she claims to be.'

'Good lord,' Jonas gasped, shuffling the papers and scanning them. 'Did Spencer send her here to stalk Jepson?'

'Seems so. She came here within weeks of Adam's arrival. Her job was to be in place when Elly arrived, and make trouble if she could. The fact that she genuinely fell for Adam helped.'

Jonas shook his head. 'And the Mirakis?'

'That was easy. I found them while I was reading up on the case, and followed their trail, and here they were. A little chat to some station hands, and then Sanderson at Longa Station, and he admitted Spencer had paid him to take them on. He didn't know why. I told him to keep the Mirakis too busy to leave Longa, which was why they didn't do more than set a few rumours going, and write that letter to Adam.'

Jonas patted Rick's shoulder. 'Your preparation and negotiation skills saved a lot of lives today, Mendham. I'm recommending you take your detective exams, and receive full hostage negotiation training.'

Rick's smile was almost rueful. 'Thanks, Sarge.'

'I'm sorry I didn't trust you, son.'

Rick swallowed before he nodded. The unusual lack of formality, calling him *son*, was deliberate—they both felt it. Belonging was as rare and important to Rick as it was to Elly. She squeezed his hand, and turned to hug him. He kissed her forehead.

When they'd signed their statements in front of the detectives from Sydney, Jonas said, 'I've never seen a display like the one you put on today, both you and Mendham.'

'You brought Spencer down in an extremely tense situation, and then saved the lives of those he attacked,' Detective Sergeant Barlow said, admiration in his voice.

'Where's Danny now?' Elly asked quietly.

'Once Martin finished treating him, we sent him to Sydney in the police plane, to a secure psychiatric facility. His mother's going with him. But Jeremiah Spencer's already made a formal complaint about his grandson's treatment, claiming Lorena isn't Danny's real mother.'

'Of course he has.' Rick sighed. 'The man's obsessed. Do a mouth swab on Danny and Lorena. That'll shut him up. He doesn't like or trust new science.'

'I still want to cuff you over the head for keeping the secret of Lorena Spencer from us,' Jonas growled, 'but there's no denying your knowledge of Spencer senior made the difference today.'

Rick shrugged. 'She's my sister.'

His boss nodded. 'I'd have done the same for my sister.' He turned to Elly. 'I'll be citing both of you, plus Jepson, for bravery awards. You saved dozens of lives today.'

Her laugh was filled with self-contempt. 'Leave the commendations for Adam and Rick. I only rectified my mistake in coming here at all.' She fingered something in the pocket of her shorts, opened her mouth and closed it. 'It's goodbye, Jonas. I'm leaving tonight.'

He sighed. 'I'm sorry for that, Elly. Macks Lake could have done with a doctor of your calibre, and a woman with your heart and love for people.' He hesitated. 'Mendham and Jepson will miss you. We all will.'

She gulped down a burning ball of pain, but Rick squeezed her hand.

After a moment, Jonas went on. 'I'll need a contact number to let you know when and where the court hearing will be.'

She nodded. 'I'd prefer to give any evidence by video or Skype. It's best Danny never sees me in person again. I'm buying a new phone tomorrow—Monday, isn't it?' She chuckled, but there was no humour in it. 'I came Tuesday. Six days ago, Macks Lake was a quiet little backwater. Now it'll hit the headlines of every newspaper in the country.' She gave Jonas a wry grin. 'You can't say I don't make an impact. Anyway, I'll text you the number.'

The senior sergeant held her hand. 'God bless you, Elly. We'll miss you.'

She shook her head. 'Not for long. I'm not exactly unforgettable, except to crazed gunmen and other selected psychopaths.' She glanced at Rick. 'See me out?'

Rick took her hand, and they walked into the velvet softness of an outback night, dotted with clear, blazing stars. 'There are potholes here. Until you know where they are, you could hurt yourself,' he said as they crossed the carpark.

She hugged him. She couldn't seem to stop. 'You risked your career for me today.'

'Of course,' he said. 'I had it all ready for when you—and Spencer—showed. It was just a matter of time. But the problem wasn't yours alone. Jen Collins saw it the first day you came—we all saw the look on Adam's face. I tried to stop them, but Baz and Simon made jokes about it. She almost sideswiped your car on her way out that day. We arrested her earlier today for stalking, two counts of malicious damage and two counts of attempted grievous bodily harm, and no doubt they'll now add identity theft to the list. She won't be getting bail this time.'

Elly blinked. 'Jen Collins dropped the tree branch, painted the fake blood in my room and shot the station window? But you said she doesn't even own a gun!'

'BB guns are quite easy to get if you know where to look—but it wasn't hers: she paid someone else to do it. Oh, and as a side point, Mrs Collins is not Mrs Collins.' Rick laughed and scratched his head. 'The real Mrs Collins died two years ago in Queensland. The death certificate was given under the name of her sister, Anne Rollings, and Anne Rollings became Jen Collins.'

Her mouth opened and closed again. 'But why? What was the point?'

'Slipping through the net. Jen Collins was a model citizen, but Anne Rollings has a record as long as your arm. Believe it or not, it was Adam being stalked here, not you. Anne Rollings has stalked more men than I've had years as a cop. She started at fourteen, and she's had fifteen complaints since.'

'Who did she pay to shoot out the station window?'

'A kid in my police youth footy team. A witness I interviewed said they'd seen a kid in the team uniform in the area at the time of the shooting. When I talked to the team, he confessed everything. The city cops who'd been following me picked Jen Collins up this afternoon after we got Spencer. They've taken her to Sydney. She won't get bail this time. We have the evidence of attempted murder and grievous bodily harm on top of the identity theft, skipping bail in Queensland, and multiple stalking charges; it should keep her away for at least five years. She's a menace, especially to tall, dark men like Adam,' he laughed.

She blinked again, and shook her head. 'She climbed that tree near the river? But its lowest branch was ten feet up!'

'I know, right? Another unbelievable fact—this case has been like a *Ripley's Believe it or Not!* show—Anne Rollings was an almost-ran for the Sydney Olympics. She was a spectacular gymnast, but her constant tantrums and harassing the boys led the coach to drop her.'

She closed her mouth, shaking her head to clear it. It didn't work. 'How did you work out the identity switch?'

'When I learned that Mrs Collins had a stalker sister, I asked for their medical and dental records. The real Mrs Collins didn't have buck teeth, and her records showed mild lung damage and osteoporosis from the steroids she'd taken for asthma. Anne Rollings is as healthy as a horse.'

'Thank you, Ricky,' she whispered, hugging him. 'I'm so sorry I suspected you.'

'Given what you've been through, it was natural. I could have told you who I was from the start, but then I'd be taken off the case. I thought I could protect you better with anonymity, by staying in the shadows until the right moment came to tell you.' He grinned ruefully. 'I also would have preferred to have our reunion in private. That's why I tried to jog your memory while we were alone.'

'It wouldn't have worked. I'd even forgotten your name until you said "Janie-jan".' She paused. 'Will you help me now? Can you take me to the nearest bus or train station that gets me to Sydney?'

'That's Mildura.' He paused, looked at her. 'Is the Beemer out of action? I was looking forward to taking it for a spin.'

'I'm leaving it here. A goodbye present for Claudius.' Tears pricked her eyes. 'He always loved fast cars.'

'Janie, we just found each other again. Can you wait a few days? Stay with me,' Rick urged. 'Adam never needs to know. Schumacher won't be able to cope once the other doctors leave—and you know they'll have to. He can look after Adam, if that's what's bothering you. I'll tell him I dropped you at Mildura when he wakes.'

'You'd lie to him?' She stared at him, touched. 'He's your best friend.'

'And you're my sister,' he said quietly, squeezing her hand. 'Please, just give us a few days before you go.'

Tears pricked her eyes. Slowly, she nodded. 'A few days.'

'If I can get more time off, I'll take you to Sydney. I have to go up soon anyway, to pick up Zoe.' He squeezed her hand again. 'Do me a favour? Go see the family. You need them now. I met them when I dropped Zoe in Sydney. They love you, Janie-jan. They deserve to see you.'

He was right. For years they'd given loyalty and love, and she'd never let them into her heart. So scarred by her father's desertion, her mother's death and Adam's marriage, she'd been blind to any suffering but her own. The Jepsons also deserved better than the ungrateful silence she'd given them the past twelve years. They'd done their best for her, tried so hard to help her … and they'd given her Adam.

'I will. I'll see them all. But do they know who you are? They'll want to meet you, too.'

'They didn't care what my name was at the time—but I'll fly up when I can.' Rick hugged her tight. 'Can't let my sister go now I've finally found her again.'

'You'll always be with me.' Her eyes filled with tears. 'I'll call or text you every day, and we can Skype.' She held him close, feeling secure in the warmth of his returned hug. 'I wish I'd known the first day,' she whispered. 'I wish I'd recognised you. But—'

'But your heart was so full of Adam, there wasn't room for me,' he said simply.

'No. *No.*' She held him even harder. 'You're my brother. That's a forever love. There will always be room for you. Always.'

After a while he murmured, 'Let's go home.'

'Can we go to the hospital first?' She had to see Adam one last time, to say the goodbye she'd never had the chance to give thirteen years before.

★ ★ ★

After checking all her other patients, and being assured the Mildura and Broken Hill doctors were here for the next twenty-four hours at least, Elly stood by the door of the room allocated to Adam. His face, grey with pale lips, had taken on the stern look she'd seen in the station that first day, when he'd given her a prim-and-proper Jepson look, judging her outfit. The ECG, still attached to his chest, printed out a reading. A massive bruise was collecting around the IV line. She'd change the IV to another vein—

She wrote it down in his patient notes. If she touched him, she'd never leave until he kicked her out.

She looked at him one last time. He stirred in his drug-induced sleep. His eyes opened a little, seeking something, as if he sensed her presence. His lips moved. *Elly?*

'I'm here.' Shaking with the need to touch him, her hands balled into fists by her sides. 'It's over. Danny's in custody, on his way to Sydney; his mother went with him. I'm fine. You and Rick saved me. Just rest now, and concentrate on getting better. Everything's going to be all right now. I promise.'

He was asleep again.

'I'm so sorry.' She turned to the door, swiping at a tear trickling down her cheek. 'Goodbye, my darling friend. I hope you find what you need to make you happy.'

Rick waited outside the door. No words necessary. He held out his hand and she took it.

CHAPTER
21

Adam awoke to a world of white. Weak, disoriented and in definite pain, centred in his neck. His head throbbed; his eyes were dry and burning. He tried to form words, but they wouldn't come.

'G'day, mate. Welcome back to the land of the living.'

Rick's quiet voice entered his consciousness, returning him to time and place. He was in Macks Lake Hospital with a shotgun wound from Danny Spencer.

Again he mouthed a word. *Zoe?*

Rick's face came into focus. 'Zoe's having a ball on the cruise. We've told the family nothing, but we'll arrange for your mother to keep Zoe once they're back. I'll go get her when you're well enough to take her home. Your great-aunt's been calling every few hours.'

Elly?

Rick's mouth twitched. 'Spencer nicked your jugular vein. You almost died. She worked on you with outdated equipment, no laser or blood, and she saved your life.'

He knew that. Even knocked out by bullet and anaesthetic he'd felt her presence, her healing touch; he'd heard her voice, begging him to live. Saying goodbye. *Where is she?*

Rick sighed. 'I dropped her off at Mildura. She got a bus north-east this morning.' He added softly, 'She can't forgive herself for what Spencer did to you. You're gonna have a hell of a job convincing her to come back—but you'll try if you know what's good for you.'

Adam closed his eyes. She'd saved his life, this time literally, and she still couldn't forgive herself for what Spencer did. Ah, his beautiful Elly. How she punished herself for burdens that didn't belong on her shoulders.

'My sister is the best thing to ever happen to you,' Rick went on fiercely. 'I wish to God I could find a woman who loves me the way she loves you. You're a bloody fool if you let her go. And Zoe needs Elly, even if you don't want a wife. And I want her here with me. But she won't come back unless you make her. You'll have to marry her to bring her back.'

Adam's eyes snapped open. *I did marry her.*

Rick's brows lifted. 'Since she only came a week ago, and this isn't Las Vegas, you can't be talking legal ceremonies. Tribal thing, huh? I didn't think you'd do something so uncivilised,' he taunted with a good-natured grin. 'The prim-and-proper Jepson clan'll have a fit. Old Sobersides Adam Jepson, married by tribal ceremony to a blackfella.'

Even though it hurt like hell, Adam grinned back. *Help me find her.*

Rick turned away, and Adam knew he was hiding something. 'Just get better, mate. We'll talk later.'

He turned back as Adam grabbed his hand.

Who attacked us? The Mirakis?

Rick grinned. 'They only wrote the nasty note, and spread the gossip around. Get ready for it, mate: it wasn't Elly causing the obsession. It was you.' Rick told him the story, laughing at his gaping horror. 'Spencer senior sent the Mirakis here, and Jen Collins. Why and how he knew about you, but didn't tell Danny, I can't fathom yet. I think he's been the abuser all along. He wanted the spotlight off Danny until he reached Elly. Probably wanted to give him enough time to rape her and make her pregnant—he's that obsessed with getting a sane heir to the Spencer holdings. ICAC is digging into the Spencer finances now.'

Adam touched his arm at the end of the strange tale, knowing, because he was a cop, just how much Rick had risked to help them. *Thank you.*

Again Rick didn't quite look at him, and Adam had the sense of something being off. 'She's my sister. I waited over a year for her to come here, plenty of time to get a few plans in place. You only had a few days.'

How could you be sure she'd come?

Rick fiddled with a pen lying on Adam's tray table. 'Your brother said she'd come, and your great-aunt. They said—' He shrugged. 'I'm sure she's told you by now.'

Yeah. Now he couldn't look at Rick. So damn *stupid.* All those years, his family had known, and he'd been blind.

'So what will you do?'

Adam tried to smile, and pointed at him. *Second wedding? Best man?*

Rick grinned. 'You bet.'

He made a fist, giving Rick's shoulder a weak punch.

His friend laughed. 'I had fun playing rogue cop, being the unknown spy, outwitting the undercovers on my tail. I might join ASIO.' He winked. 'Well, mate, I told you months ago you needed a shake-up, and you got it. You can't say life with my sister will be boring. She'll keep you on the run till you're ninety, I reckon.' He winked. 'Not to mention other sundry members of the family.'

He winced with the pain his laugh of agreement brought. Never could two lives be less reconciled than the ones he'd lived. Life with Sharon had been a carousel: quiet, steady, predictable, but constantly coming back around to tension and regret. If he continued to bring up Zoe the way Sharon had wanted him to, he'd lose her. Zoe was *his* daughter, with the adventurous streak that could either be repressed to the point of rebellion, or nourished to make her life pure joy.

Life with Elly was a roller coaster—but experiencing the joy of every minute with her was more than worth living through the downs that had come, and would be sure to come again, if not so dramatically as this time.

The last chains around his heart snapped and fell. At last, he'd escaped his self-inflicted prison – and Zoe was young enough to ensure she'd never remember it, thank God. He was alive again, and he'd stay that way—so long as Elly was by his side. His every memory of happiness came from her. Doctoring those bedraggled critters of hers, running wild on the grass, climbing trees, stealing tractors and apples. Riding the highway in fast convertibles, eating pizza, skinny-dipping. Seeing the love in her eyes as she looked at his daughter.

A passion he'd never known before. Watching her come to vivid life under his touch; reaching out for him again and again, in unashamed wonder and desire. Talking about his hopes and dreams, knowing she not only listened, but shared in every one of them, and would help to make them come true if she could. Setting up the clinic together would be a challenge he'd treasure for life—so long as he had Elly beside him.

His face broke out in a crazy grin that made him wince in pain. Finally he realised why his marriage had been so traumatic for him and Sharon both; at last he understood what he suspected Sharon had known the whole time. Loving, adventurous Elly-May was the love of his life, and always had been.

Now to find her, and convince her he was worth another try.

★ ★ ★

'I think he knows,' Rick said as he found Elly in the doctor's office. 'At least he knows something's not right. Someone's going to say something about you before long.'

She sighed and rubbed her forehead. 'I thought you'd find it hard to lie to him. Can you take me to the bus tomorrow?'

'He loves you, Janie.'

She almost winced. 'Sometimes that isn't enough.'

'Why not?' Her brother held her gaze. 'He wants you to stay here, Janie—and so do the townsfolk. So do I.'

She walked around the desk to him, hugging him as fiercely as he did her. 'I want to stay.'

He kissed the top of her head. 'Then stay, little sis.'

Tears stung her eyes again. So emotional lately. 'Not while Danny's alive. Not while none of us can stop Jeremiah.'

Rick sighed. The media had already reported the so-called 'witch hunt' of the Spencer family, thanks to Jeremiah's barristers and friends on the High Court. Lorena Spencer had been given a court order to keep her away from Danny. 'It's only been a few days. Give us some time, and we'll—'

She shook her head. 'You did more than anyone could, but five people died, and Simon is still critical. Adam will never be the same, and Jeremiah gets away with it all again. You can't take on the whole system and win, Ricky. Adam almost died this time. I can't risk him—or you. If I lost you again …'

'Not going to happen.' He lifted her up as if she were a child, holding her hard against him. 'It's hard for you to believe, but I'm here for life. I love you, Janie-jan.'

'I'm wetting your shirt,' she whispered, hiccuping.

'Ruin the damn thing, and I'll still love you.'

Every word he spoke was a balm on her soul. He knew she couldn't say it back yet, and didn't mind. He'd had the stable family life and love. 'I'll let you know when I change phone numbers.'

He sighed. 'I can't stop you?'

'It's *for* you.'

He sighed again. 'You just won't see it, will you? We'd rather risk it all to have you with us. I wish I'd found you years ago, before you stopped believing people could love you.'

Eyes and throat stinging, she held him so hard he probably couldn't breathe. 'I believe you love me, Ricky.' There was no way she could deny it, after all he'd done.

'Just not anyone else?'

One shoulder lifted, and fell. Not lying, just unable to tell the truth.

'If we can stop Jeremiah Spencer, you'd come back to us?'

She wished she knew. 'I'll always be your sister.'

His jaw worked. 'Go pack, little sis. I think there's a flight tonight from here to Bankstown.'

★   ★   ★

Seven days later, Rick came in the hospital room to find Adam dressed, his bags beside him. 'You're off, then?'

He nodded. 'I tried to quit, but Sarge gave me indefinite leave until I come back.' Though he could speak now, more than a week after the siege, his voice still rasped and his throat hurt like hell. 'I'll get the car, then I'm off to the Southern Highlands to see Zoe. Then I'm heading to Sydney.'

Rick tossed him the keys. 'I brought the Beemer in. I had a feeling you'd be off today. Since I have to be in Sydney by Monday for the hostage negotiation course and the D exam, I thought I'd hitch a ride with you. I need to see my fiancée, or she might run off with another Prince Eric lookalike.'

He tossed the keys back. 'You drive.'

His friend grinned. 'What'll you do when you find her?'

'Marry her, bring her home to Macks Lake and set up a mobile medical clinic together. I'm signing up for flying lessons and upgrading my first aid from basic.'

Rick laughed. 'When you get out of your rut, you don't muck around. Good thing for both of us, as well as the town. I'll be glad to have her nearby.' He gripped Adam's hand. 'Welcome to the family, bro.'

'Don't get emotional on me. My throat still hurts.'

Rick laughed, then sobered. 'She answers my calls, but won't tell me where she is. By the time I get the tower she's calling from, she's gone somewhere else. She knows I'm visiting you, so she's locking me out. I'll go meet my family while I'm in Sydney; I'll get more information from them than you could, and I'm sure she's with one of them.'

His throat thickened. 'Thanks, mate.'

'Brother,' Rick amended softly.

He nodded. After years alone, he had acceptance, family. Thanks to Elly. 'Brother.'

'You know Spencer's put the wheels in motion to have Danny removed to his care? We've got to find her—fast—or she'll leave the country.'

'Don't worry,' Adam replied, just as taut. 'I'll find her.'

He signed himself out of the hospital. Rick slung their bags into the boot of the BMW. 'I'll be looking for her as soon as they have a replacement for one of us. Let's find her, mate.'

CHAPTER
22

Adam slammed down the phone for at least the fiftieth time. 'Where the hell is she?'

His mother touched his arm. 'You'll find her.'

'How? Either every single member of both her family and mine are lying through their teeth, or she left them months ago without trace! Even Rick isn't answering my calls now. He's with her, I know he is, but he won't talk to me.' He was at his mum's on a fly-ing visit to see Zoe before he tried another friend, another relative, anyone who might know Elly's whereabouts. He'd been running around for over two months now.

'Would it help to talk about it, Adam?' his mother asked quietly.

His gaze fell. 'It's—hard for me—'

'Except with Janie.' Mum's smile was sad, but accepting. 'It was always that way. Your father was wrong to keep you apart.' She shrugged as he looked up in sudden fury. 'You know how much your father wanted for you and Jared. The Jepsons have always been a respectable family. When Jared went into corporate law and married Hannah, and then took over the farm, your father was content. But you always worried him. Being a policeman, especially in the Federal Police, was enough to frighten him. Your feelings for Janie, though—they terrified him.'

'Her Koori background,' he said flatly.

'Give your father some credit,' his mother snapped. 'No, he wasn't fond of it, and that was obvious to us all, but he got used to it. But he could never feel safe around her. It was all the things he saw she was bringing to life in you—that passion for living, and disregard for consequences—your wildness when you were with her scared him. So before Janie was old enough for you to get serious with her, he arranged for you to meet Sharon. She was everything he wanted for you: a lady, a teacher, a daughter of a friend in the Southern Highlands Council.'

'And I fell for it. I wanted Dad to be proud of me for once.' He met his mother's eyes. 'Sharon and I were never suited. We were miserable together.'

'I know. It hurt me to see you and Sharon so unhappy. It hurt your father, too, the way you buried yourself in work, taking so many risks.' She added quietly, 'Avoiding him and Sharon.'

'Yeah,' he said. 'I even avoided the kids.'

'He knew he was wrong to do what he did, but a man of his pride couldn't admit it, or tell you he was sorry, even when he was dying.' His mother gulped, and smiled. 'But you're still young. So find your Elly, and give me more babies to fuss over. I'll be happy to move to Macks Lake to help out with babysitting while you two play Flying Doctors. It's time you learned to fly again, son.'

'I'll do my best, on both counts.' He hugged her, feeling closer to his mother than he had in many years.

His phone rang. After checking the caller ID, he snatched it up. 'Aunty Hat, how are you?'

'We have no time for that,' Aunty Hat snapped. 'I assume you'd like to know where Janie is? Or did you merely use her?'

'You know where Elly is? Is she with you?'

'She was here for a fortnight. I lied every time you came or called, just as her family all did. She doesn't want to see you.' His great-aunt sounded belligerent. 'Promise to do the right thing by her, Adam, or I hang up now!'

He laughed, giddy with relief. 'I already did the right thing, Aunty Hat, I swear!'

'Hmph. A tribal marriage?' His aunt sniffed. 'I want a ceremony I can see, in a church or a garden, with all the family. Swear to it, Adam, or she'll be gone before you can find her.'

'Anything Elly wants is hers. Aunty Hat, please tell me where she is,' he pleaded. 'I might have hurt her, but I never used her. I love her.'

'I always knew that,' his great-aunt said. 'I'm glad you finally know it, too, darling.'

A sudden suspicion hit him. 'Did you play Cupid on us, Aunty Hat?'

'What do you think?' She gave a wise chuckle. 'When you wouldn't come out of your grief and guilt, I only knew of one person you'd respond to.' She sighed. ' I lost the love of my life. I didn't want you to lose yours. I just want you to be happy, Adam. Janie's always loved you, the way you deserve to be loved—and she deserves everything she wants.'

Gruff with embarrassment, he said, 'I don't know about deserving her. But I'm not letting her go again.'

'Good boy.' To his surprise, his great-aunt giggled. 'How many stiff-necked Jepsons do you think will boycott the wedding?'

'I don't care. Please, just tell me where she is!'

Aunty Hat sighed again. 'She's flying out to the Congo tonight to join a volunteer medical team in the war zone.'

He gasped again. '*The Congo?* What the hell—I mean, what for?'

'You don't know? Haven't you watched the news?' Aunty Hat sounded frightened. 'Detective Sergeant Barlow called her three days ago. Jeremiah Spencer paid an actor with a strong resemblance to his grandson to get a job as a wardsman at the place Spencer was being held, and then swap places with him. Spencer's been on the loose for seven days now. The actor was arrested, but they let him go. Apparently he thought he was on one of those reality shows—Jeremiah Spencer even had a fake TV contract drawn up for him. Danny swapped clothes with the wardsman, changed his hair and put in contacts the wardsman gave him, and was gone by the next check. They believe he had inside help. Three members of the security staff have emptied their bank accounts and disappeared. But Jeremiah Spencer has at last stepped over the line. He's been charged— something to do with aiding and abetting a known criminal.'

'My God,' he gasped. Why the hell hadn't Sarge told him? *Because I haven't answered the phone unless a member of the family was calling. Because I don't want to be a cop anymore.*

'Janie panicked, and called a friend who'd signed up with the Medicin Sans Frontières team. They always need more medical staff. She said this time, even if Spencer's grandfather could get him a fake passport, he'd have to get through a war zone to find her.'

He collapsed into a chair. 'Maybe she's right. She'll never be safe in Australia with Spencer on the loose.'

'Go to the airport, Adam,' Aunty Hat said gently. 'You need to see her before you make the decision to let her go.'

His trained ears picking up her urgent stress on the word 'see', he growled, 'What's happened to her, Aunty Hat?'

She sighed. 'I promised her I wouldn't tell. But if you see her, you'll know what to do.'

'Thanks.' About to hang up, he added, 'Love you, Aunty Hat.'

She gave a rippling laugh. 'Just find her, Adam. Take your badge. It's the flight via Johannesburg.'

He dropped the phone. 'Call any of the family who can make it to the airport in time, Mum. I'll need all the help I can get to make Elly agree to come back to me.'

Zoe had been bouncing from foot to foot through the conversation. 'Are you going to get Annelly now, Daddy?'

Adam nodded, swinging her up onto his hip.

Zoe kissed his face repeatedly. 'Bring her here, Daddy, so we can go home! She wants to go home. She told me.'

He frowned, staring at his daughter. 'What? When did Aunt Elly call you?'

Zoe giggled. 'All the time, Daddy. The last times—this many—' she held up a hand full of fingers '—from Uncle Rick's phone. She said it's our special secret.'

He couldn't feel anger; he understood and forgave, even though it hurt that Elly and Rick had both lied to him. They loved Zoe, and Rick would do anything for his sister—as Elly would for him … for them both. She was willing to sacrifice herself to save him. Again.

'Will you do me a favour?' he asked, and when he told his daughter what it was, she laughed and grabbed his phone from him. At almost five, she could work the damned thing better than he could.

After kissing Zoe a final time, he went for the BMW at a run. The dust swirled around the old farm as he screeched away without a backward glance. But he made a final call, to reinforce the local cops who were watching his mother and daughter, night and day.

★　★　★

By the time he'd reached the outskirts of Sydney, Adam knew he was being followed. Every time he glanced in the rear-vision mirror, the silver turbo sedan was the same distance behind him. If he slowed down or sped up, it copied his action.

He had less than three hours to lose the tail and find Elly. Though he still had his police ID, he didn't have a gun. He hoped to God Rick had his. He'd tipped off the airport police, giving his name and rank, and told them they could probably find Danny Spencer at the gate with the flight to Kinshasa via Johannesburg. He also reported the tail.

He called Rick, but it went straight to message, as usual. He called Elly's grandmother, and her cousin Kara, with the same result. *Please, let them all be with her.*

He took the quickest route to the airport through backstreets he'd found during his time as a city cop. He drove as fast as he could without risking injury to anyone. *Come on, God, where are the cops around here?*

His prayer was answered. A few minutes later, sirens wailed behind him. He stopped, flashed his badge and immediately recruited new allies. They chased the silver car, calling for backup as their quarry roared off.

A stretch limo fell in behind him at the airport turn-off from the Princes Highway, but he paid it no more attention than necessary before he roared into the international terminal, parking in the emergency section. He flashed his badge again; the security guards watched both the car and the entrance, in case Danny Spencer escaped the cops on his tail.

Having flashed his badge at check-in, Adam soon found out she hadn't even checked in yet. He looked everywhere. At last he found her in a café bar near her check-in desk, surrounded by family, both Larkins and Jepson. He blew out a sigh of relief, sending up a silent prayer of thanks that she hadn't yet gone through security to the gates, and for his mother's quick work in sending half the family he had in Sydney.

For almost a minute he stood at a distance, watching her, almost scared by what he saw. His vivid, laughing Elly sat thin and subdued, neither moving nor speaking. His colourful Elly was in a loose jumpsuit, hair pulled back in a tight band. She seemed defeated, alone despite her family's presence, less his untamed tigress than the kicked puppy he'd once seen in her. There was little trace of the impudent woman who'd come to him in cuffs, laughing in the face of his starchy disapproval. Her head lay on her grandmother's shoulder. Rick stood behind her, his hand on her other shoulder. She held the hand of a dark, pretty girl—her cousin Kara, he guessed—who could never have eclipsed Elly a few months back. Most men would think Kara outshone her now—but she was still his Elly, who'd risked her life to save him.

'Elly!'

He had no need to repeat himself. Her head snapped up, eyes zeroing in on him. Her skin paled to a sick shade. His heart contracted at the terror in her eyes.

'No. Not you. Not you! Turn around. Walk out of here. Run. Now!'

'No.' His voice was hoarse. 'You can't go. I won't let you leave me!' *Good one, Jepson. See her for the first time in months, and order her around.* 'Elle, darlin', please, can't we talk about this?'

Her eyes closed when she heard the loving nickname, but he caught the flash of pain in the coffee depths. 'There's nothing left to say. Please, if you ever cared for me at all, go!'

He blinked. Of all the greetings he'd envisaged, this wasn't one. 'Can't you forgive me for letting you down? Do you hate me so much?'

'Hate you? You idiot,' she hissed, 'I'm trying to save your life! If Danny sees you—'

He almost closed his eyes. Yes, thank God, it was still there, the love that would sacrifice everything for him. Now it was his turn to show his love in return. 'He thinks we're just foster brother and sister. He won't—'

Hysterical laughter interrupted him. 'He won't now. Not now!'

He blinked. 'What—?'

'Just *go*!' she cried. 'I almost got you killed last time!'

'Elly, you did nothing to hurt me. You're the one who saved my life after he shot me! You have to stop taking the rap for what Spencer—' As he approached her, he received a shove so hard he fell into a chair.

Rick stood over him, fists clenched, an aggressive glint in his eyes. 'You jerk. You didn't tell me you'd knocked her up before she left. You're going to marry her now, or I'll break both your arms.'

'Ricky, stop it. I told you it was me,' Elly hissed, with a flash of her old fire, but she remained half-hidden behind the café bench, and the girl who held her.

'Good try, sis, but you're a pathetic liar. I'm pretty sure he was there, too.'

Adam staggered to his feet, feeling the wind knocked out of him in more ways than one. 'Knocked up?' His stunned gaze settled on Elly. 'You're pregnant?'

She drew herself up, lifting her chin and looking at him steadily with shimmering eyes. Pride and pain and haunting uncertainty— and love, so much love. 'Aunty Hat didn't tell you?'

He shook his head. 'We're having a baby?'

Throwing off her grandmother's and the girl's hands, Elly got to her feet. She waved Rick aside. The fullness of her belly was unmistakable.

'So what are you going to—'

'I said *back off,* Ricky,' Elly snapped. 'This is between Adam and me.'

He stood frozen. An impatient airport passenger pushed past him, knocking him over. He got to his feet, and started walking to her. Another passenger put a suitcase in the space between tables in front of him, and he walked right into it. He barely noticed as Rick, now laughing at him, helped steady him—his whole focus was on Elly.

'We're having a baby?' he repeated, feeling stupid.

'Two, actually.' She still looked wary.

'Twins?' he croaked. Would his voice ever return to normal?

She looked at him as if he was stupid. 'That's what two babies adds up to. I wouldn't be this large at three months otherwise.'

He moved closer, absurd joy and pride combating inside him. More inevitability. Of course Elly was having his children. Everything he'd been too young and stupid to dream of. 'There's no way I'm letting you go now.'

'I have to. Don't you see?' The look in her eyes turned pleading. 'If Danny sees me pregnant, he'll connect it to you.'

'They're my children. You're staying if I have to force you with a court order,' he snapped. He fished an envelope from his pocket and pushed it into her hand. 'Sign this, and we're legally married—but we're getting married again, Elly-May, this time in front of everyone, and forever. Do you hear me?'

'I imagine half the airport heard it,' she replied, in a voice of ice. 'What a romantic proposal, Detective Sergeant Jepson. Is this how you wooed your first wife?'

He couldn't help grinning, even as he acknowledged her pain with a tender kiss to her cheek. 'You know I've always been a tactless sod. Ah, Elle, don't you know I—' Then the sixth sense that had saved his life more than once made him turn. 'Elly, sit down again. Hide it.'

But Elly was already looking beyond him, eyes wide, face pale. Her mouth worked, as if she would throw up. 'Mr Spencer.'

A scent touched Adam's nose, expensive, woodsy and masculine. Success in a bottle.

He spun around. The white-haired man in the impeccable suit he'd noticed more than once as he'd searched the airport for Elly stood behind him, his burning eyes fixed on the loose jumpsuit she wore, the slight bulge at her belly proclaiming her impending maternity.

The man nodded, a slow smile growing.

'Ah, good girl.' He held out a packet. 'There's no need for you to leave Australia, Miss Larkins. No need at all. After the wedding, my grandson will no longer be a problem for you. He'll be in a safe facility, and you'll live at Gundawin with me.'

Elly stepped past Adam, facing Danny's grandfather as she had the grandson months ago: head high, showing no fear. 'Why will Danny no longer be a problem?'

'You know why, Miss Larkins. Daniel will be safe, but will hurt no one else until the day he dies. You and my great-grandson will be safe at Gundawin. He will be nowhere near you.' Jeremiah Spencer's cold eyes glimmered, but the storm clouds beneath were held in with absolute self-control. It was a look Adam had seen before, in his years as an inner-city cop. Tainted blood and mind. Was he even aware of his problems, or had he spent his entire life blaming anyone and everyone else for his insane moments?

Wherever Jeremiah Spencer had hidden Danny away, nobody would ever find him. Being right, being in control, was everything to this man. The old man cared nothing for his grandson. The ultimate narcissist, everything in life related only to his wants and needs—even his poor, suffering only grandchild.

Adam glanced at Rick, and saw the wheels turning in his friend's head. He'd obviously had a plan for dealing with *Danny* Spencer, not Jeremiah, and was playing catch-ups in his head. They needed to know what the hell was going on, and where Danny was right now—nearby with an arsenal of weapons, or locked away for life. With a dozen private security guards surrounding Spencer, the airport police no doubt looking for Danny instead of this old man, and the family to think of, the two of them alone had to wait for backup.

Give us a few minutes, Elly. Stall Spencer. String him along.

But for once, Elly didn't seem to be on his wavelength. 'I won't take your money, Mr Spencer. Yes, I'm pregnant, but Danny is not the father.'

Sick paleness crossed his face, a mirror of Elly's face in its haunted fear—but after a moment, Spencer smiled again. 'Come on, dear, be honest. I had you investigated. You're a selective girl who has never slept around. For a girl of your … background, you're highly intelligent, and have kept yourself clean. That's why I encouraged Daniel to pursue his interest with you. You only reunited with Detective Jepson three months ago, the only possible worry to my plans—and you look at be at least five months pregnant to me.'

Rick glanced at Adam, blank and desperate. What the hell were they going to do? *Give us a minute, Elly! Buy into Spencer's delusions!*

From her copious medical bag that was never far from her, Elly handed Spencer an envelope of her own. 'Note the date, Mr Spencer, and the report. I'm thirteen weeks pregnant with twins—and the father is my husband, Adam Jepson.'

Spencer's eyes were obsidian, boring into her. 'So you paid for a hoax ultrasound. I don't blame you. Daniel has passed all bounds with you. I understand that, if he does not.' He didn't notice the phalanx of police closing in. Adam supposed he didn't have to, with his own arsenal of protection. 'I've had Births, Deaths and Marriages checked regularly. As lately as this morning, Miss Larkins, you were still single. There was a request for marriage papers, but they were never turned in. Now please stop irritating me with your fairy tales. Detective Jepson is still too damaged by his wife's death to notice you ... though I believe you tried your best.' His smile was too cold to be nasty, or even triumphant. Jeremiah Spencer was so sure of success he didn't need to crow over her, or anyone.

'Where's Danny?' she asked, holding Jeremiah's gaze. When he didn't answer, she closed her eyes. 'You had him killed. You killed your own grandson.'

The elegant old man looked a touch pained. 'Really, my dear, there's no need to descend into melodrama. I did mention your upcoming wedding to Daniel. I arranged his release from that awful place, and now have him safe.'

'And got arrested into the bargain?'

He shrugged. 'A small price to pay to see the succession fulfilled. As to Daniel, he is as well as can be expected. You will see him as often as you wish to—or as little. He'll be happy knowing you're his wife, safe on Gundawin, and that I'm protecting you from the attentions of other men.'

Cautiously, the airport's security guards moved into place. Adam noted police pouring in through the doors and up the escalators.

Jeremiah's security men had no need to fight. They stepped aside. He wouldn't be armed; he was the kind of man who always won with money and power, and a flotilla of barristers.

People milled around them. Some stopped to watch the drama. Others passed on. Somewhere nearby, a dog barked once, and made snuffling sounds.

Elly shifted on her feet. 'Mr Spencer, there will be no wedding, and I refuse to come to Gundawin. I told you the truth. I'm thirteen weeks pregnant with twins, and Adam's the father.'

The utter steadiness in her voice must have sowed a seed of doubt in the old man's confidence. Frowning, he shifted his gaze to Adam. 'Well, boy?'

He nodded. 'The marriage certificate will go in as soon as El— Janie signs it, but we've already had the ceremony. I am the father of her children.'

Spencer's frown deepened. 'You can't know for certain.'

Adam offered him a grim smile. 'I am absolutely, one hundred per cent certain that your grandson was *never* my wife's lover.'

Suddenly he looked every day of his eighty-two years. The storm clouds came in and his eyes unfocused, Danny in replica. Plans and certainty crumbling, nothing left, nowhere to go. He stared at Elly, uncomprehending. 'You've ruined everything. I had it all set up … paying the Mirakis and Ms Rollings to create alibis for Daniel until he got you pregnant. But you played the harlot. No—this can't happen. The child will be mine! Daniel will father no child now … his mother, the silly slut, ruined it …'

He grabbed her hands. Shuddering, Elly tried to pull away. 'I did all this for you—for my great-grandson. I even underwent the indignity of arrest to keep Daniel away from you, from my heir …'

She jerked her hands away. 'My babies are not your heirs, Mr Spencer.'

'He can be.' The old man's gaze shifted from Elly to Adam and back, eager need hidden beneath the imperious demand. 'They'll inherit everything. I've already written your child into the will. You're young and healthy—you can have more children. Just leave one boy with me. You can take the other. Your son will be one of the richest people in the nation.'

Neither answered; they didn't have to. Spencer read the revulsion in their expressions with the unerring ability of the long-term businessman, and stepped back. The man who'd never known defeat, or how to accept it, lifted his head, eyes frozen. Manipulating people like pieces on a chessboard, as Rick had told him he would. 'I can force the situation, you know. You are rather simple people, and I have unlimited funds.'

In the stunned quiet, Rick stepped beside Adam. 'Not in this age of DNA testing, Mr Spencer. Adam is my sister's children's father, and it's easily proven.'

'I have unlimited funds,' Jeremiah Spencer replied, a little smile playing on his features. 'And to be raised on Gundawin with me is clearly best for the child. I'm a very wealthy man. I have many friends in government, both at state and federal levels. They'll understand that I can give the child everything you can't.'

Rick's gaze narrowed. 'You've overlooked one thing, Mr Spencer. The day of paternalism in government is dying. Yes, we are Aboriginal people, and the Australian government spent decades stealing our children from us. But it's now well known that most of those children were subjected to slavery and physical, emotional and sexual abuse. If you try to take either of my sister's children, we'll take it to the High Court, the international courts and the press. We can force several independent DNA tests to prove the babies' paternity. You can't pay them all off. The government can't afford to side with you this time, no matter how much money or how many high-powered barristers you have. You will not take my sister from her family, or steal my niece or nephew—not while any member of our family is alive to stop you. We'll get every single organisation behind us, the press, whatever it takes. I'll prove your mental instability, and your abuse of Danny and Lorena Spencer, not to mention the animals whose throats you slit. I've already found two jackaroos willing to testify that you paid them off to lie about who was behind the killings.'

The words exploded from Rick with all the ferocity of a man denied family too long; all the intensity of his nature, dammed up too long, had burst forth. As one, the crowd gasped.

Jeremiah Spencer made a sound—short, horrible, strangled. His eyes turned dark. 'Boy, you don't want me for an enemy,' he forced out. 'If you knew the powerful people I have in my pocket ... what I can do to those who cross me ...'

Elly's hand moved back, fingers twining with Rick's.

'Like poor Lorena?' Rick lifted his phone. 'Go ahead, Mr Spencer, call me "boy" again. Keep on threatening me, and my family. I've recorded every word so far, including your tacit admission that you accept my sister's babies are not related to you in any way. Go ahead and make your threats. Two-dozen people have videotaped this whole thing. Your tirade will be on YouTube and Facebook by tonight. Do you know what they are, the power they have?'

Spencer's eyes swivelled from face to avid face, phone to phone. Unfamiliar territory for a man who worked in the dark, used to making his bribes and threats behind closed doors. 'They wouldn't dare ... if they knew who I am ...'

Rick shrugged. 'No doubt you can buy the people we don't know. But to us, you're just the crazy old man trying to take a member of our family. You can't buy everyone, and you can't gag all of us with court orders in time. It's an abuse of free speech.'

The old man waved a hand. 'Haskins, Jones, take their phones. All of them.'

As the security men moved forward, Adam said, 'Are you really going to attempt to assault and steal from two serving police officers?'

The men moved back so fast it was comical. Spencer stared at first Adam, and then Rick, at a clear loss.

Dropping Elly's hand, Rick played with his phone for a few moments. Then he held it up again, smiling. 'There you go. Five seconds, and it's on YouTube. "Rich man threatens to use wealth and influence with the government to steal Aboriginal children."'

He pressed another button. 'It'll appear on my Facebook, Instagram and Twitter feeds any second—and I have a lot of friends. By the time you have a court order to remove the post, over a hundred thousand people will have seen it and shared their outrage with a million others.'

As Spencer made that awful gobbling sound again, Rick grinned, and it was a thing of beauty in its nasty cheek. 'Welcome to the age of social media, Mr Spencer, where everyone's free to post—and once it's out there, no amount of wealth or power can stop it.'

The old man's jaw snapped closed. His eyes moved as he worked out what to say. 'I'll sue you … I'll sue you all!'

Adam stepped in, his smile every bit as triumphant as Rick's. 'The trouble with that threat is you've condemned yourself out of your own mouth, threatening to take our child from us—and we have visual and audio evidence of your threat to use the government against us. Nobody will dare back your case now.'

Elly moved toward Spencer, her face alive with pity. 'You've lost, Mr Spencer. Accept it. Go home. Look after Danny. Treat him with love and compassion, and he might heal in time, find another woman to love, and give you your own great-grandchildren.'

But the old man glared at her. 'You stupid harlot! When I told him you were pregnant, I thought he'd be happy, but I found him the next morning—he'd hanged himself. You've ruined everything! I *need* a great-grandson! Why didn't you just take the deal? I'd have kept Daniel away from you. You'd have lived in luxury for life. Why, *why*?'

As the old man lifted a fist to her, Adam and Rick grabbed his wrists, bearing them down. His security men stepped forward, and then back. Adam tipped his head, and the police on the periphery approached. Pulling his hands behind his back, they used the traditional words of arrest, mentioning extortion, intimidation and threats. Jeremiah Spencer spoke with cold control about calling his barrister, who made more in an hour than the police did in a year.

As he was led away, his security men followed, looking helpless. One was using his phone, no doubt calling a barrister.

A moment of hush, followed by shocked murmurs. Family members stopped recording.

'So Danny's dead at last. Poor Danny.' Elly let out a hurting cry. 'Did you hear him? Talking of Danny's death like it was an inconvenience to his plans. Poor Danny … he wasn't worth anything to anyone, except to the mother he barely knew.'

Adam pulled her close. 'I know, but you couldn't have saved him, Elle. He'd have lived forever in a padded cell. This way is best. It's all over now. The nightmare's over. Danny's at rest. Spencer can't hurt or abuse him or you again. You're free at last.'

'I–I …' She looked up at him in strange, desperate grief as members of the police waited to interview them, the security guards and passers-by still filming. Suddenly, she turned to Rick. 'Where's Lorena? What's he done to her?'

Rick said quietly, 'I'll call her, sis.' Rick walked off, dialling. Moments later he was talking, his face sad, words consoling, but he gave Elly the thumbs-up. Lorena was at least alive, but Adam felt Elly shaking in his arms. 'Poor Lorena...'

He kissed her forehead. 'I know.'

'She has no one now,' she whispered.

Knowing she'd need to do something about the poor woman, he murmured, 'We'll help her, Elle. We'll see she gets a good life.'

She sighed and rested her head on his shoulder for a moment. 'Poor Lorena. Poor Danny.'

'I know—but it was inevitable, love. Do you remember that poor run-over wombat we found on the road near Grandpa's farm? We had to have it put down.' She nodded. 'Danny was too sick to save.

If he was a dog we'd have put him out of his misery years ago.' He pulled back to gaze reassuringly into her eyes. 'Don't let his death haunt you, Elle. The nightmare's over now. It's time to focus on living. Your life and dreams can all come true. All of them.' He smiled, tracing her mouth with his finger. 'And that includes me—if you still want me.'

Elly gave him an unreadable look, and wrenched out of his arms, turning to her grandmother. 'Nana? Are you okay?'

Rick was back, and supporting their grandmother. Dot Larkins gave Elly a shaky smile. 'Nice fella,' she remarked, in grand understatement. 'Glad no relation to that man is the father of my great-grandchildren, Janie.'

Elly laughed through her tears, causing a bout of hiccups. Everyone laughed, breaking the odd tension hovering in the air.

Dot looked at Adam, having to crane her neck to meet his eyes. 'Daresay you don't want my advice, but here it is: marry the girl, take her home and have your babies before any other nutcase gets funny ideas about her.'

Adam grinned. 'Great advice, Mrs Larkins—but we already got married.'

Dot Larkins sniffed, much as Aunty Hat had done. 'Not in front of me, you didn't—and call me Nana.'

Moved, he kissed the old woman's cheek. 'Can you set up a quick wedding, Nana? I've got a licence ready.'

Dot nodded briskly, her eyes shining with approval. 'Good boy. This weekend?'

'Whatever you and Elly want. If my family can make it, great, if they can't, they already saw me get married once.'

The pretty girl piped up. 'First take on bridesmaid, Janie—uh, Elly.'

'I'm getting married? I don't remember anyone asking me,' she remarked casually.

Hearing the challenge in her voice, Adam grimaced. 'Come on, Elle ...'

A haughty stare. Oh yeah, she was determined not to make it easy for him. 'So you're doing the right thing—the *Jepson* thing— for the babies ... even if it means taking me on?'

'Come on, Elle,' he said again, desperate and embarrassed. 'Why else would I be here but for you? You know I've been looking for you since I left hospital. You've been the one avoiding me for months. I only found out you were pregnant when I got here.'

A brow lifted. 'So?'

The family crowded around. Smothered laughs and whispers filled the air.

He glanced around, and grimaced. 'You want the whole hog, don't you?'

Her mouth pursed and her eyes narrowed. 'Bones, teeth and all, babe.'

He groaned, and looked at the avid faces surrounding them. He blew out a sigh. It was obvious no one would give them space right now. The whole debacle would be on social media by tonight—but no way would Elly take that as an excuse. Thinking of their crazy history, all she'd been through, she deserved no less than his abject embarrassment, and a hell of a lot more.

He closed his eyes and nodded. Here it went: the whole hog, bones, teeth and all.

'I came for you, Elly. I've loved you since I was fifteen, and everyone knew it but me.' He hesitated, then added, 'Even Sharon knew if I was near you much longer, I'd have worked it out. She spent the whole nine years not just trying to keep me from you, but trying to make me something I wasn't. It was never like that with you, and she knew it.' He nuzzled her cheek, feeling the tender little purr in response. 'When I'm with you, there's no expectation, just happiness. Don't leave me, Elle. Don't condemn me to the living death I existed in before you came back to me. I love you. I need you. Marry me.' He trailed a line of feather-light kisses to her mouth.

'What about Zoe?' she asked quietly.

He chuckled. 'Here's her opinion.' He pulled out his phone, turned on the camera, and pressed *Play*. Zoe's face filled the screen until they could see up her nose. Elly laughed.

'Annelly, you gotta come home. You said you wanted to come wif us. Don't you wanna be somebody's mummy?' The wistfulness in his daughter's voice brought a lump to his throat, even though he'd already heard it. 'You can be my mummy, Annelly, and we'll have pizza and make pea-boats *all the time!*'

After a few moments, she sniffed and bit her lip, frowning hard at him. 'It's not me crying. It's the pregnancy. Your children—all three of them—are making me *emotional*.' She wiped her eyes, staring at him in odd defiance. Flooded with tenderness, he smiled at her. She lifted her chin. 'You did love Sharon.'

With a soft laugh, he nodded. 'You know me so well. Yeah, I did love her for a little while, with a boy's first intense love. It was like a dream, the sort of feeling that should have been a nice memory after I married the right woman.' He grinned. 'When she became a woman, that is.'

She remained silent, waiting for the rest of his public declaration with a little smile.

He touched her face. 'You know the rest. It was always you, and everyone knew it but me. Part of me must have always known I loved you. That's why I felt so guilty and confused when you came back into my life.' He drew in a breath, then went down on one knee before the laughing crowd, red-faced but grinning. 'Jane Ann Elly-May Larkins, please marry me. I know Africa needs doctors, but I need *you*. I want the life we talked about—the pilot's licence, the plane, the clinic in Macks Lake. I want to work beside you, with you day and night. I want to spend my life with you, and our kids.'

From his pocket he withdrew a box. 'This is Grandma's engagement ring, to match the wedding ring I gave you. Please wear it, not because you're becoming a Jepson, but because you love me. Because you want to marry me.'

'*Stupid* hormones,' she complained, wiping her eyes before putting out her left hand. He noticed it still bore his ring. 'And what if I say I'm committed to working overseas?'

'Then we'll come with you,' he declared without hesitation, sliding the ring on.

She gasped. 'Adam, it's a war zone. We can't take Zoe there!'

'Then we can't take our babies there, either.' From where he knelt, he smoothed a hand over her belly. 'Your basic idea's great, so let's just change the geography. You can change destination, can't you? Are you contracted to this scheme?'

'No. They didn't give me a contract because of my pregnancy. They'll have a contract waiting for me when I get there, but it's only a month-to-month thing, in case of medical problems in the pregnancy, or if I want to give birth in Australia.'

'So pick another place you'll be useful, just minus the war.'

'You'd come with me, just like that?' she whispered, staring at him as if he was a mirage. 'You'd give up your life, your home and job, just to be with me?'

'Absolutely.' He got to his feet, and took her hands in his. 'I'm not letting you out of my sight again, woman. You're too dangerous on the loose—and so am I, it seems. I reckon we'd better get married quick before any other infatuated psychos decide we're their perfect match.'

Caught off guard, she laughed—and then, face softly radiant, she stepped to him, hands barely touching his arms. Wonder and joy in her fingers. He did the same, laying his forehead on hers, breathing her in. Shampoo, powder and forever love. Inevitability. Elly.

'Don't ever leave me again,' he whispered. 'I'm not me without you.'

'I know.' Just standing there, breathing him in too.

'So are we celebrating or not?' Nana Larkins wanted to know.

He turned to her and smiled. 'Get that wedding going, Nana.'

The old lady grinned. 'Good boy.'

As if in unspoken agreement, both sides of the family moved a little apart from them.

'I've quit the service, by the way,' he murmured, fingers moving on her arms in delicate wonder. His woman, his wife at last. 'You realise you're marrying an unemployed person.'

'So I'll support you until you get your pilot's licence, huh? Now I know why you came,' she mock-complained. The fingers of one hand locked with his, holding on tight. She wouldn't lose the fear of losing him for a long time. He didn't mind. He had a lifetime to prove to her he wasn't going anywhere.

'I have long-service leave,' he retorted, smiling. 'God forbid any woman ever supports a Jepson!'

She laughed. 'That sounds about right … Claudius.'

He grinned, thrilled to hear that *stupid* nickname once more. He'd be hearing it for the rest of his life—and nothing could make him a happier man. 'Right. Aunty Hat and Nana Larkins have both decreed we get married again, in front of them, and they're going to outgun us every time. Do you think Minyenbarra would come up here to do a second ceremony?'

She shrugged. 'I don't know. We can ask.' But her smile was filled with approval and joy.

He nuzzled her cheek again. 'I'd like that—but this time a fully legal ceremony, with me actually participating in the wedding.'

'That's the Jepson in you coming out *again*. Life with you will be so tame,' she sighed.

He put his forehead back on hers, smiling into her upturned face. 'Everyone thinks I'm insane, dumping an underpaid but well-respected job as a detective to become a bush pilot.' He grinned. 'A pilot for a pregnant doctor. Terrific job security!'

'It's an *adventure*, Claudius.' Her eyes sparkled. 'If we get the contract, we'll set up base while we wait for the babies. Some of my mates from college might like to join in the challenge. If any others have kids, we could try each filling the job on a part-time basis.'

'Mum's offered to move to Macks Lake to be our babysitter so you can keep working, part time at least.'

Elly looked up, her eyes wide. 'Aunt Susan—'

He closed her mouth with a gentle finger. 'Always knew, and she's ordered us to give her more grandchildren.' He grinned. 'She'll be thrilled when we tell her about the twins. That'll give her something to brag about with the whole clan.'

Elly frowned. 'Are you sure? When the family finds out—'

'Look around, Elle. I think you missed something in all the excitement.' He turned her to face the crowd.

Slowly, as if noticing the others for the first time, she looked around. Eight Jepsons stood watching them. Aunt Bea, whose immaculate outfit hinted that she must have come from one of her society fundraisers. Aunt Ginny, wife of Uncle Fred the barrister, who always looked (and was) like a ship in full sail. His cousin Craig, a managing partner in a major Sydney accountancy firm. His cousins Jenny and Ben, who ran a busy florist business in Newtown;

they must have closed it to come. And Uncle Mike, the retired state politician, and his wife, Adelaide, were here.

At the back stood his sister-in-law, Hannah, beside his sensible, respectable brother, Jared. Gentle, blonde Hannah, the girl next door, the one so ideal to Stephen Jepson's tastes he'd found a clone of her for his second son to marry.

And, true to form, generous-hearted Hannah stepped out first. 'Welcome home, Janie—and welcome back to the family,' she said, affection in every syllable. 'Jared and I hope you and Adam and Zoe will come to visit us at the farm soon. It hasn't changed much since you lived there. We wanted it kept much the same as Grandma and Grandpa Jepson had it. We all have such happy memories of our childhood times there … and Rachel and Jake would love to play with their cousins.'

Elly smiled at her. 'I've got good memories of living there, too, and I'm sure Zoe would love it.' Her eyes met Adam's, a wealth of tenderness in them. 'Thank you, Hannah. But please, call me Elly.'

'Elly,' Hannah repeated, smiling. 'It will take a little getting used to. Anyway, I was wondering … I believe you're not religious?'

Frowning, Elly shook her head.

'If you'd like it, I've made a clearing in the old orchard that might be nice for a family wedding, under that tree you loved …?'

Her teeth pressing down on her lip, Elly turned back to Adam. He smiled again. 'I can't think of a better place for us to marry.'

Hannah held out her arms, and Elly hugged her. Old times forgotten, the sister she should always have been. More healing.

Then Jared came forward and kissed her. 'Welcome back to the family, Janie—uh, Elly.' He winked at Adam. 'Way to go, mate. It's about time you got it right. We've only been waiting for this event the past three years!'

'Yeah, yeah, I was always a bit slow.' Adam grinned at his brother, drawing Elly close to him.

'I'm best man, I hope.'

'We'll see. You have competition.' He laughed, and motioned Rick forward. 'This is my best mate and soon-to-be brother-in-law, Rick.'

Jared lifted a brow. 'You're kidding! You found Janie's long-lost brother?'

'He found us.'

Jared shook his head, eyes wide. 'He found you, and you're best friends with him? You don't do things by halves, mate. There's a story in this, right?'

Adam laughed again. It seemed he'd never stop. 'One you'll hear after a few beers.'

Finally Aunt Ginny asked the question on all their minds. 'So, is the wedding this weekend? Fred and I usually like prior notice— but of course family comes first.' She pinched Adam's cheek. 'You have yourself a fine girl here, Adam. I always liked her. She's got fire and guts and spirit. The family could do with a bit of that in the bloodline. My brother always was a bit foolish about things like that.'

Aunt Ginny's bluntness was legendary in the family—and he blessed his aunt for saying the exact words Elly needed to hear. 'The wedding's this weekend, Aunt Ginny. I'm not waiting for anyone. Be there or be square.'

'Well said.' Aunt Ginny nodded and turned to Elly's grandmother. 'Mrs Larkins—Dot, is it?—I'm Ginny. It seems Adam and Janie have chosen the venue. Of course your family is welcome to stay at the farm from now until the wedding—there's loads of room.' She didn't so much as glance at Jared and Hannah as she made the invitation. 'Would you like to help with the catering, the flowers and so on?'

Dot Larkins gave the perfectly groomed woman a reluctant smile. 'Seems they have—but I think I'll be able to work out the rest.'

Dot's grandchildren, who knew her irascible nature and love of control, bit back laughs and grinned at each other. It would snow in the Barrier Reef before an outsider muscled in on any family function of Dot's.

As the awkward greetings between the families continued, Elly turned back to Adam, and he saw the healing begin. Little Janie Larkins was finally a Jepson, with all the fierce loyalty the name entailed; and she was a Larkins, loved and accepted. As was Rick. She had her brother at last, and this time he'd be in her life every day. Full circle had come.

Elly's distant cousin and close friend stepped forward. 'You're going to need nurses as well as doctors on shift at this new clinic, unless you want to have a breakdown. I'd love to work with you again, Elly, and I can't think of a better way than treating our people on the Flying Doctor circuit.'

Adam put out a hand to her. 'Hi. I'm Adam, and we'd love to have some more family along for the ride.'

She grinned, turning their joined hands to make a high five. 'Hi, new cuz. I'm Kara, and I promise I won't break in on any honeymoon you two might be planning. I know how to be tactful … when I put my mind to it. I can even babysit for you. I love kids. Has Macks Lake got many available men? I might finally find the love of my life.'

'Kara's as picky as me, and as determined,' Elly murmured dreamily.

Kara grinned, unabashed. 'A family trait, my dear.' She slanted a slight glance to Adam's left, a look of intense interest, then she turned away, biting her lip.

Rick turned to talk to the cops, but the stiffness of his back said there was a story to this. He'd have to ask Elly about it when they were alone at last.

'Excuse me, Detective Sergeant Jepson, if we could speak to you and the lady now? We'll need to take your statements.'

He waved the cops off. 'I'll bring her in later.' He was glad he hadn't yet put in his resignation. 'My wife's pregnant with twins. She needs a rest after what she's just been through. She's in shock.'

'I'm not in shock, and I don't want to rest,' Elly murmured as the constable backed off, the respect for a fellow cop's family clear in his eyes. 'But I really need a distraction. Right here and now would be pretty good for me. How about it, Claudius? You game?'

Kara must have overheard, because she walked away, fast—obviously putting that tact to work.

'From a river shack to a city airport?' he whispered with a loving smile. 'Woman, you pick the strangest places to turn me on. What happened to that five-star hotel you wanted?'

'There's one around the corner from here. Alas, no harbour view, but I can wait for that.' Her smile turned wicked. 'I'd rather have a full weekend—no, make that a week, or two—at the shack. A picnic basket or three, a jar of honey and a river—and a working fire. What more could we want?'

'A new bed. Warm chocolate,' he whispered in her ear. 'Whipped cream.'

She giggled. 'Yum. And I can think of some great places to eat dessert,' she murmured, her fingers trailing down his chest and stomach. 'And I'm *starving*, Claudius. Eating for three, you know. You'll have to feed me—often.'

In that smile, Adam had a sudden vision of their future: love and joy and faith, a lifetime of giving to others; a shared passion for healing and for each other mingling with laughter and the spice of the unexpected. 'I think I can manage that, darlin'.'

A voice came over the loudspeaker. 'If there are any doctors or nurses in the terminal, please report to the security desk. We have an injured man outside the entrance to Terminal 1.'

Kara grinned as Elly grabbed her medical bag and strode off. 'She'll always do that to you, you know.'

'Thank God for that.' He laughed in sheer relief. Kara wasn't a cop, and couldn't know he'd half-expected Elly to collapse in tears, or miscarry their babies in a guilt/grief reaction to the events of the day—to the past two years. That Elly could still laugh, still want to live and reach out to help others, made him so damn proud to be her man he thought he'd burst with it. 'She always has, for people or her critters.' His gaze never left her. 'It's why I nicknamed her Elly-May—and it's why I love her.'

Kara laughed, a silvery, infectious rush of sound. 'Just as well, or she'd drive you nuts. I'll go and help her. I took a pledge, too.' She dashed off after her cousin.

As he and Rick followed her together, he heard Aunt Ginny ask the police in a voice of command, 'Can we *please* have a fortifying cup of tea before coming in to give our statements? It's been a very strange hour.'

'We're old ladies, and in shock. We could have a heart attack!' he heard Dot Larkins add.

Adam winked at Rick, who grinned. 'I defy the entire police force to stand up to the women of our combined families, when they stand together.'

Outside the terminal, watching the two women working in harmony on a courier who'd fallen off his bike and been sideswiped by a car, Adam saw his future: a life with constant interruptions to their private life; calls for help, day and night. Elly would always respond to that call. She'd always have to drive or fly off some-where, and he'd have to take her. They'd live a life of hard work and dedication, and raise their children in an area where they were truly needed.

He could hardly wait.

AUTHOR'S NOTE

I'm so proud to have *Beneath the Skin* as my debut Mira release. I wrote the first version of this book many years ago, not long after being 'recognised' as Koori by locals in the town where I lived, and a lot of missing pieces fell into place. I studied Aboriginal history at university, and learned true stories that became the kernel for my three published books with Aboriginal characters (there's still at least two more yet to go). I'm passionate about history in all forms, especially of the people I relate to, and I know that truth is often stranger than fiction. I believe in doing as much research as possible to get the story right. I'm also passionate about reading, and getting kids to read, and discover whole new worlds.

Because of that, I am donating 5 per cent of all royalties for this book to the Indigenous Literacy Foundation. This fantastic charity was founded and set up by members of the Australian book industry in 2005. It draws on the skills and expertise of the book industry to address children's literacy levels in remote Aboriginal and Torres Strait Islander communities. Their work is done through three core programs: Book Supply, Book Buzz and community literacy projects. The ILF also advocates lifting community awareness of Indigenous literacy issues. Since 2011, the ILF has worked as a not-for-profit charity without *any* government support or major corporate funding. It works with the support of the Australian Publishers Association, the Australian Booksellers Association and the Australian Society of Authors, along with a team of ambassadors, volunteers, and five full-time staff members.

I will also donate 5 per cent of all royalties of this book to the Royal Flying Doctor Service. This wonderful unsung hero of the Outback people plays a part in this book. It's one of the largest and most comprehensive aeromedical organisations in the world, providing extensive primary health care and 24-hour emergency service to people over an area of 7.3 million square kilometres. Delivered by a dedicated team of professionals, using the latest in aviation, medical and communications technology, and supported by a vast number of volunteers and supporters, the RFDS is vital for those who live, work and travel in rural and remote Australia. Their work is extraordinary, and they need and deserve as much support as possible.

Deepest respect to both organisations, fighting hard to bring better lives to the people of the massive, untamed land we simply call 'the Outback'.

I hope you enjoyed *Beneath the Skin*.

Melissa

talk about it

Let's talk about books.

Join the conversation:

 on facebook.com/harlequinaustralia

 on Twitter @harlequinaus

www.harlequinbooks.com.au

If you love reading and want to know about our authors and titles, then let's talk about it.